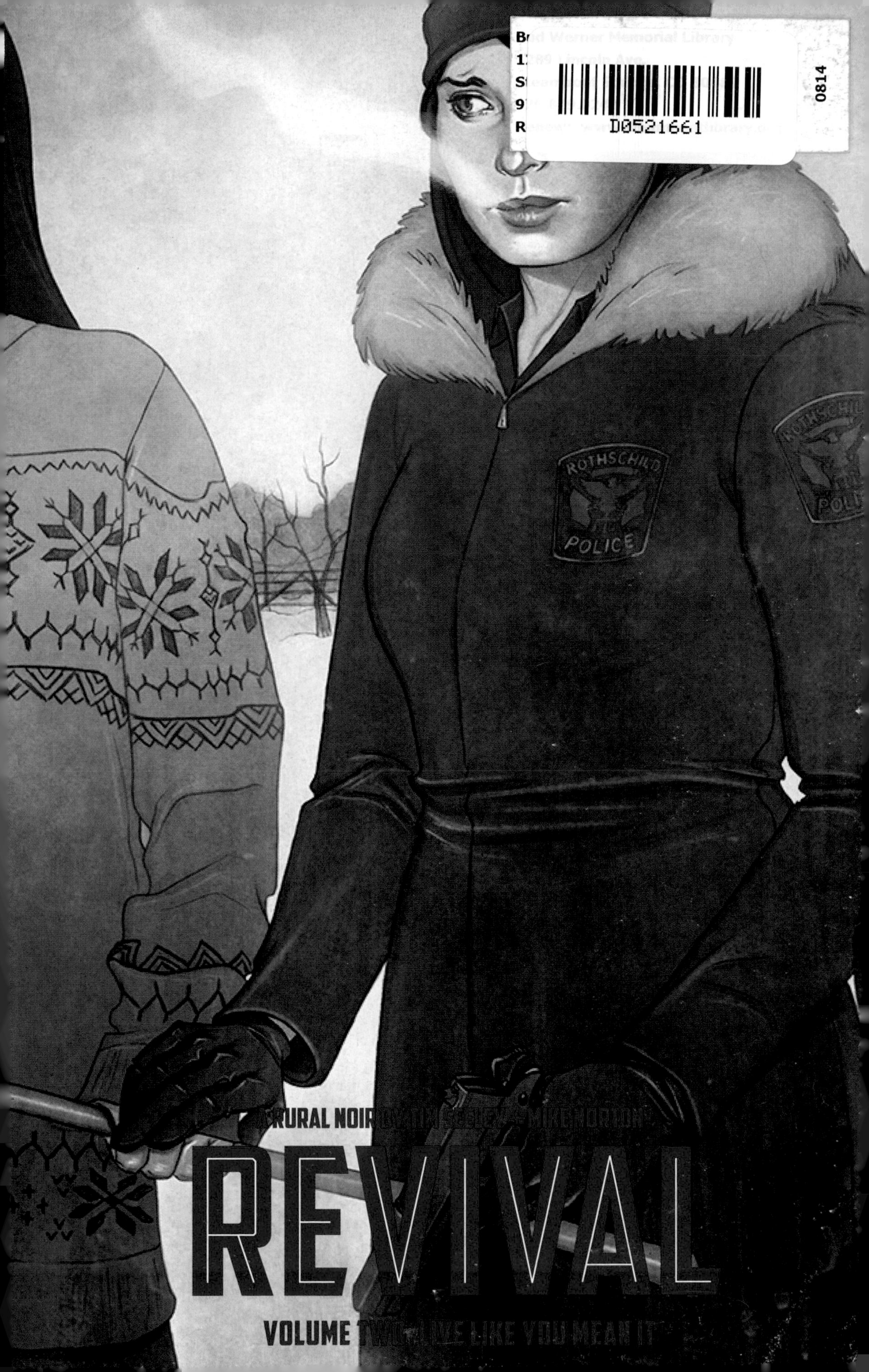
A RURAL NOIR BY TIM SEELEY & MIKE NORTON
REVIVAL
VOLUME TWO: LIVE LIKE YOU MEAN IT
ROTHSCHILD POLICE

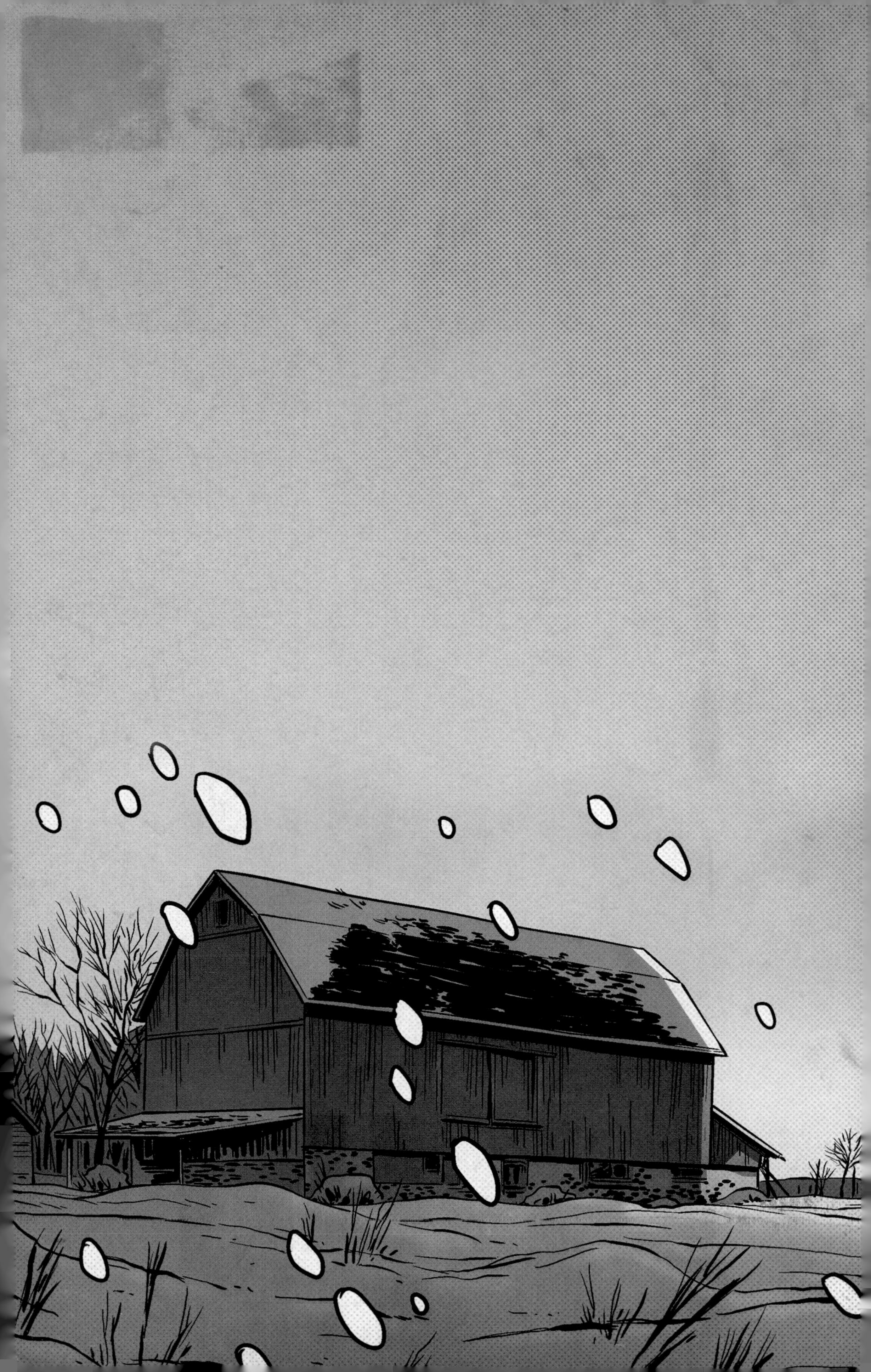

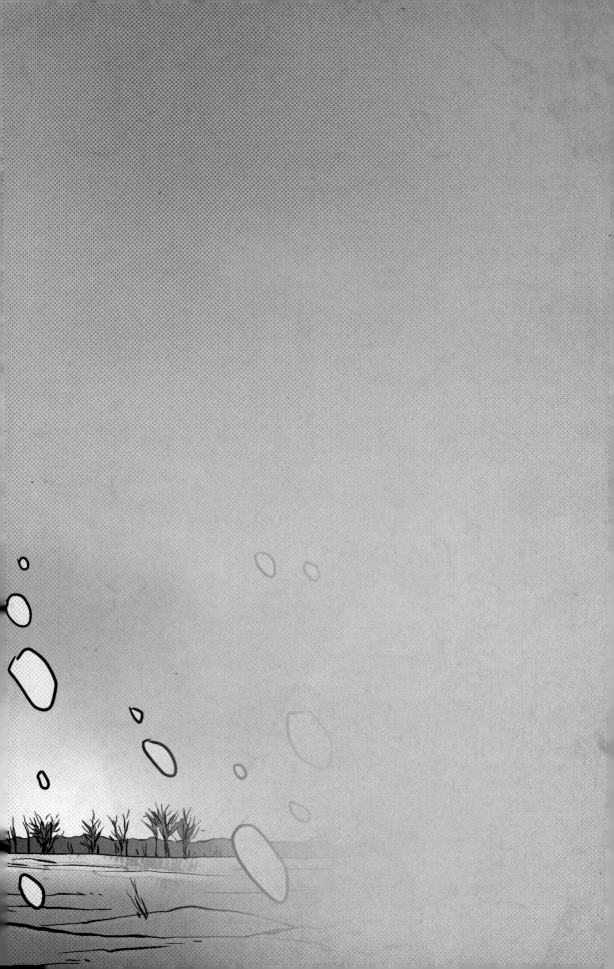

STORY BY
TIM SEELEY

ART BY
MIKE NORTON

COLORS BY
MARK ENGLERT

LETTERS BY
CRANK!

CHAPTER ART BY
JENNY FRISON

EDITED BY
4 STAR STUDIOS

DESIGN BY
SEAN DOVE

FOR MORE INFO CHECK OUT
WWW.REVIVALCOMIC.COM

ALSO CHECK OUT THE SOUNDTRACK BY
SONO MORTI AT **SONOMORTI.BANDCAMP.COM**

IMAGE COMICS, INC.
Robert Kirkman - chief operating officer
Erik Larsen - chief financial officer
Todd McFarlane - president
Marc Silvestri - chief executive officer
Jim Valentino - vice-president

Eric Stephenson - publisher
Ron Richards - director of business development
Jennifer de Guzman - pr & marketing director
Branwyn Bigglestone - accounts manager
Emily Miller - accounting assistant
Jamie Parreno - marketing assistant
Emilio Bautista - sales assistant
Susie Giroux - administrative assistant
Kevin Yuen - digital rights coordinator
Tyler Shainline - events coordinator
David Brothers - contents manager
Jonathan Chan - production manager
Drew Gill - art director
Jana Cook - print manager
Monica Garcia - senior production artist
Vincent Kukua - production artist
Jenna Savage - production artist
www.imagecomics.com

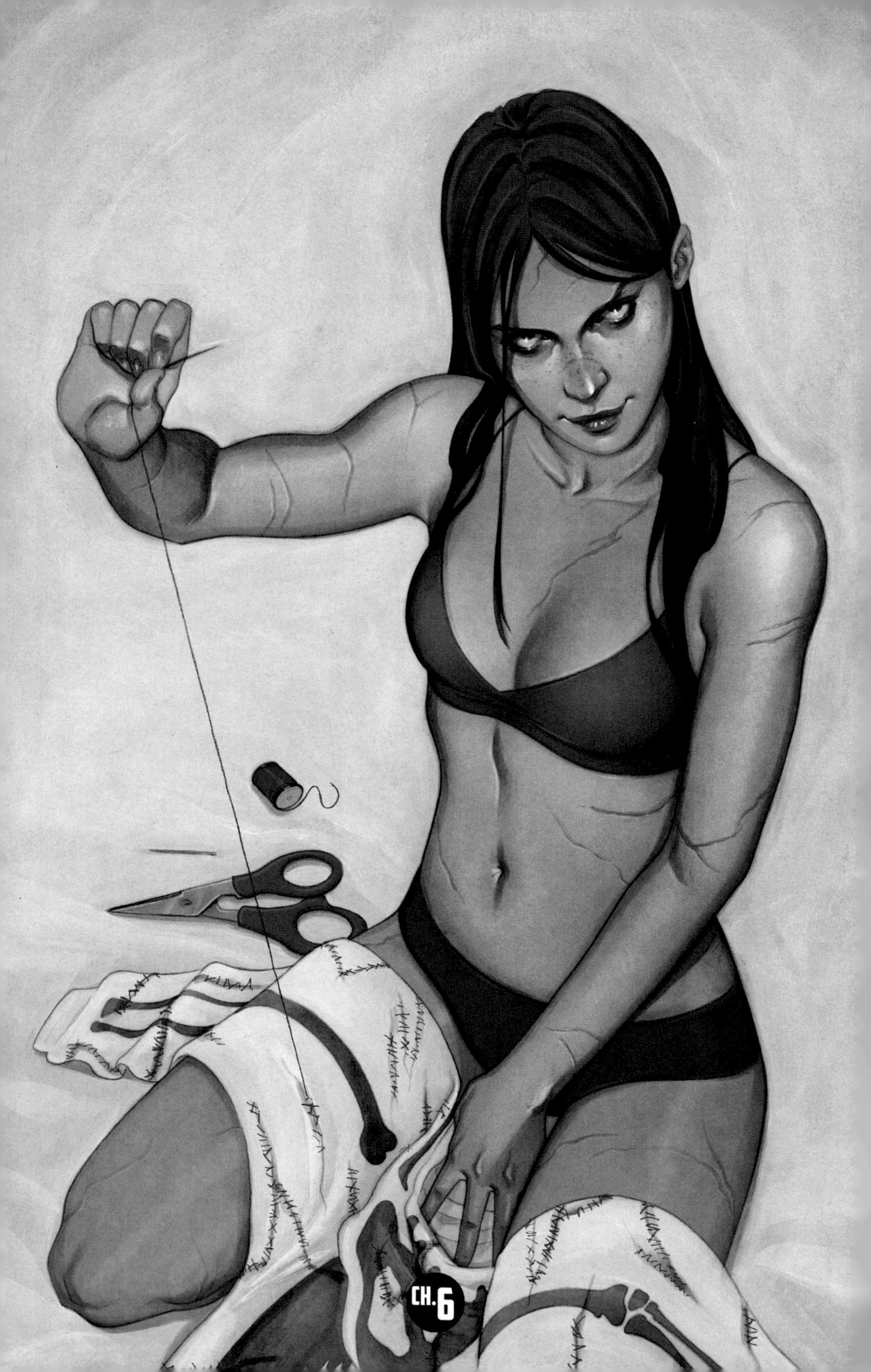
CH.6

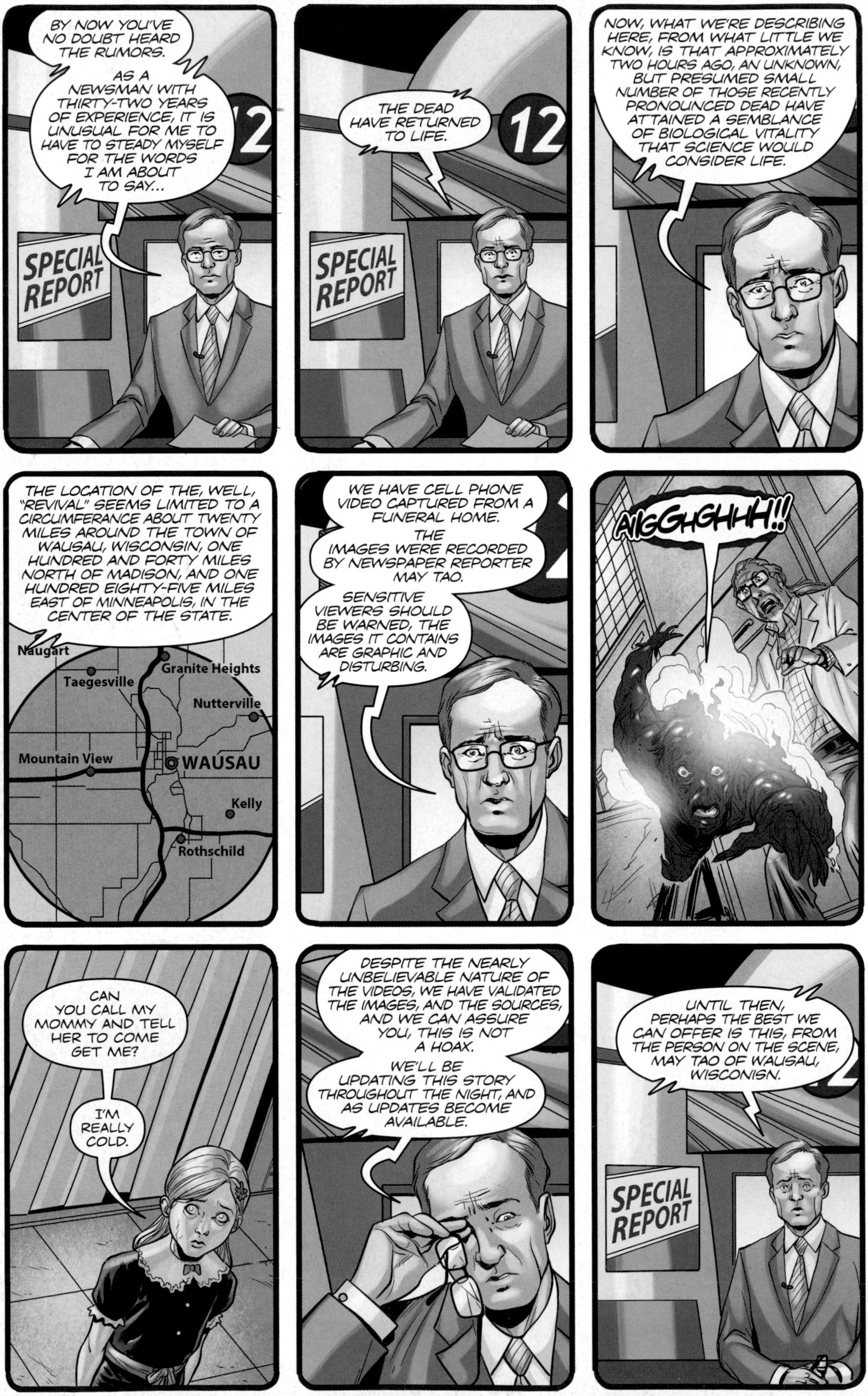
BY NOW YOU'VE NO DOUBT HEARD THE RUMORS.
AS A NEWSMAN WITH THIRTY-TWO YEARS OF EXPERIENCE, IT IS UNUSUAL FOR ME TO HAVE TO STEADY MYSELF FOR THE WORDS I AM ABOUT TO SAY...
12
SPECIAL REPORT
THE DEAD HAVE RETURNED TO LIFE.
12
SPECIAL REPORT
NOW, WHAT WE'RE DESCRIBING HERE, FROM WHAT LITTLE WE KNOW, IS THAT APPROXIMATELY TWO HOURS AGO, AN UNKNOWN, BUT PRESUMED SMALL NUMBER OF THOSE RECENTLY PRONOUNCED DEAD HAVE ATTAINED A SEMBLANCE OF BIOLOGICAL VITALITY THAT SCIENCE WOULD CONSIDER LIFE.
THE LOCATION OF THE, WELL, "REVIVAL" SEEMS LIMITED TO A CIRCUMFERANCE ABOUT TWENTY MILES AROUND THE TOWN OF WAUSAU, WISCONSIN, ONE HUNDRED AND FORTY MILES NORTH OF MADISON, AND ONE HUNDRED EIGHTY-FIVE MILES EAST OF MINNEAPOLIS, IN THE CENTER OF THE STATE.
Naugart
Taegesville
Granite Heights
Nutterville
Mountain View
WAUSAU
Kelly
Rothschild
WE HAVE CELL PHONE VIDEO CAPTURED FROM A FUNERAL HOME.
THE IMAGES WERE RECORDED BY NEWSPAPER REPORTER MAY TAO.
SENSITIVE VIEWERS SHOULD BE WARNED, THE IMAGES IT CONTAINS ARE GRAPHIC AND DISTURBING.
AIGGHGHHH!!
CAN YOU CALL MY MOMMY AND TELL HER TO COME GET ME?
I'M REALLY COLD.
DESPITE THE NEARLY UNBELIEVABLE NATURE OF THE VIDEOS, WE HAVE VALIDATED THE IMAGES, AND THE SOURCES, AND WE CAN ASSURE YOU, THIS IS NOT A HOAX.
WE'LL BE UPDATING THIS STORY THROUGHOUT THE NIGHT, AND AS UPDATES BECOME AVAILABLE.
UNTIL THEN, PERHAPS THE BEST WE CAN OFFER IS THIS, FROM THE PERSON ON THE SCENE, MAY TAO OF WAUSAU, WISCONISN.
SPECIAL REPORT

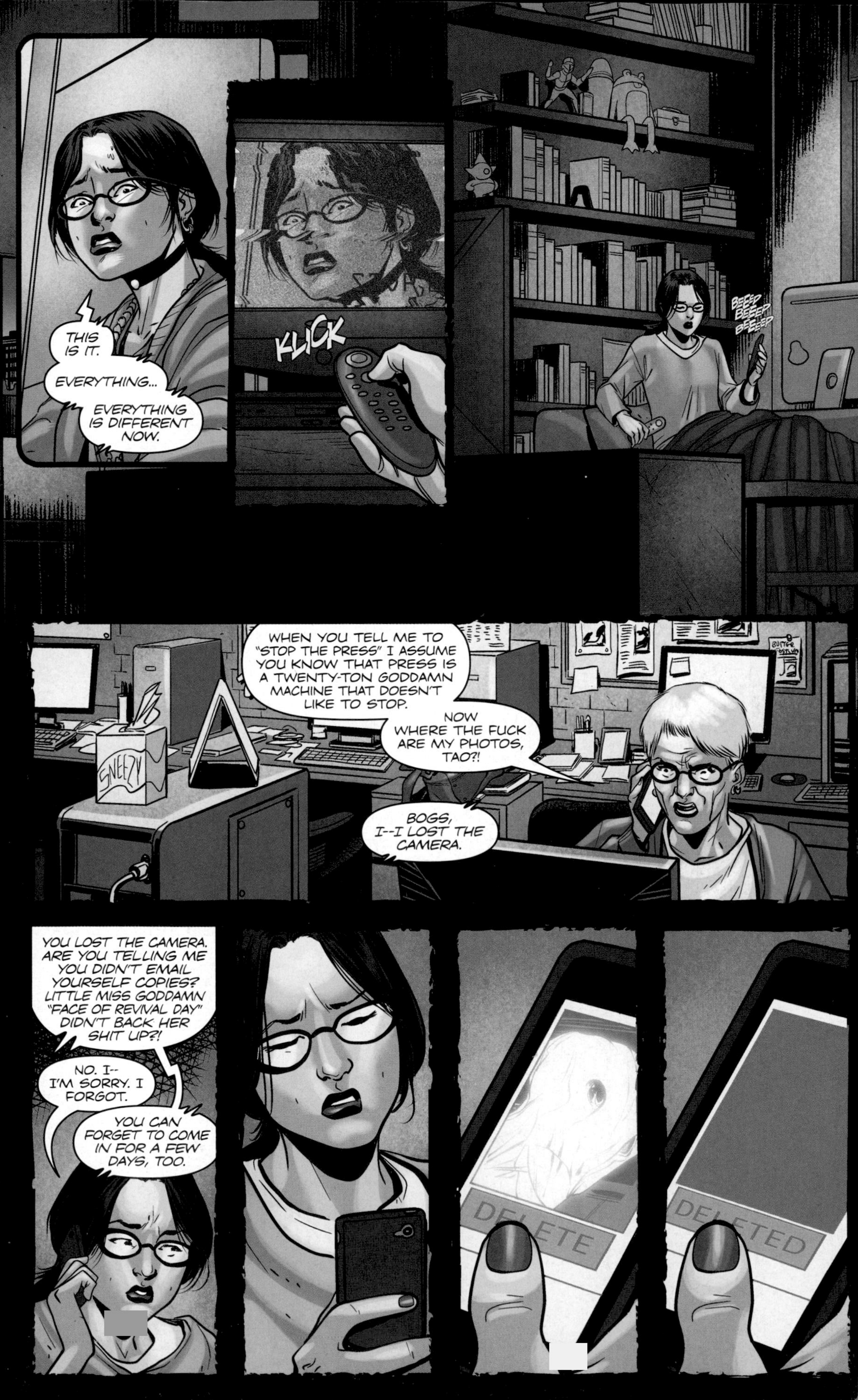

THIS IS IT.
EVERYTHING...
EVERYTHING IS DIFFERENT NOW.
KLICK
BEEEP BEEEP BEEEP
WHEN YOU TELL ME TO "STOP THE PRESS" I ASSUME YOU KNOW THAT PRESS IS A TWENTY-TON GODDAMN MACHINE THAT DOESN'T LIKE TO STOP.
NOW WHERE THE FUCK ARE MY PHOTOS, TAO?!
BOGS, I--I LOST THE CAMERA.
SNEEZY
YOU LOST THE CAMERA. ARE YOU TELLING ME YOU DIDN'T EMAIL YOURSELF COPIES? LITTLE MISS GODDAMN "FACE OF REVIVAL DAY" DIDN'T BACK HER SHIT UP?!
NO. I-- I'M SORRY. I FORGOT.
YOU CAN FORGET TO COME IN FOR A FEW DAYS, TOO.
DELETE
DELETED

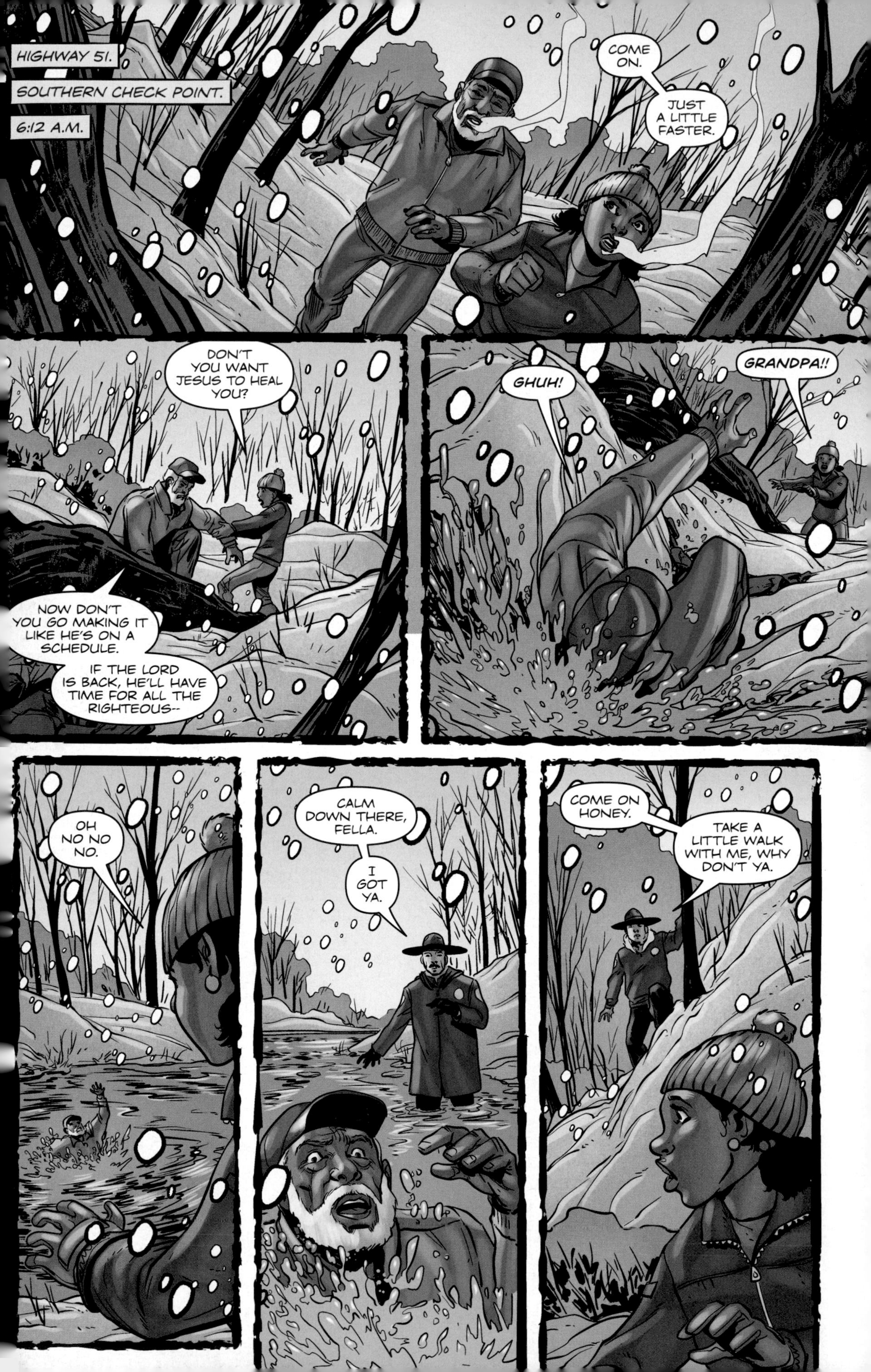
HIGHWAY 51.
SOUTHERN CHECK POINT.
6:12 A.M.
COME ON.
JUST A LITTLE FASTER.
DON'T YOU WANT JESUS TO HEAL YOU?
NOW DON'T YOU GO MAKING IT LIKE HE'S ON A SCHEDULE.
IF THE LORD IS BACK, HE'LL HAVE TIME FOR ALL THE RIGHTEOUS--
GHUH!
GRANDPA!!
OH NO NO NO.
CALM DOWN THERE, FELLA.
I GOT YA.
COME ON HONEY.
TAKE A LITTLE WALK WITH ME, WHY DON'T YA.

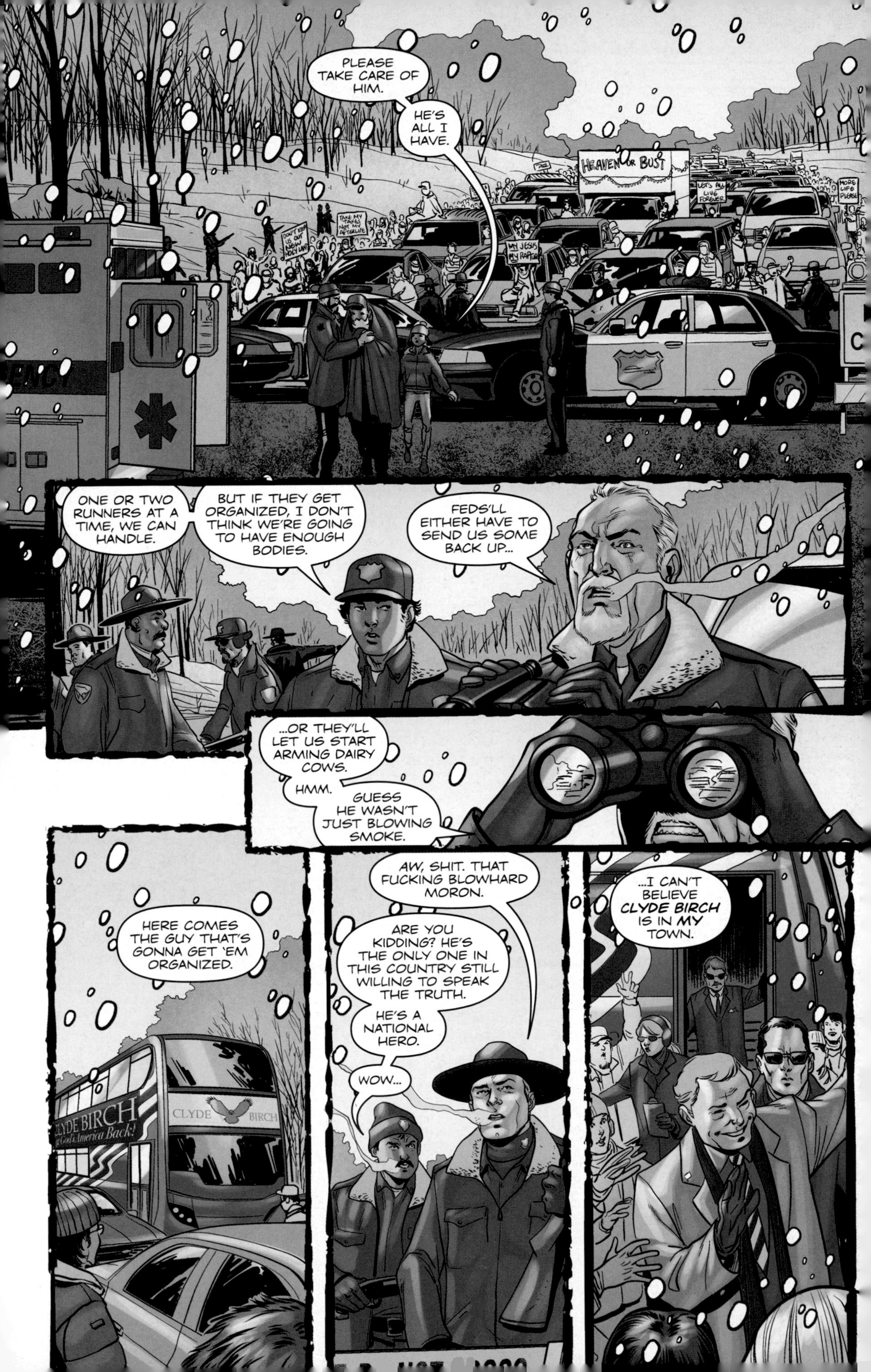
PLEASE TAKE CARE OF HIM.
HE'S ALL I HAVE.
HEAVEN OR BUST
ONE OR TWO RUNNERS AT A TIME, WE CAN HANDLE.
BUT IF THEY GET ORGANIZED, I DON'T THINK WE'RE GOING TO HAVE ENOUGH BODIES.
FEDS'LL EITHER HAVE TO SEND US SOME BACK UP...
...OR THEY'LL LET US START ARMING DAIRY COWS.
HMM.
GUESS HE WASN'T JUST BLOWING SMOKE.
HERE COMES THE GUY THAT'S GONNA GET 'EM ORGANIZED.
CLYDE BIRCH
AW, SHIT. THAT FUCKING BLOWHARD MORON.
ARE YOU KIDDING? HE'S THE ONLY ONE IN THIS COUNTRY STILL WILLING TO SPEAK THE TRUTH.
HE'S A NATIONAL HERO.
WOW...
...I CAN'T BELIEVE ***CLYDE BIRCH*** IS IN ***MY*** TOWN.

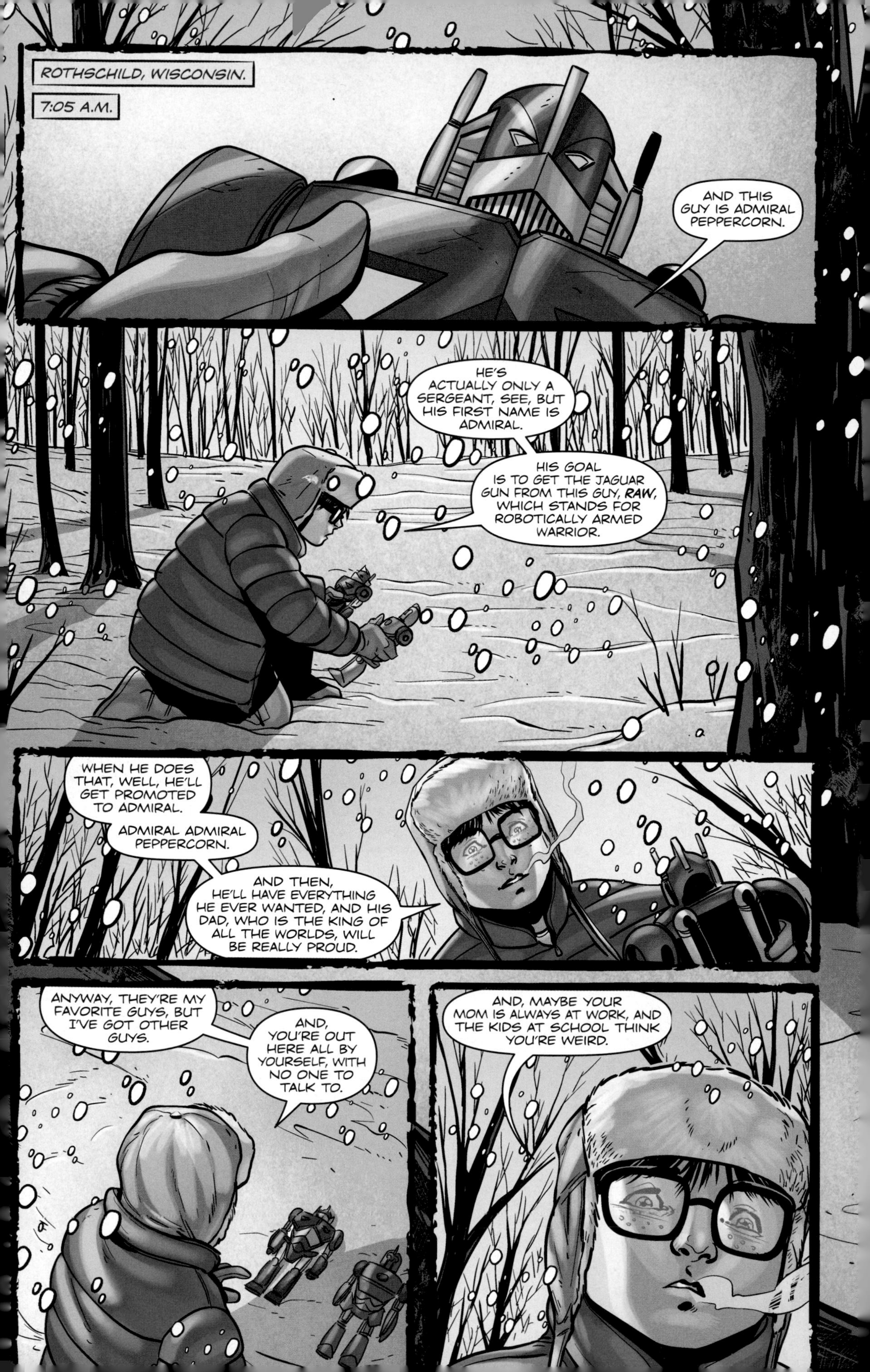
ROTHSCHILD, WISCONSIN.
7:05 A.M.
AND THIS GUY IS ADMIRAL PEPPERCORN.
HE'S ACTUALLY ONLY A SERGEANT, SEE, BUT HIS FIRST NAME IS ADMIRAL.
HIS GOAL IS TO GET THE JAGUAR GUN FROM THIS GUY, RAW, WHICH STANDS FOR ROBOTICALLY ARMED WARRIOR.
WHEN HE DOES THAT, WELL, HE'LL GET PROMOTED TO ADMIRAL.
ADMIRAL ADMIRAL PEPPERCORN.
AND THEN, HE'LL HAVE EVERYTHING HE EVER WANTED, AND HIS DAD, WHO IS THE KING OF ALL THE WORLDS, WILL BE REALLY PROUD.
ANYWAY, THEY'RE MY FAVORITE GUYS, BUT I'VE GOT OTHER GUYS.
AND, YOU'RE OUT HERE ALL BY YOURSELF, WITH NO ONE TO TALK TO.
AND, MAYBE YOUR MOM IS ALWAYS AT WORK, AND THE KIDS AT SCHOOL THINK YOU'RE WEIRD.

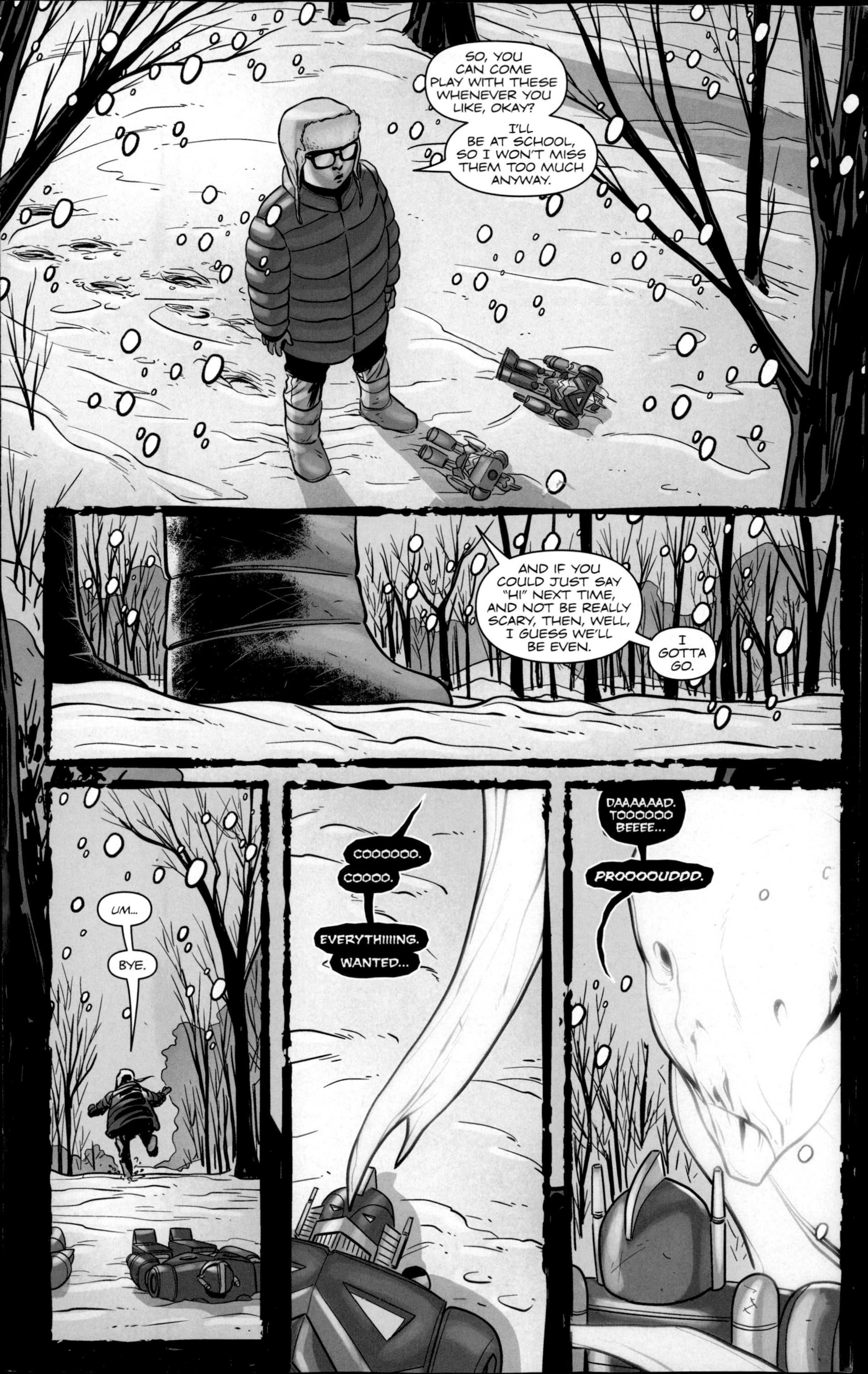
SO, YOU CAN COME PLAY WITH THESE WHENEVER YOU LIKE, OKAY?
I'LL BE AT SCHOOL, SO I WON'T MISS THEM TOO MUCH ANYWAY.
AND IF YOU COULD JUST SAY "HI" NEXT TIME, AND NOT BE REALLY SCARY, THEN, WELL, I GUESS WE'LL BE EVEN.
I GOTTA GO.
UM...
BYE.
COOOOOO.
COOOO.
EVERYTHIIIING.
WANTED...
DAAAAAAD. TOOOOOO BEEEE...
PROOOOUDDD.

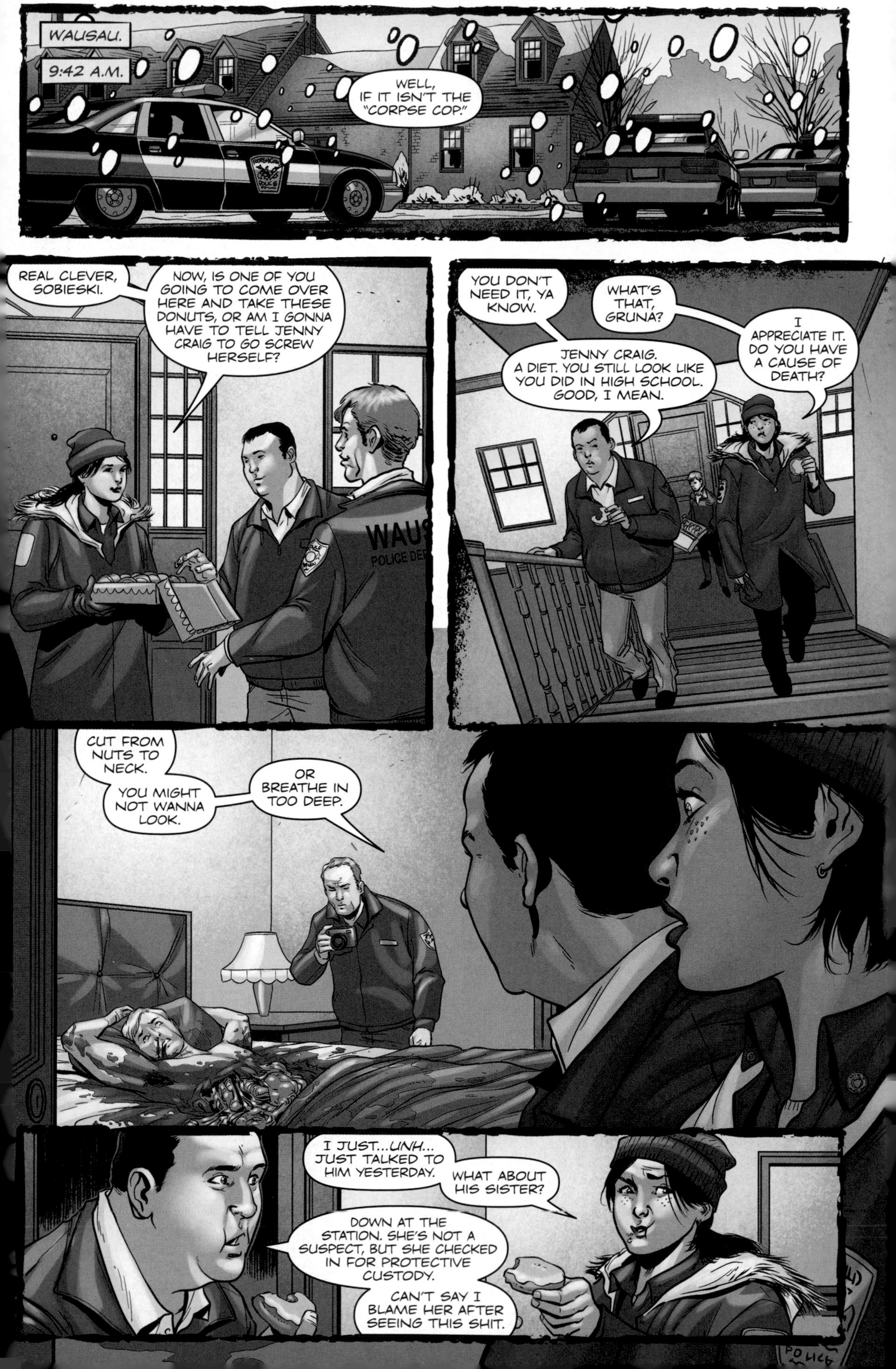
WAUSAU.
9:42 A.M.
WELL, IF IT ISN'T THE "CORPSE COP."
REAL CLEVER, SOBIESKI.
NOW, IS ONE OF YOU GOING TO COME OVER HERE AND TAKE THESE DONUTS, OR AM I GONNA HAVE TO TELL JENNY CRAIG TO GO SCREW HERSELF?
WAUS
POLICE DEP
YOU DON'T NEED IT, YA KNOW.
WHAT'S THAT, GRUNA?
JENNY CRAIG. A DIET. YOU STILL LOOK LIKE YOU DID IN HIGH SCHOOL. GOOD, I MEAN.
I APPRECIATE IT. DO YOU HAVE A CAUSE OF DEATH?
CUT FROM NUTS TO NECK.
YOU MIGHT NOT WANNA LOOK.
OR BREATHE IN TOO DEEP.
I JUST...UNH... JUST TALKED TO HIM YESTERDAY.
WHAT ABOUT HIS SISTER?
DOWN AT THE STATION. SHE'S NOT A SUSPECT, BUT SHE CHECKED IN FOR PROTECTIVE CUSTODY.
CAN'T SAY I BLAME HER AFTER SEEING THIS SHIT.

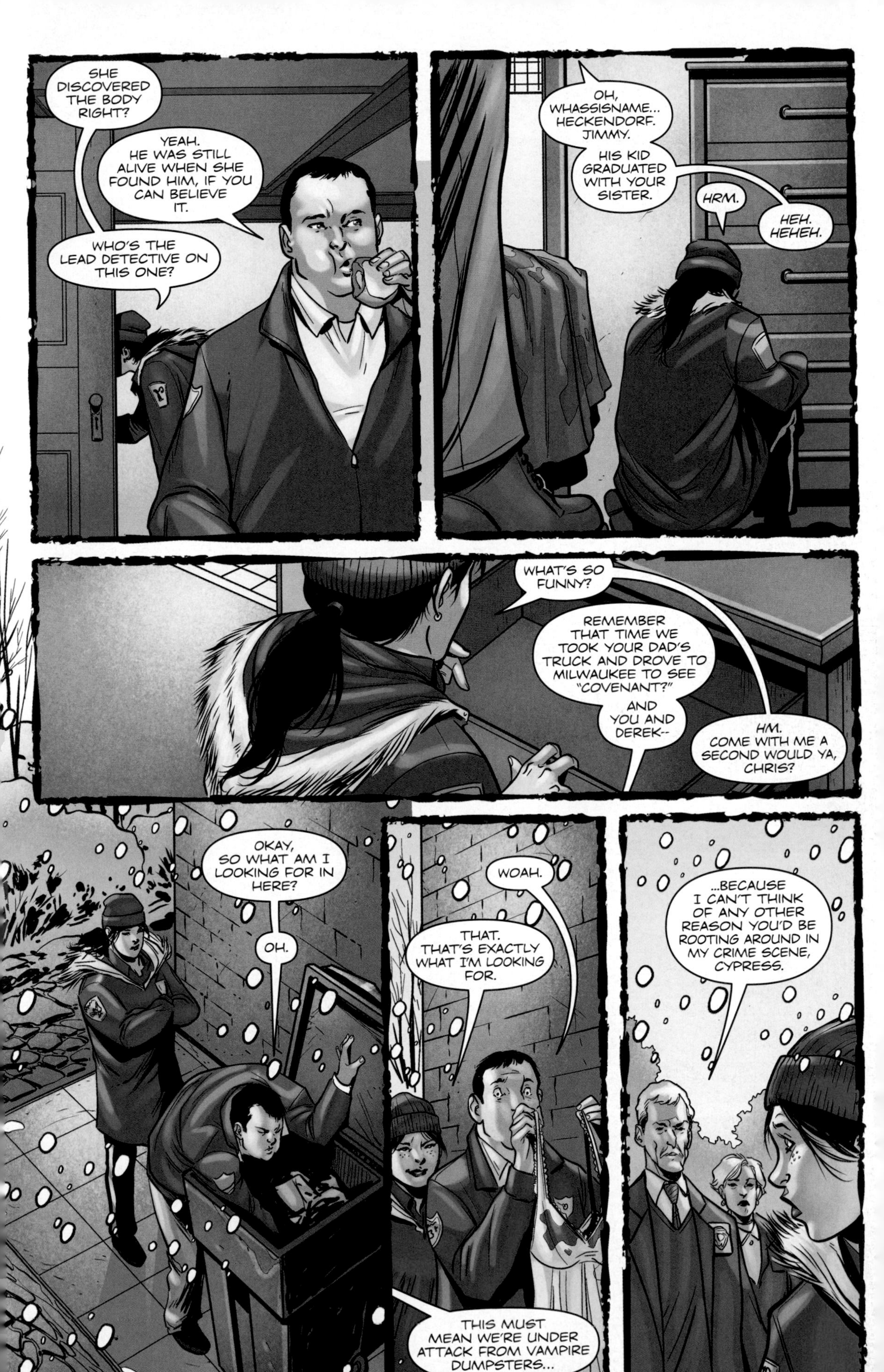

SHE DISCOVERED THE BODY RIGHT?
YEAH. HE WAS STILL ALIVE WHEN SHE FOUND HIM, IF YOU CAN BELIEVE IT.
WHO'S THE LEAD DETECTIVE ON THIS ONE?
OH, WHASSISNAME... HECKENDORF. JIMMY.
HIS KID GRADUATED WITH YOUR SISTER.
HRM.
HEH. HEHEH.
WHAT'S SO FUNNY?
REMEMBER THAT TIME WE TOOK YOUR DAD'S TRUCK AND DROVE TO MILWAUKEE TO SEE "COVENANT?"
AND YOU AND DEREK--
HM. COME WITH ME A SECOND WOULD YA, CHRIS?
OKAY, SO WHAT AM I LOOKING FOR IN HERE?
OH.
WOAH.
THAT. THAT'S EXACTLY WHAT I'M LOOKING FOR.
THIS MUST MEAN WE'RE UNDER ATTACK FROM VAMPIRE DUMPSTERS...
...BECAUSE I CAN'T THINK OF ANY OTHER REASON YOU'D BE ROOTING AROUND IN MY CRIME SCENE, CYPRESS.

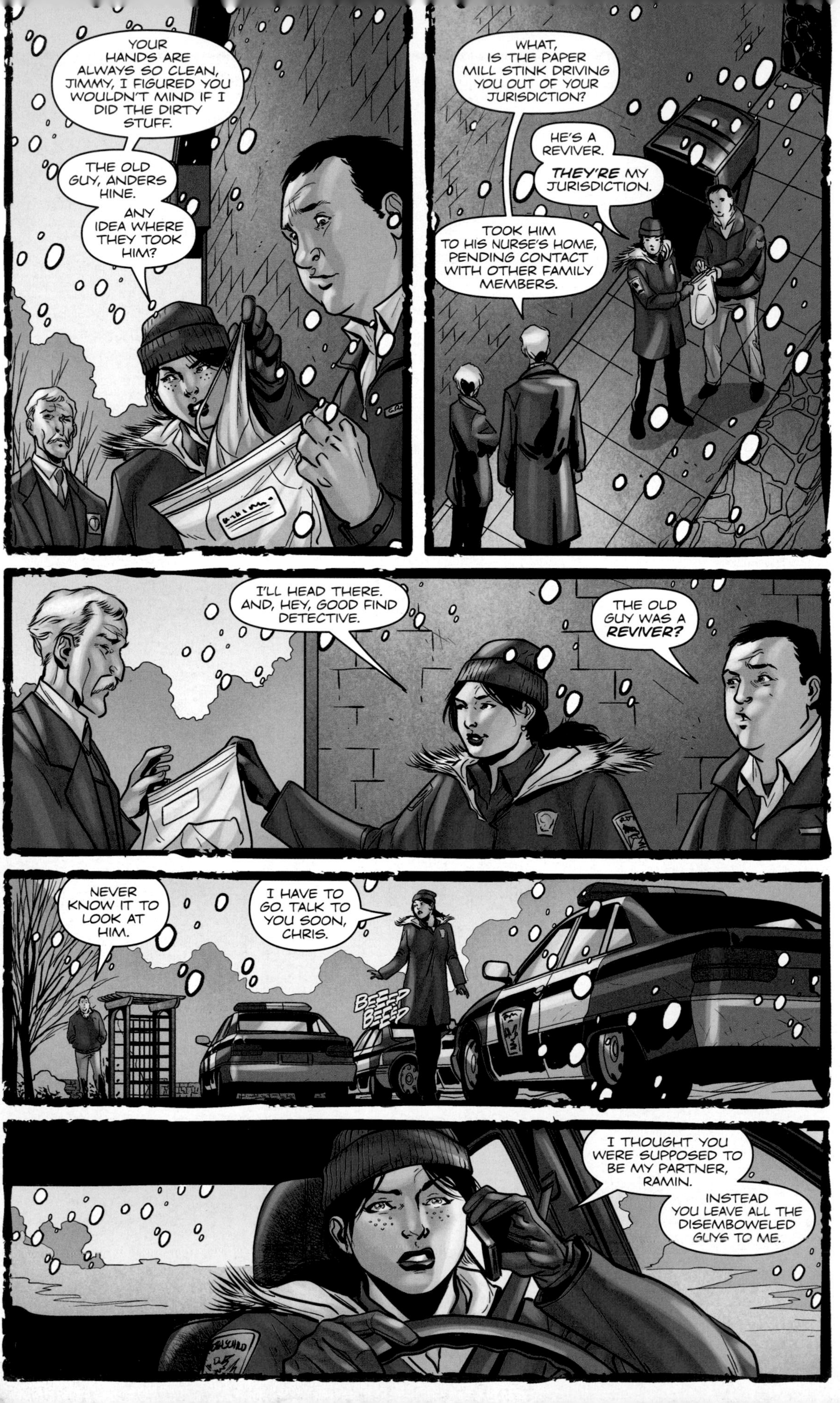
YOUR HANDS ARE ALWAYS SO CLEAN, JIMMY, I FIGURED YOU WOULDN'T MIND IF I DID THE DIRTY STUFF.
THE OLD GUY, ANDERS HINE.
ANY IDEA WHERE THEY TOOK HIM?
WHAT, IS THE PAPER MILL STINK DRIVING YOU OUT OF YOUR JURISDICTION?
HE'S A REVIVER.
THEY'RE MY JURISDICTION.
TOOK HIM TO HIS NURSE'S HOME, PENDING CONTACT WITH OTHER FAMILY MEMBERS.
I'LL HEAD THERE. AND, HEY, GOOD FIND DETECTIVE.
THE OLD GUY WAS A *REVIVER?*
NEVER KNOW IT TO LOOK AT HIM.
I HAVE TO GO. TALK TO YOU SOON, CHRIS.
BEEEP BEEEP
I THOUGHT YOU WERE SUPPOSED TO BE MY PARTNER, RAMIN.
INSTEAD YOU LEAVE ALL THE DISEMBOWELED GUYS TO ME.

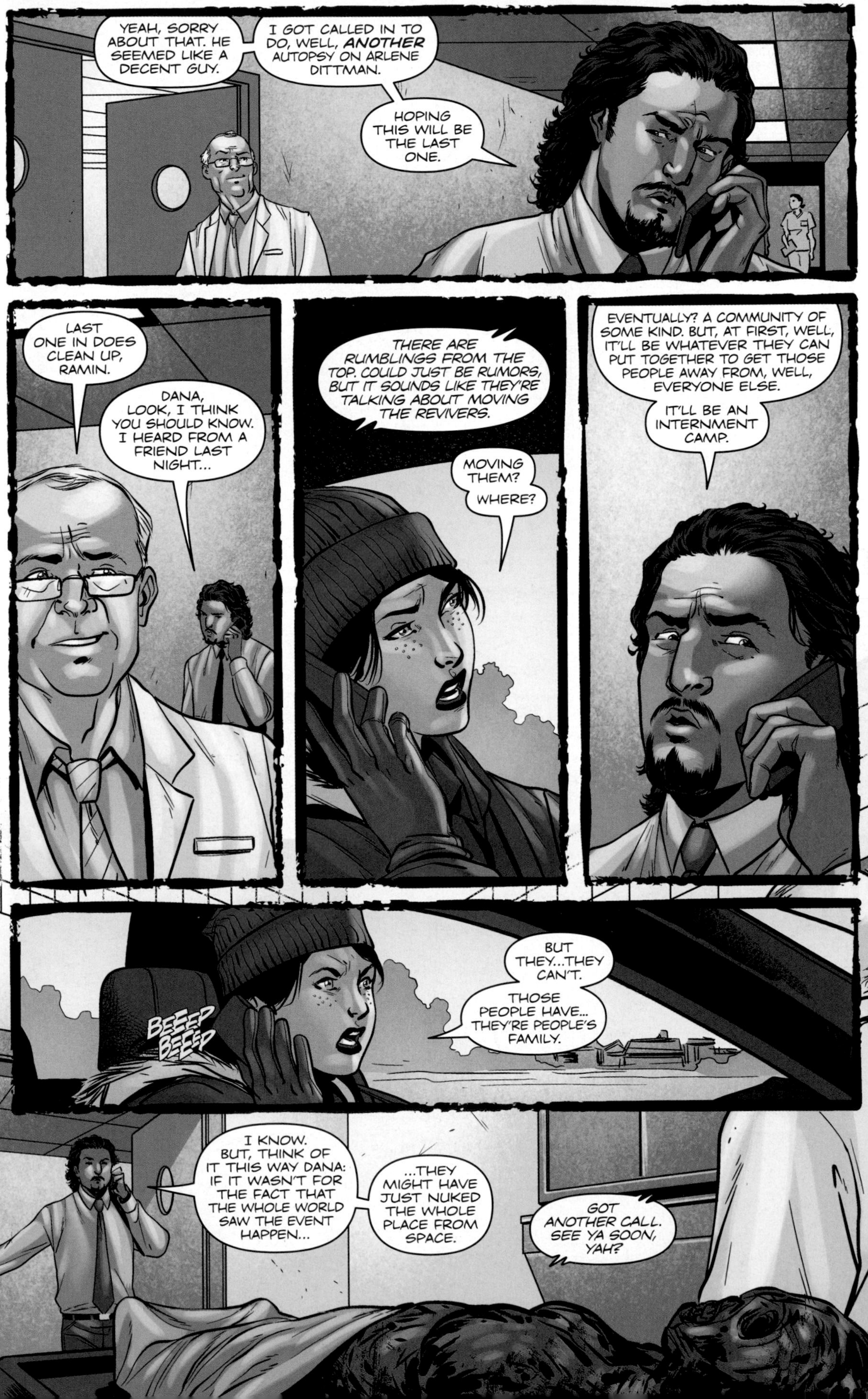

YEAH, SORRY ABOUT THAT. HE SEEMED LIKE A DECENT GUY.
I GOT CALLED IN TO DO, WELL, ANOTHER AUTOPSY ON ARLENE DITTMAN.
HOPING THIS WILL BE THE LAST ONE.
LAST ONE IN DOES CLEAN UP, RAMIN.
DANA, LOOK, I THINK YOU SHOULD KNOW. I HEARD FROM A FRIEND LAST NIGHT...
THERE ARE RUMBLINGS FROM THE TOP. COULD JUST BE RUMORS, BUT IT SOUNDS LIKE THEY'RE TALKING ABOUT MOVING THE REVIVERS.
MOVING THEM?
WHERE?
EVENTUALLY? A COMMUNITY OF SOME KIND. BUT, AT FIRST, WELL, IT'LL BE WHATEVER THEY CAN PUT TOGETHER TO GET THOSE PEOPLE AWAY FROM, WELL, EVERYONE ELSE.
IT'LL BE AN INTERNMENT CAMP.
BEEEP BEEEP
BUT THEY...THEY CAN'T.
THOSE PEOPLE HAVE... THEY'RE PEOPLE'S FAMILY.
I KNOW. BUT, THINK OF IT THIS WAY DANA: IF IT WASN'T FOR THE FACT THAT THE WHOLE WORLD SAW THE EVENT HAPPEN...
...THEY MIGHT HAVE JUST NUKED THE WHOLE PLACE FROM SPACE.
GOT ANOTHER CALL. SEE YA SOON, YAH?

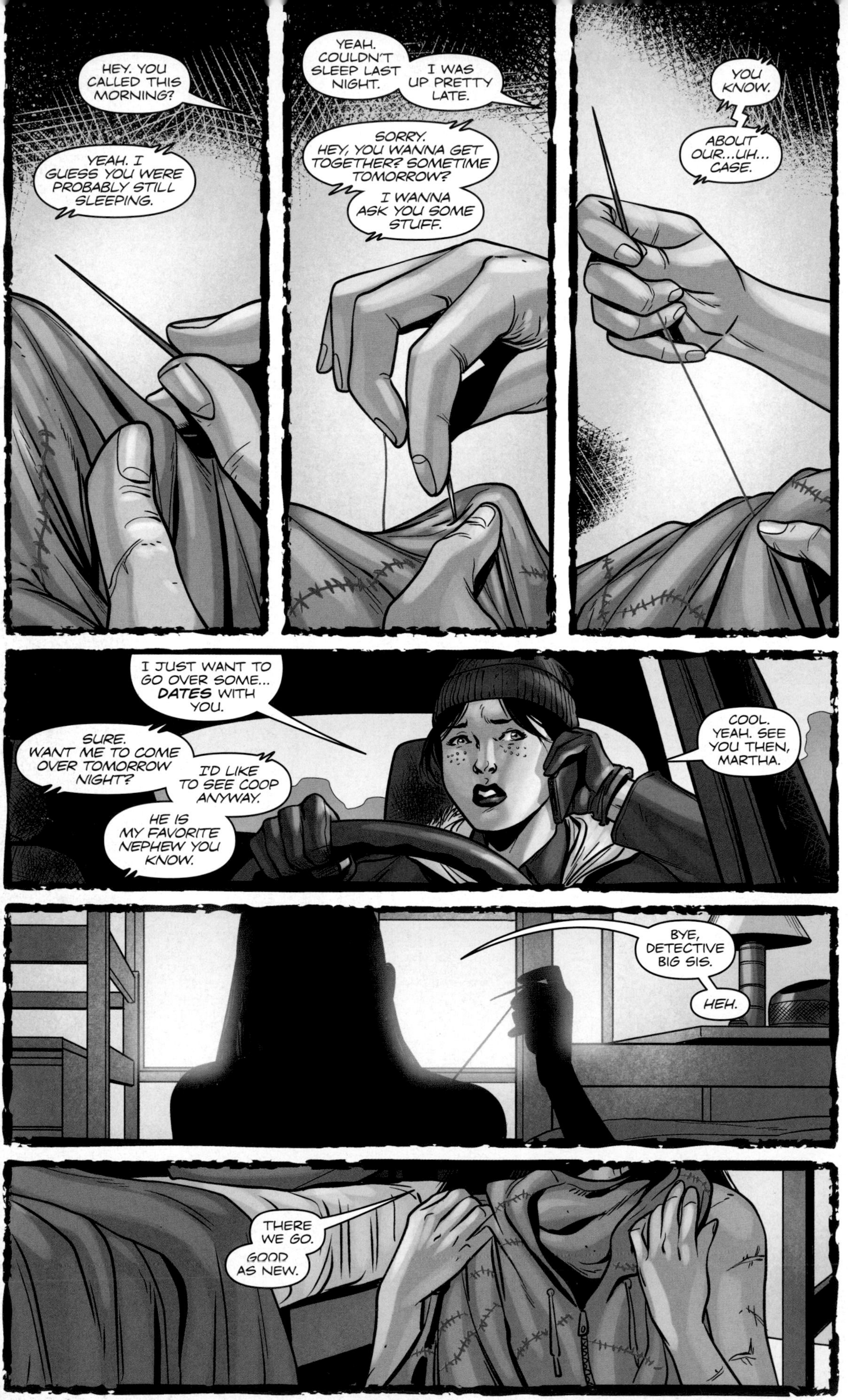
HEY. YOU CALLED THIS MORNING?
YEAH. I GUESS YOU WERE PROBABLY STILL SLEEPING.
YEAH. COULDN'T SLEEP LAST NIGHT.
I WAS UP PRETTY LATE.
SORRY. HEY, YOU WANNA GET TOGETHER? SOMETIME TOMORROW?
I WANNA ASK YOU SOME STUFF.
YOU KNOW.
ABOUT OUR...UH... CASE.
I JUST WANT TO GO OVER SOME... DATES WITH YOU.
SURE. WANT ME TO COME OVER TOMORROW NIGHT?
I'D LIKE TO SEE COOP ANYWAY.
HE IS MY FAVORITE NEPHEW YOU KNOW.
COOL. YEAH. SEE YOU THEN, MARTHA.
BYE, DETECTIVE BIG SIS.
HEH.
THERE WE GO.
GOOD AS NEW.

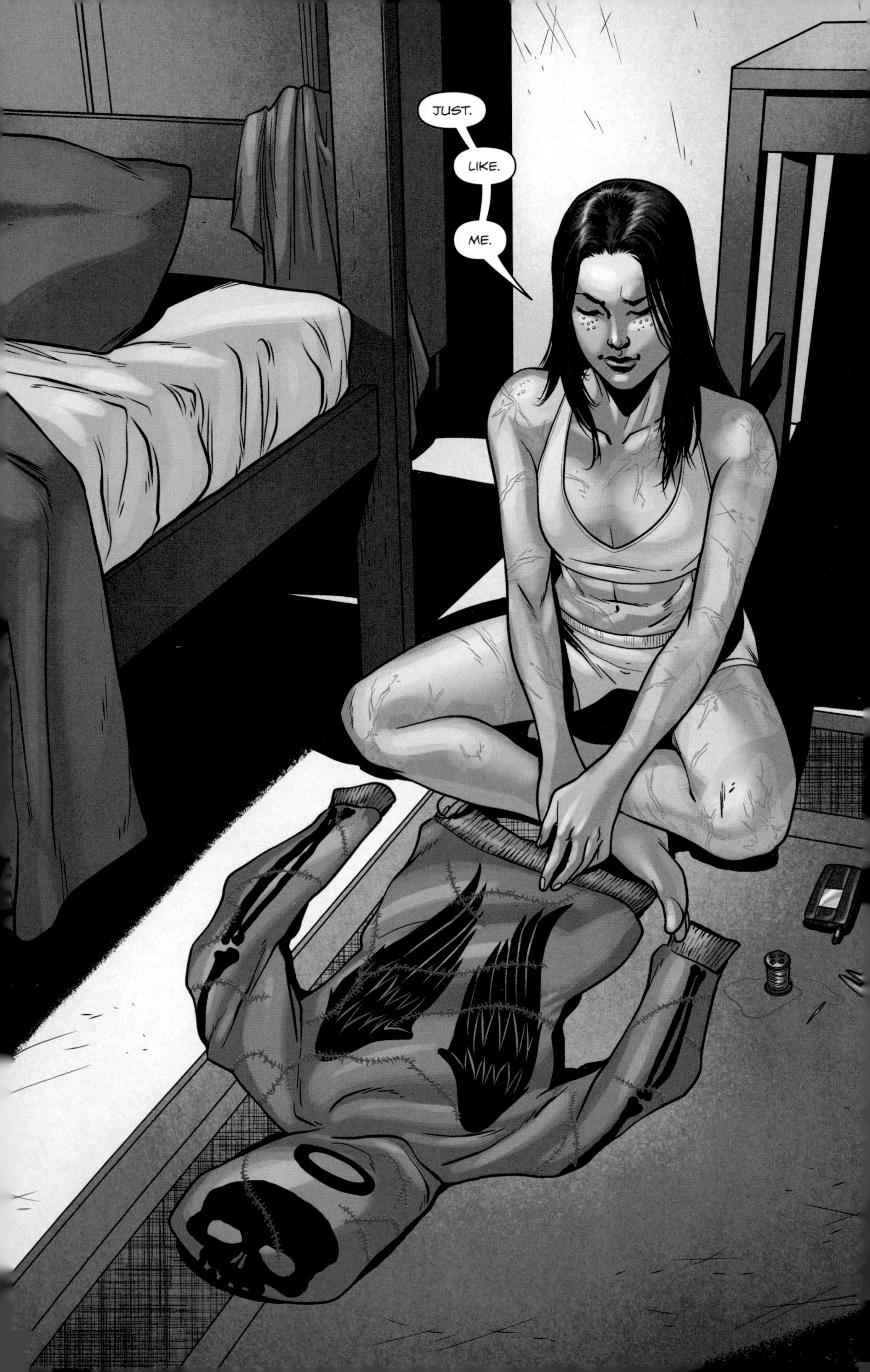
JUST.
LIKE.
ME.

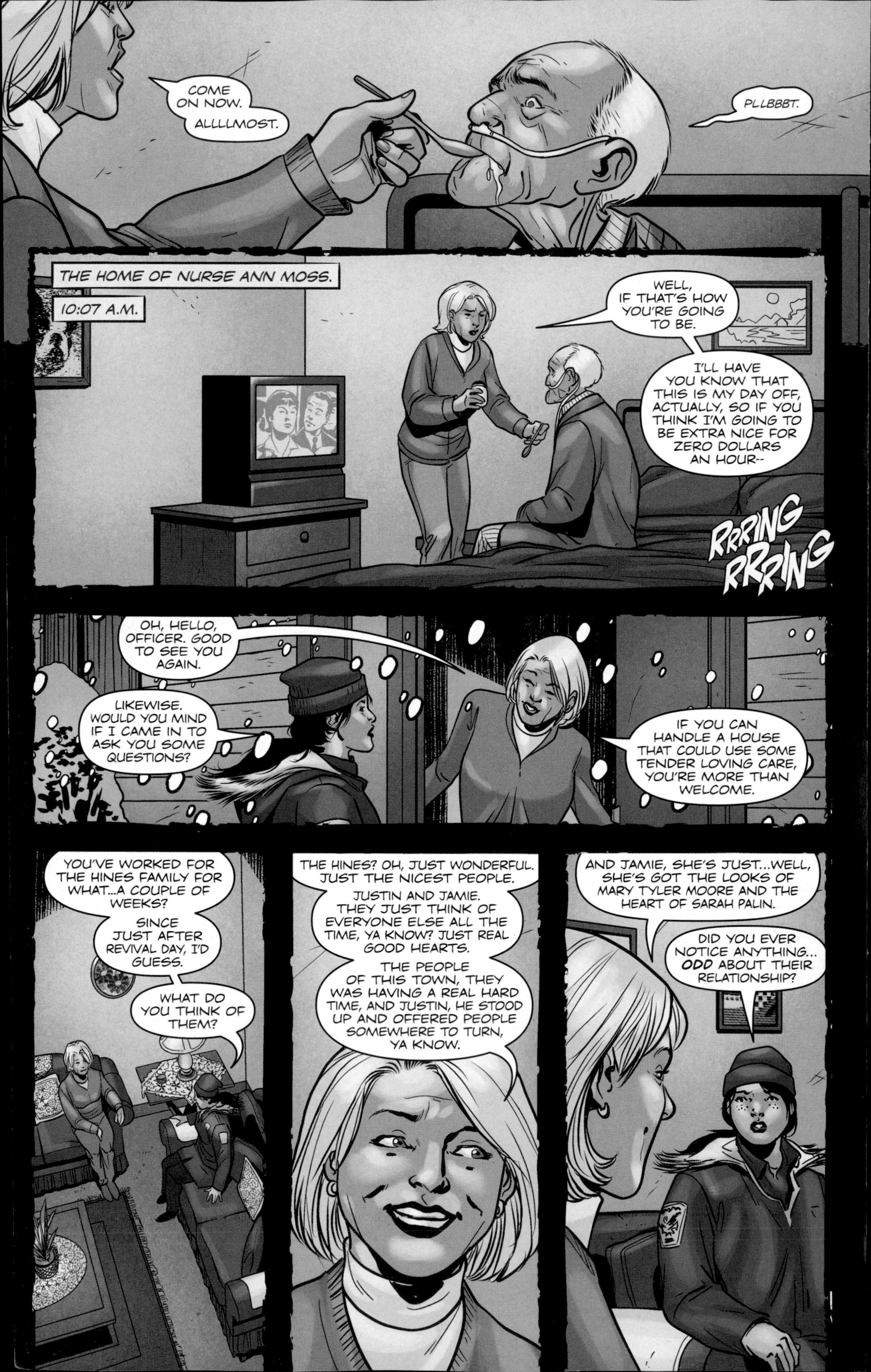
COME ON NOW. ALLLLMOST.
PLLBBBT.
THE HOME OF NURSE ANN MOSS.
10:07 A.M.
WELL, IF THAT'S HOW YOU'RE GOING TO BE.
I'LL HAVE YOU KNOW THAT THIS IS MY DAY OFF, ACTUALLY, SO IF YOU THINK I'M GOING TO BE EXTRA NICE FOR ZERO DOLLARS AN HOUR--
RRRING RRRING
OH, HELLO, OFFICER. GOOD TO SEE YOU AGAIN.
LIKEWISE. WOULD YOU MIND IF I CAME IN TO ASK YOU SOME QUESTIONS?
IF YOU CAN HANDLE A HOUSE THAT COULD USE SOME TENDER LOVING CARE, YOU'RE MORE THAN WELCOME.
YOU'VE WORKED FOR THE HINES FAMILY FOR WHAT...A COUPLE OF WEEKS?
SINCE JUST AFTER REVIVAL DAY, I'D GUESS.
WHAT DO YOU THINK OF THEM?
THE HINES? OH, JUST WONDERFUL. JUST THE NICEST PEOPLE.
JUSTIN AND JAMIE. THEY JUST THINK OF EVERYONE ELSE ALL THE TIME, YA KNOW? JUST REAL GOOD HEARTS.
THE PEOPLE OF THIS TOWN, THEY WAS HAVING A REAL HARD TIME, AND JUSTIN, HE STOOD UP AND OFFERED PEOPLE SOMEWHERE TO TURN, YA KNOW.
AND JAMIE, SHE'S JUST...WELL, SHE'S GOT THE LOOKS OF MARY TYLER MOORE AND THE HEART OF SARAH PALIN.
DID YOU EVER NOTICE ANYTHING... ODD ABOUT THEIR RELATIONSHIP?

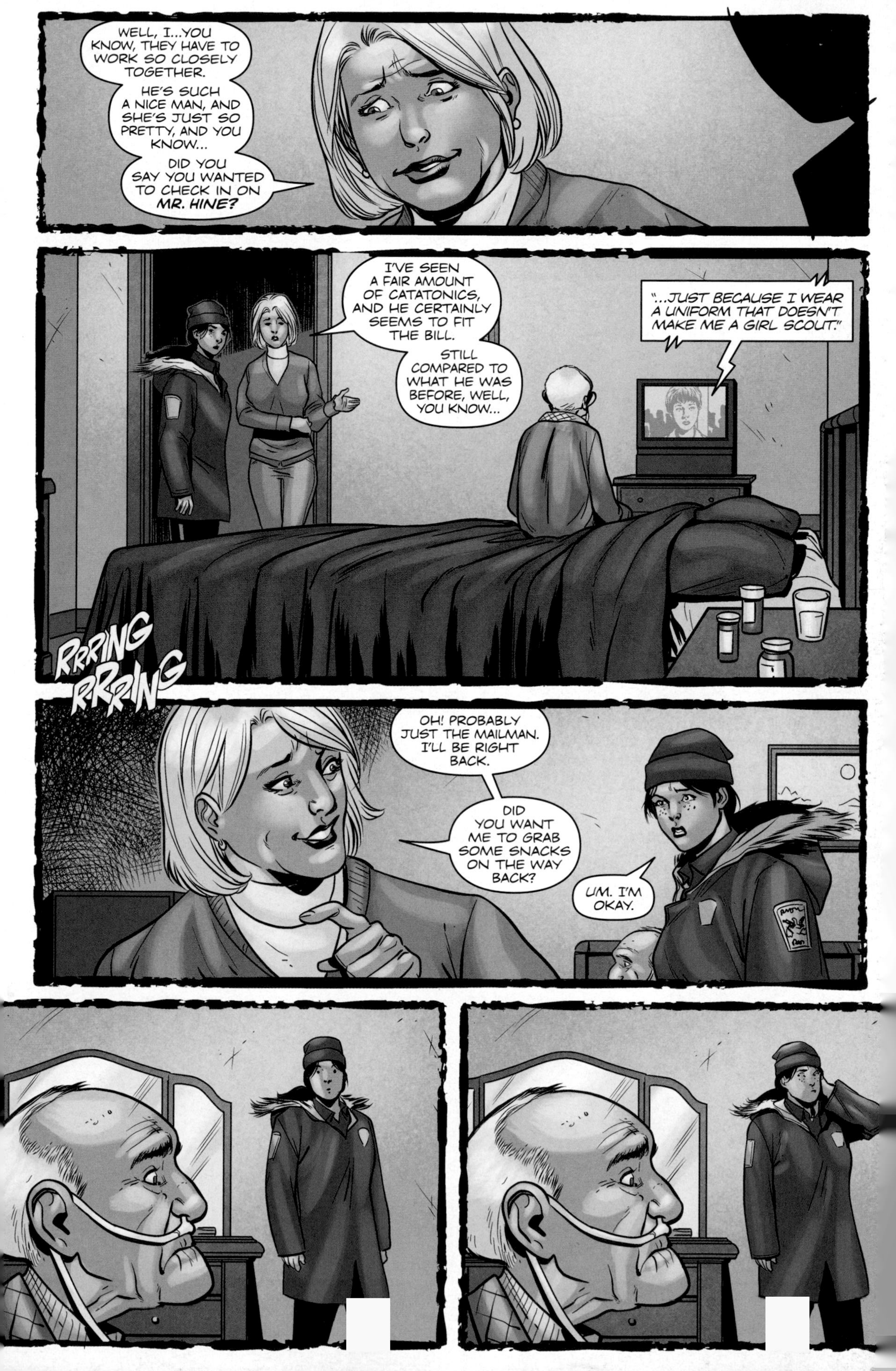
WELL, I...YOU KNOW, THEY HAVE TO WORK SO CLOSELY TOGETHER.
HE'S SUCH A NICE MAN, AND SHE'S JUST SO PRETTY, AND YOU KNOW...
DID YOU SAY YOU WANTED TO CHECK IN ON MR. HINE?
I'VE SEEN A FAIR AMOUNT OF CATATONICS, AND HE CERTAINLY SEEMS TO FIT THE BILL.
STILL COMPARED TO WHAT HE WAS BEFORE, WELL, YOU KNOW...
"...JUST BECAUSE I WEAR A UNIFORM THAT DOESN'T MAKE ME A GIRL SCOUT."
RRRING RRRING
OH! PROBABLY JUST THE MAILMAN. I'LL BE RIGHT BACK.
DID YOU WANT ME TO GRAB SOME SNACKS ON THE WAY BACK?
UM. I'M OKAY.

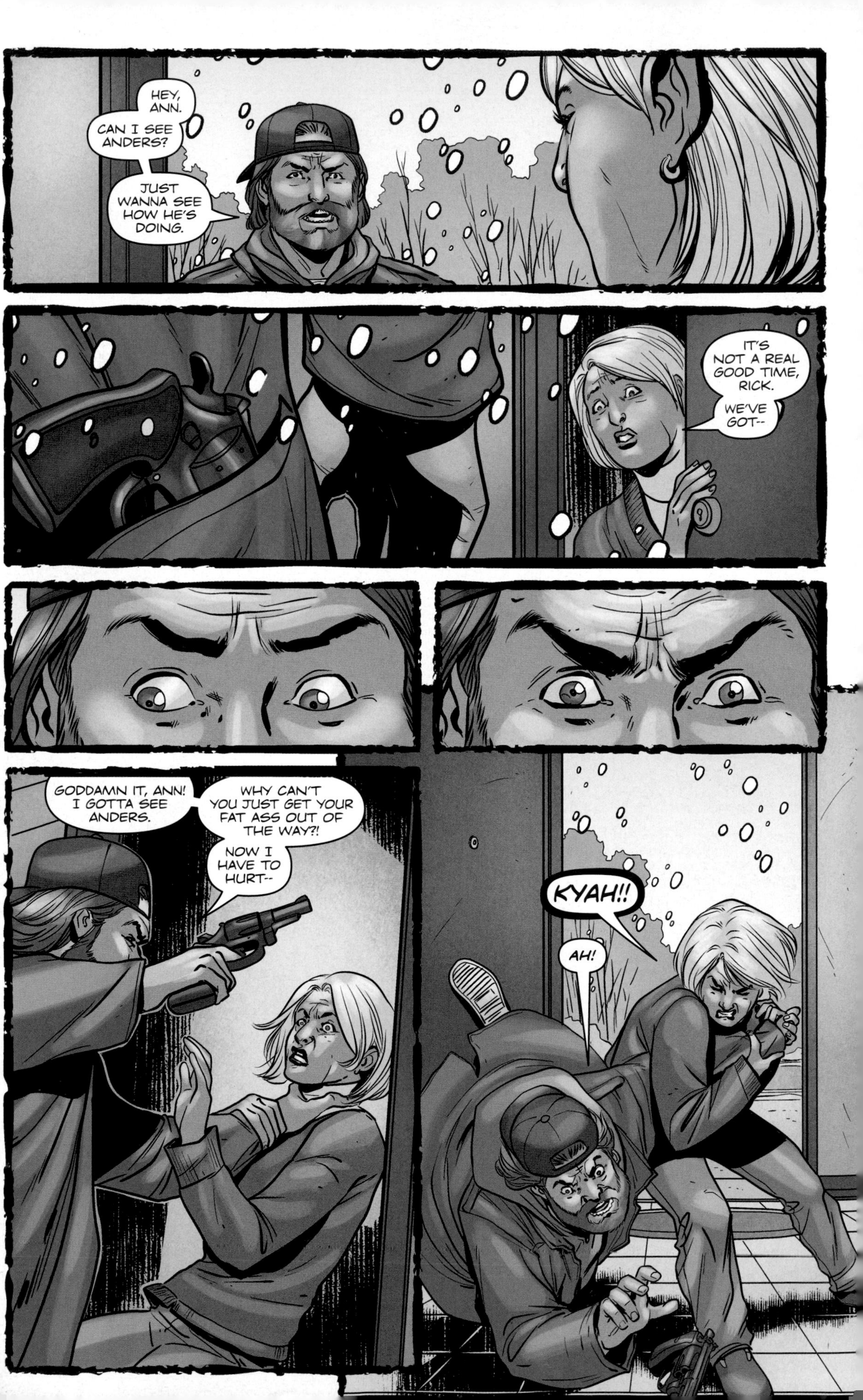
HEY, ANN.
CAN I SEE ANDERS?
JUST WANNA SEE HOW HE'S DOING.
IT'S NOT A REAL GOOD TIME, RICK.
WE'VE GOT--
GODDAMN IT, ANN! I GOTTA SEE ANDERS.
WHY CAN'T YOU JUST GET YOUR FAT ASS OUT OF THE WAY?!
NOW I HAVE TO HURT--
KYAH!!
AH!

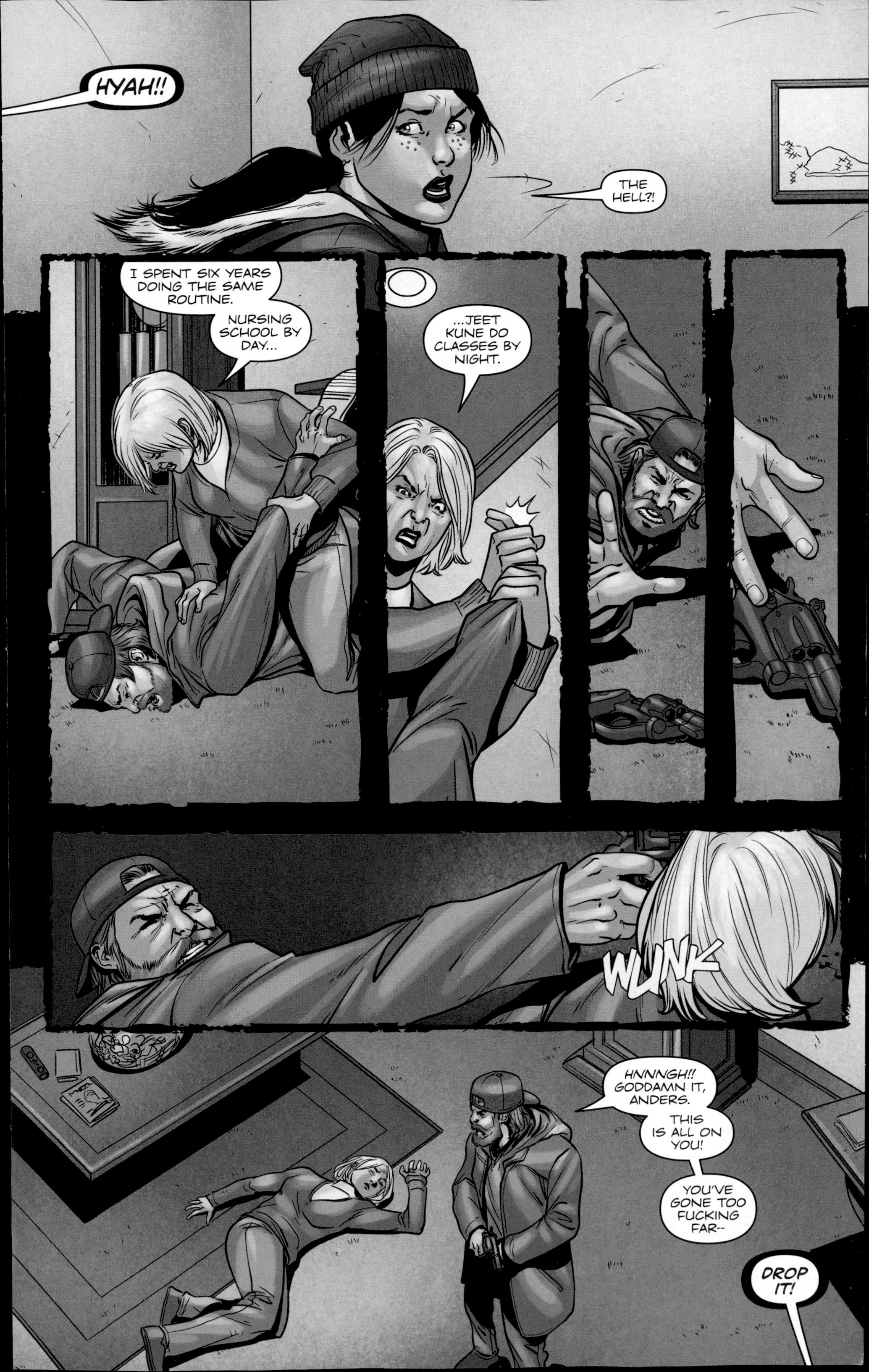
HYAH!!
THE HELL?!
I SPENT SIX YEARS DOING THE SAME ROUTINE.
NURSING SCHOOL BY DAY...
...JEET KUNE DO CLASSES BY NIGHT.
WUNK
HNNNGH!! GODDAMN IT, ANDERS.
THIS IS ALL ON YOU!
YOU'VE GONE TOO FUCKING FAR--
DROP IT!

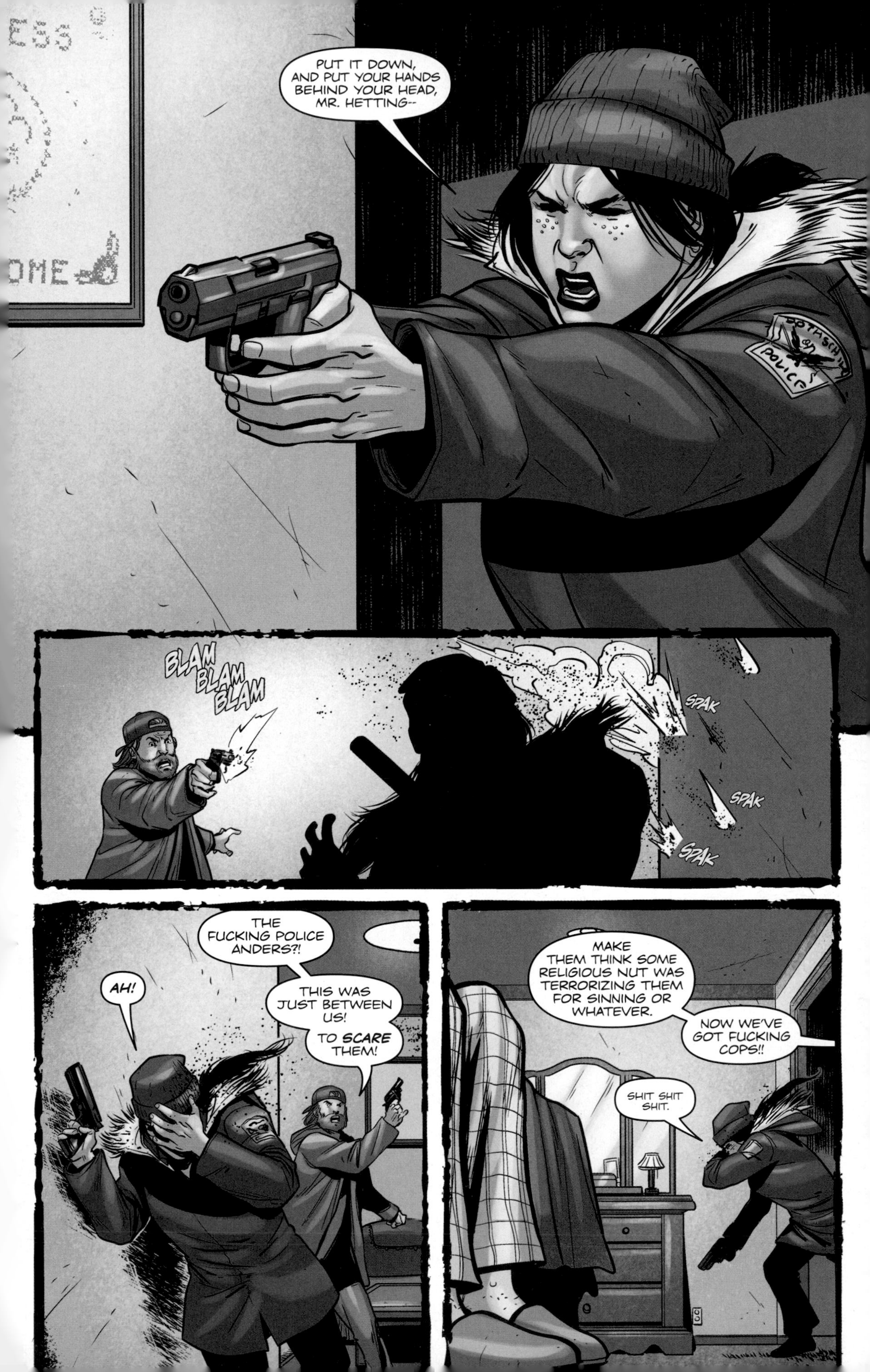
PUT IT DOWN, AND PUT YOUR HANDS BEHIND YOUR HEAD, MR. HETTING--
BLAM BLAM BLAM
SPAK
SPAK
SPAK
AH!
THE FUCKING POLICE ANDERS?!
THIS WAS JUST BETWEEN US!
TO SCARE THEM!
MAKE THEM THINK SOME RELIGIOUS NUT WAS TERRORIZING THEM FOR SINNING OR WHATEVER.
NOW WE'VE GOT FUCKING COPS!!
SHIT SHIT SHIT.

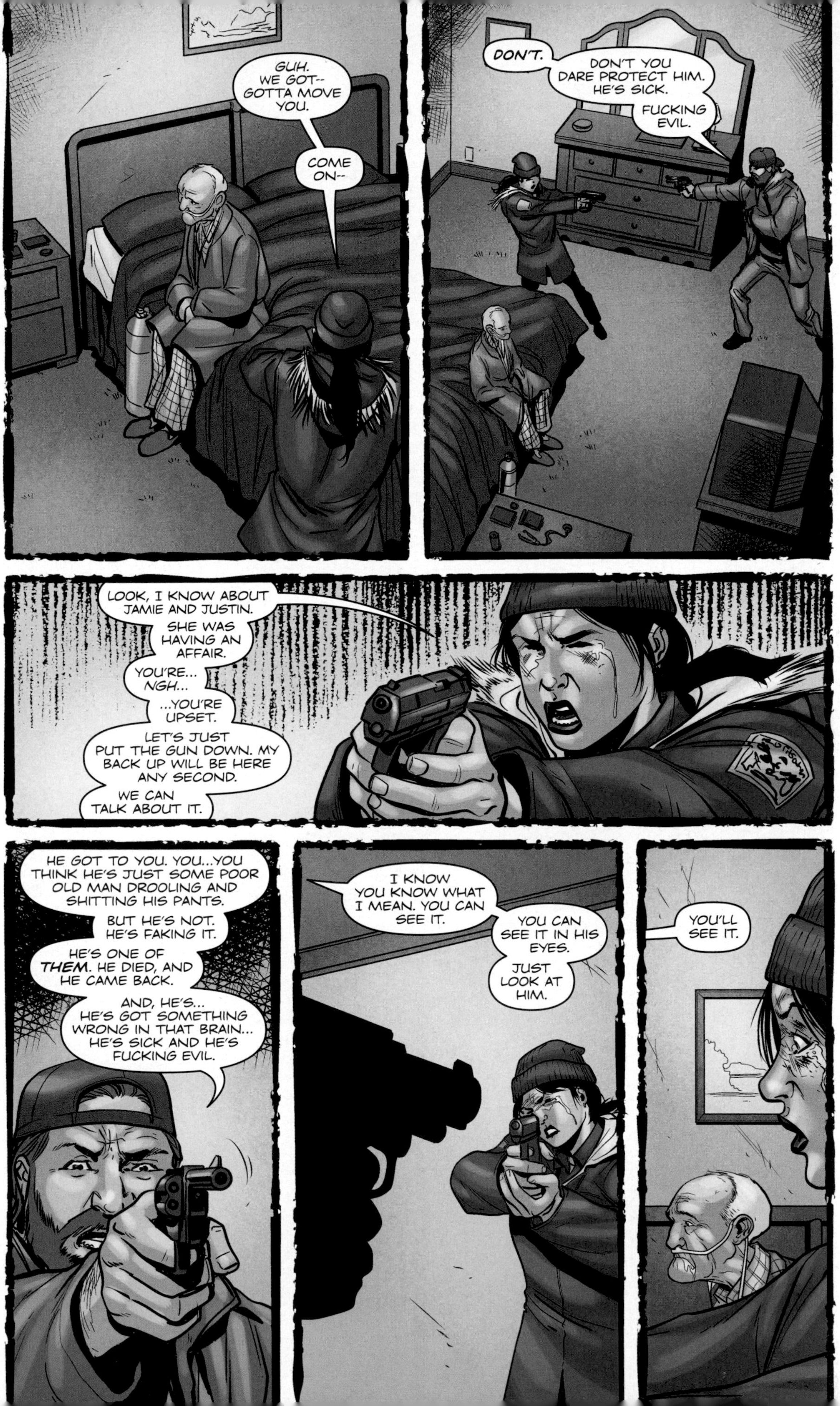
GUH. WE GOT-- GOTTA MOVE YOU.
COME ON--
DON'T.
DON'T YOU DARE PROTECT HIM. HE'S SICK.
FUCKING EVIL.
LOOK, I KNOW ABOUT JAMIE AND JUSTIN.
SHE WAS HAVING AN AFFAIR.
YOU'RE... NGH...
...YOU'RE UPSET.
LET'S JUST PUT THE GUN DOWN. MY BACK UP WILL BE HERE ANY SECOND.
WE CAN TALK ABOUT IT.
HE GOT TO YOU. YOU...YOU THINK HE'S JUST SOME POOR OLD MAN DROOLING AND SHITTING HIS PANTS.
BUT HE'S NOT. HE'S FAKING IT.
HE'S ONE OF THEM. HE DIED, AND HE CAME BACK.
AND, HE'S... HE'S GOT SOMETHING WRONG IN THAT BRAIN... HE'S SICK AND HE'S FUCKING EVIL.
I KNOW YOU KNOW WHAT I MEAN. YOU CAN SEE IT.
YOU CAN SEE IT IN HIS EYES.
JUST LOOK AT HIM.
YOU'LL SEE IT.

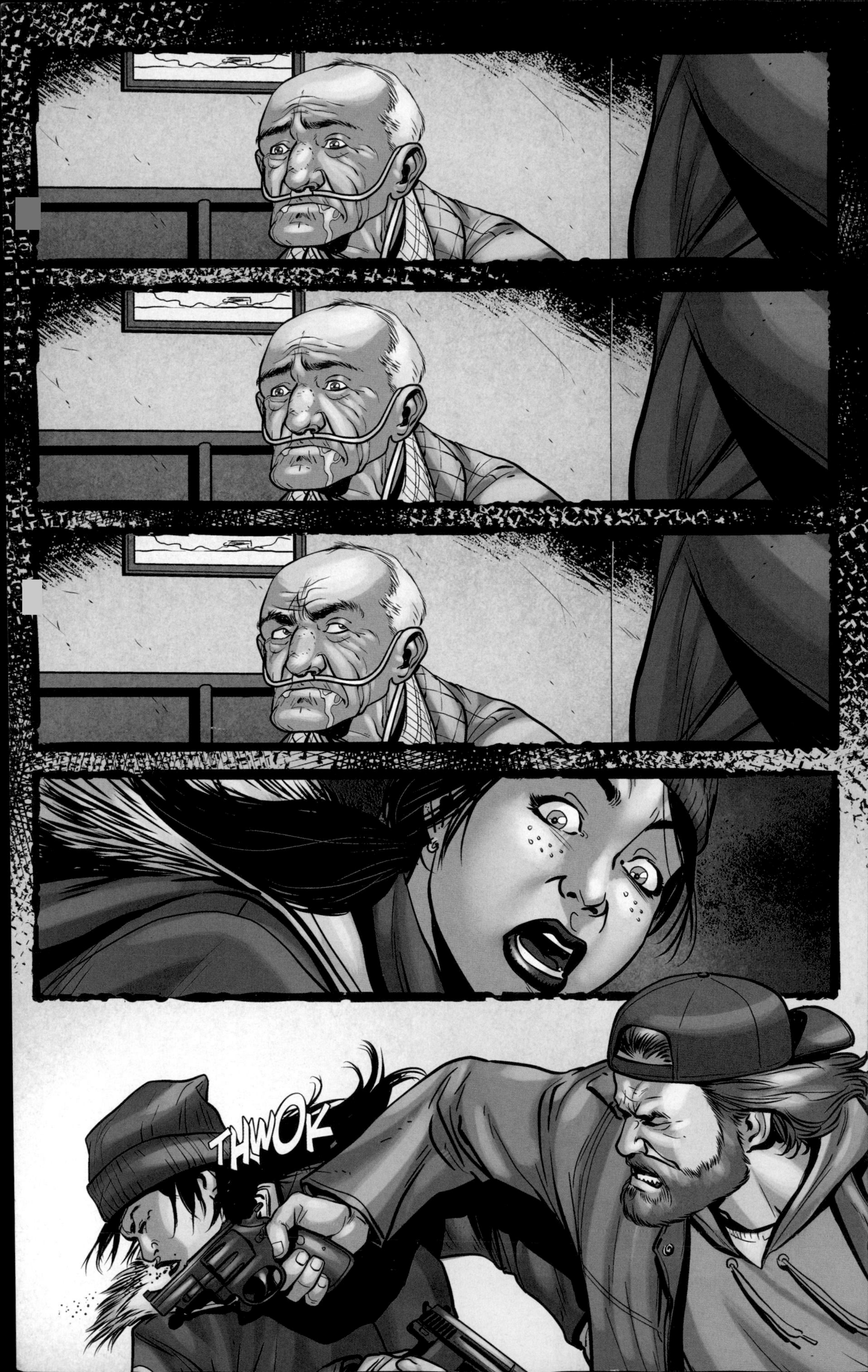
THWOK

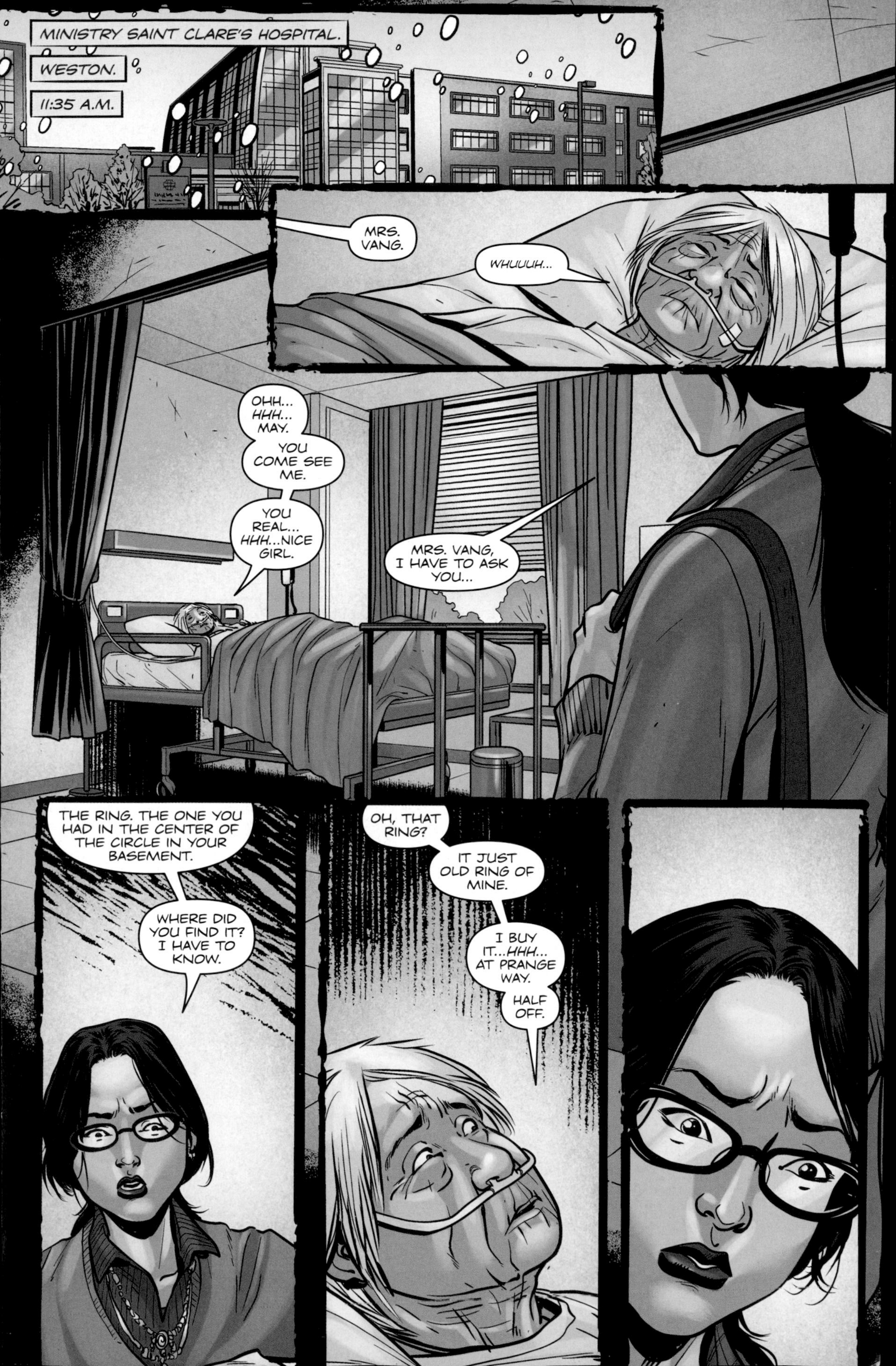
MINISTRY SAINT CLARE'S HOSPITAL.
WESTON.
11:35 A.M.
MRS. VANG.
WHUUUH...
OHH... HHH... MAY.
YOU COME SEE ME.
YOU REAL... HHH...NICE GIRL.
MRS. VANG, I HAVE TO ASK YOU...
THE RING. THE ONE YOU HAD IN THE CENTER OF THE CIRCLE IN YOUR BASEMENT.
WHERE DID YOU FIND IT? I HAVE TO KNOW.
OH, THAT RING?
IT JUST OLD RING OF MINE.
I BUY IT...HHH... AT PRANGE WAY.
HALF OFF.

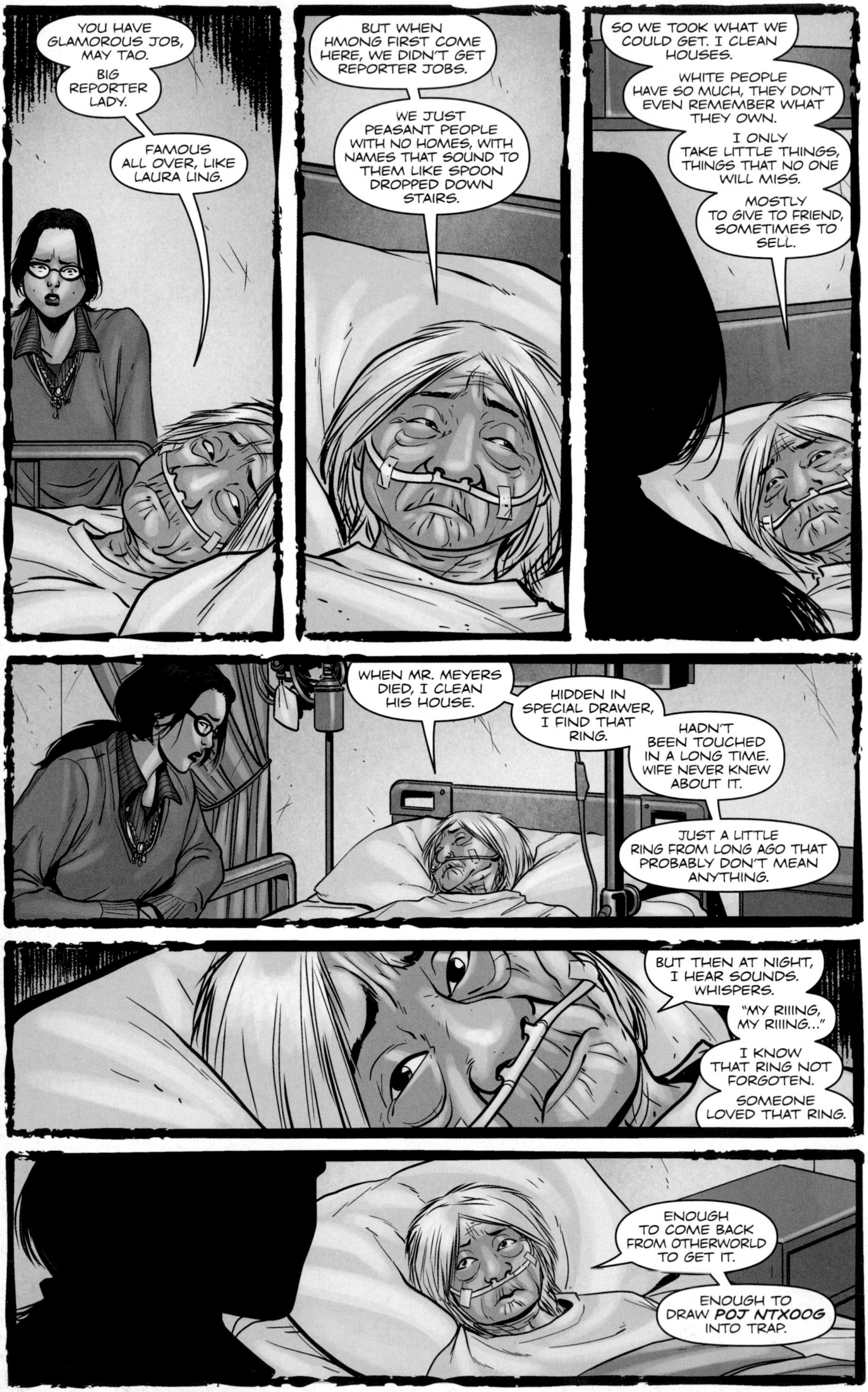
YOU HAVE GLAMOROUS JOB, MAY TAO.
BIG REPORTER LADY.
FAMOUS ALL OVER, LIKE LAURA LING.
BUT WHEN HMONG FIRST COME HERE, WE DIDN'T GET REPORTER JOBS.
WE JUST PEASANT PEOPLE WITH NO HOMES, WITH NAMES THAT SOUND TO THEM LIKE SPOON DROPPED DOWN STAIRS.
SO WE TOOK WHAT WE COULD GET. I CLEAN HOUSES.
WHITE PEOPLE HAVE SO MUCH, THEY DON'T EVEN REMEMBER WHAT THEY OWN.
I ONLY TAKE LITTLE THINGS, THINGS THAT NO ONE WILL MISS.
MOSTLY TO GIVE TO FRIEND, SOMETIMES TO SELL.
WHEN MR. MEYERS DIED, I CLEAN HIS HOUSE.
HIDDEN IN SPECIAL DRAWER, I FIND THAT RING.
HADN'T BEEN TOUCHED IN A LONG TIME. WIFE NEVER KNEW ABOUT IT.
JUST A LITTLE RING FROM LONG AGO THAT PROBABLY DON'T MEAN ANYTHING.
BUT THEN AT NIGHT, I HEAR SOUNDS. WHISPERS.
"MY RIIING, MY RIIING..."
I KNOW THAT RING NOT FORGOTEN.
SOMEONE LOVED THAT RING.
ENOUGH TO COME BACK FROM OTHERWORLD TO GET IT.
ENOUGH TO DRAW ***POJ NTXOOG*** INTO TRAP.

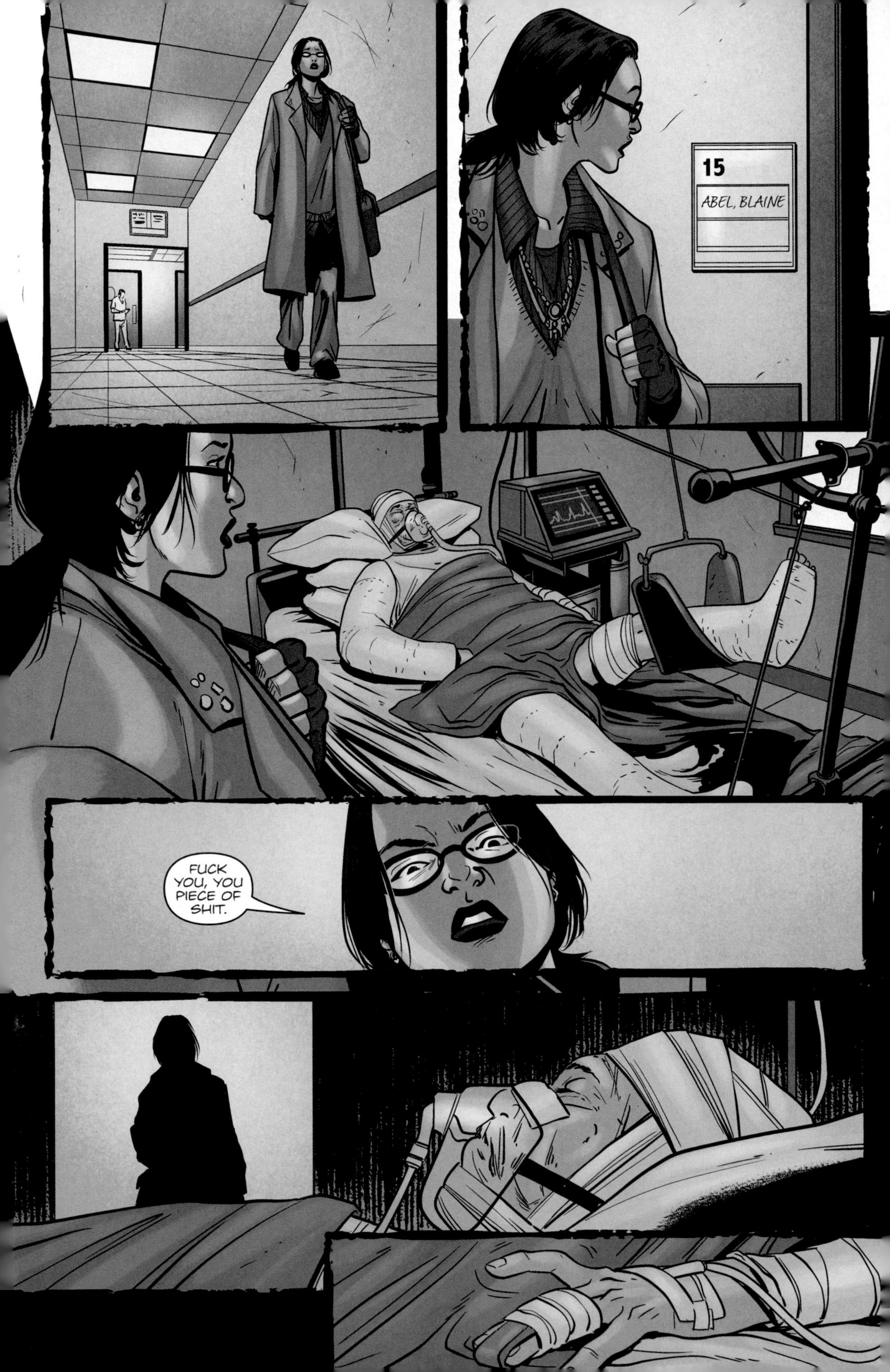
15
ABEL, BLAINE
FUCK YOU, YOU PIECE OF SHIT.

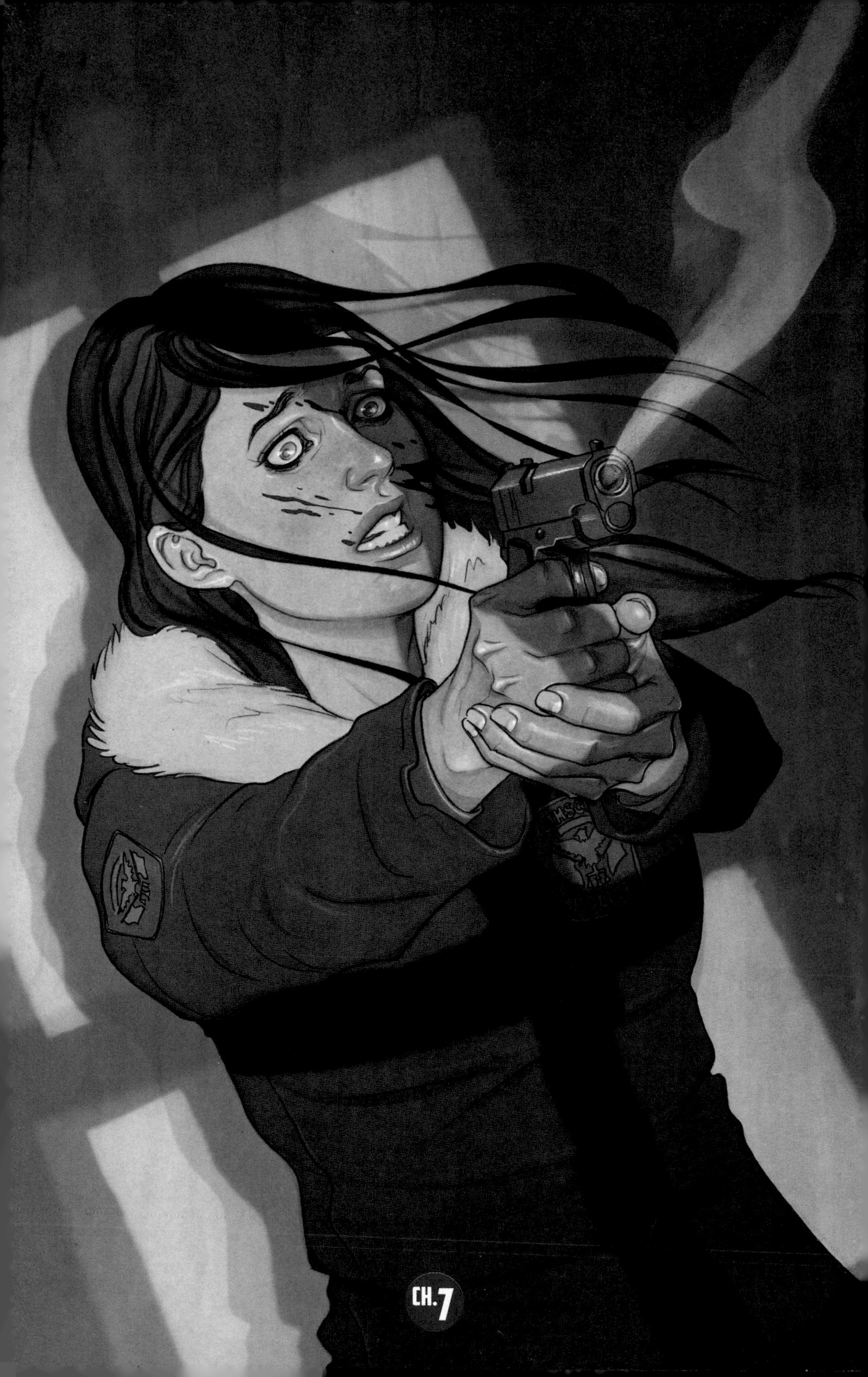
CH. 7

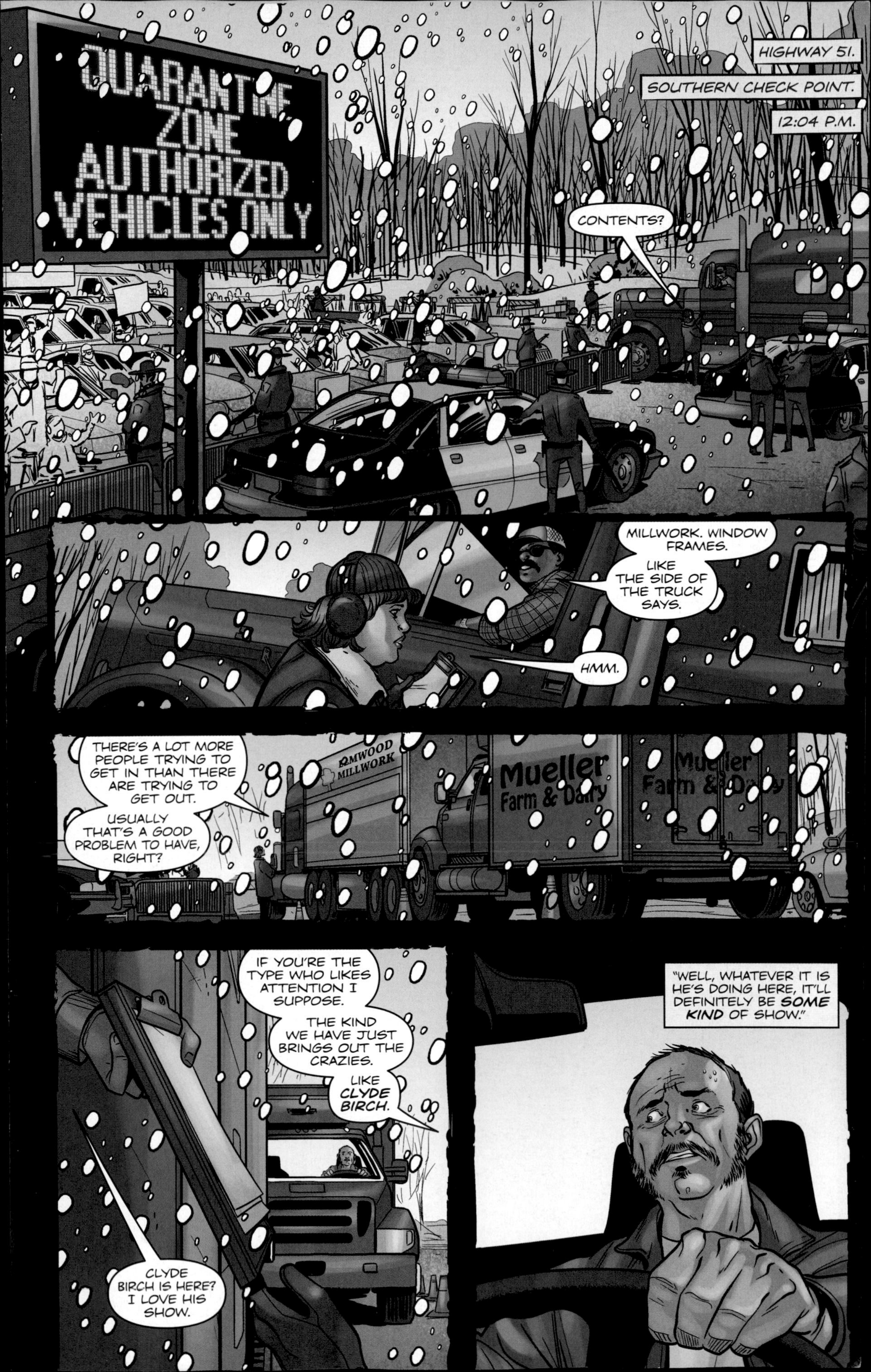
QUARANTINE ZONE AUTHORIZED VEHICLES ONLY
HIGHWAY 51.
SOUTHERN CHECK POINT.
12:04 P.M.
CONTENTS?
MILLWORK. WINDOW FRAMES.
LIKE THE SIDE OF THE TRUCK SAYS.
HMM.
THERE'S A LOT MORE PEOPLE TRYING TO GET IN THAN THERE ARE TRYING TO GET OUT.
USUALLY THAT'S A GOOD PROBLEM TO HAVE, RIGHT?
MILLWORK
Mueller Farm & Dairy
Mueller Farm & Dairy
IF YOU'RE THE TYPE WHO LIKES ATTENTION I SUPPOSE.
THE KIND WE HAVE JUST BRINGS OUT THE CRAZIES.
LIKE CLYDE BIRCH.
CLYDE BIRCH IS HERE? I LOVE HIS SHOW.
"WELL, WHATEVER IT IS HE'S DOING HERE, IT'LL DEFINITELY BE SOME KIND OF SHOW."

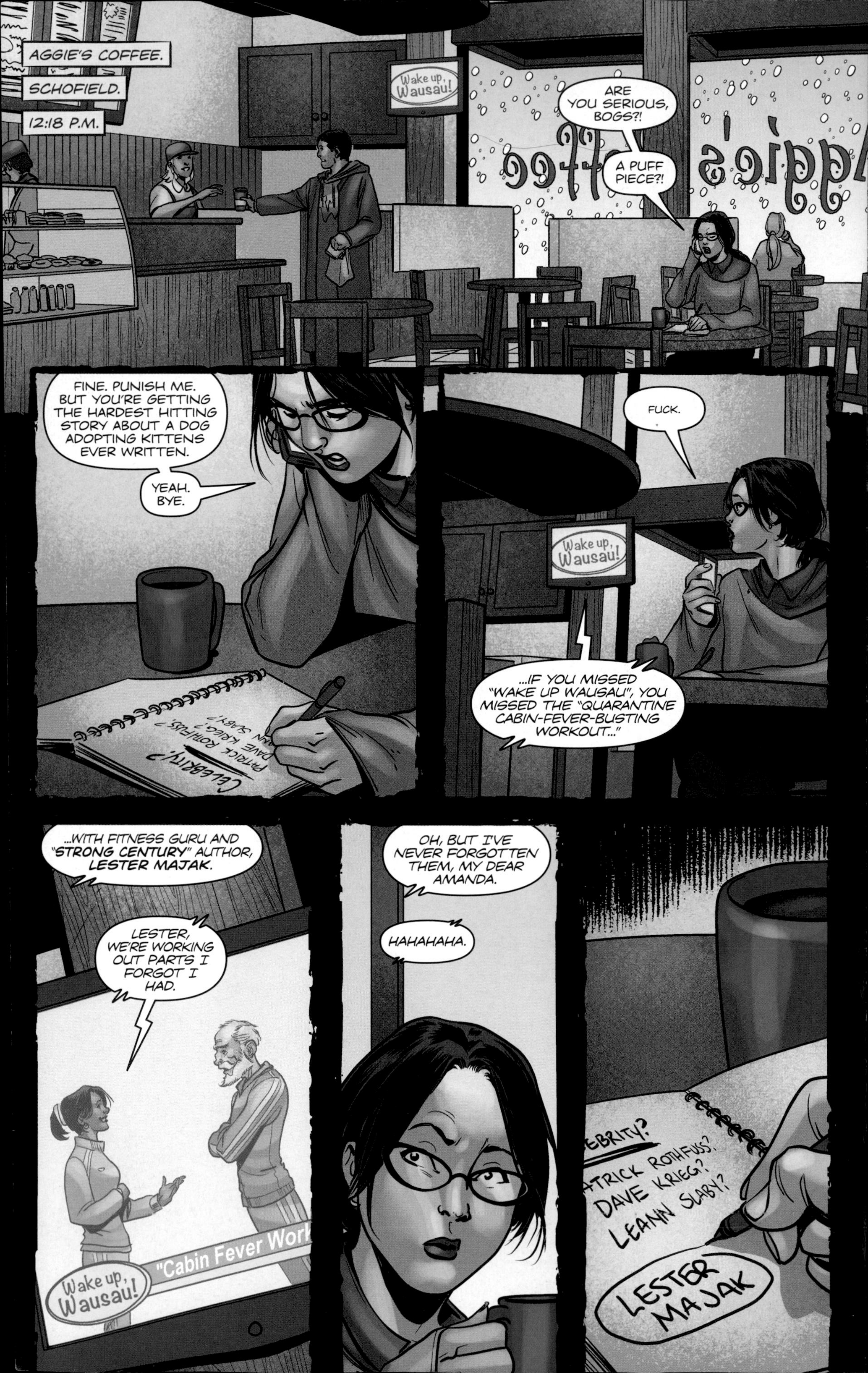
AGGIE'S COFFEE.
SCHOFIELD.
12:18 P.M.
Wake up, Wausau!
ARE YOU SERIOUS, BOGS?!
A PUFF PIECE?!
FINE. PUNISH ME. BUT YOU'RE GETTING THE HARDEST HITTING STORY ABOUT A DOG ADOPTING KITTENS EVER WRITTEN.
YEAH. BYE.
FUCK.
Wake up, Wausau!
...IF YOU MISSED "WAKE UP WAUSAU", YOU MISSED THE "QUARANTINE CABIN-FEVER-BUSTING WORKOUT..."
...WITH FITNESS GURU AND "STRONG CENTURY" AUTHOR, LESTER MAJAK.
LESTER, WE'RE WORKING OUT PARTS I FORGOT I HAD.
"Cabin Fever Work
Wake up, Wausau!
OH, BUT I'VE NEVER FORGOTTEN THEM, MY DEAR AMANDA.
HAHAHAHA.
EBRITY?
ATRICK ROTHFUSS?
DAVE KRIEG?
LEANN SLABY?
LESTER MAJAK

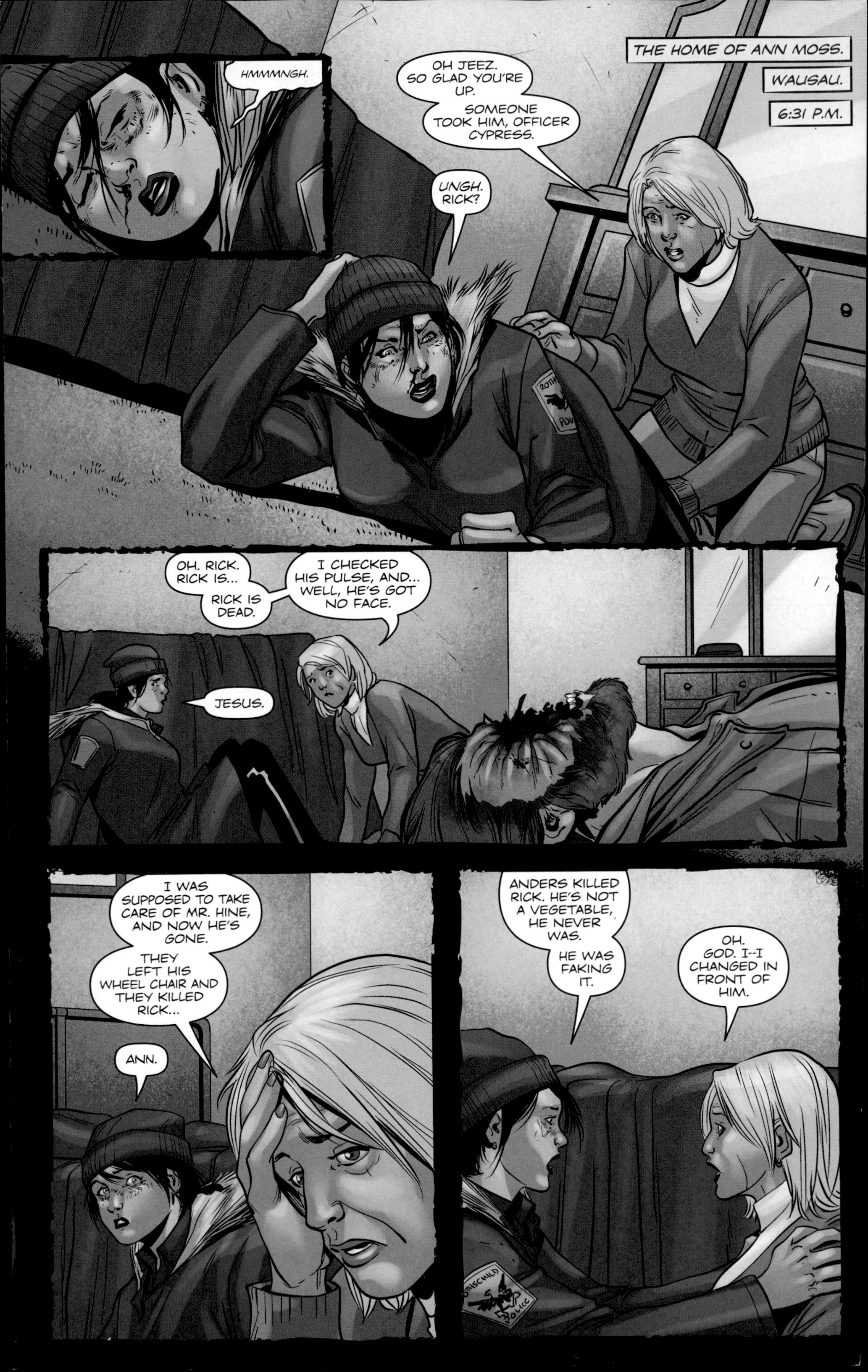
THE HOME OF ANN MOSS.
WAUSAU.
6:31 P.M.
HMMMNGH.
OH JEEZ. SO GLAD YOU'RE UP.
SOMEONE TOOK HIM, OFFICER CYPRESS.
UNGH. RICK?
OH. RICK. RICK IS...
RICK IS DEAD.
I CHECKED HIS PULSE, AND... WELL, HE'S GOT NO FACE.
JESUS.
I WAS SUPPOSED TO TAKE CARE OF MR. HINE, AND NOW HE'S GONE.
THEY LEFT HIS WHEEL CHAIR AND THEY KILLED RICK...
ANN.
ANDERS KILLED RICK. HE'S NOT A VEGETABLE, HE NEVER WAS.
HE WAS FAKING IT.
OH. GOD. I--I CHANGED IN FRONT OF HIM.

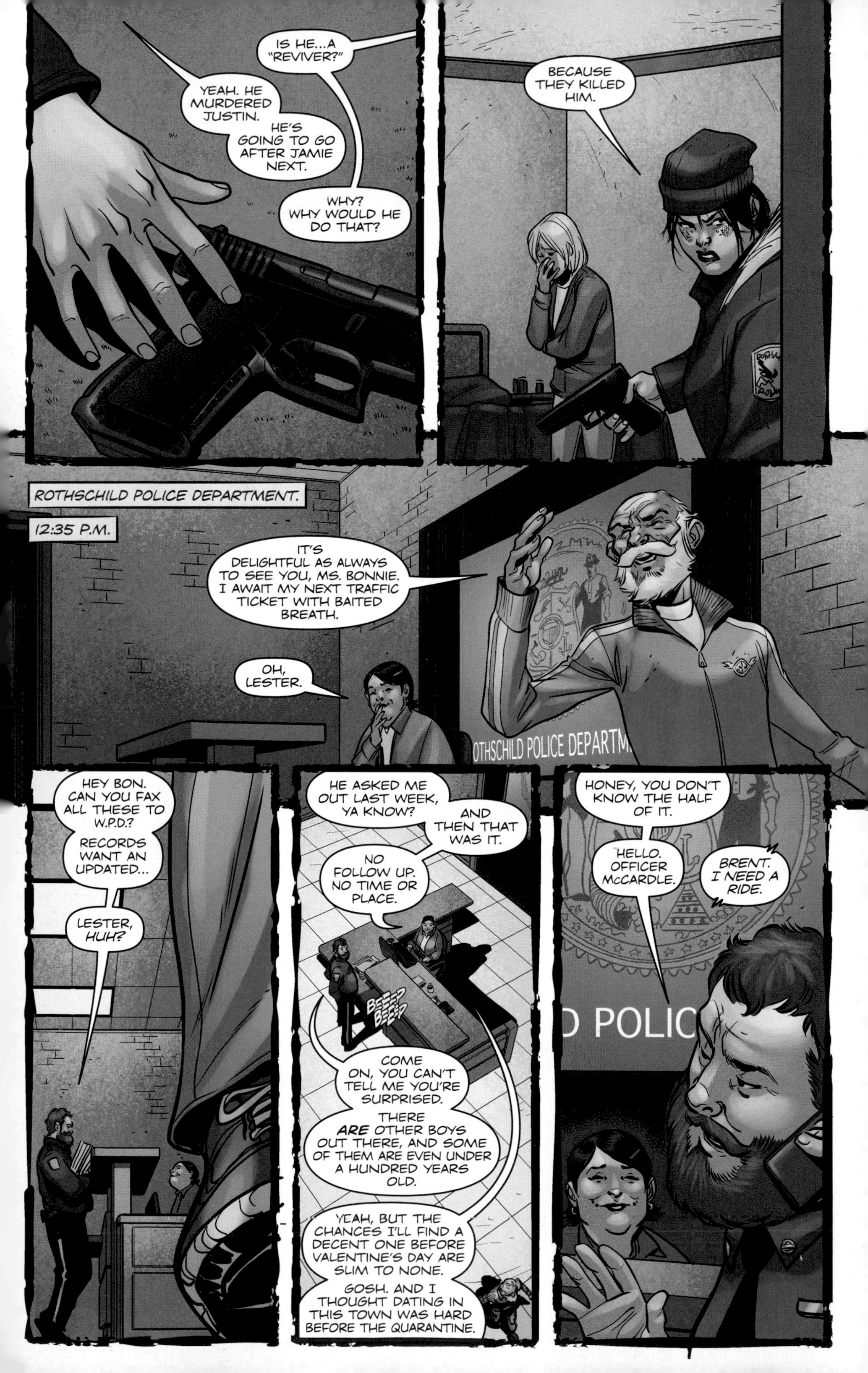
IS HE...A "REVIVER?"
YEAH. HE MURDERED JUSTIN.
HE'S GOING TO GO AFTER JAMIE NEXT.
WHY? WHY WOULD HE DO THAT?
BECAUSE THEY KILLED HIM.
ROTHSCHILD POLICE DEPARTMENT.
12:35 P.M.
IT'S DELIGHTFUL AS ALWAYS TO SEE YOU, MS. BONNIE. I AWAIT MY NEXT TRAFFIC TICKET WITH BAITED BREATH.
OH, LESTER.
OTHSCHILD POLICE DEPARTM
HEY BON. CAN YOU FAX ALL THESE TO W.P.D.?
RECORDS WANT AN UPDATED...
LESTER, HUH?
HE ASKED ME OUT LAST WEEK, YA KNOW?
AND THEN THAT WAS IT.
NO FOLLOW UP. NO TIME OR PLACE.
BEEEP BEEEP
COME ON, YOU CAN'T TELL ME YOU'RE SURPRISED.
THERE ARE OTHER BOYS OUT THERE, AND SOME OF THEM ARE EVEN UNDER A HUNDRED YEARS OLD.
YEAH, BUT THE CHANCES I'LL FIND A DECENT ONE BEFORE VALENTINE'S DAY ARE SLIM TO NONE.
GOSH. AND I THOUGHT DATING IN THIS TOWN WAS HARD BEFORE THE QUARANTINE.
HONEY, YOU DON'T KNOW THE HALF OF IT.
HELLO. OFFICER McCARDLE.
BRENT. I NEED A RIDE.
D POLIC

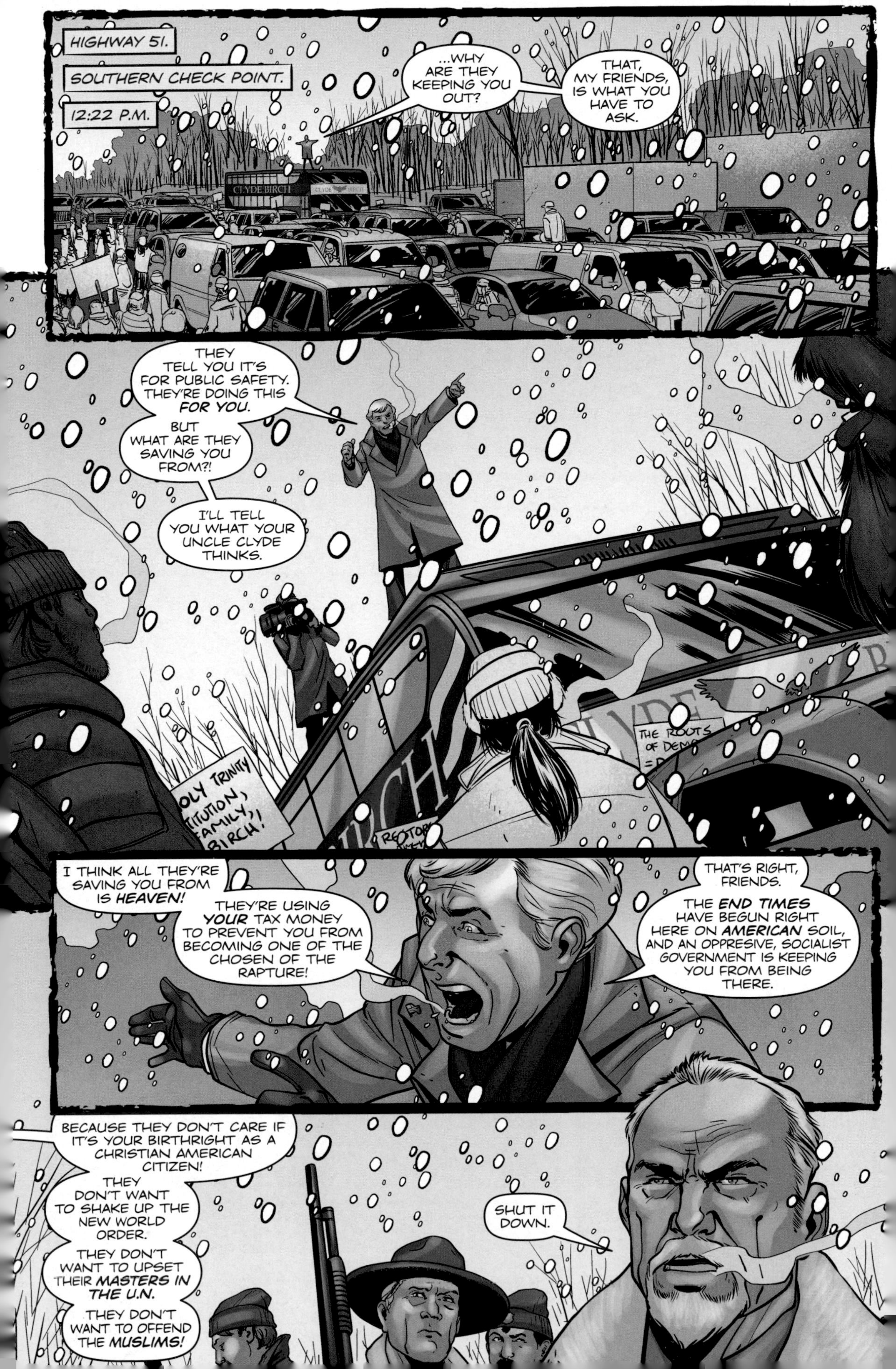

HIGHWAY 51.
SOUTHERN CHECK POINT.
12:22 P.M.
CLYDE BIRCH
...WHY ARE THEY KEEPING YOU OUT?
THAT, MY FRIENDS, IS WHAT YOU HAVE TO ASK.
THEY TELL YOU IT'S FOR PUBLIC SAFETY. THEY'RE DOING THIS FOR YOU.
BUT WHAT ARE THEY SAVING YOU FROM?!
I'LL TELL YOU WHAT YOUR UNCLE CLYDE THINKS.
I THINK ALL THEY'RE SAVING YOU FROM IS HEAVEN!
THEY'RE USING YOUR TAX MONEY TO PREVENT YOU FROM BECOMING ONE OF THE CHOSEN OF THE RAPTURE!
THAT'S RIGHT, FRIENDS.
THE END TIMES HAVE BEGUN RIGHT HERE ON AMERICAN SOIL, AND AN OPPRESIVE, SOCIALIST GOVERNMENT IS KEEPING YOU FROM BEING THERE.
BECAUSE THEY DON'T CARE IF IT'S YOUR BIRTHRIGHT AS A CHRISTIAN AMERICAN CITIZEN!
THEY DON'T WANT TO SHAKE UP THE NEW WORLD ORDER.
THEY DON'T WANT TO UPSET THEIR MASTERS IN THE U.N.
THEY DON'T WANT TO OFFEND THE MUSLIMS!
SHUT IT DOWN.

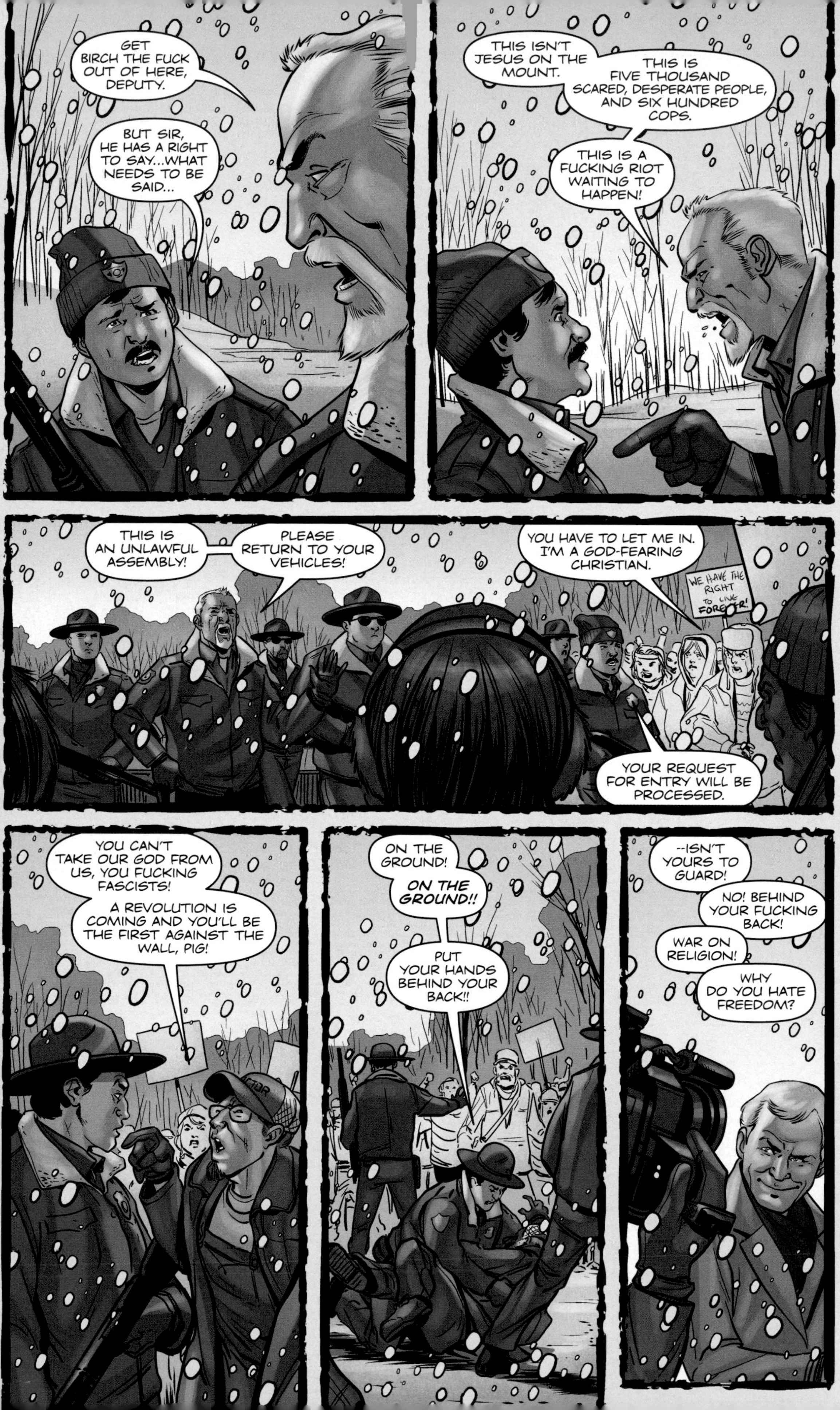
GET BIRCH THE FUCK OUT OF HERE, DEPUTY.
BUT SIR, HE HAS A RIGHT TO SAY...WHAT NEEDS TO BE SAID...
THIS ISN'T JESUS ON THE MOUNT.
THIS IS FIVE THOUSAND SCARED, DESPERATE PEOPLE, AND SIX HUNDRED COPS.
THIS IS A FUCKING RIOT WAITING TO HAPPEN!
THIS IS AN UNLAWFUL ASSEMBLY!
PLEASE RETURN TO YOUR VEHICLES!
YOU HAVE TO LET ME IN. I'M A GOD-FEARING CHRISTIAN.
WE HAVE THE RIGHT TO LIVE FOREVER!
YOUR REQUEST FOR ENTRY WILL BE PROCESSED.
YOU CAN'T TAKE OUR GOD FROM US, YOU FUCKING FASCISTS!
A REVOLUTION IS COMING AND YOU'LL BE THE FIRST AGAINST THE WALL, PIG!
ON THE GROUND!
ON THE GROUND!!
PUT YOUR HANDS BEHIND YOUR BACK!!
--ISN'T YOURS TO GUARD!
NO! BEHIND YOUR FUCKING BACK!
WAR ON RELIGION!
WHY DO YOU HATE FREEDOM?

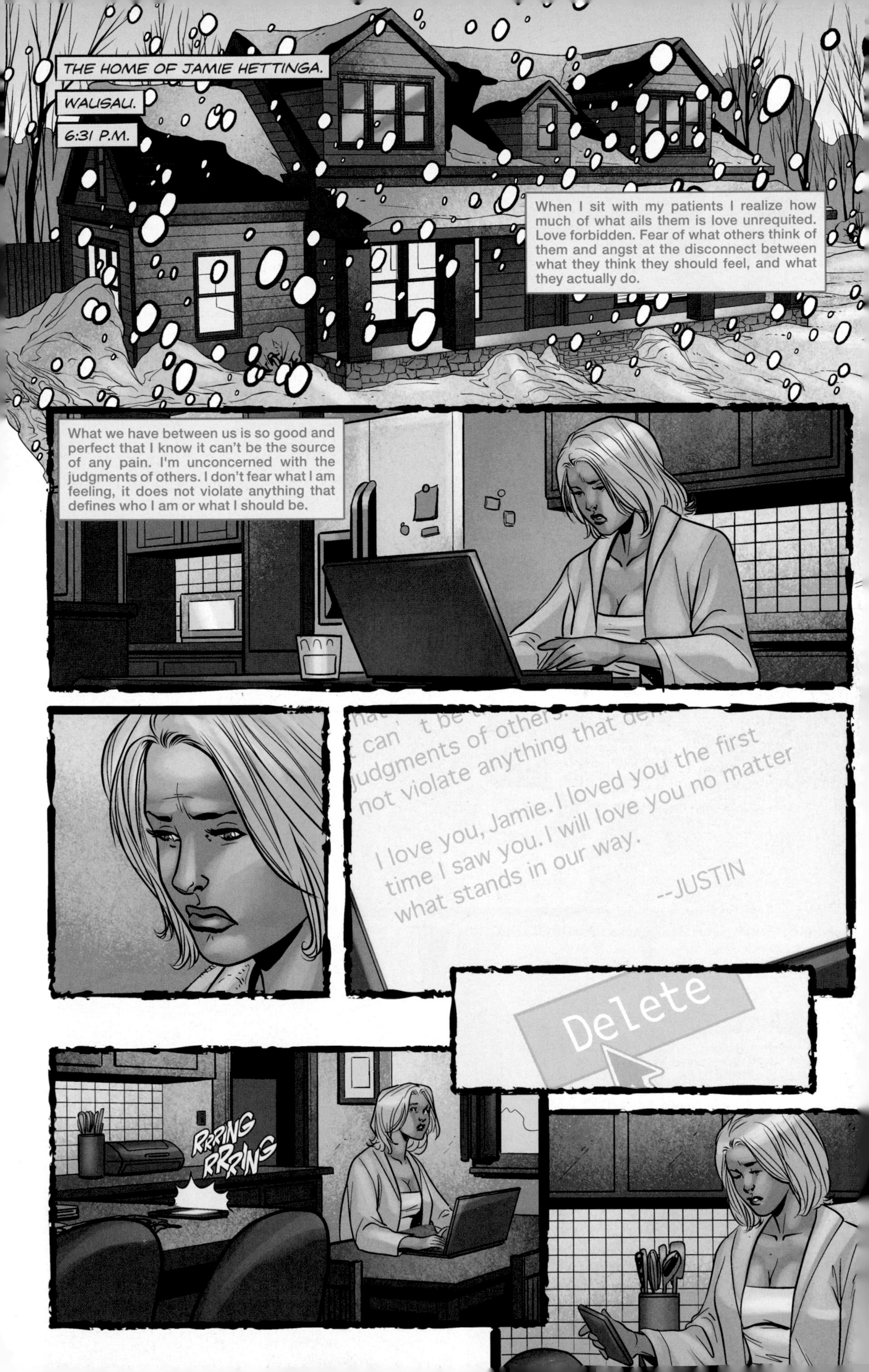
THE HOME OF JAMIE HETTINGA.
WAUSAU.
6:31 P.M.
When I sit with my patients I realize how much of what ails them is love unrequited. Love forbidden. Fear of what others think of them and angst at the disconnect between what they think they should feel, and what they actually do.
What we have between us is so good and perfect that I know it can't be the source of any pain. I'm unconcerned with the judgments of others. I don't fear what I am feeling, it does not violate anything that defines who I am or what I should be.
judgments of others.
not violate anything that
I love you, Jamie. I loved you the first time I saw you. I will love you no matter what stands in our way.
--JUSTIN
Delete
RRRING
RRRING

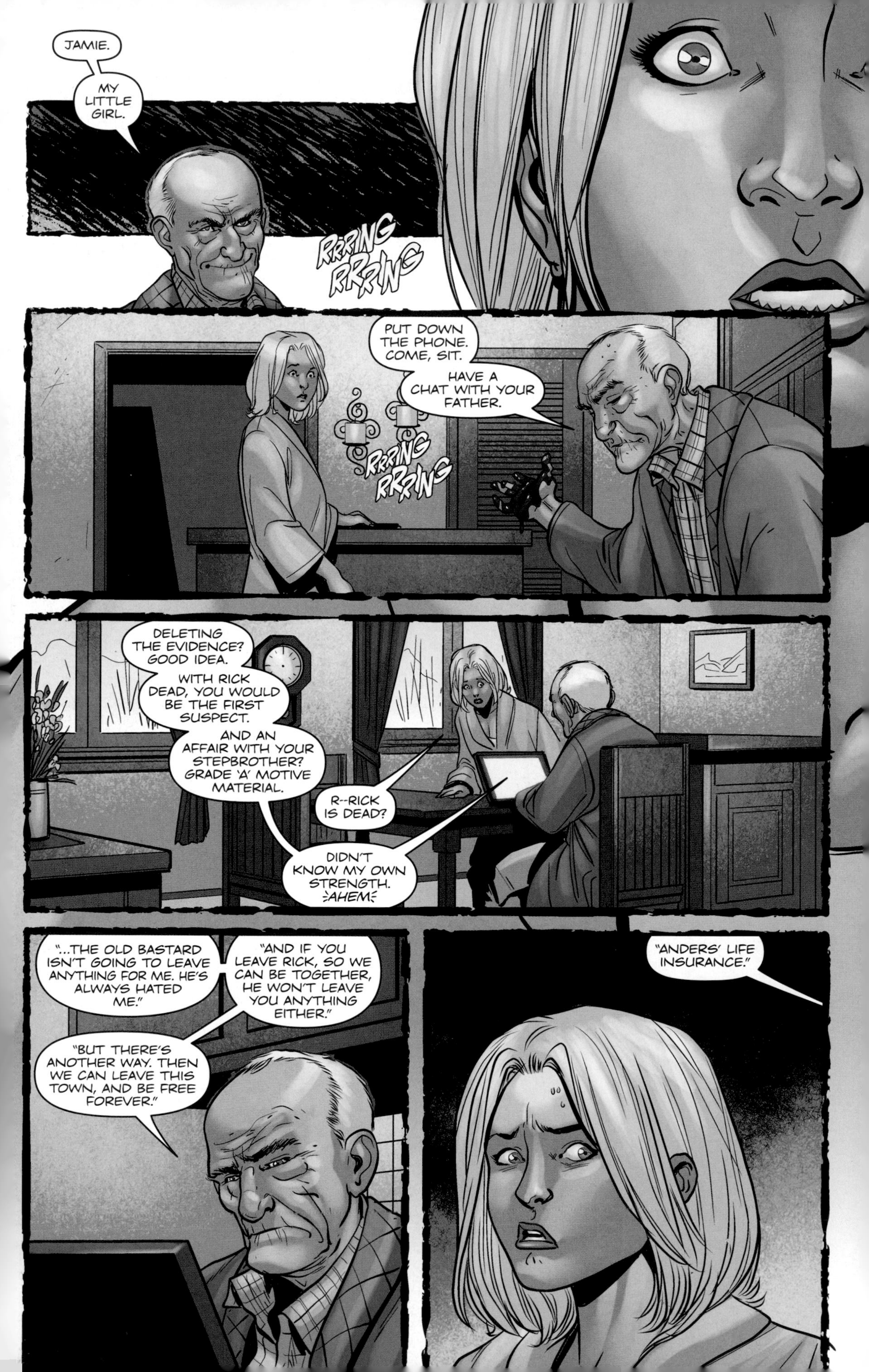
JAMIE.
MY LITTLE GIRL.
RRRING RRRING
PUT DOWN THE PHONE. COME, SIT.
HAVE A CHAT WITH YOUR FATHER.
RRRING RRRING
DELETING THE EVIDENCE? GOOD IDEA.
WITH RICK DEAD, YOU WOULD BE THE FIRST SUSPECT.
AND AN AFFAIR WITH YOUR STEPBROTHER? GRADE 'A' MOTIVE MATERIAL.
R--RICK IS DEAD?
DIDN'T KNOW MY OWN STRENGTH. AHEM
"...THE OLD BASTARD ISN'T GOING TO LEAVE ANYTHING FOR ME. HE'S ALWAYS HATED ME."
"AND IF YOU LEAVE RICK, SO WE CAN BE TOGETHER, HE WON'T LEAVE YOU ANYTHING EITHER."
"BUT THERE'S ANOTHER WAY. THEN WE CAN LEAVE THIS TOWN, AND BE FREE FOREVER."
"ANDERS' LIFE INSURANCE."

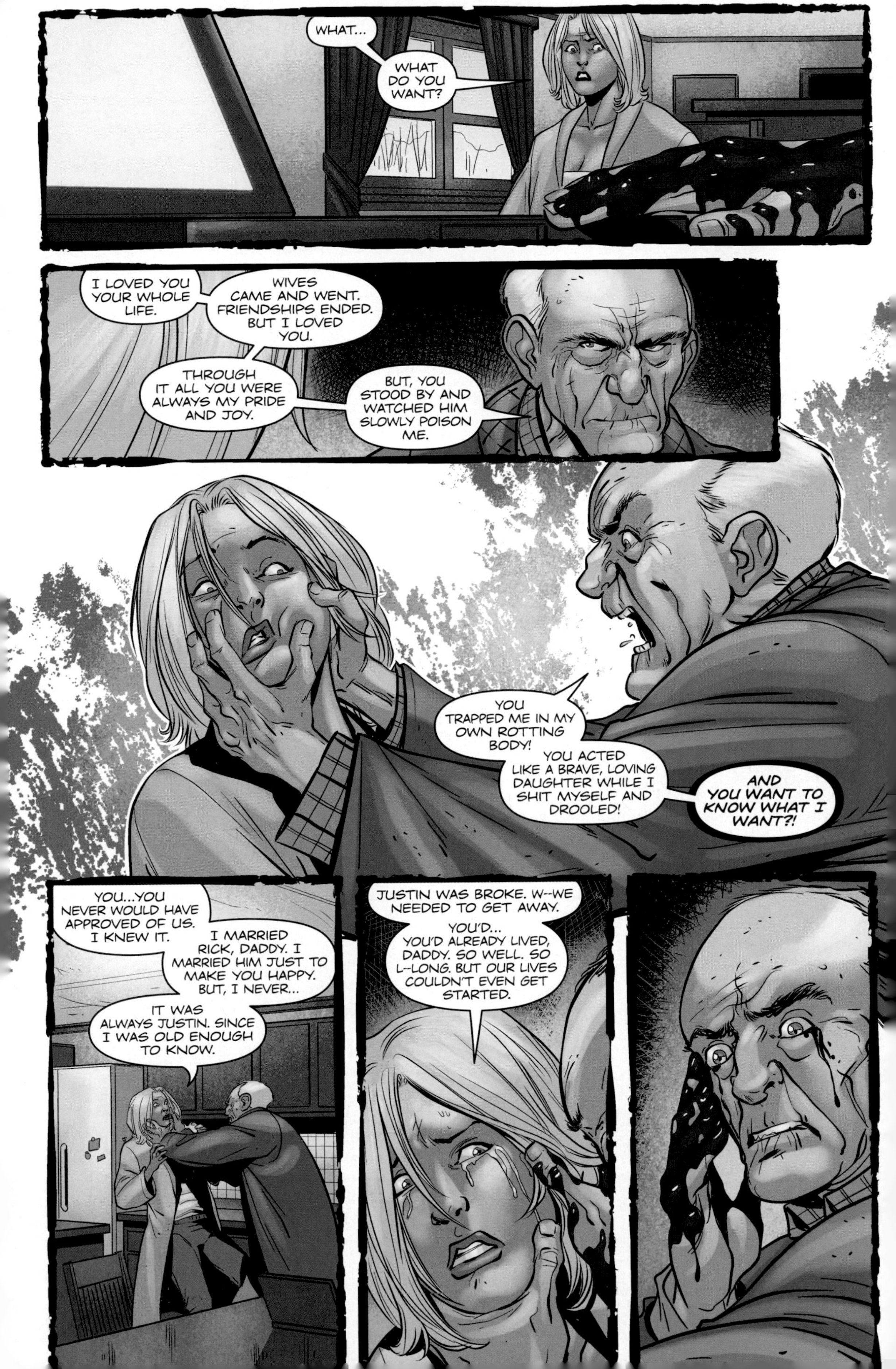
WHAT...
WHAT DO YOU WANT?
I LOVED YOU YOUR WHOLE LIFE.
WIVES CAME AND WENT. FRIENDSHIPS ENDED. BUT I LOVED YOU.
THROUGH IT ALL YOU WERE ALWAYS MY PRIDE AND JOY.
BUT, YOU STOOD BY AND WATCHED HIM SLOWLY POISON ME.
YOU TRAPPED ME IN MY OWN ROTTING BODY!
YOU ACTED LIKE A BRAVE, LOVING DAUGHTER WHILE I SHIT MYSELF AND DROOLED!
AND YOU WANT TO KNOW WHAT I WANT?!
YOU...YOU NEVER WOULD HAVE APPROVED OF US. I KNEW IT.
I MARRIED RICK, DADDY. I MARRIED HIM JUST TO MAKE YOU HAPPY. BUT, I NEVER...
IT WAS ALWAYS JUSTIN. SINCE I WAS OLD ENOUGH TO KNOW.
JUSTIN WAS BROKE. W--WE NEEDED TO GET AWAY.
YOU'D... YOU'D ALREADY LIVED, DADDY. SO WELL. SO L--LONG. BUT OUR LIVES COULDN'T EVEN GET STARTED.

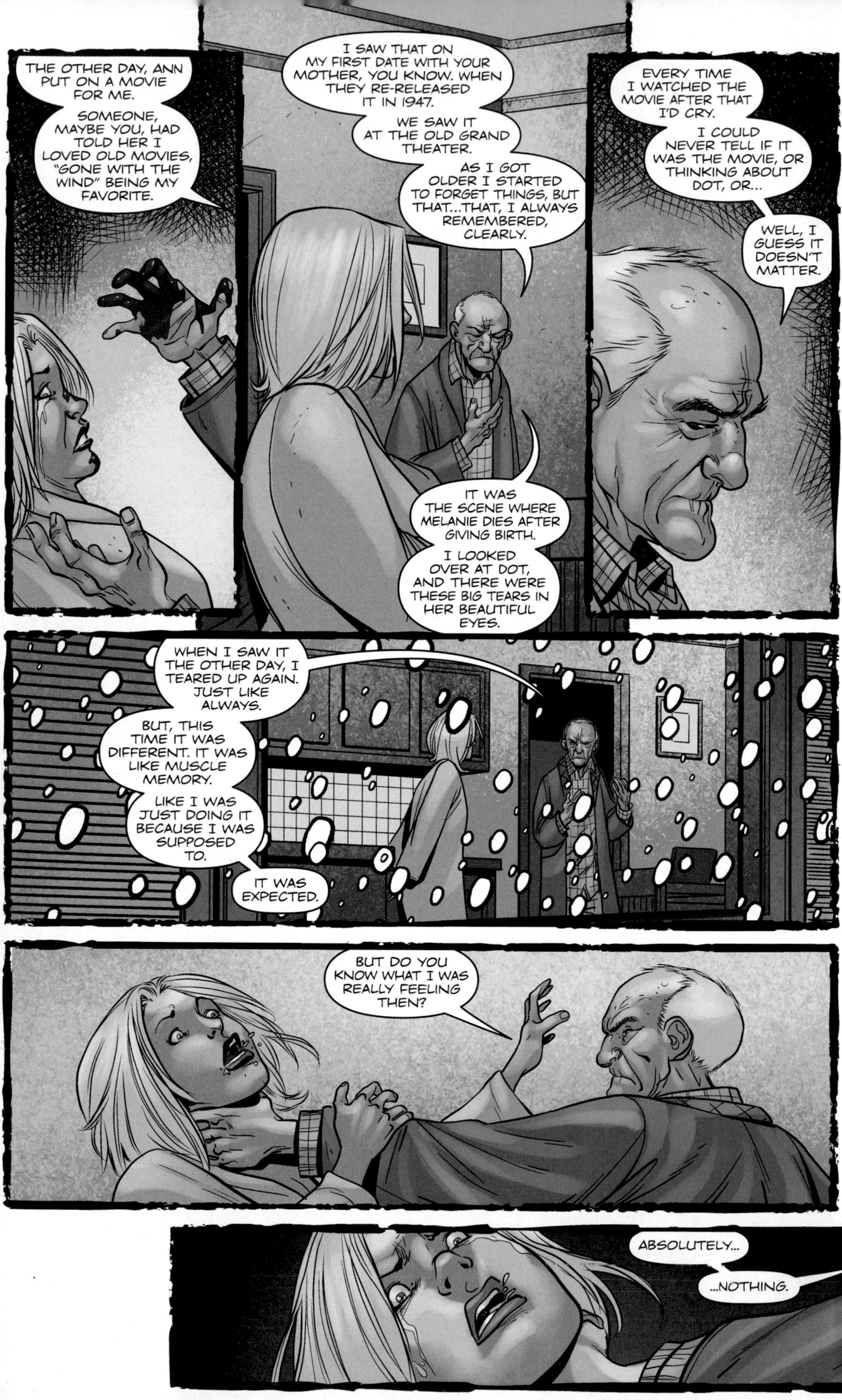
THE OTHER DAY, ANN PUT ON A MOVIE FOR ME.
SOMEONE, MAYBE YOU, HAD TOLD HER I LOVED OLD MOVIES, "GONE WITH THE WIND" BEING MY FAVORITE.
I SAW THAT ON MY FIRST DATE WITH YOUR MOTHER, YOU KNOW. WHEN THEY RE-RELEASED IT IN 1947.
WE SAW IT AT THE OLD GRAND THEATER.
AS I GOT OLDER I STARTED TO FORGET THINGS, BUT THAT...THAT, I ALWAYS REMEMBERED, CLEARLY.
IT WAS THE SCENE WHERE MELANIE DIES AFTER GIVING BIRTH.
I LOOKED OVER AT DOT, AND THERE WERE THESE BIG TEARS IN HER BEAUTIFUL EYES.
EVERY TIME I WATCHED THE MOVIE AFTER THAT I'D CRY.
I COULD NEVER TELL IF IT WAS THE MOVIE, OR THINKING ABOUT DOT, OR...
WELL, I GUESS IT DOESN'T MATTER.
WHEN I SAW IT THE OTHER DAY, I TEARED UP AGAIN. JUST LIKE ALWAYS.
BUT, THIS TIME IT WAS DIFFERENT. IT WAS LIKE MUSCLE MEMORY.
LIKE I WAS JUST DOING IT BECAUSE I WAS SUPPOSED TO.
IT WAS EXPECTED.
BUT DO YOU KNOW WHAT I WAS REALLY FEELING THEN?
ABSOLUTELY...
...NOTHING.

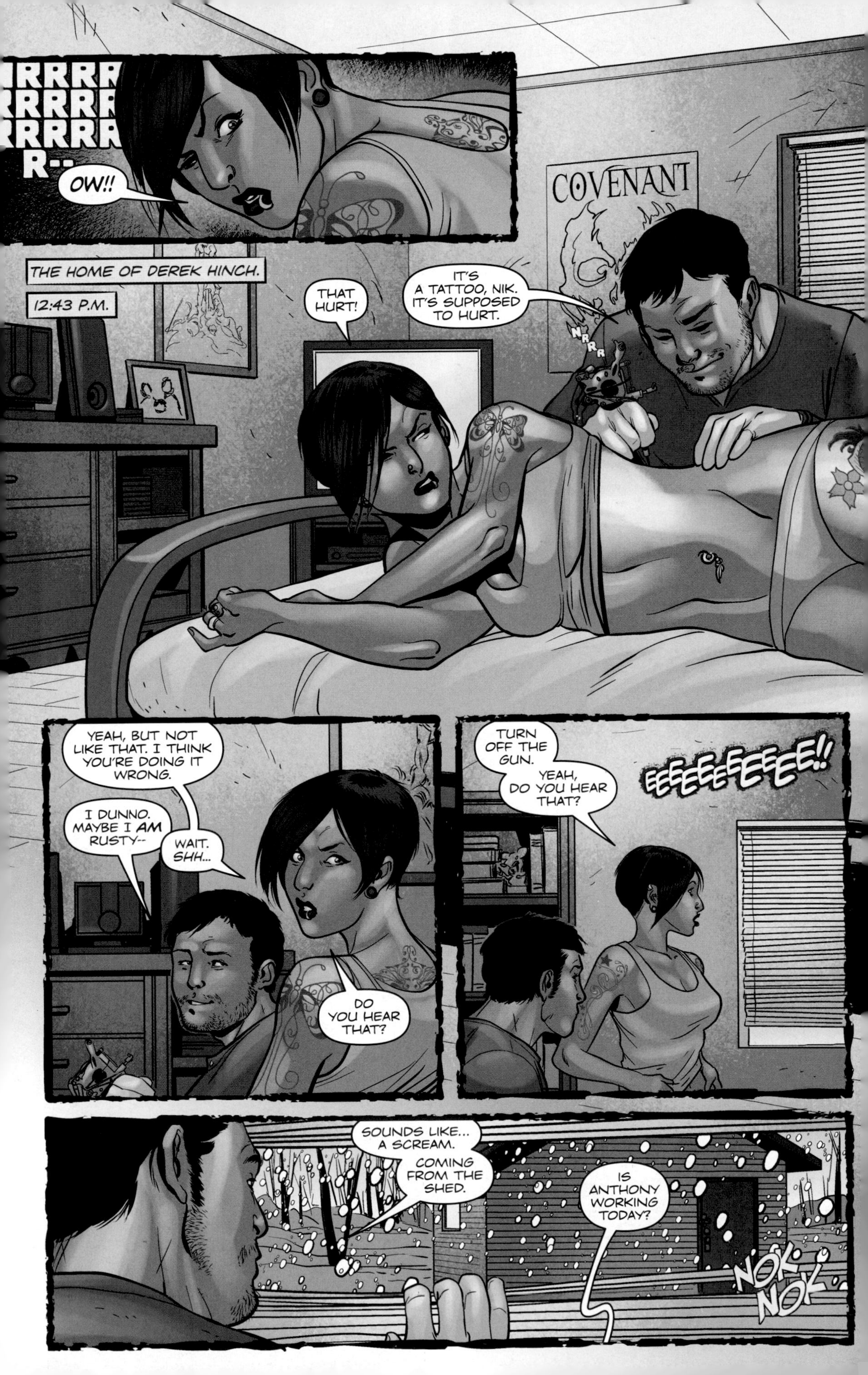
RRRRR RRRRR RRRRR R..
OW!!
THE HOME OF DEREK HINCH.
12:43 P.M.
THAT HURT!
IT'S A TATTOO, NIK. IT'S SUPPOSED TO HURT.
NRRR
COVENANT
YEAH, BUT NOT LIKE THAT. I THINK YOU'RE DOING IT WRONG.
I DUNNO. MAYBE I AM RUSTY--
WAIT. SHH...
DO YOU HEAR THAT?
TURN OFF THE GUN.
YEAH, DO YOU HEAR THAT?
EEEEEEEEEEEE!!
SOUNDS LIKE... A SCREAM.
COMING FROM THE SHED.
IS ANTHONY WORKING TODAY?
NOK NOK

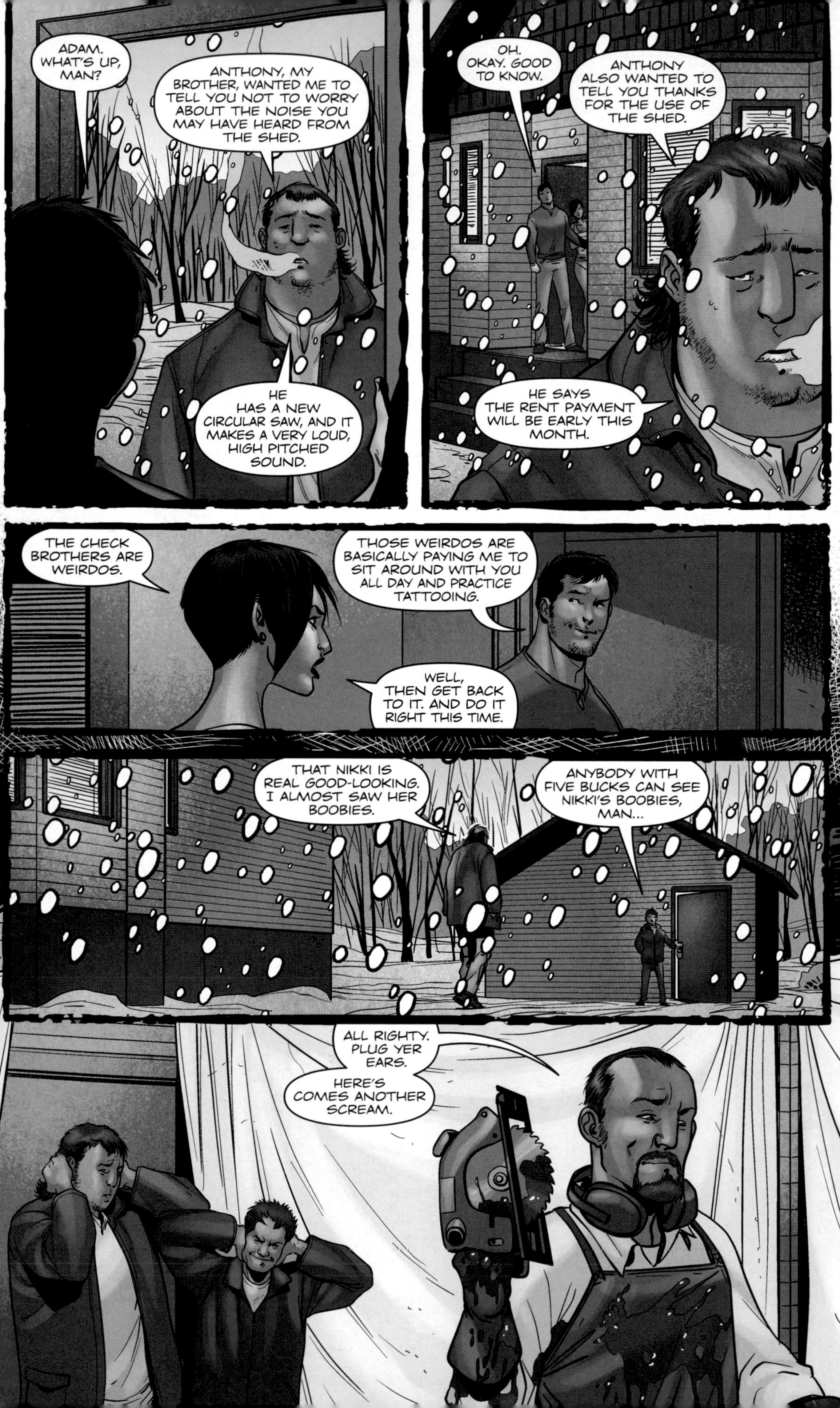

ADAM. WHAT'S UP, MAN?
ANTHONY, MY BROTHER, WANTED ME TO TELL YOU NOT TO WORRY ABOUT THE NOISE YOU MAY HAVE HEARD FROM THE SHED.
HE HAS A NEW CIRCULAR SAW, AND IT MAKES A VERY LOUD, HIGH PITCHED SOUND.
OH. OKAY. GOOD TO KNOW.
ANTHONY ALSO WANTED TO TELL YOU THANKS FOR THE USE OF THE SHED.
HE SAYS THE RENT PAYMENT WILL BE EARLY THIS MONTH.
THE CHECK BROTHERS ARE WEIRDOS.
THOSE WEIRDOS ARE BASICALLY PAYING ME TO SIT AROUND WITH YOU ALL DAY AND PRACTICE TATTOOING.
WELL, THEN GET BACK TO IT. AND DO IT RIGHT THIS TIME.
THAT NIKKI IS REAL GOOD-LOOKING. I ALMOST SAW HER BOOBIES.
ANYBODY WITH FIVE BUCKS CAN SEE NIKKI'S BOOBIES, MAN...
ALL RIGHTY. PLUG YER EARS.
HERE'S COMES ANOTHER SCREAM.

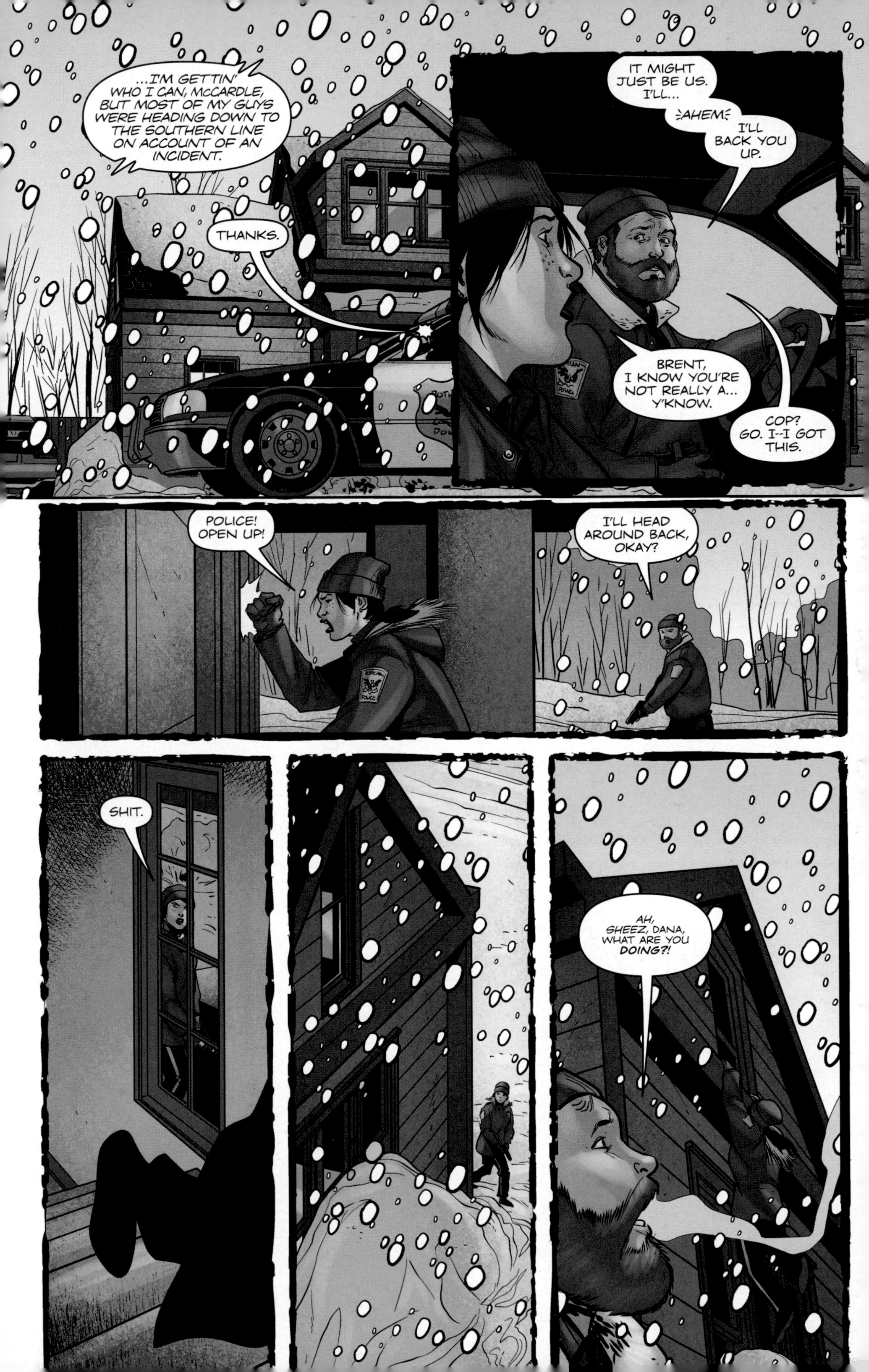
...I'M GETTIN' WHO I CAN, McCARDLE, BUT MOST OF MY GUYS WERE HEADING DOWN TO THE SOUTHERN LINE ON ACCOUNT OF AN INCIDENT.
THANKS.
IT MIGHT JUST BE US. I'LL...
AHEM
I'LL BACK YOU UP.
BRENT, I KNOW YOU'RE NOT REALLY A... Y'KNOW.
COP? GO. I--I GOT THIS.
POLICE! OPEN UP!
I'LL HEAD AROUND BACK, OKAY?
SHIT.
AH, SHEEZ, DANA, WHAT ARE YOU DOING?!

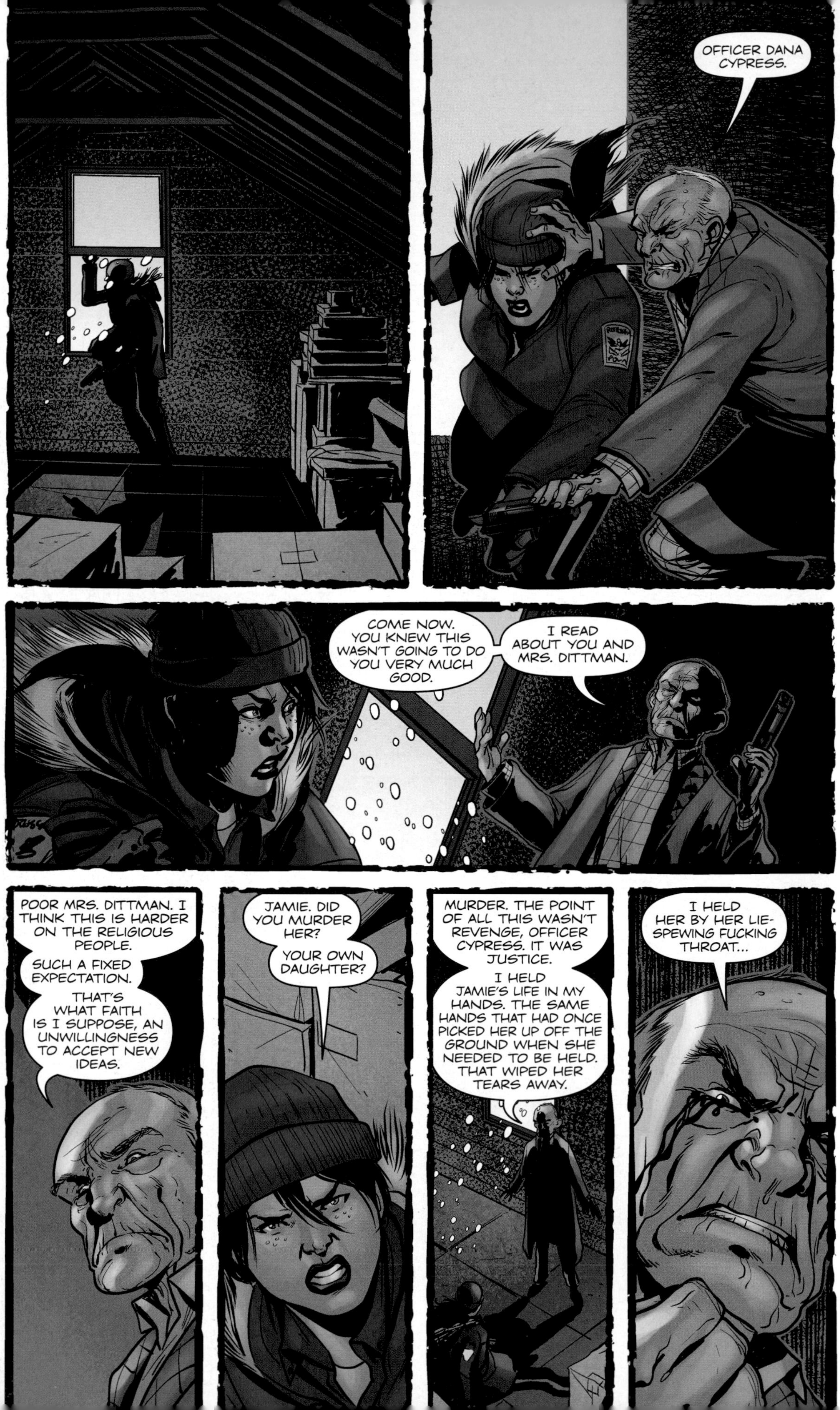
OFFICER DANA CYPRESS.
COME NOW. YOU KNEW THIS WASN'T GOING TO DO YOU VERY MUCH GOOD.
I READ ABOUT YOU AND MRS. DITTMAN.
POOR MRS. DITTMAN. I THINK THIS IS HARDER ON THE RELIGIOUS PEOPLE.
SUCH A FIXED EXPECTATION.
THAT'S WHAT FAITH IS I SUPPOSE, AN UNWILLINGNESS TO ACCEPT NEW IDEAS.
JAMIE. DID YOU MURDER HER?
YOUR OWN DAUGHTER?
MURDER. THE POINT OF ALL THIS WASN'T REVENGE, OFFICER CYPRESS. IT WAS JUSTICE.
I HELD JAMIE'S LIFE IN MY HANDS. THE SAME HANDS THAT HAD ONCE PICKED HER UP OFF THE GROUND WHEN SHE NEEDED TO BE HELD. THAT WIPED HER TEARS AWAY.
I HELD HER BY HER LIE-SPEWING FUCKING THROAT...

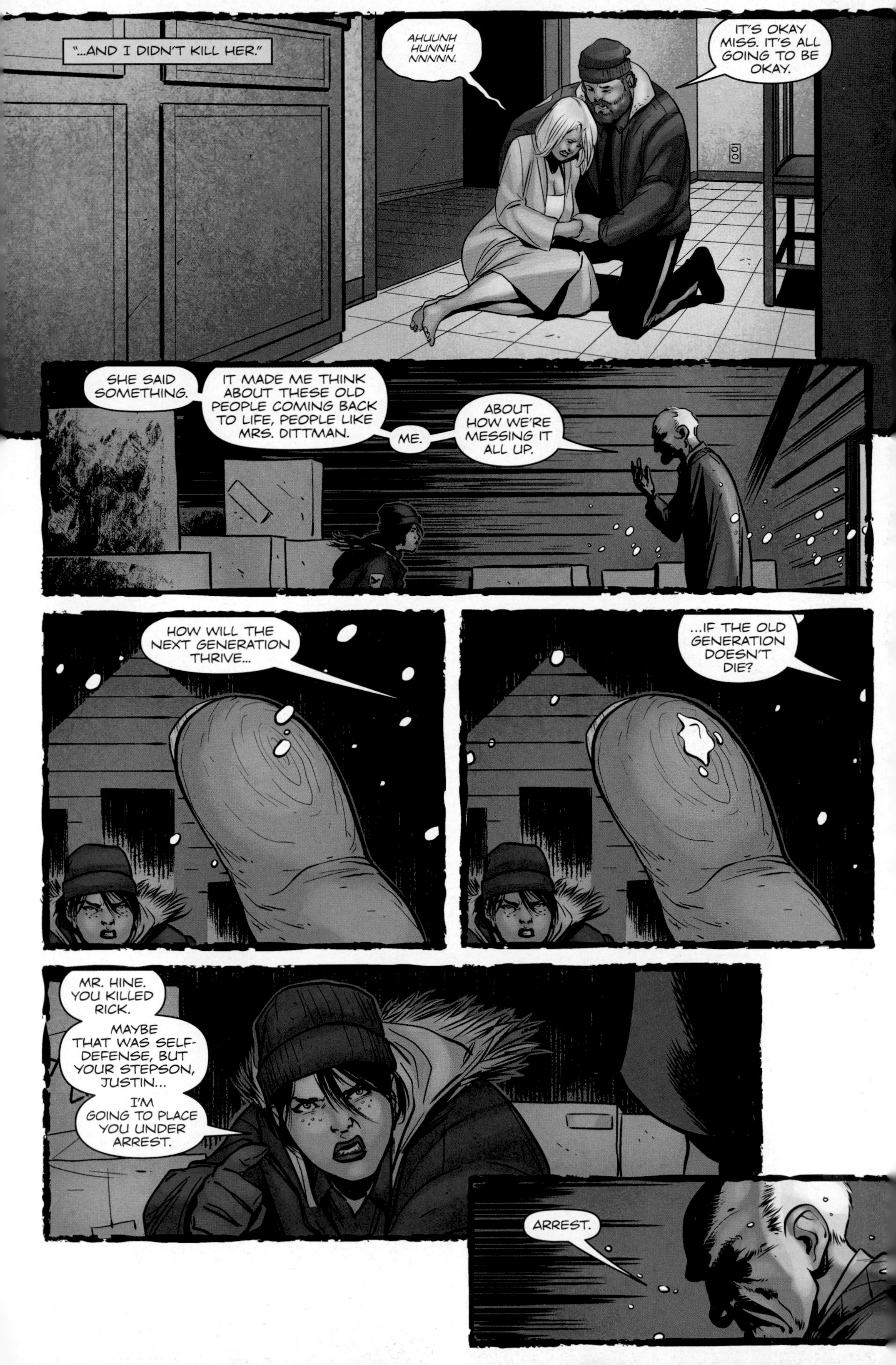
"...AND I DIDN'T KILL HER."
AHUUNH HUNNH NNNNN.
IT'S OKAY MISS. IT'S ALL GOING TO BE OKAY.
SHE SAID SOMETHING.
IT MADE ME THINK ABOUT THESE OLD PEOPLE COMING BACK TO LIFE, PEOPLE LIKE MRS. DITTMAN.
ME.
ABOUT HOW WE'RE MESSING IT ALL UP.
HOW WILL THE NEXT GENERATION THRIVE...
...IF THE OLD GENERATION DOESN'T DIE?
MR. HINE. YOU KILLED RICK.
MAYBE THAT WAS SELF-DEFENSE, BUT YOUR STEPSON, JUSTIN...
I'M GOING TO PLACE YOU UNDER ARREST.
ARREST.

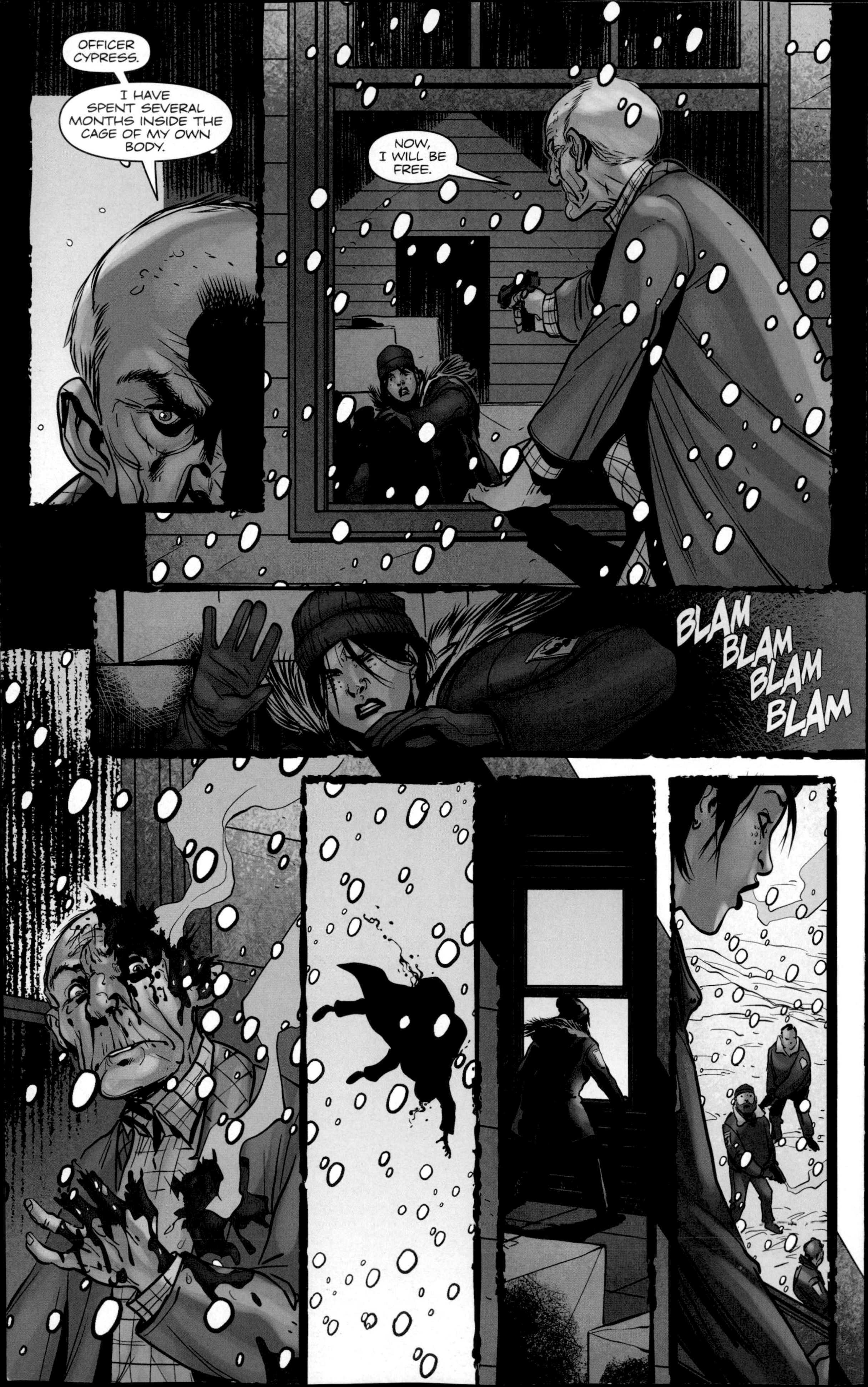
OFFICER CYPRESS.
I HAVE SPENT SEVERAL MONTHS INSIDE THE CAGE OF MY OWN BODY.
NOW, I WILL BE FREE.
BLAM BLAM BLAM BLAM

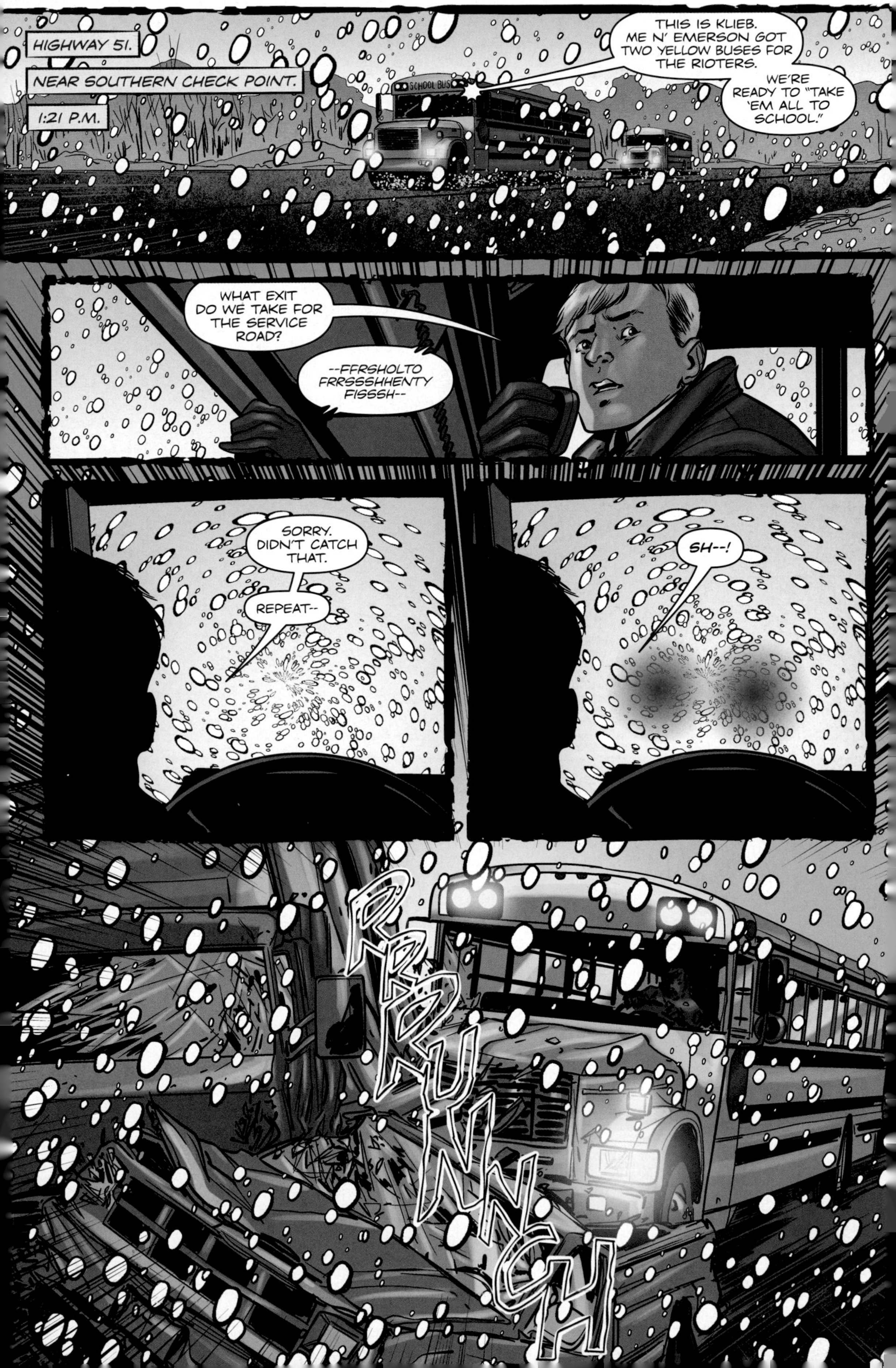
HIGHWAY 51.
NEAR SOUTHERN CHECK POINT.
1:21 P.M.
SCHOOL BUS
THIS IS KLIEB. ME N' EMERSON GOT TWO YELLOW BUSES FOR THE RIOTERS.
WE'RE READY TO "TAKE 'EM ALL TO SCHOOL."
WHAT EXIT DO WE TAKE FOR THE SERVICE ROAD?
--FFRSHOLTO FRRSSSHHENTY FISSSH--
SORRY. DIDN'T CATCH THAT.
REPEAT--
SH--!
RRRUNNNCH

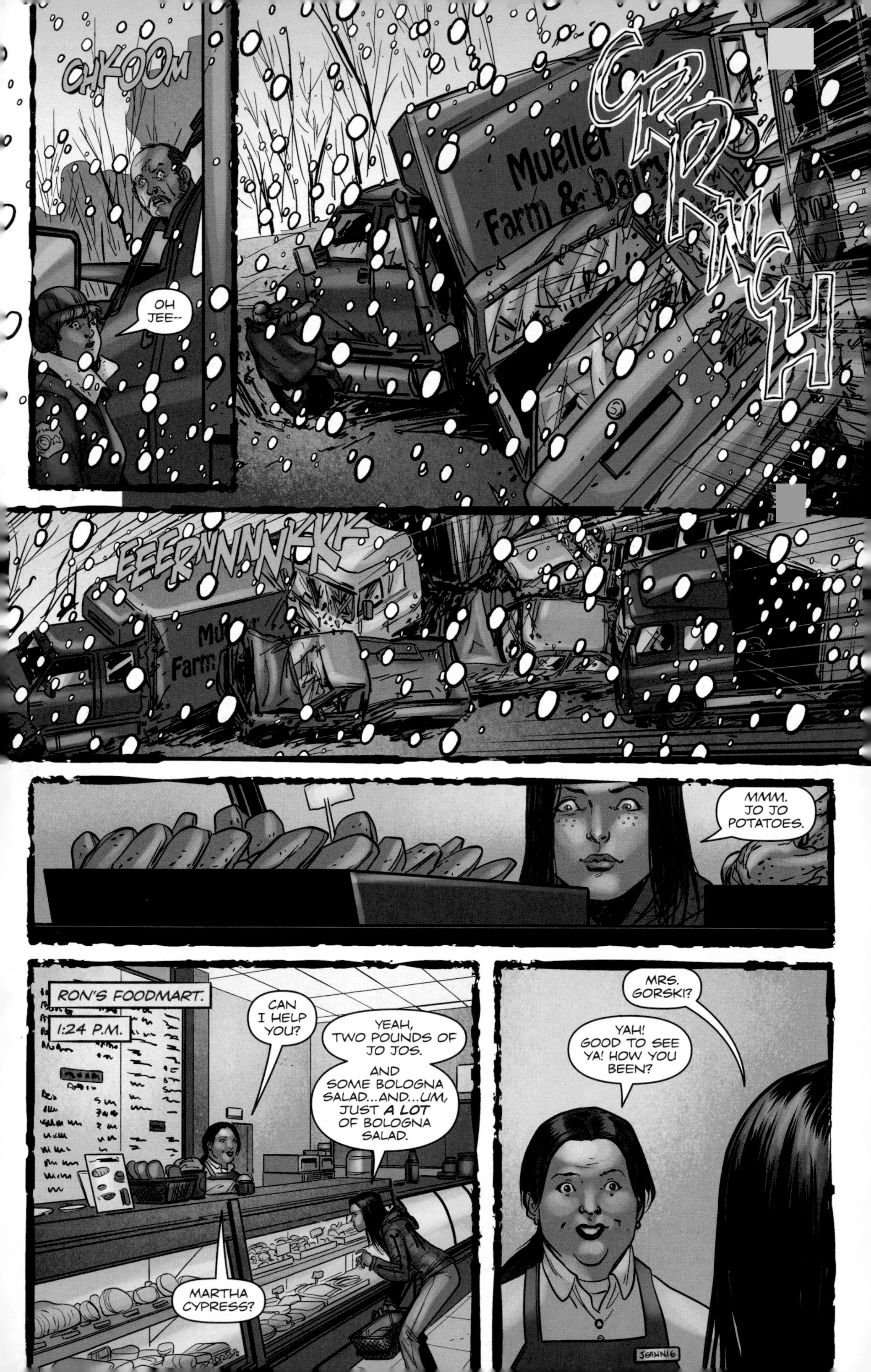
CHKOOM
OH JEE--
Mueller Farm & Dairy
CRRUNCH
STOP
EEERNNNNKKK
Mueller Farm
MMM. JO JO POTATOES.
RON'S FOODMART.
1:24 P.M.
CAN I HELP YOU?
YEAH, TWO POUNDS OF JO JOS.
AND SOME BOLOGNA SALAD...AND...UM, JUST A LOT OF BOLOGNA SALAD.
MARTHA CYPRESS?
MRS. GORSKI?
YAH! GOOD TO SEE YA! HOW YOU BEEN?
JEANNIE

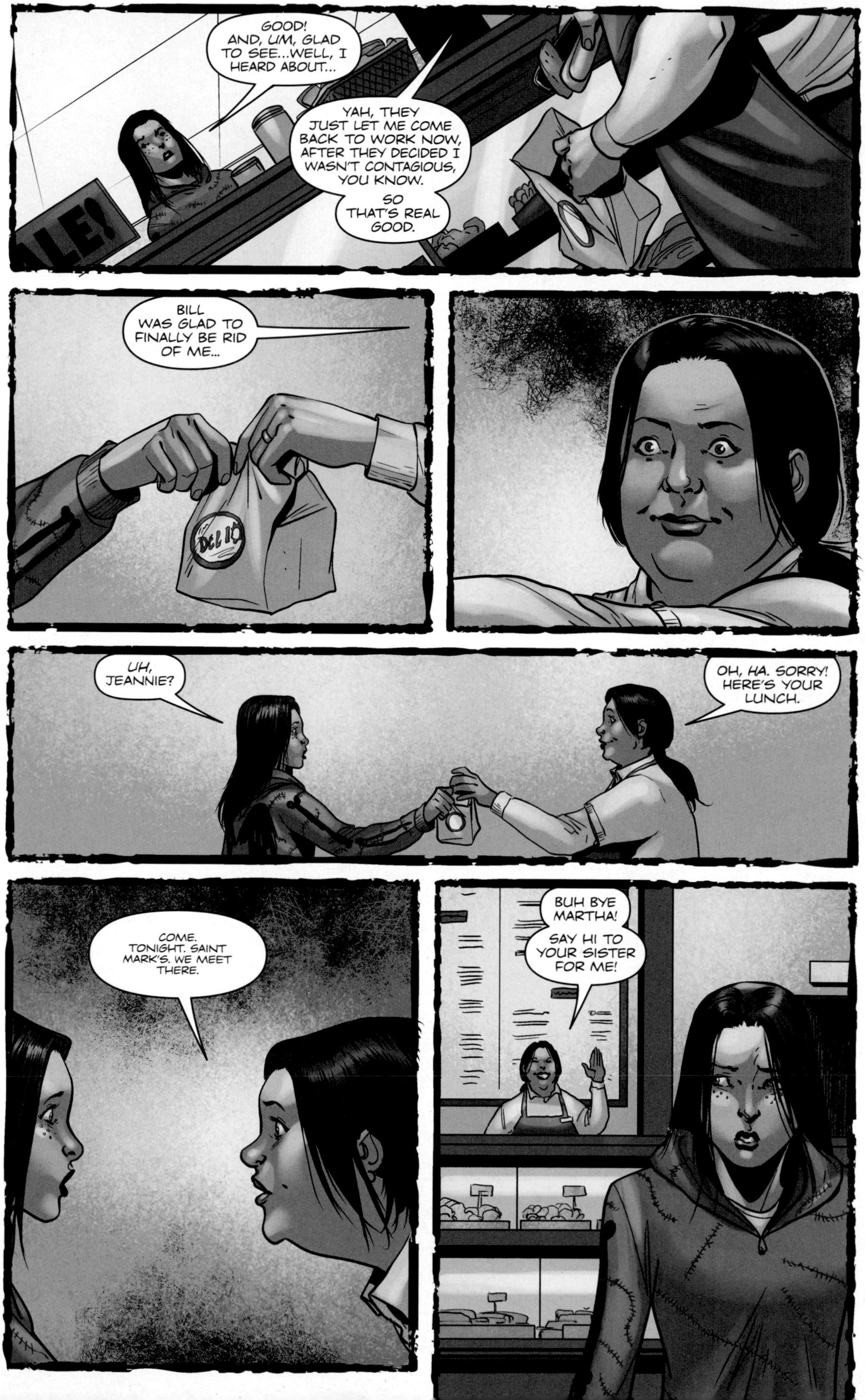

GOOD! AND, UM, GLAD TO SEE...WELL, I HEARD ABOUT...
YAH, THEY JUST LET ME COME BACK TO WORK NOW, AFTER THEY DECIDED I WASN'T CONTAGIOUS, YOU KNOW.
SO THAT'S REAL GOOD.
ALE!
BILL WAS GLAD TO FINALLY BE RID OF ME...
DELI
UH, JEANNIE?
OH, HA. SORRY! HERE'S YOUR LUNCH.
COME. TONIGHT. SAINT MARK'S. WE MEET THERE.
BUH BYE MARTHA!
SAY HI TO YOUR SISTER FOR ME!

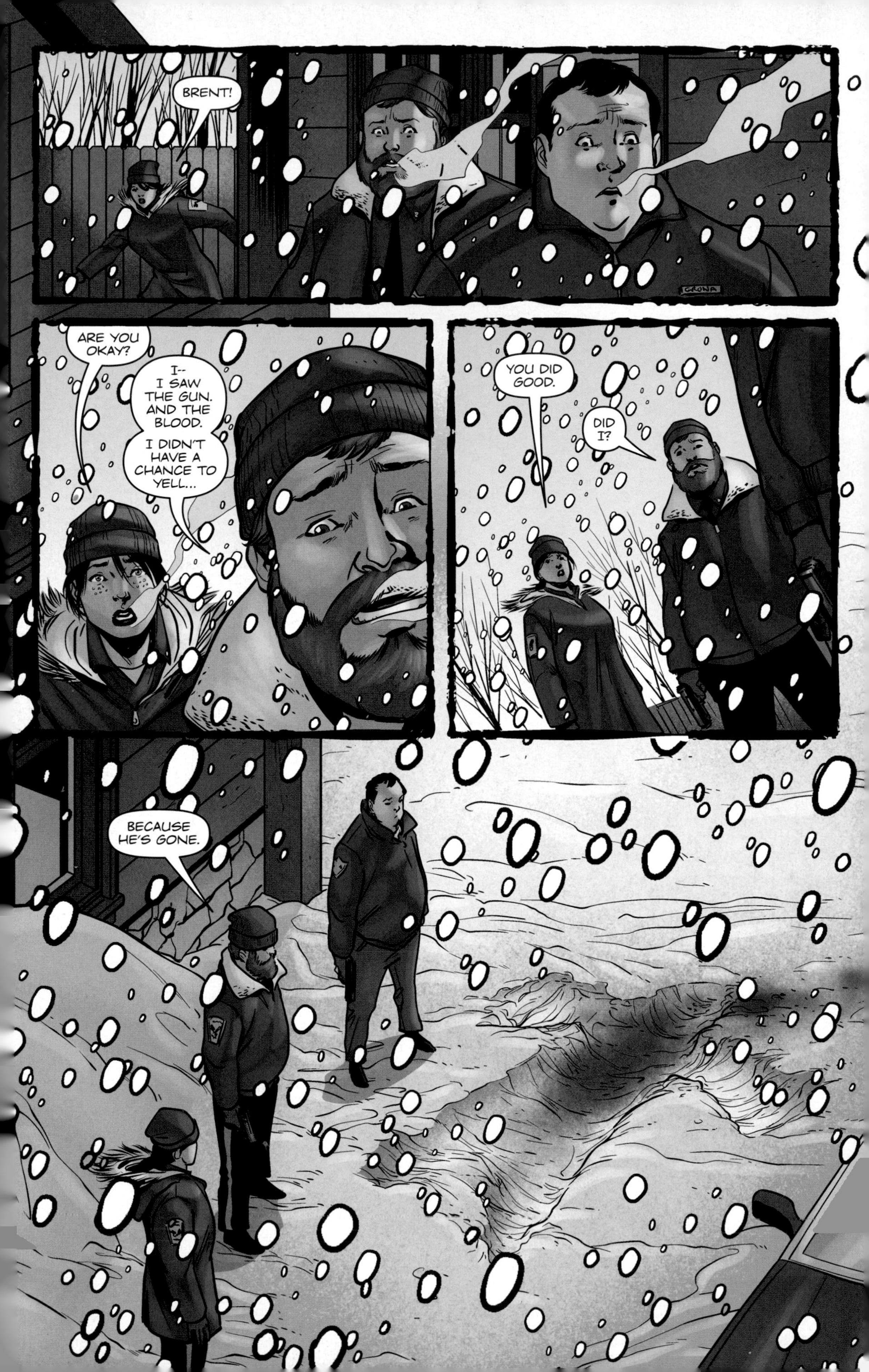
BRENT!
ARE YOU OKAY?
I-- I SAW THE GUN. AND THE BLOOD.
I DIDN'T HAVE A CHANCE TO YELL...
YOU DID GOOD.
DID I?
BECAUSE HE'S GONE.

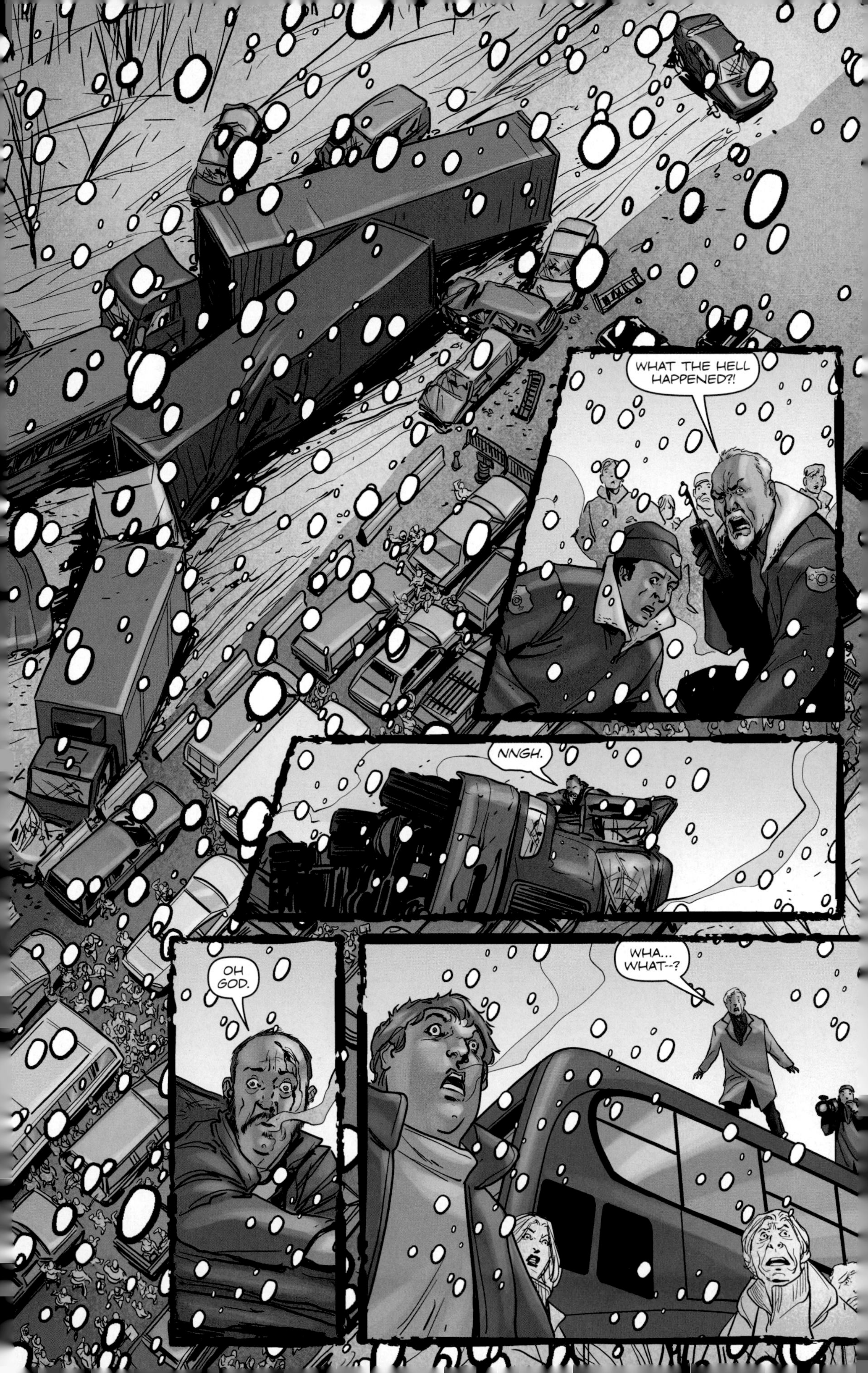
WHAT THE HELL HAPPENED?!
NNGH.
OH GOD.
WHA... WHAT--?

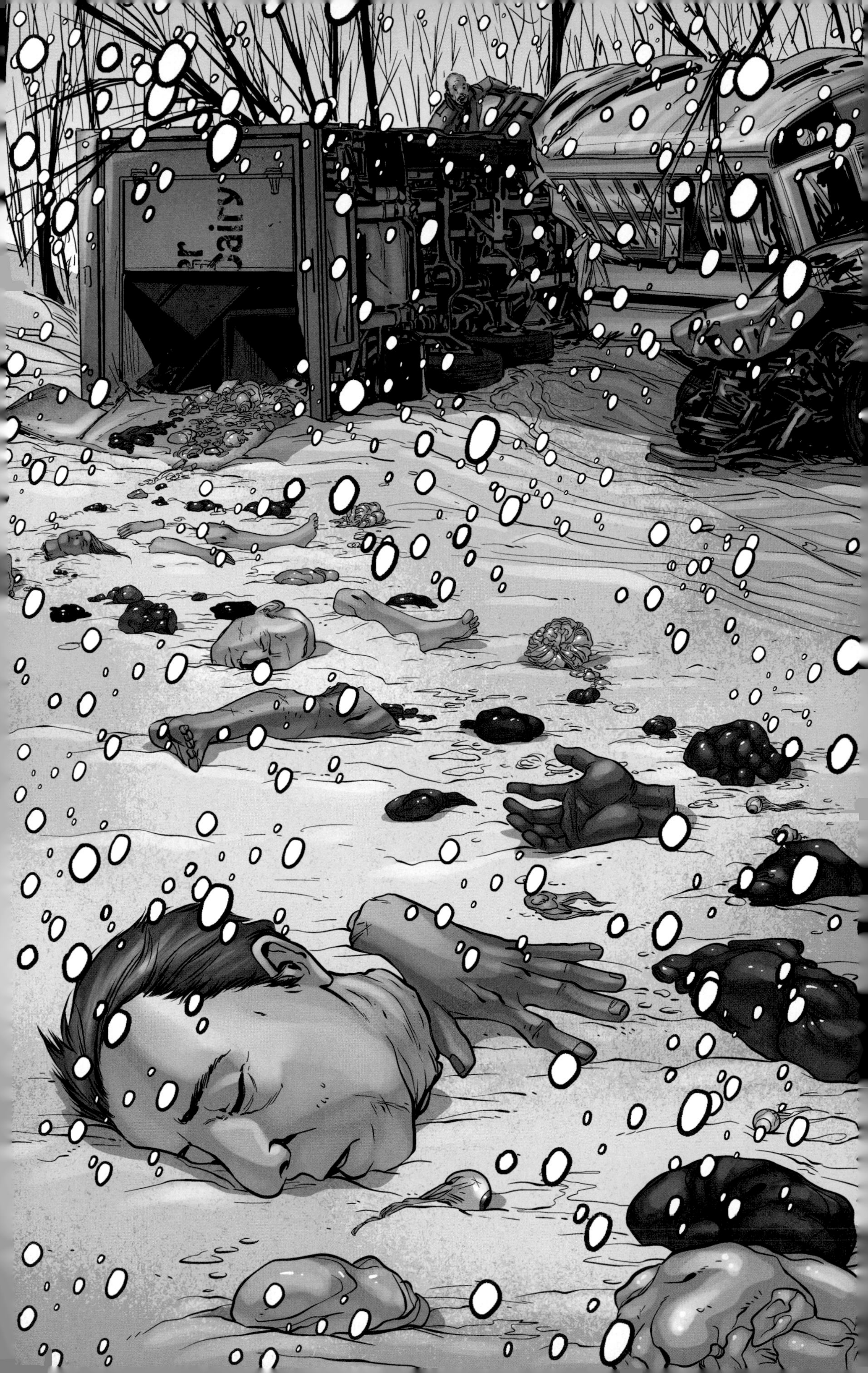
Dairy

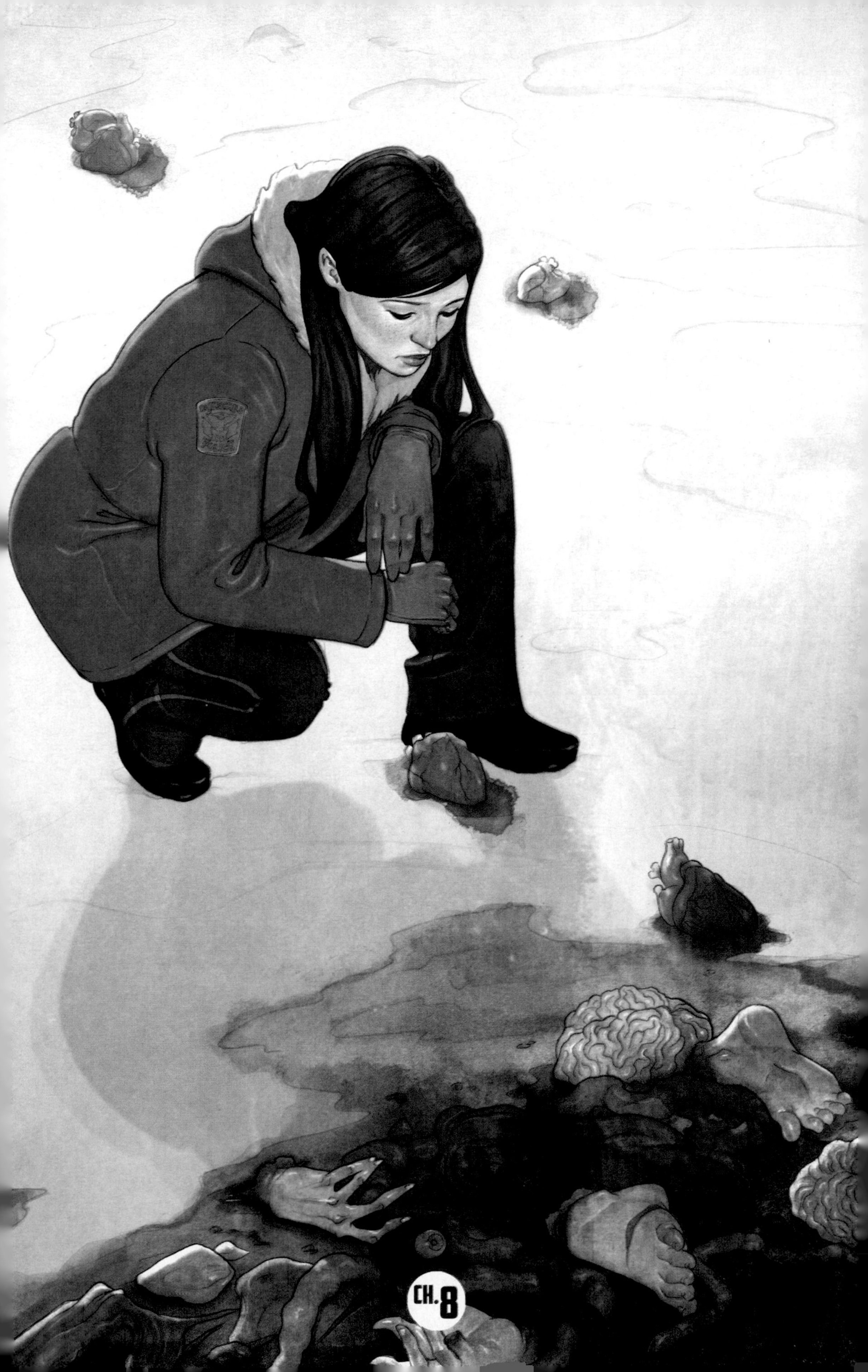
CH. 8

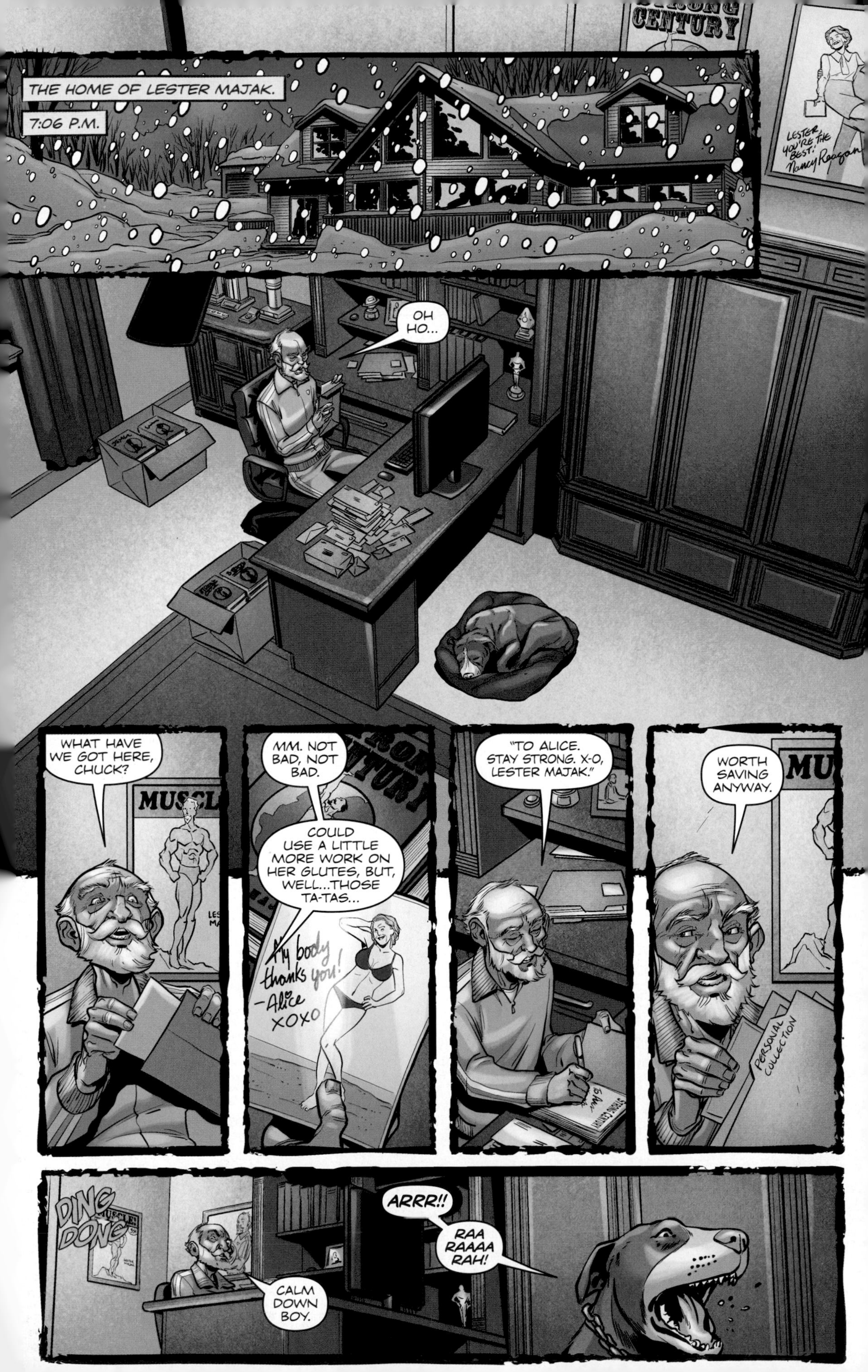

STRONG CENTURY
LESTER YOU'RE THE BEST! Nancy Reagan
THE HOME OF LESTER MAJAK.
7:06 P.M.
OH HO...
WHAT HAVE WE GOT HERE, CHUCK?
MUSCLE
MM. NOT BAD, NOT BAD.
COULD USE A LITTLE MORE WORK ON HER GLUTES, BUT, WELL...THOSE TA-TAS...
My body thanks you! -Alice XOXO
"TO ALICE. STAY STRONG. X-O, LESTER MAJAK."
WORTH SAVING ANYWAY.
PERSONAL COLLECTION
DING DONG
ARRR!!
RAA RAAAA RAH!
CALM DOWN BOY.

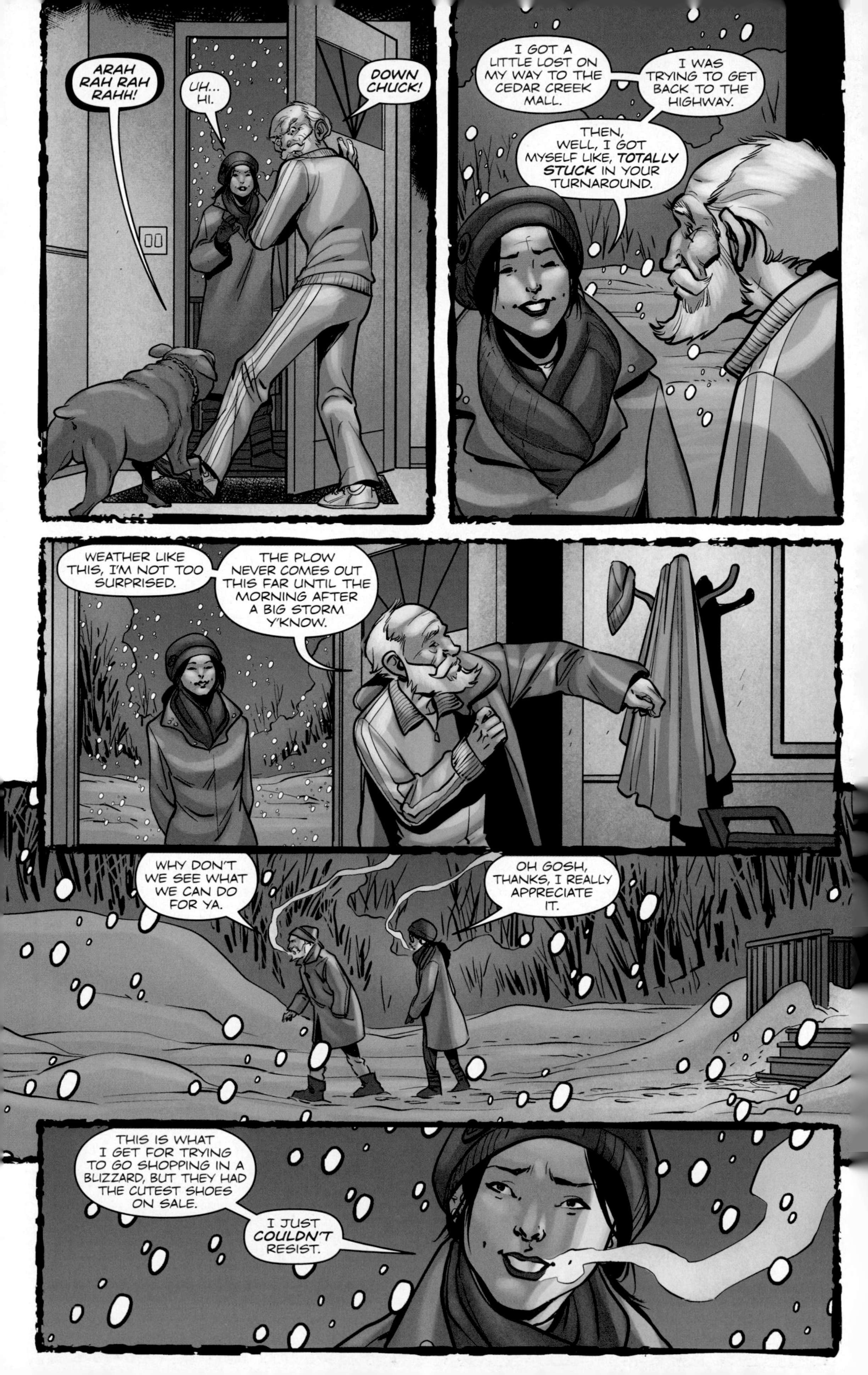
ARAH RAH RAH RAHH!
UH... HI.
DOWN CHUCK!
I GOT A LITTLE LOST ON MY WAY TO THE CEDAR CREEK MALL.
I WAS TRYING TO GET BACK TO THE HIGHWAY.
THEN, WELL, I GOT MYSELF LIKE, TOTALLY STUCK IN YOUR TURNAROUND.
WEATHER LIKE THIS, I'M NOT TOO SURPRISED.
THE PLOW NEVER COMES OUT THIS FAR UNTIL THE MORNING AFTER A BIG STORM Y'KNOW.
WHY DON'T WE SEE WHAT WE CAN DO FOR YA.
OH GOSH, THANKS, I REALLY APPRECIATE IT.
THIS IS WHAT I GET FOR TRYING TO GO SHOPPING IN A BLIZZARD, BUT THEY HAD THE CUTEST SHOES ON SALE.
I JUST COULDN'T RESIST.

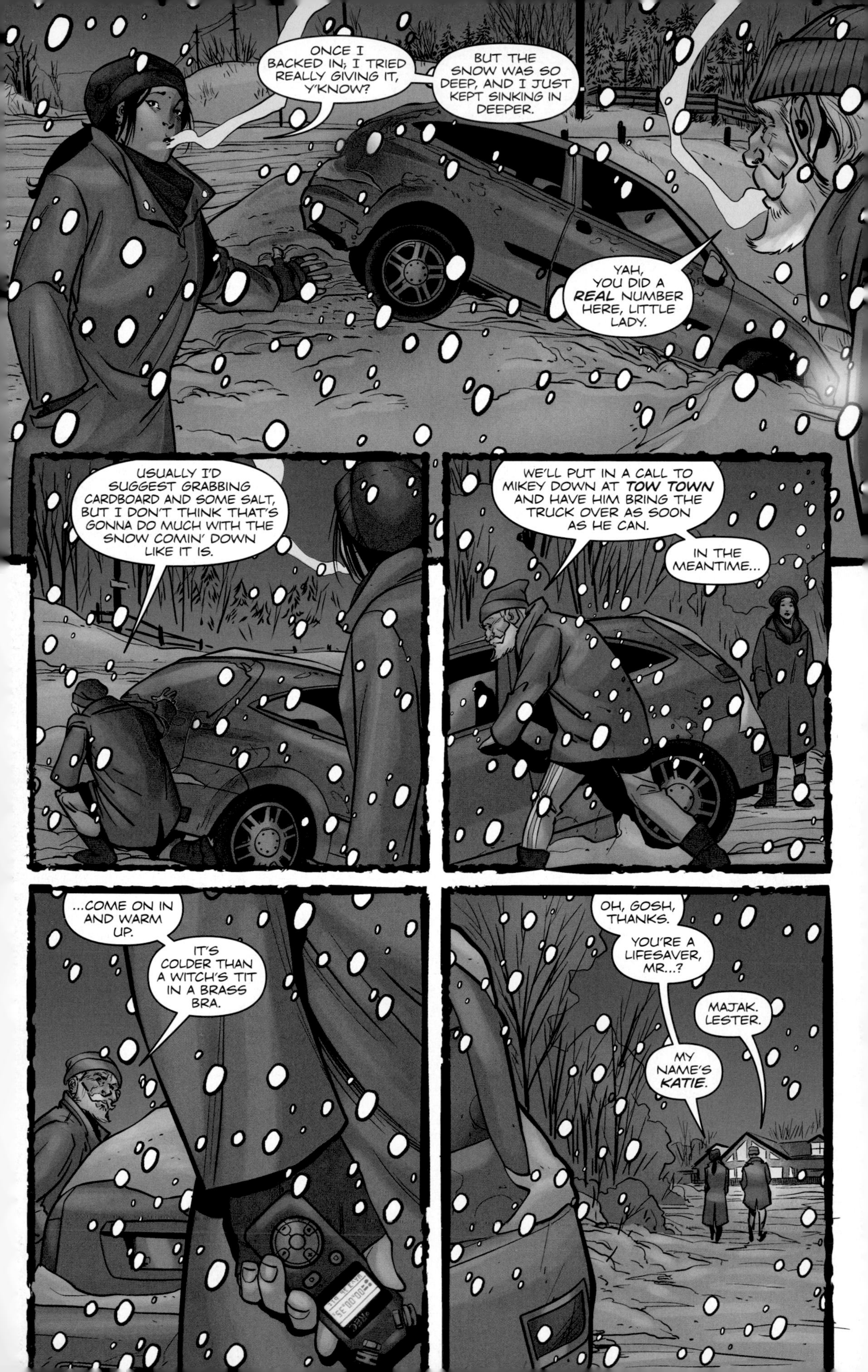
ONCE I BACKED IN; I TRIED REALLY GIVING IT, Y'KNOW?
BUT THE SNOW WAS SO DEEP, AND I JUST KEPT SINKING IN DEEPER.
YAH, YOU DID A REAL NUMBER HERE, LITTLE LADY.
USUALLY I'D SUGGEST GRABBING CARDBOARD AND SOME SALT, BUT I DON'T THINK THAT'S GONNA DO MUCH WITH THE SNOW COMIN' DOWN LIKE IT IS.
WE'LL PUT IN A CALL TO MIKEY DOWN AT TOW TOWN AND HAVE HIM BRING THE TRUCK OVER AS SOON AS HE CAN.
IN THE MEANTIME...
...COME ON IN AND WARM UP.
IT'S COLDER THAN A WITCH'S TIT IN A BRASS BRA.
OH, GOSH, THANKS.
YOU'RE A LIFESAVER, MR...?
MAJAK. LESTER.
MY NAME'S KATIE.

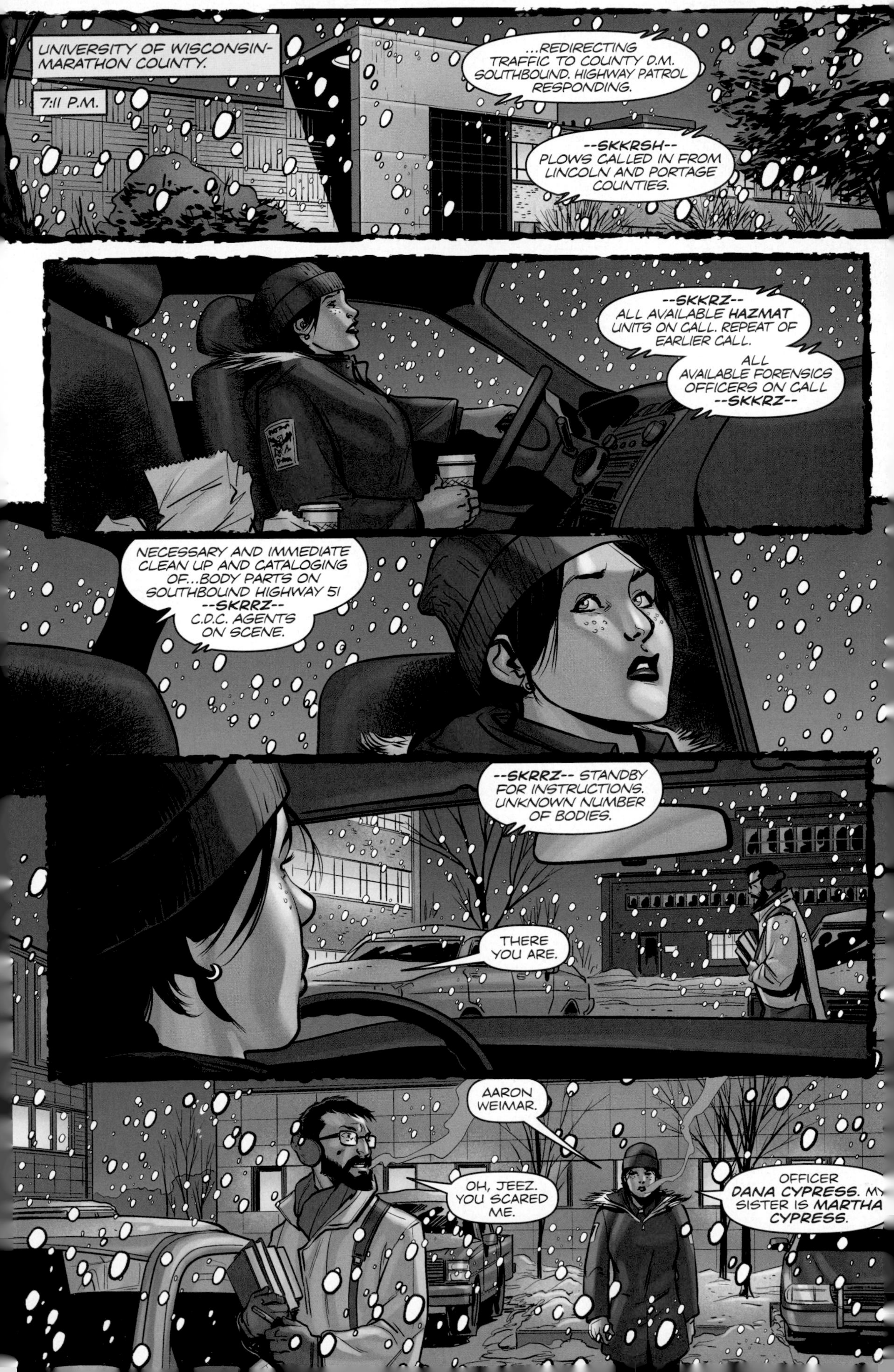
UNIVERSITY OF WISCONSIN-MARATHON COUNTY.
7:11 P.M.
...REDIRECTING TRAFFIC TO COUNTY D.M. SOUTHBOUND. HIGHWAY PATROL RESPONDING.
--SKKRSH-- PLOWS CALLED IN FROM LINCOLN AND PORTAGE COUNTIES.
--SKKRZ-- ALL AVAILABLE HAZMAT UNITS ON CALL. REPEAT OF EARLIER CALL.
ALL AVAILABLE FORENSICS OFFICERS ON CALL --SKKRZ--
NECESSARY AND IMMEDIATE CLEAN UP AND CATALOGING OF...BODY PARTS ON SOUTHBOUND HIGHWAY 51 --SKRRZ-- C.D.C. AGENTS ON SCENE.
--SKRRZ-- STANDBY FOR INSTRUCTIONS. UNKNOWN NUMBER OF BODIES.
THERE YOU ARE.
AARON WEIMAR.
OH, JEEZ. YOU SCARED ME.
OFFICER DANA CYPRESS. MY SISTER IS MARTHA CYPRESS.

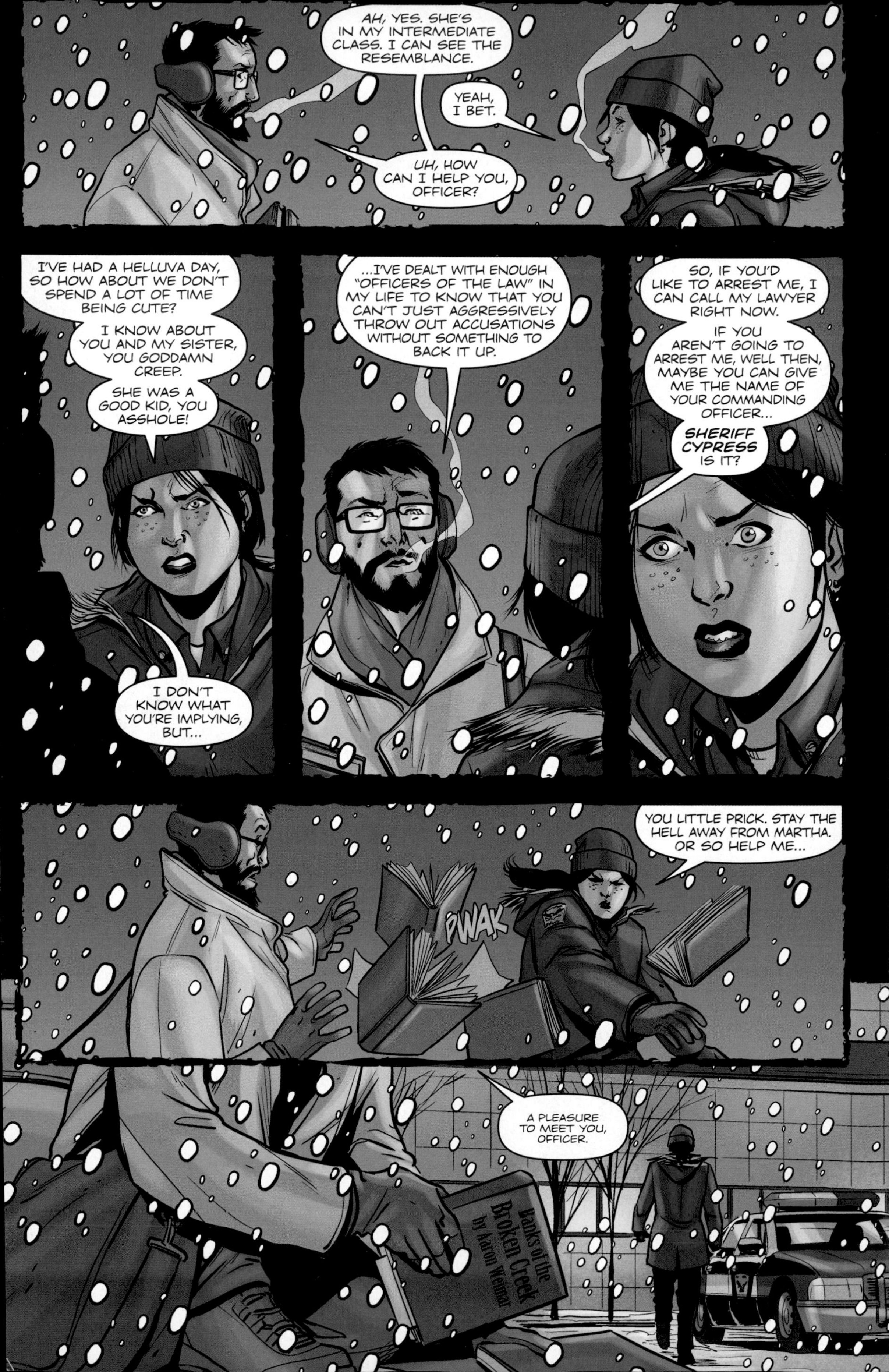
AH, YES. SHE'S IN MY INTERMEDIATE CLASS. I CAN SEE THE RESEMBLANCE.
YEAH, I BET.
UH, HOW CAN I HELP YOU, OFFICER?
I'VE HAD A HELLUVA DAY, SO HOW ABOUT WE DON'T SPEND A LOT OF TIME BEING CUTE?
I KNOW ABOUT YOU AND MY SISTER, YOU GODDAMN CREEP.
SHE WAS A GOOD KID, YOU ASSHOLE!
I DON'T KNOW WHAT YOU'RE IMPLYING, BUT...
...I'VE DEALT WITH ENOUGH "OFFICERS OF THE LAW" IN MY LIFE TO KNOW THAT YOU CAN'T JUST AGGRESSIVELY THROW OUT ACCUSATIONS WITHOUT SOMETHING TO BACK IT UP.
SO, IF YOU'D LIKE TO ARREST ME, I CAN CALL MY LAWYER RIGHT NOW.
IF YOU AREN'T GOING TO ARREST ME, WELL THEN, MAYBE YOU CAN GIVE ME THE NAME OF YOUR COMMANDING OFFICER...
SHERIFF CYPRESS IS IT?
YOU LITTLE PRICK. STAY THE HELL AWAY FROM MARTHA. OR SO HELP ME...
PWAK
A PLEASURE TO MEET YOU, OFFICER.
Banks of the Broken Creek by Aaron Weimar

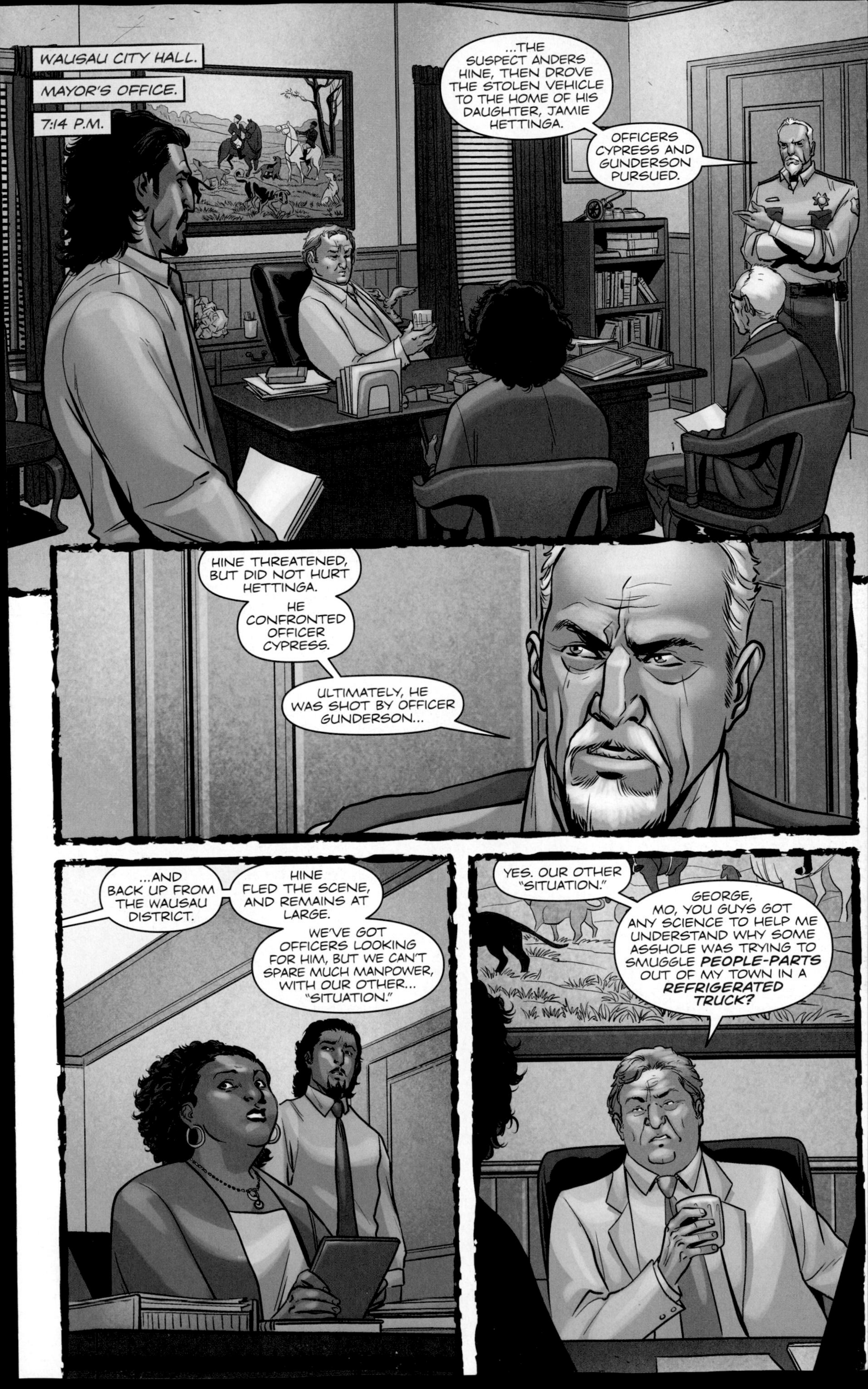

WAUSAU CITY HALL.
MAYOR'S OFFICE.
7:14 P.M.
...THE SUSPECT ANDERS HINE, THEN DROVE THE STOLEN VEHICLE TO THE HOME OF HIS DAUGHTER, JAMIE HETTINGA.
OFFICERS CYPRESS AND GUNDERSON PURSUED.
HINE THREATENED, BUT DID NOT HURT HETTINGA.
HE CONFRONTED OFFICER CYPRESS.
ULTIMATELY, HE WAS SHOT BY OFFICER GUNDERSON...
...AND BACK UP FROM THE WAUSAU DISTRICT.
HINE FLED THE SCENE, AND REMAINS AT LARGE.
WE'VE GOT OFFICERS LOOKING FOR HIM, BUT WE CAN'T SPARE MUCH MANPOWER, WITH OUR OTHER... "SITUATION."
YES. OUR OTHER "SITUATION."
GEORGE, MO, YOU GUYS GOT ANY SCIENCE TO HELP ME UNDERSTAND WHY SOME ASSHOLE WAS TRYING TO SMUGGLE **PEOPLE-PARTS** OUT OF MY TOWN IN A ***REFRIGERATED*** TRUCK?

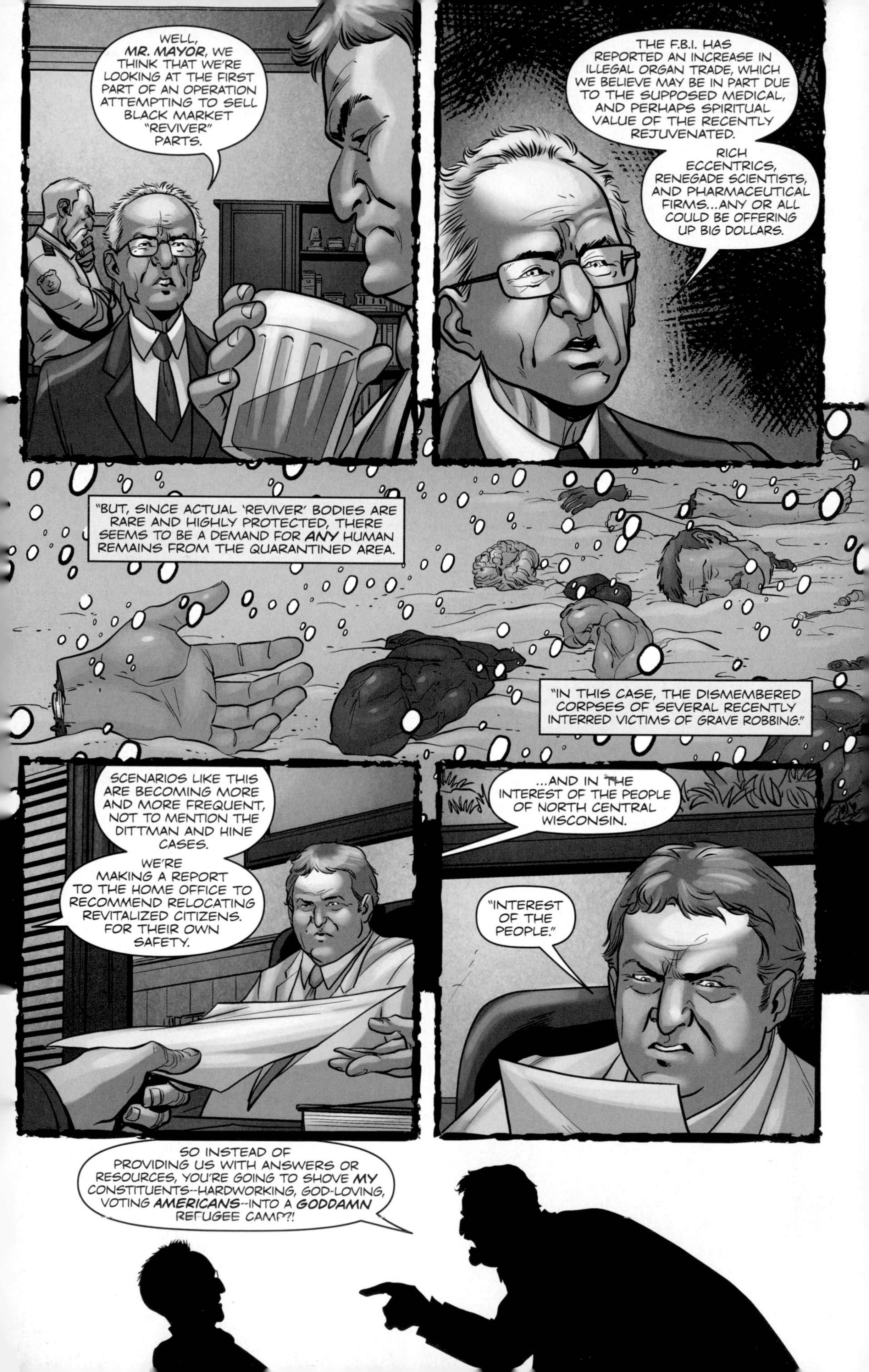

WELL, MR. MAYOR, WE THINK THAT WE'RE LOOKING AT THE FIRST PART OF AN OPERATION ATTEMPTING TO SELL BLACK MARKET "REVIVER" PARTS.
THE F.B.I. HAS REPORTED AN INCREASE IN ILLEGAL ORGAN TRADE, WHICH WE BELIEVE MAY BE IN PART DUE TO THE SUPPOSED MEDICAL, AND PERHAPS SPIRITUAL VALUE OF THE RECENTLY REJUVENATED.
RICH ECCENTRICS, RENEGADE SCIENTISTS, AND PHARMACEUTICAL FIRMS...ANY OR ALL COULD BE OFFERING UP BIG DOLLARS.
"BUT, SINCE ACTUAL 'REVIVER' BODIES ARE RARE AND HIGHLY PROTECTED, THERE SEEMS TO BE A DEMAND FOR ANY HUMAN REMAINS FROM THE QUARANTINED AREA.
"IN THIS CASE, THE DISMEMBERED CORPSES OF SEVERAL RECENTLY INTERRED VICTIMS OF GRAVE ROBBING."
SCENARIOS LIKE THIS ARE BECOMING MORE AND MORE FREQUENT, NOT TO MENTION THE DITTMAN AND HINE CASES.
WE'RE MAKING A REPORT TO THE HOME OFFICE TO RECOMMEND RELOCATING REVITALIZED CITIZENS. FOR THEIR OWN SAFETY.
...AND IN THE INTEREST OF THE PEOPLE OF NORTH CENTRAL WISCONSIN.
"INTEREST OF THE PEOPLE."
SO INSTEAD OF PROVIDING US WITH ANSWERS OR RESOURCES, YOU'RE GOING TO SHOVE MY CONSTITUENTS--HARDWORKING, GOD-LOVING, VOTING AMERICANS--INTO A GODDAMN REFUGEE CAMP?!

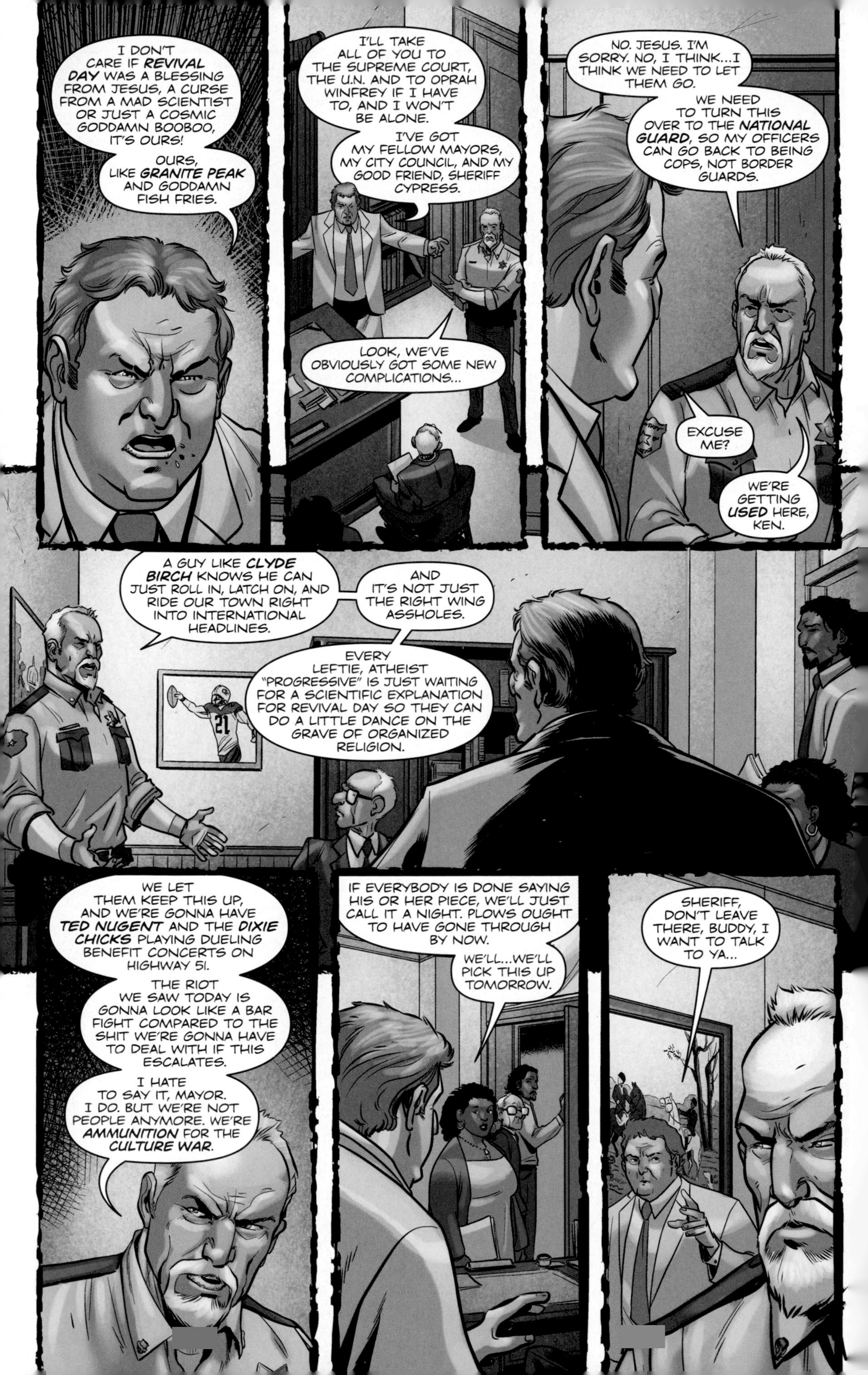

I DON'T CARE IF REVIVAL DAY WAS A BLESSING FROM JESUS, A CURSE FROM A MAD SCIENTIST OR JUST A COSMIC GODDAMN BOOBOO, IT'S OURS!
OURS, LIKE GRANITE PEAK AND GODDAMN FISH FRIES.
I'LL TAKE ALL OF YOU TO THE SUPREME COURT, THE U.N. AND TO OPRAH WINFREY IF I HAVE TO, AND I WON'T BE ALONE.
I'VE GOT MY FELLOW MAYORS, MY CITY COUNCIL, AND MY GOOD FRIEND, SHERIFF CYPRESS.
LOOK, WE'VE OBVIOUSLY GOT SOME NEW COMPLICATIONS...
NO. JESUS. I'M SORRY. NO, I THINK...I THINK WE NEED TO LET THEM GO.
WE NEED TO TURN THIS OVER TO THE NATIONAL GUARD, SO MY OFFICERS CAN GO BACK TO BEING COPS, NOT BORDER GUARDS.
EXCUSE ME?
WE'RE GETTING USED HERE, KEN.
A GUY LIKE CLYDE BIRCH KNOWS HE CAN JUST ROLL IN, LATCH ON, AND RIDE OUR TOWN RIGHT INTO INTERNATIONAL HEADLINES.
AND IT'S NOT JUST THE RIGHT WING ASSHOLES.
EVERY LEFTIE, ATHEIST "PROGRESSIVE" IS JUST WAITING FOR A SCIENTIFIC EXPLANATION FOR REVIVAL DAY SO THEY CAN DO A LITTLE DANCE ON THE GRAVE OF ORGANIZED RELIGION.
WE LET THEM KEEP THIS UP, AND WE'RE GONNA HAVE TED NUGENT AND THE DIXIE CHICKS PLAYING DUELING BENEFIT CONCERTS ON HIGHWAY 51.
THE RIOT WE SAW TODAY IS GONNA LOOK LIKE A BAR FIGHT COMPARED TO THE SHIT WE'RE GONNA HAVE TO DEAL WITH IF THIS ESCALATES.
I HATE TO SAY IT, MAYOR. I DO. BUT WE'RE NOT PEOPLE ANYMORE. WE'RE AMMUNITION FOR THE CULTURE WAR.
IF EVERYBODY IS DONE SAYING HIS OR HER PIECE, WE'LL JUST CALL IT A NIGHT. PLOWS OUGHT TO HAVE GONE THROUGH BY NOW.
WE'LL...WE'LL PICK THIS UP TOMORROW.
SHERIFF, DON'T LEAVE THERE, BUDDY, I WANT TO TALK TO YA...

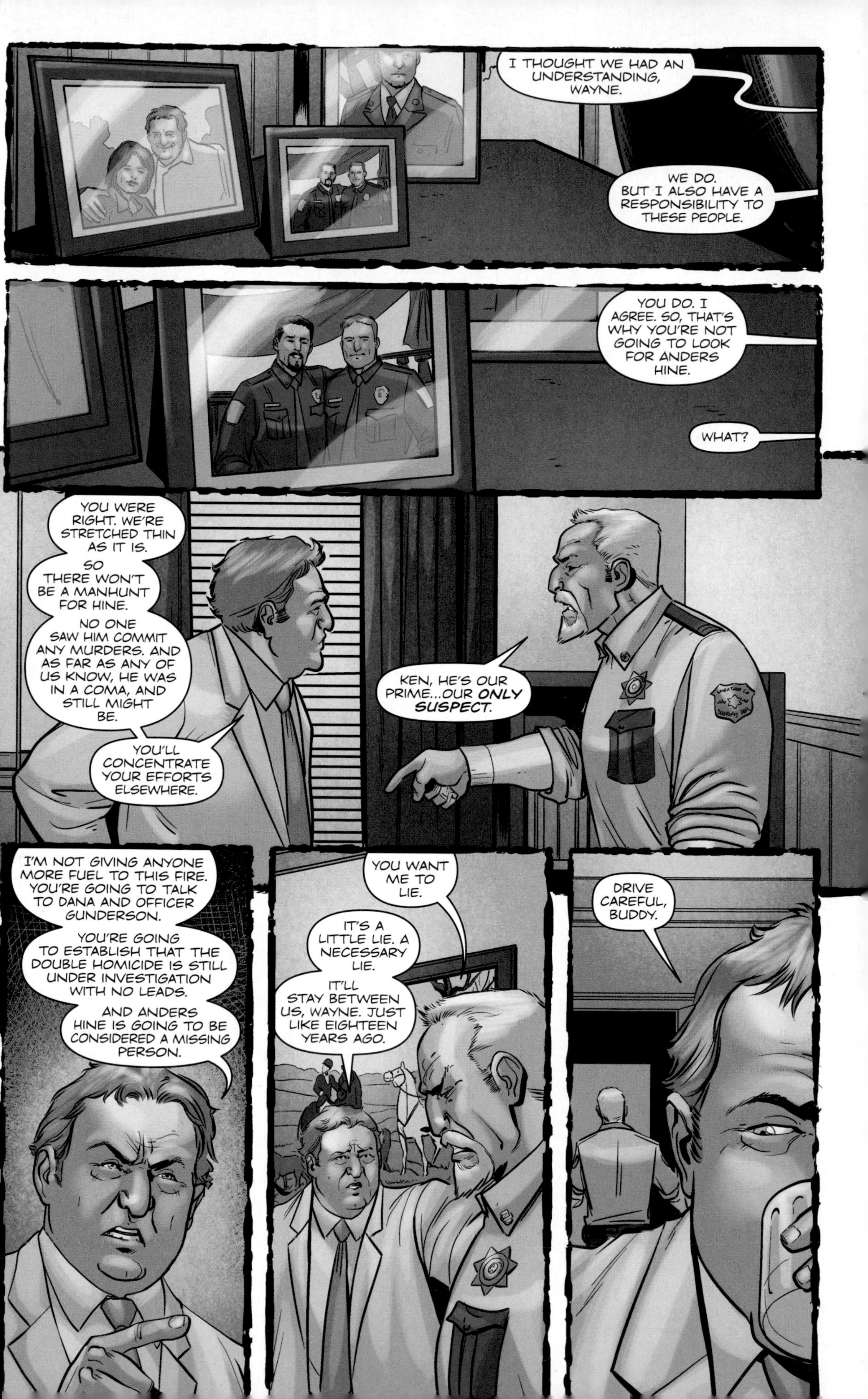
I THOUGHT WE HAD AN UNDERSTANDING, WAYNE.
WE DO. BUT I ALSO HAVE A RESPONSIBILITY TO THESE PEOPLE.
YOU DO. I AGREE. SO, THAT'S WHY YOU'RE NOT GOING TO LOOK FOR ANDERS HINE.
WHAT?
YOU WERE RIGHT. WE'RE STRETCHED THIN AS IT IS.
SO THERE WON'T BE A MANHUNT FOR HINE.
NO ONE SAW HIM COMMIT ANY MURDERS. AND AS FAR AS ANY OF US KNOW, HE WAS IN A COMA, AND STILL MIGHT BE.
YOU'LL CONCENTRATE YOUR EFFORTS ELSEWHERE.
KEN, HE'S OUR PRIME...OUR **ONLY SUSPECT**.
I'M NOT GIVING ANYONE MORE FUEL TO THIS FIRE. YOU'RE GOING TO TALK TO DANA AND OFFICER GUNDERSON.
YOU'RE GOING TO ESTABLISH THAT THE DOUBLE HOMICIDE IS STILL UNDER INVESTIGATION WITH NO LEADS.
AND ANDERS HINE IS GOING TO BE CONSIDERED A MISSING PERSON.
YOU WANT ME TO LIE.
IT'S A LITTLE LIE. A NECESSARY LIE.
IT'LL STAY BETWEEN US, WAYNE. JUST LIKE EIGHTEEN YEARS AGO.
DRIVE CAREFUL, BUDDY.

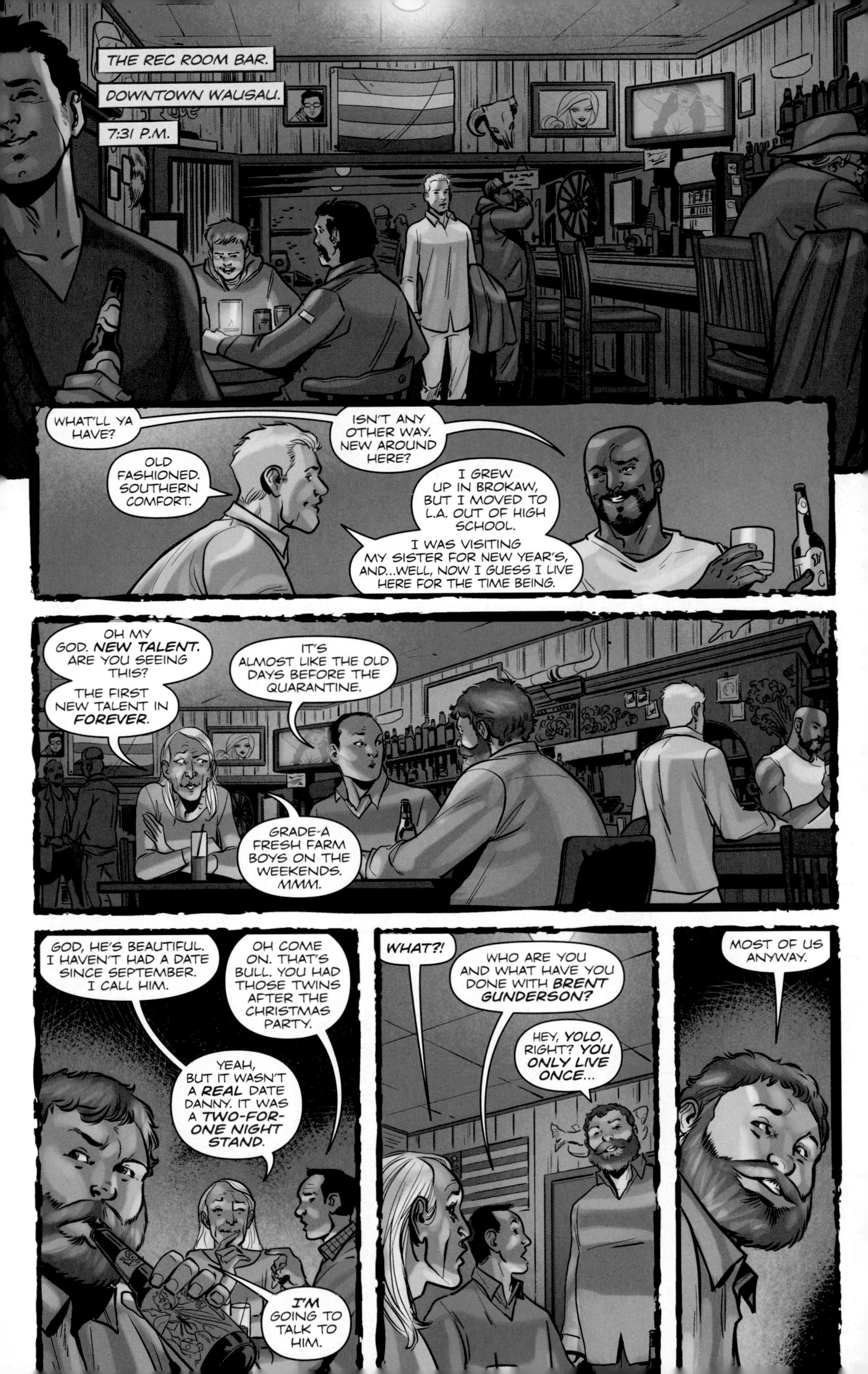
THE REC ROOM BAR.
DOWNTOWN WAUSAU.
7:31 P.M.
WHAT'LL YA HAVE?
OLD FASHIONED. SOUTHERN COMFORT.
ISN'T ANY OTHER WAY. NEW AROUND HERE?
I GREW UP IN BROKAW, BUT I MOVED TO L.A. OUT OF HIGH SCHOOL.
I WAS VISITING MY SISTER FOR NEW YEAR'S, AND...WELL, NOW I GUESS I LIVE HERE FOR THE TIME BEING.
OH MY GOD. NEW TALENT. ARE YOU SEEING THIS?
THE FIRST NEW TALENT IN FOREVER.
IT'S ALMOST LIKE THE OLD DAYS BEFORE THE QUARANTINE.
GRADE-A FRESH FARM BOYS ON THE WEEKENDS. MMM.
GOD, HE'S BEAUTIFUL. I HAVEN'T HAD A DATE SINCE SEPTEMBER. I CALL HIM.
OH COME ON. THAT'S BULL. YOU HAD THOSE TWINS AFTER THE CHRISTMAS PARTY.
YEAH, BUT IT WASN'T A REAL DATE DANNY. IT WAS A TWO-FOR-ONE NIGHT STAND.
I'M GOING TO TALK TO HIM.
WHAT?!
WHO ARE YOU AND WHAT HAVE YOU DONE WITH BRENT GUNDERSON?
HEY, YOLO, RIGHT? YOU ONLY LIVE ONCE...
MOST OF US ANYWAY.

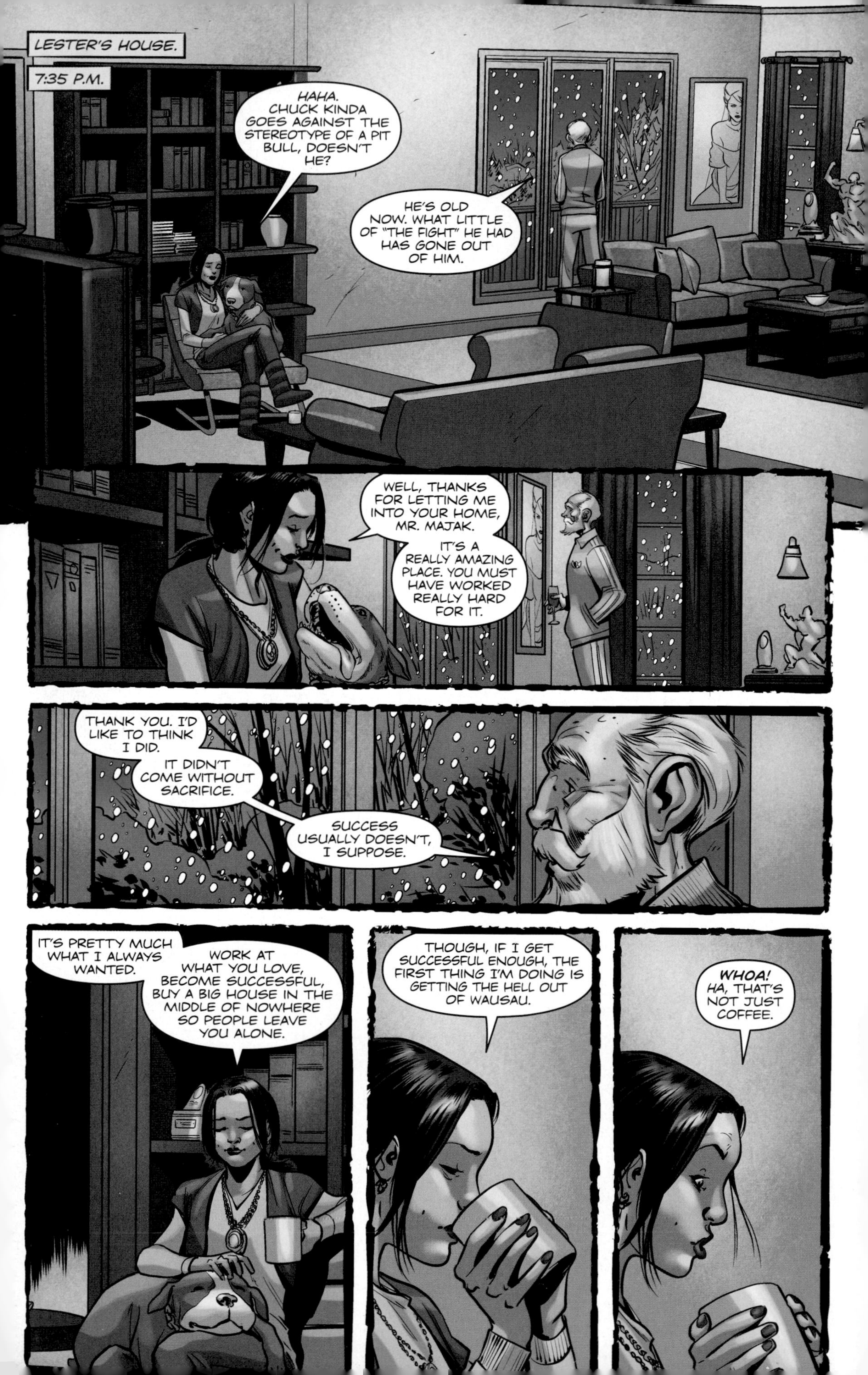
LESTER'S HOUSE.
7:35 P.M.
HAHA. CHUCK KINDA GOES AGAINST THE STEREOTYPE OF A PIT BULL, DOESN'T HE?
HE'S OLD NOW. WHAT LITTLE OF "THE FIGHT" HE HAD HAS GONE OUT OF HIM.
WELL, THANKS FOR LETTING ME INTO YOUR HOME, MR. MAJAK.
IT'S A REALLY AMAZING PLACE. YOU MUST HAVE WORKED REALLY HARD FOR IT.
THANK YOU. I'D LIKE TO THINK I DID.
IT DIDN'T COME WITHOUT SACRIFICE.
SUCCESS USUALLY DOESN'T, I SUPPOSE.
IT'S PRETTY MUCH WHAT I ALWAYS WANTED.
WORK AT WHAT YOU LOVE, BECOME SUCCESSFUL, BUY A BIG HOUSE IN THE MIDDLE OF NOWHERE SO PEOPLE LEAVE YOU ALONE.
THOUGH, IF I GET SUCCESSFUL ENOUGH, THE FIRST THING I'M DOING IS GETTING THE HELL OUT OF WAUSAU.
WHOA! HA, THAT'S NOT JUST COFFEE.

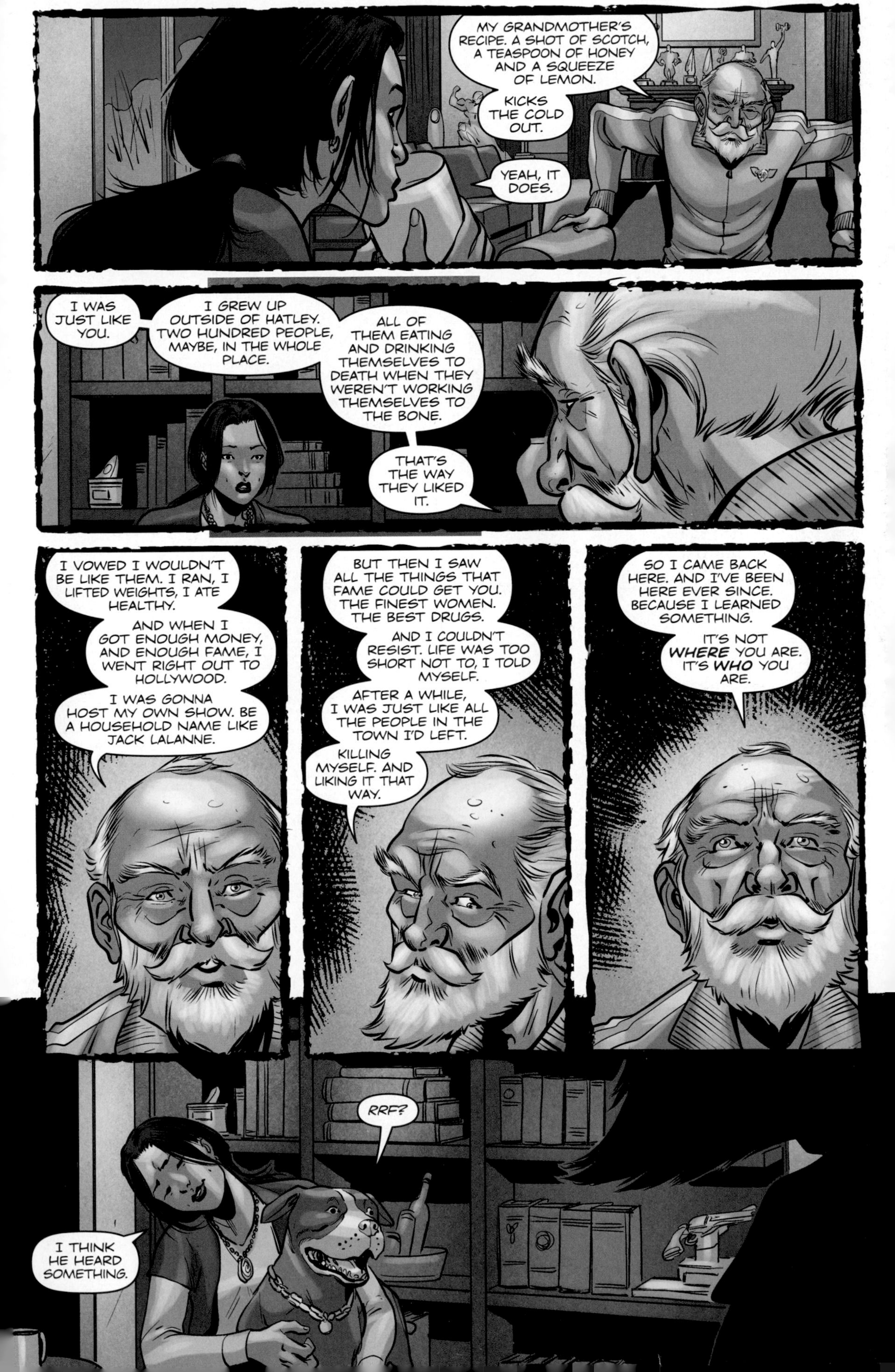
MY GRANDMOTHER'S RECIPE. A SHOT OF SCOTCH, A TEASPOON OF HONEY AND A SQUEEZE OF LEMON.
KICKS THE COLD OUT.
YEAH, IT DOES.
I WAS JUST LIKE YOU.
I GREW UP OUTSIDE OF HATLEY. TWO HUNDRED PEOPLE, MAYBE, IN THE WHOLE PLACE.
ALL OF THEM EATING AND DRINKING THEMSELVES TO DEATH WHEN THEY WEREN'T WORKING THEMSELVES TO THE BONE.
THAT'S THE WAY THEY LIKED IT.
I VOWED I WOULDN'T BE LIKE THEM. I RAN, I LIFTED WEIGHTS, I ATE HEALTHY.
AND WHEN I GOT ENOUGH MONEY, AND ENOUGH FAME, I WENT RIGHT OUT TO HOLLYWOOD.
I WAS GONNA HOST MY OWN SHOW. BE A HOUSEHOLD NAME LIKE JACK LALANNE.
BUT THEN I SAW ALL THE THINGS THAT FAME COULD GET YOU. THE FINEST WOMEN. THE BEST DRUGS.
AND I COULDN'T RESIST. LIFE WAS TOO SHORT NOT TO, I TOLD MYSELF.
AFTER A WHILE, I WAS JUST LIKE ALL THE PEOPLE IN THE TOWN I'D LEFT.
KILLING MYSELF. AND LIKING IT THAT WAY.
SO I CAME BACK HERE. AND I'VE BEEN HERE EVER SINCE. BECAUSE I LEARNED SOMETHING.
IT'S NOT *WHERE* YOU ARE. IT'S *WHO* YOU ARE.
RRF?
I THINK HE HEARD SOMETHING.

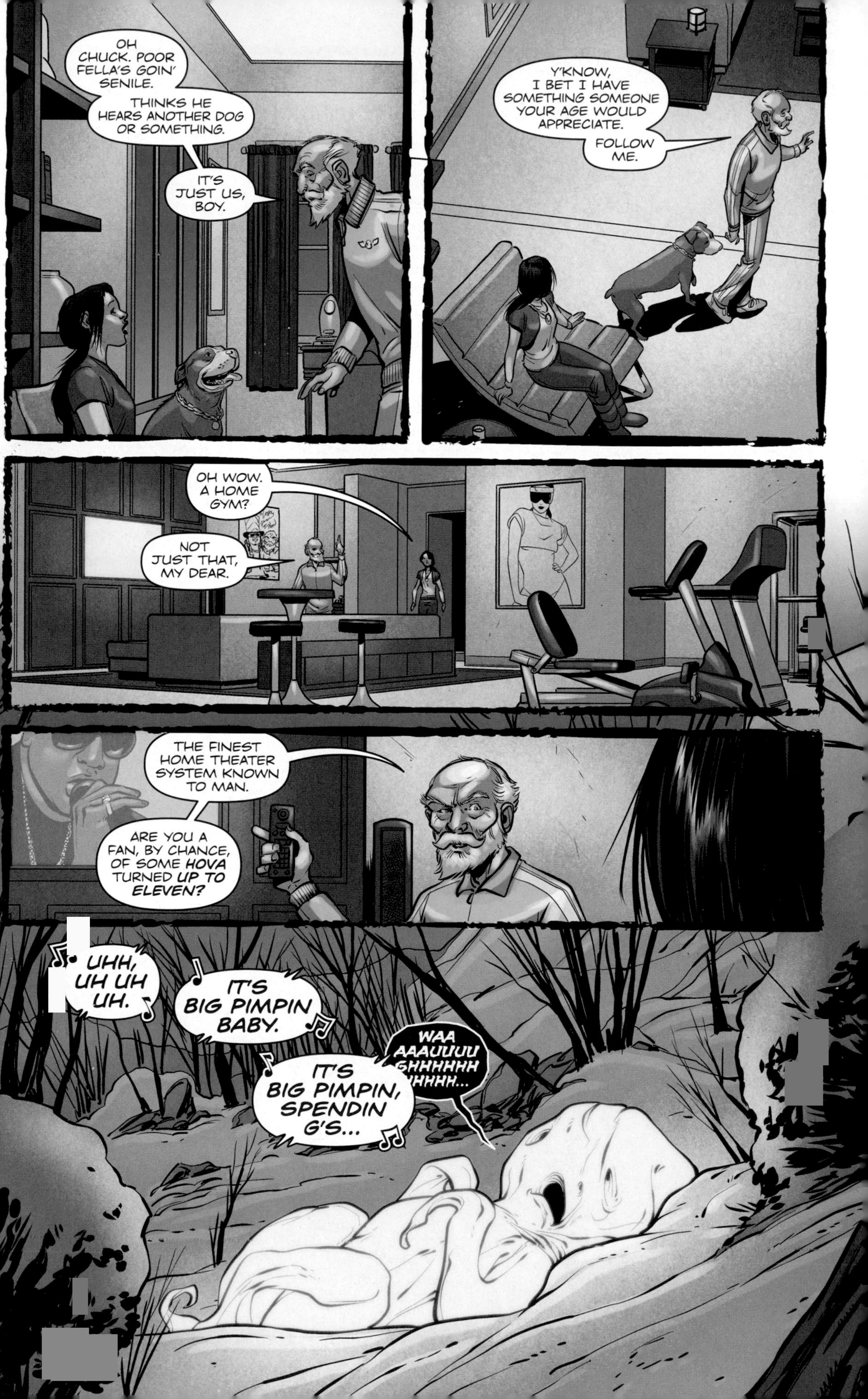
OH CHUCK. POOR FELLA'S GOIN' SENILE.
THINKS HE HEARS ANOTHER DOG OR SOMETHING.
IT'S JUST US, BOY.
Y'KNOW, I BET I HAVE SOMETHING SOMEONE YOUR AGE WOULD APPRECIATE.
FOLLOW ME.
OH WOW. A HOME GYM?
NOT JUST THAT, MY DEAR.
THE FINEST HOME THEATER SYSTEM KNOWN TO MAN.
ARE YOU A FAN, BY CHANCE, OF SOME HOVA TURNED UP TO ELEVEN?
UHH, UH UH UH.
IT'S BIG PIMPIN BABY.
IT'S BIG PIMPIN, SPENDIN G'S...
WAA AAAUUUU GHHHHHH HHHHH...

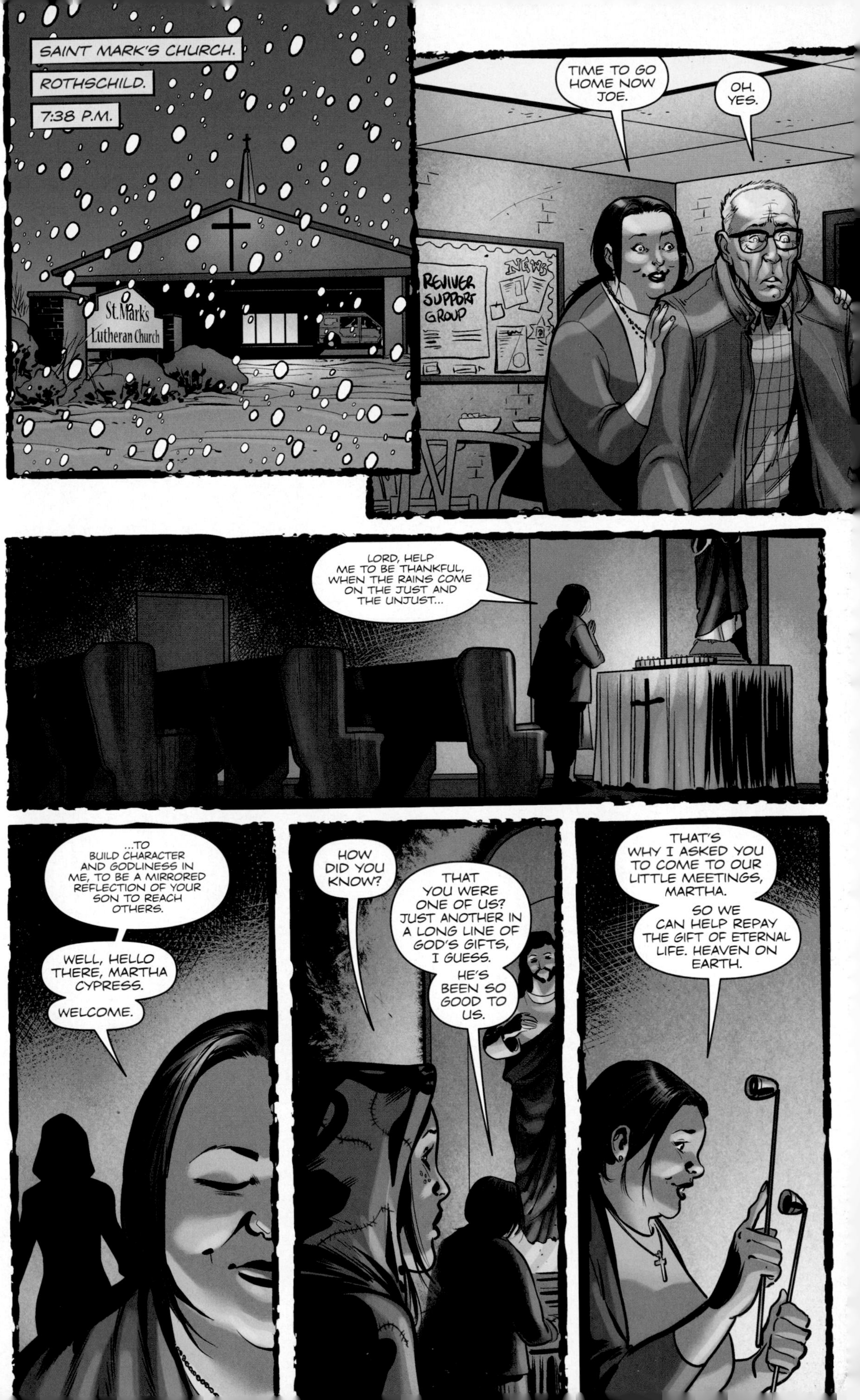
SAINT MARK'S CHURCH.
ROTHSCHILD.
7:38 P.M.
St. Mark's Lutheran Church
TIME TO GO HOME NOW JOE.
OH. YES.
REVIVER SUPPORT GROUP
NEWS
LORD, HELP ME TO BE THANKFUL, WHEN THE RAINS COME ON THE JUST AND THE UNJUST...
...TO BUILD CHARACTER AND GODLINESS IN ME, TO BE A MIRRORED REFLECTION OF YOUR SON TO REACH OTHERS.
WELL, HELLO THERE, MARTHA CYPRESS.
WELCOME.
HOW DID YOU KNOW?
THAT YOU WERE ONE OF US? JUST ANOTHER IN A LONG LINE OF GOD'S GIFTS, I GUESS.
HE'S BEEN SO GOOD TO US.
THAT'S WHY I ASKED YOU TO COME TO OUR LITTLE MEETINGS, MARTHA.
SO WE CAN HELP REPAY THE GIFT OF ETERNAL LIFE. HEAVEN ON EARTH.

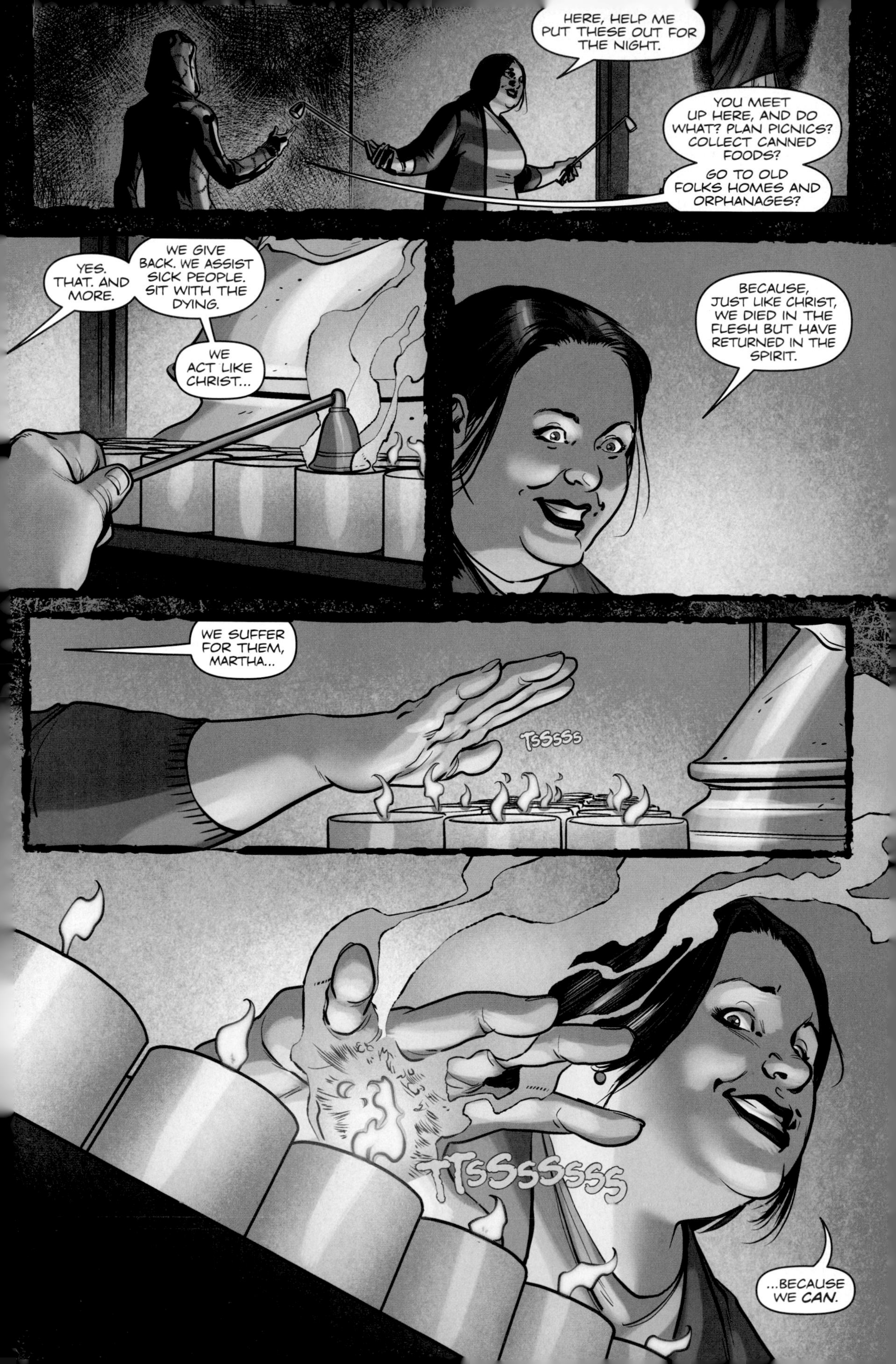
HERE, HELP ME PUT THESE OUT FOR THE NIGHT.
YOU MEET UP HERE, AND DO WHAT? PLAN PICNICS? COLLECT CANNED FOODS?
GO TO OLD FOLKS HOMES AND ORPHANAGES?
YES. THAT. AND MORE.
WE GIVE BACK. WE ASSIST SICK PEOPLE. SIT WITH THE DYING.
WE ACT LIKE CHRIST...
BECAUSE, JUST LIKE CHRIST, WE DIED IN THE FLESH BUT HAVE RETURNED IN THE SPIRIT.
WE SUFFER FOR THEM, MARTHA...
TSSSSS
TTSSSSSSSS
...BECAUSE WE CAN.

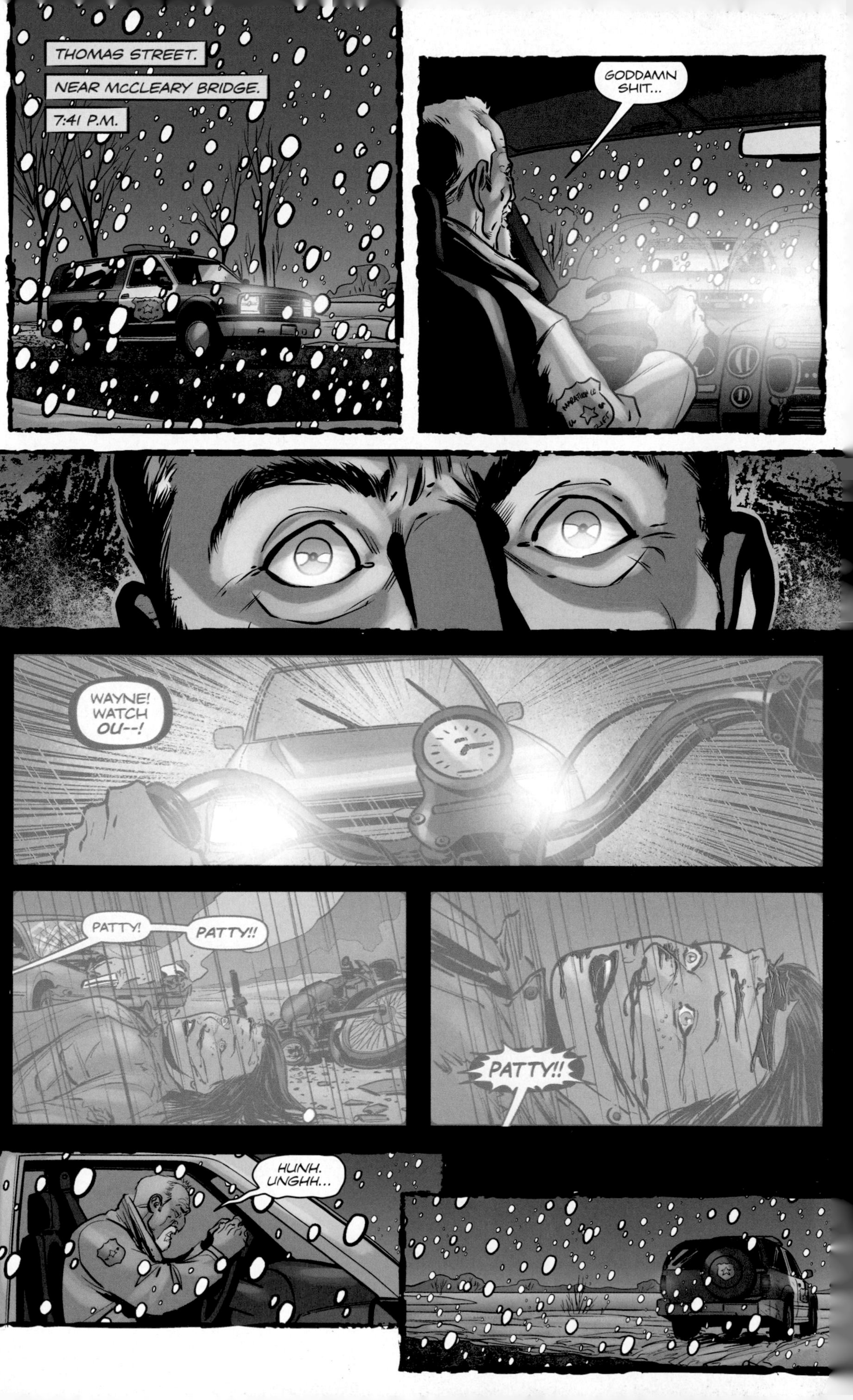
THOMAS STREET.
NEAR McCLEARY BRIDGE.
7:41 P.M.
GODDAMN SHIT...
WAYNE! WATCH OU--!
PATTY!
PATTY!!
PATTY!!
HUNH. UNGHH...

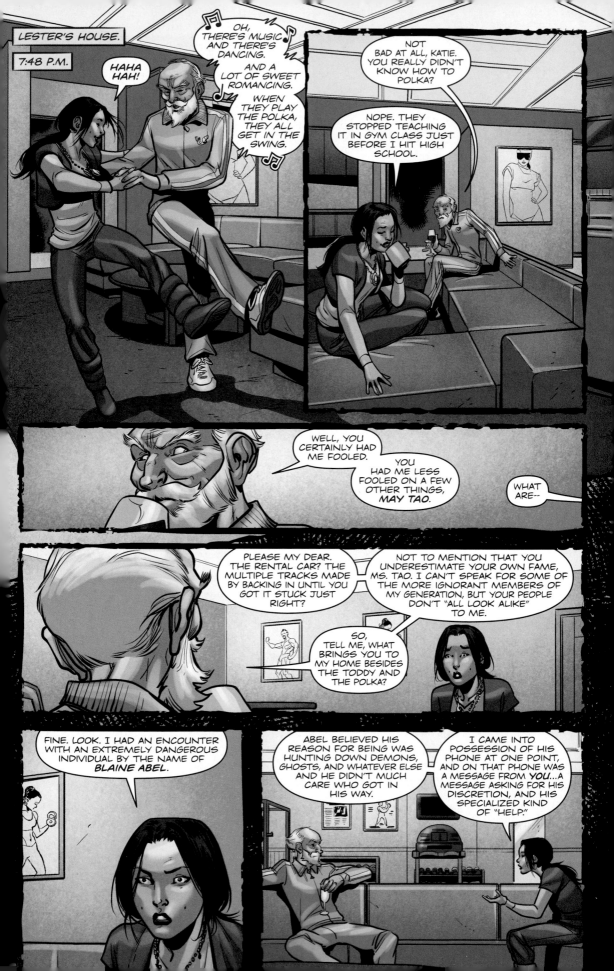

LESTER'S HOUSE.

7:48 P.M.

HAHA HAH!

♪ OH, THERE'S MUSIC AND THERE'S DANCING. ♫ AND A LOT OF SWEET ROMANCING. WHEN THEY PLAY THE POLKA, THEY ALL GET IN THE SWING.

NOT BAD AT ALL, KATIE. YOU REALLY DIDN'T KNOW HOW TO POLKA?

NOPE. THEY STOPPED TEACHING IT IN GYM CLASS JUST BEFORE I HIT HIGH SCHOOL.

WELL, YOU CERTAINLY HAD ME FOOLED.

YOU HAD ME LESS FOOLED ON A FEW OTHER THINGS, MAY TAO.

WHAT ARE--

PLEASE MY DEAR. THE RENTAL CAR? THE MULTIPLE TRACKS MADE BY BACKING IN UNTIL YOU GOT IT STUCK JUST RIGHT?

NOT TO MENTION THAT YOU UNDERESTIMATE YOUR OWN FAME, MS. TAO. I CAN'T SPEAK FOR SOME OF THE MORE IGNORANT MEMBERS OF MY GENERATION, BUT YOUR PEOPLE DON'T "ALL LOOK ALIKE" TO ME.

SO, TELL ME, WHAT BRINGS YOU TO MY HOME BESIDES THE TODDY AND THE POLKA?

FINE. LOOK. I HAD AN ENCOUNTER WITH AN EXTREMELY DANGEROUS INDIVIDUAL BY THE NAME OF BLAINE ABEL.

ABEL BELIEVED HIS REASON FOR BEING WAS HUNTING DOWN DEMONS, GHOSTS, AND WHATEVER ELSE AND HE DIDN'T MUCH CARE WHO GOT IN HIS WAY.

I CAME INTO POSSESSION OF HIS PHONE AT ONE POINT, AND ON THAT PHONE WAS A MESSAGE FROM YOU...A MESSAGE ASKING FOR HIS DISCRETION, AND HIS SPECIALIZED KIND OF "HELP."

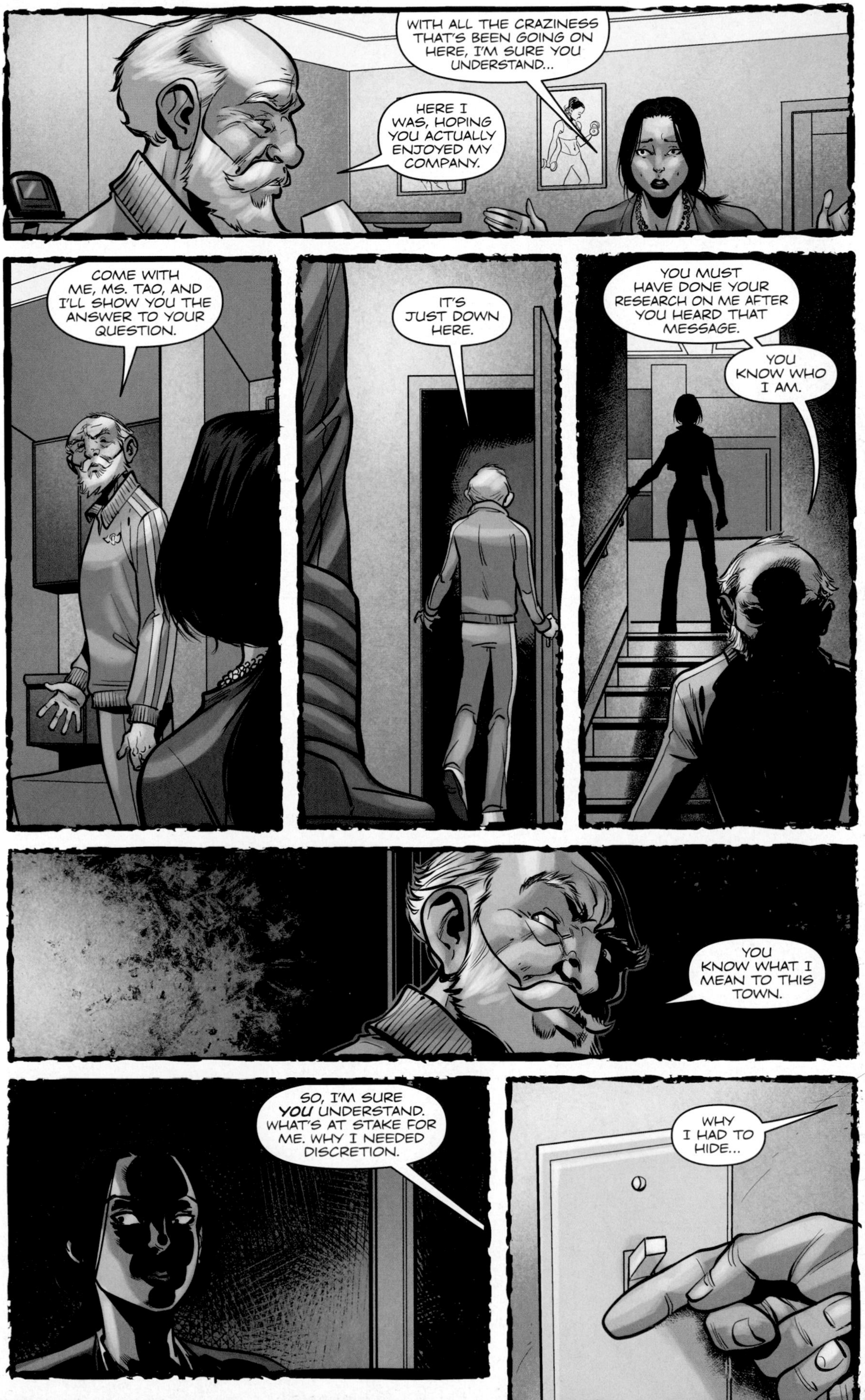
WITH ALL THE CRAZINESS THAT'S BEEN GOING ON HERE, I'M SURE YOU UNDERSTAND...
HERE I WAS, HOPING YOU ACTUALLY ENJOYED MY COMPANY.
COME WITH ME, MS. TAO, AND I'LL SHOW YOU THE ANSWER TO YOUR QUESTION.
IT'S JUST DOWN HERE.
YOU MUST HAVE DONE YOUR RESEARCH ON ME AFTER YOU HEARD THAT MESSAGE.
YOU KNOW WHO I AM.
YOU KNOW WHAT I MEAN TO THIS TOWN.
SO, I'M SURE YOU UNDERSTAND. WHAT'S AT STAKE FOR ME. WHY I NEEDED DISCRETION.
WHY I HAD TO HIDE...

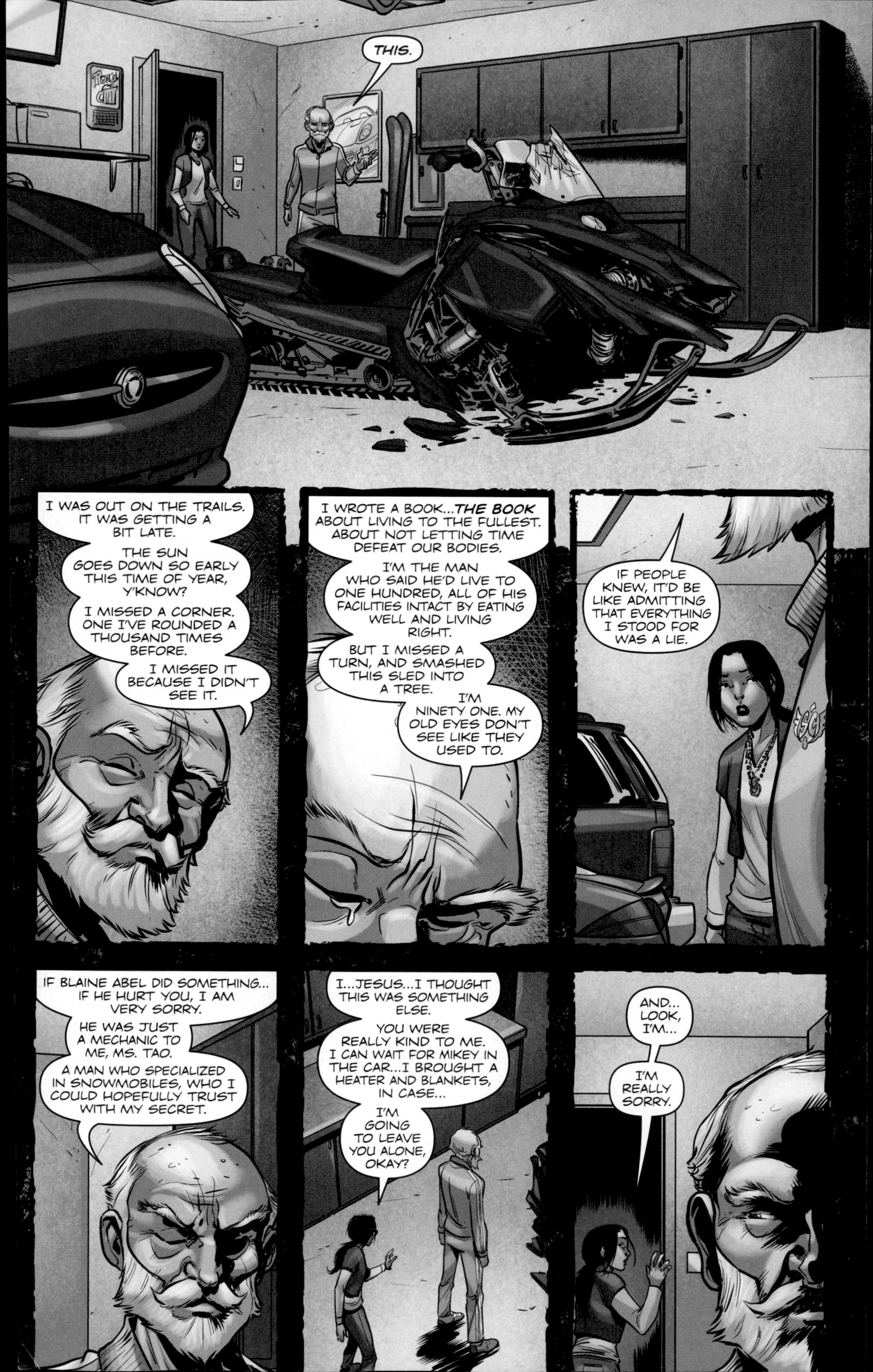
THIS.
I WAS OUT ON THE TRAILS. IT WAS GETTING A BIT LATE.
THE SUN GOES DOWN SO EARLY THIS TIME OF YEAR, Y'KNOW?
I MISSED A CORNER. ONE I'VE ROUNDED A THOUSAND TIMES BEFORE.
I MISSED IT BECAUSE I DIDN'T SEE IT.
I WROTE A BOOK...THE BOOK ABOUT LIVING TO THE FULLEST. ABOUT NOT LETTING TIME DEFEAT OUR BODIES.
I'M THE MAN WHO SAID HE'D LIVE TO ONE HUNDRED, ALL OF HIS FACILITIES INTACT BY EATING WELL AND LIVING RIGHT.
BUT I MISSED A TURN, AND SMASHED THIS SLED INTO A TREE.
I'M NINETY ONE. MY OLD EYES DON'T SEE LIKE THEY USED TO.
IF PEOPLE KNEW, IT'D BE LIKE ADMITTING THAT EVERYTHING I STOOD FOR WAS A LIE.
IF BLAINE ABEL DID SOMETHING... IF HE HURT YOU, I AM VERY SORRY.
HE WAS JUST A MECHANIC TO ME, MS. TAO.
A MAN WHO SPECIALIZED IN SNOWMOBILES, WHO I COULD HOPEFULLY TRUST WITH MY SECRET.
I...JESUS...I THOUGHT THIS WAS SOMETHING ELSE.
YOU WERE REALLY KIND TO ME. I CAN WAIT FOR MIKEY IN THE CAR...I BROUGHT A HEATER AND BLANKETS, IN CASE...
I'M GOING TO LEAVE YOU ALONE, OKAY?
AND... LOOK, I'M...
I'M REALLY SORRY.

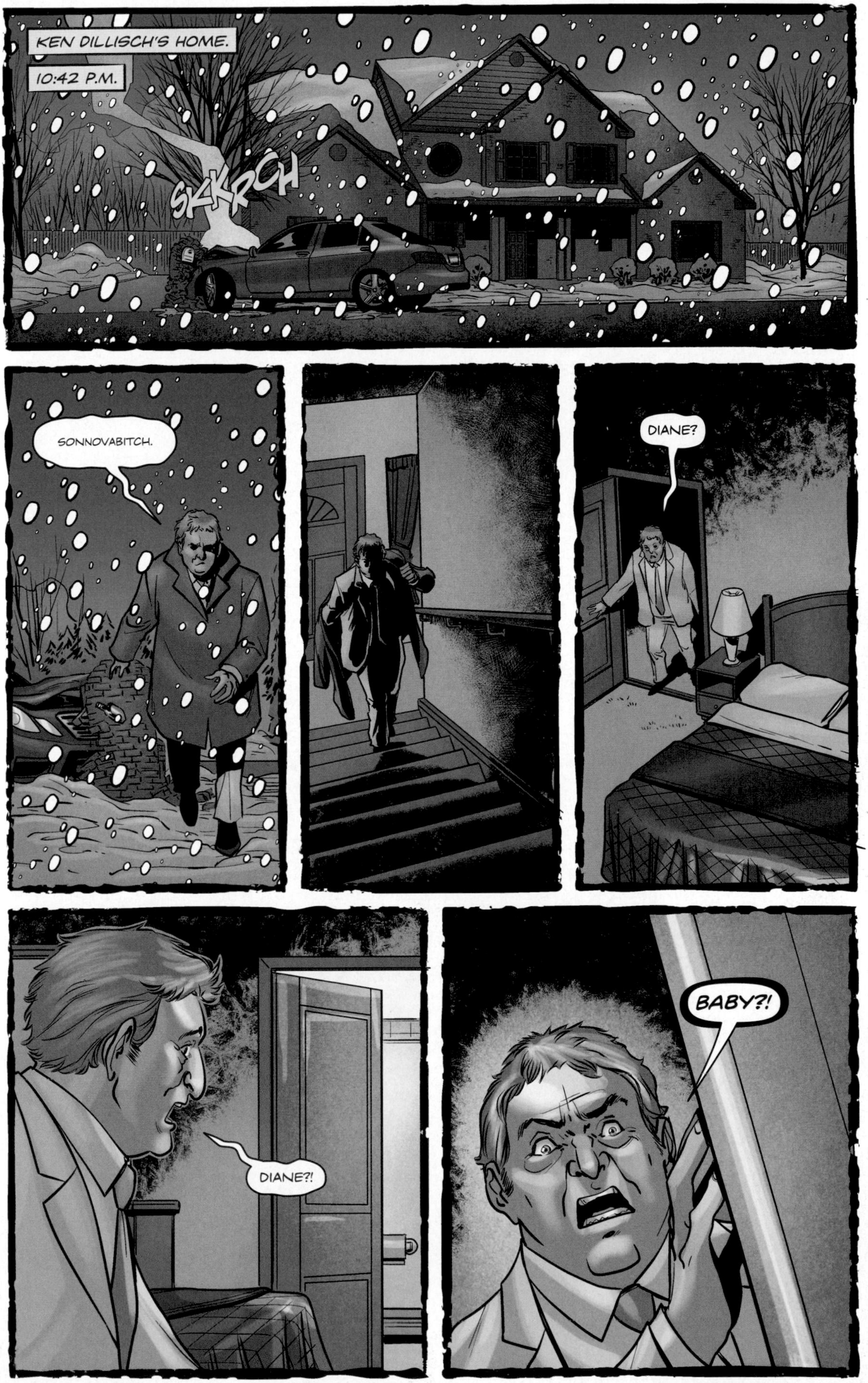
KEN DILLISCH'S HOME.
10:42 P.M.
SKKRCH
SONNOVABITCH.
DIANE?
DIANE?!
BABY?!

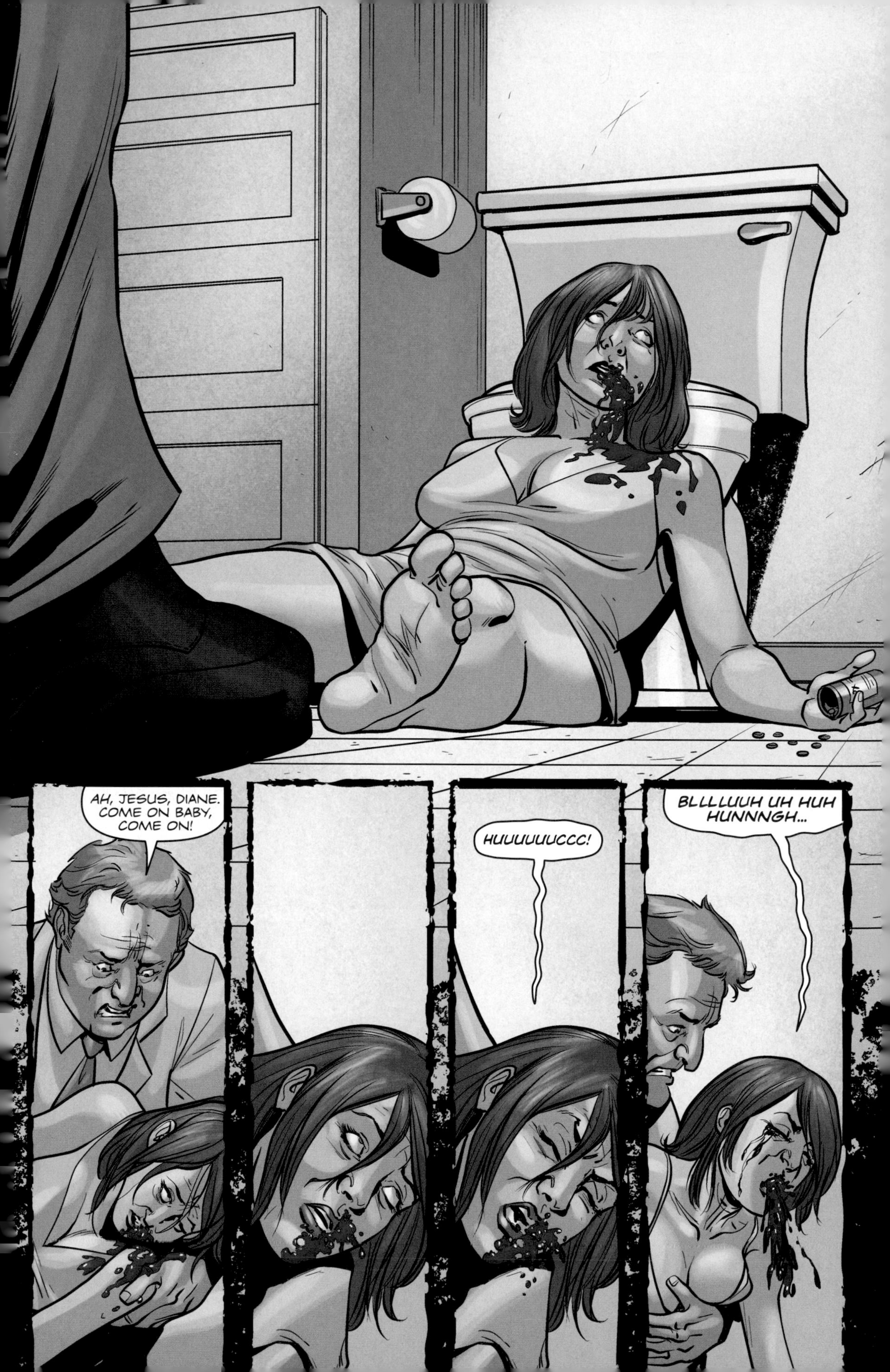
AH, JESUS, DIANE.
COME ON BABY,
COME ON!
HUUUUUUCCC!
BLLLLUUH UH HUH
HUNNNGH...

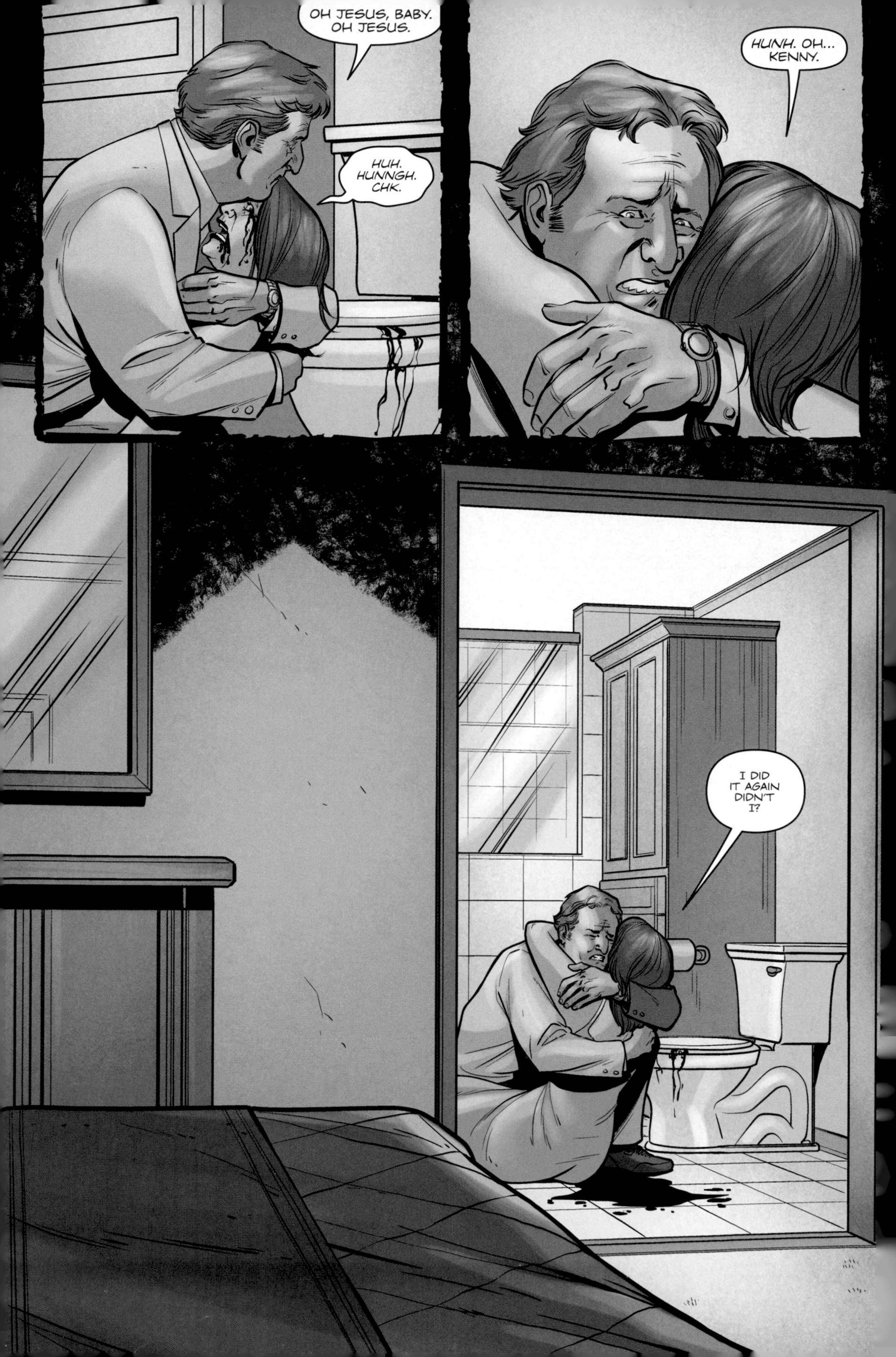
OH JESUS, BABY. OH JESUS.
HUH. HUNNGH. CHK.
HUNH. OH... KENNY.
I DID IT AGAIN DIDN'T I?

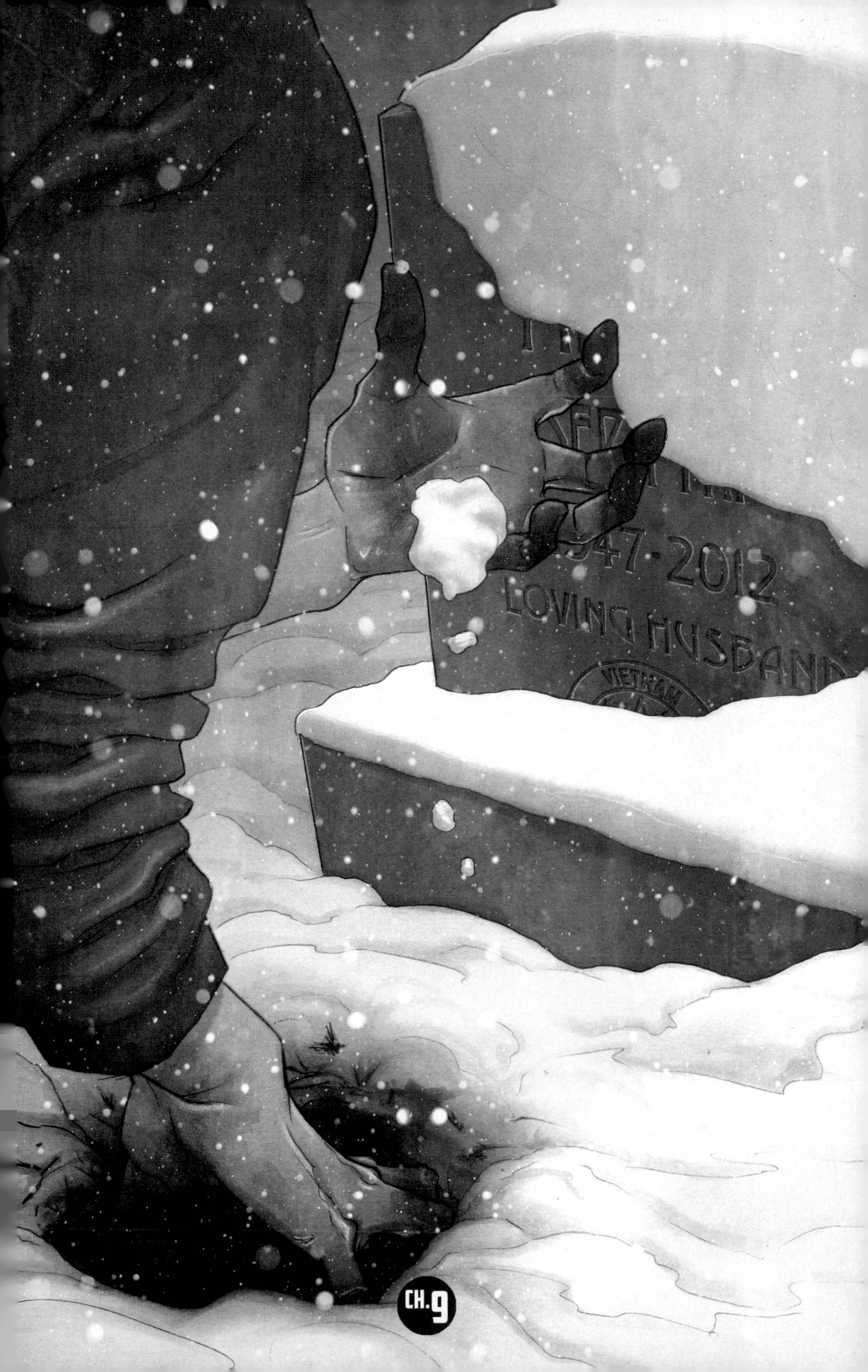
947-2012
LOVING HUSBAN
VIETNAM
CH.9

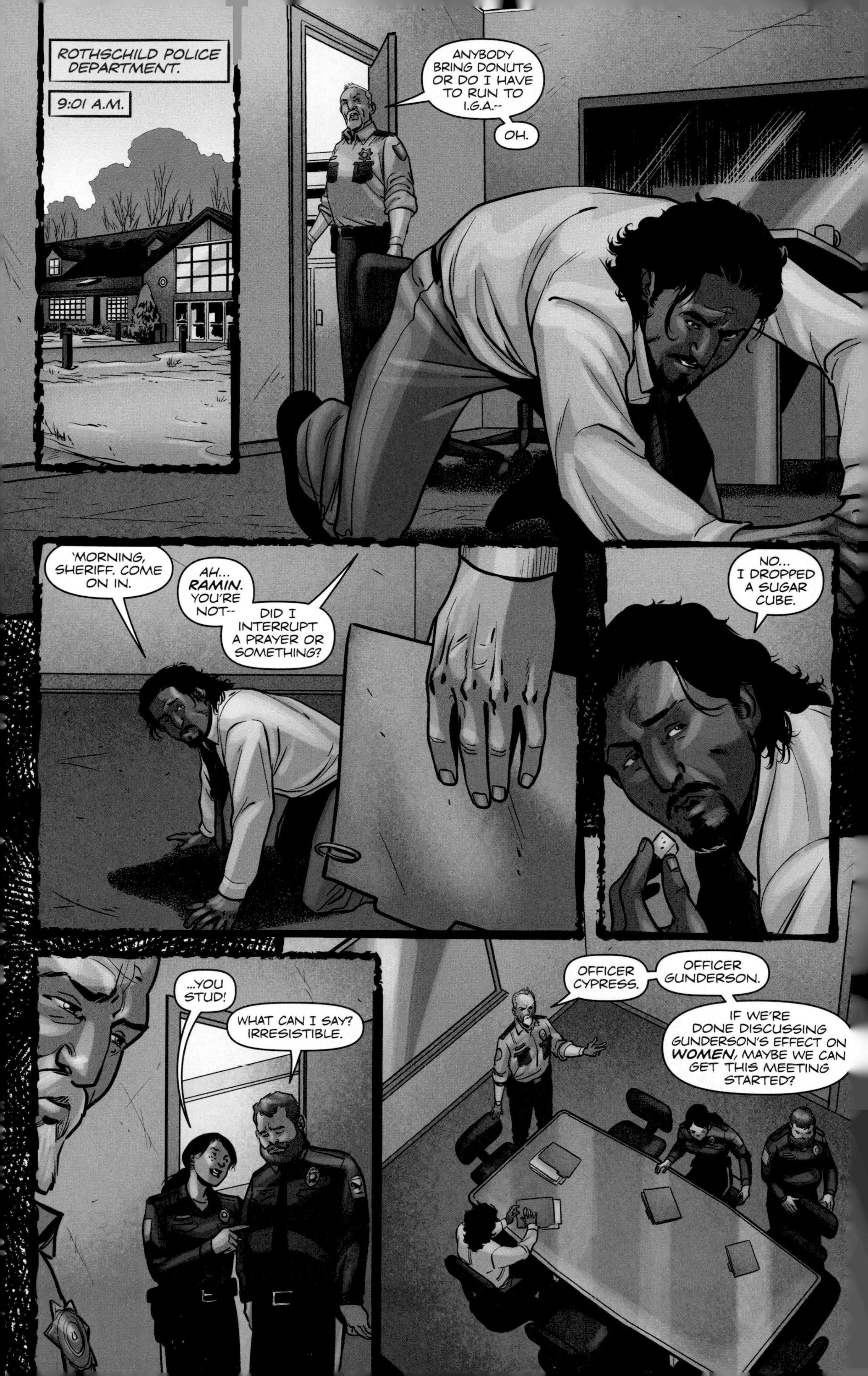
ROTHSCHILD POLICE DEPARTMENT.
9:01 A.M.
ANYBODY BRING DONUTS OR DO I HAVE TO RUN TO I.G.A.--
OH.
'MORNING, SHERIFF. COME ON IN.
AH... **RAMIN**. YOU'RE NOT--
DID I INTERRUPT A PRAYER OR SOMETHING?
NO... I DROPPED A SUGAR CUBE.
...YOU STUD!
WHAT CAN I SAY? IRRESISTIBLE.
OFFICER CYPRESS.
OFFICER GUNDERSON.
IF WE'RE DONE DISCUSSING GUNDERSON'S EFFECT ON **WOMEN**, MAYBE WE CAN GET THIS MEETING STARTED?

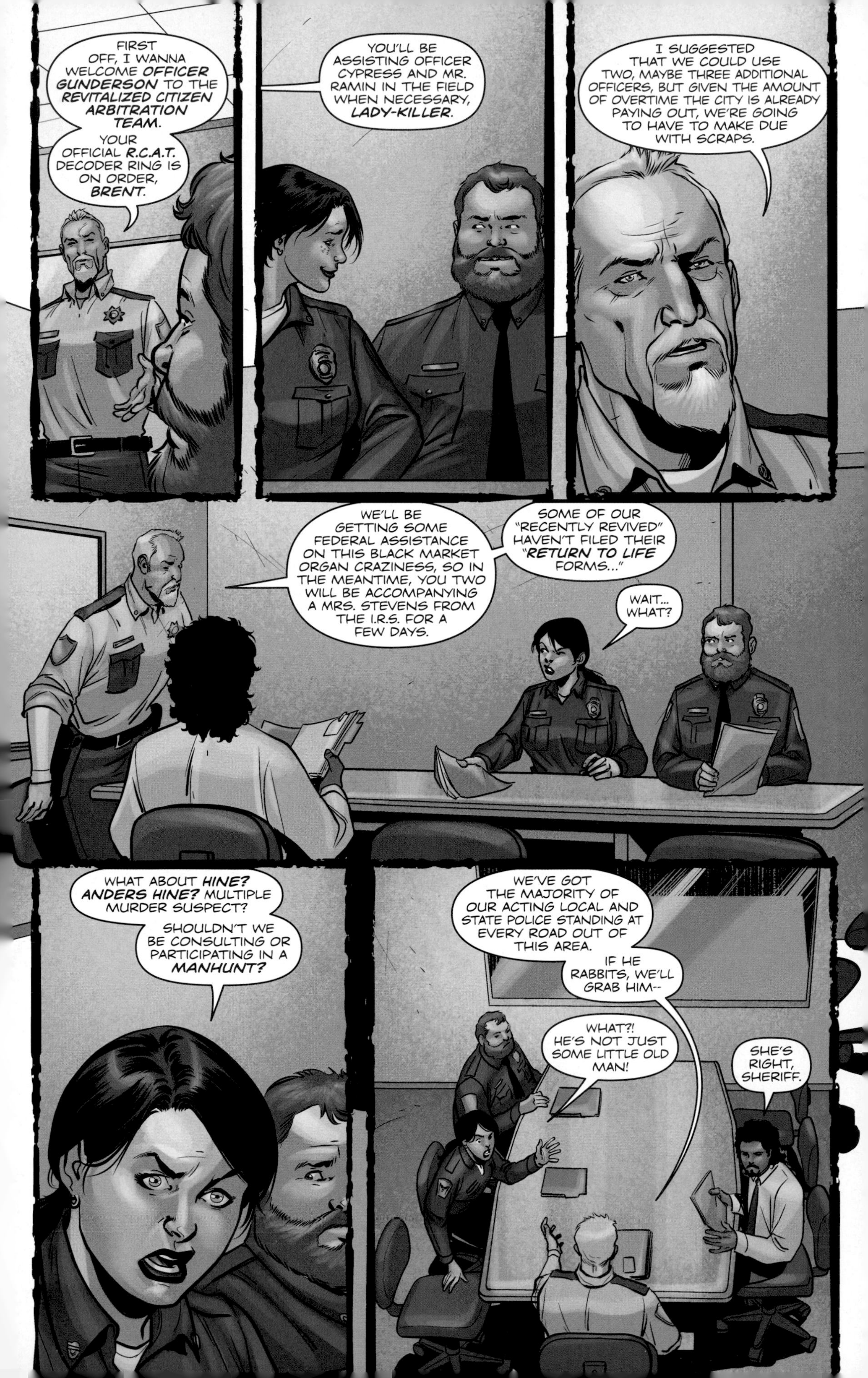
FIRST OFF, I WANNA WELCOME OFFICER GUNDERSON TO THE REVITALIZED CITIZEN ARBITRATION TEAM.
YOUR OFFICIAL R.C.A.T. DECODER RING IS ON ORDER, BRENT.
YOU'LL BE ASSISTING OFFICER CYPRESS AND MR. RAMIN IN THE FIELD WHEN NECESSARY, LADY-KILLER.
I SUGGESTED THAT WE COULD USE TWO, MAYBE THREE ADDITIONAL OFFICERS, BUT GIVEN THE AMOUNT OF OVERTIME THE CITY IS ALREADY PAYING OUT, WE'RE GOING TO HAVE TO MAKE DUE WITH SCRAPS.
WE'LL BE GETTING SOME FEDERAL ASSISTANCE ON THIS BLACK MARKET ORGAN CRAZINESS, SO IN THE MEANTIME, YOU TWO WILL BE ACCOMPANYING A MRS. STEVENS FROM THE I.R.S. FOR A FEW DAYS.
SOME OF OUR "RECENTLY REVIVED" HAVEN'T FILED THEIR "RETURN TO LIFE FORMS..."
WAIT... WHAT?
WHAT ABOUT HINE? ANDERS HINE? MULTIPLE MURDER SUSPECT?
SHOULDN'T WE BE CONSULTING OR PARTICIPATING IN A MANHUNT?
WE'VE GOT THE MAJORITY OF OUR ACTING LOCAL AND STATE POLICE STANDING AT EVERY ROAD OUT OF THIS AREA.
IF HE RABBITS, WE'LL GRAB HIM--
WHAT?! HE'S NOT JUST SOME LITTLE OLD MAN!
SHE'S RIGHT, SHERIFF.

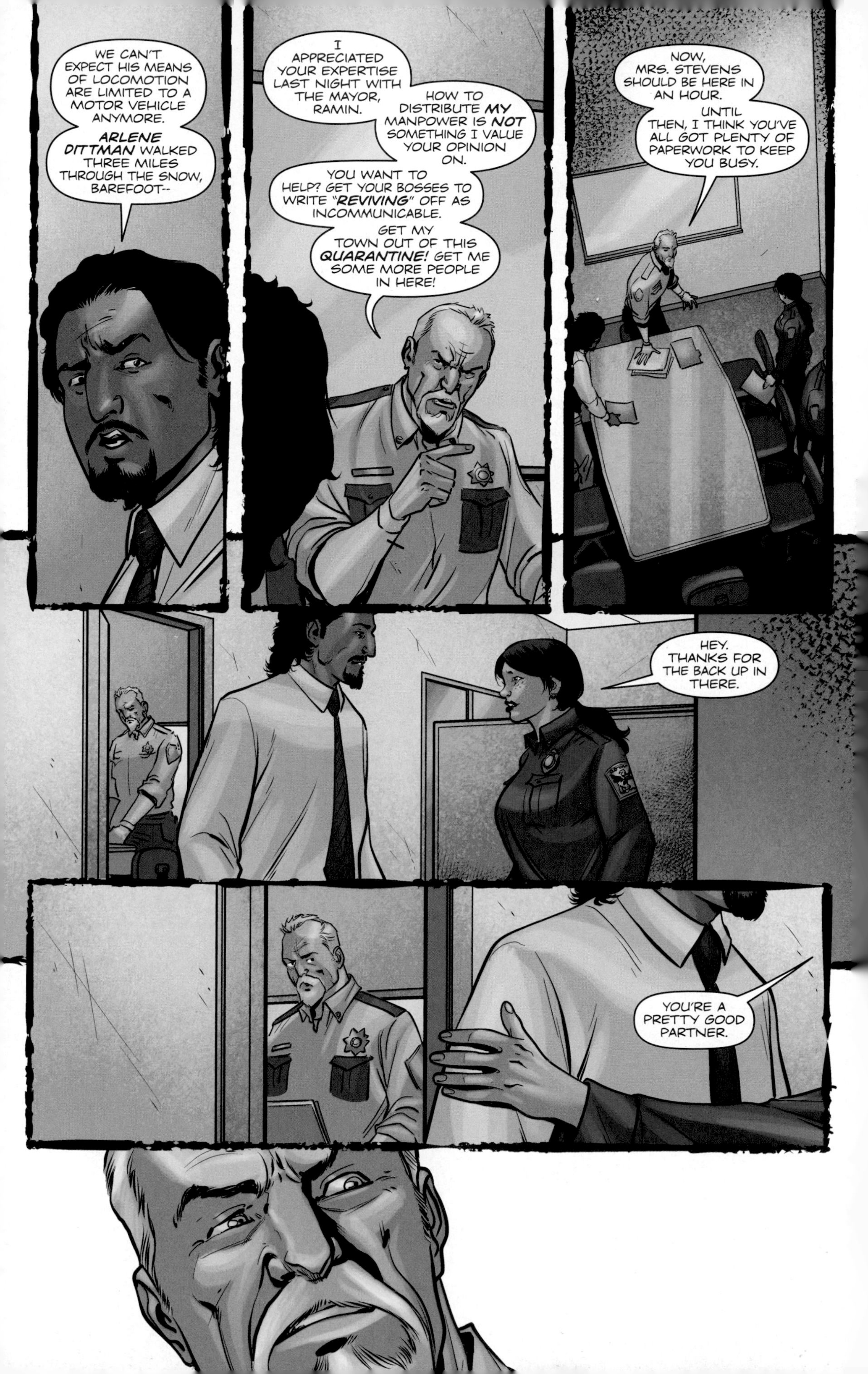
WE CAN'T EXPECT HIS MEANS OF LOCOMOTION ARE LIMITED TO A MOTOR VEHICLE ANYMORE.
ARLENE DITTMAN WALKED THREE MILES THROUGH THE SNOW, BAREFOOT--
I APPRECIATED YOUR EXPERTISE LAST NIGHT WITH THE MAYOR, RAMIN.
HOW TO DISTRIBUTE MY MANPOWER IS NOT SOMETHING I VALUE YOUR OPINION ON.
YOU WANT TO HELP? GET YOUR BOSSES TO WRITE "REVIVING" OFF AS INCOMMUNICABLE.
GET MY TOWN OUT OF THIS QUARANTINE! GET ME SOME MORE PEOPLE IN HERE!
NOW, MRS. STEVENS SHOULD BE HERE IN AN HOUR.
UNTIL THEN, I THINK YOU'VE ALL GOT PLENTY OF PAPERWORK TO KEEP YOU BUSY.
HEY. THANKS FOR THE BACK UP IN THERE.
YOU'RE A PRETTY GOOD PARTNER.

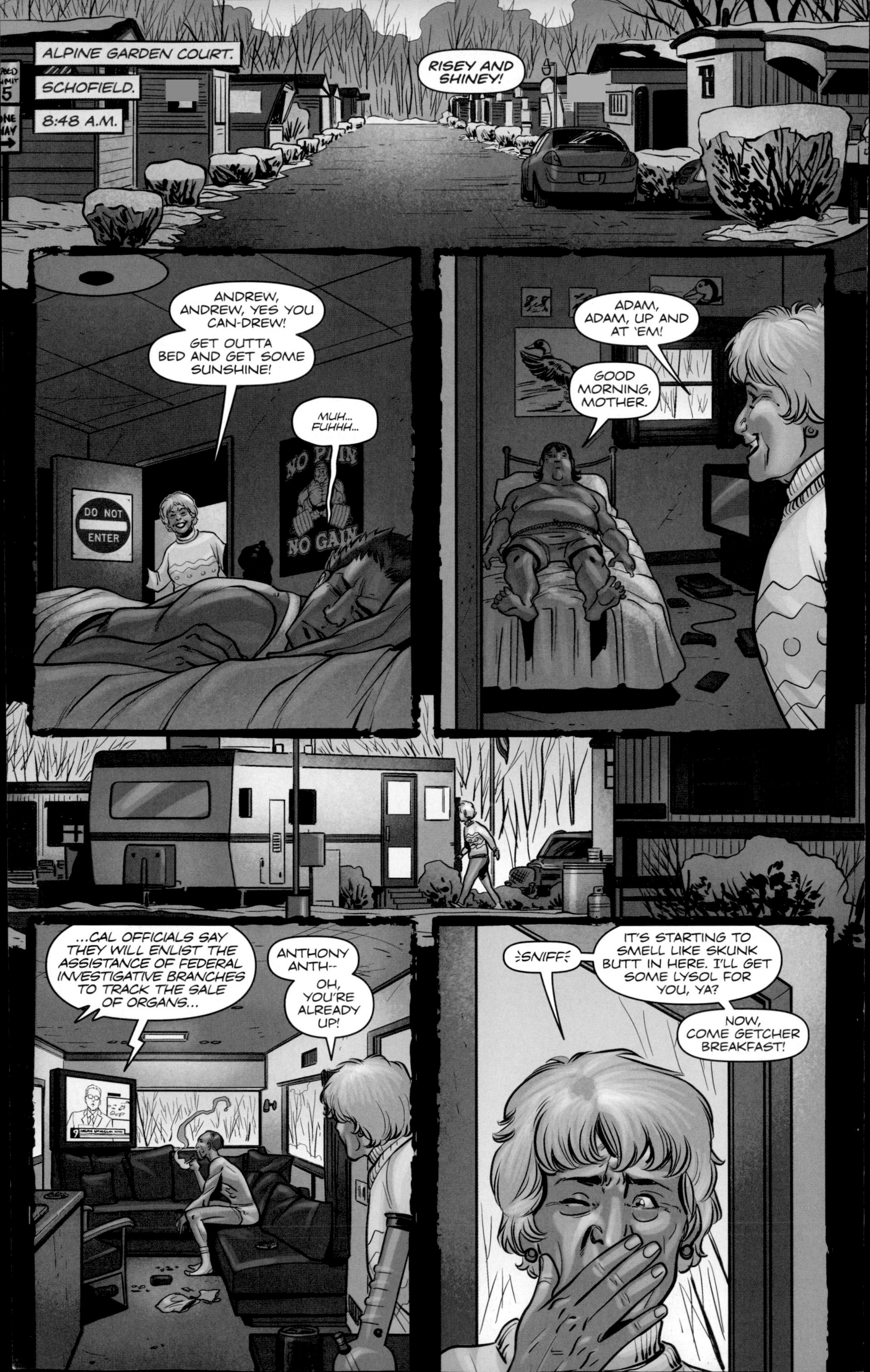

ALPINE GARDEN COURT.
SCHOFIELD.
8:48 A.M.
RISEY AND SHINEY!
ANDREW, ANDREW, YES YOU CAN-DREW!
GET OUTTA BED AND GET SOME SUNSHINE!
MUH... FUHHH...
DO NOT ENTER
NO PAIN NO GAIN
ADAM, ADAM, UP AND AT 'EM!
GOOD MORNING, MOTHER.
...CAL OFFICIALS SAY THEY WILL ENLIST THE ASSISTANCE OF FEDERAL INVESTIGATIVE BRANCHES TO TRACK THE SALE OF ORGANS...
ANTHONY ANTH--
OH, YOU'RE ALREADY UP!
SNIFF
IT'S STARTING TO SMELL LIKE SKUNK BUTT IN HERE. I'LL GET SOME LYSOL FOR YOU, YA?
NOW, COME GETCHER BREAKFAST!

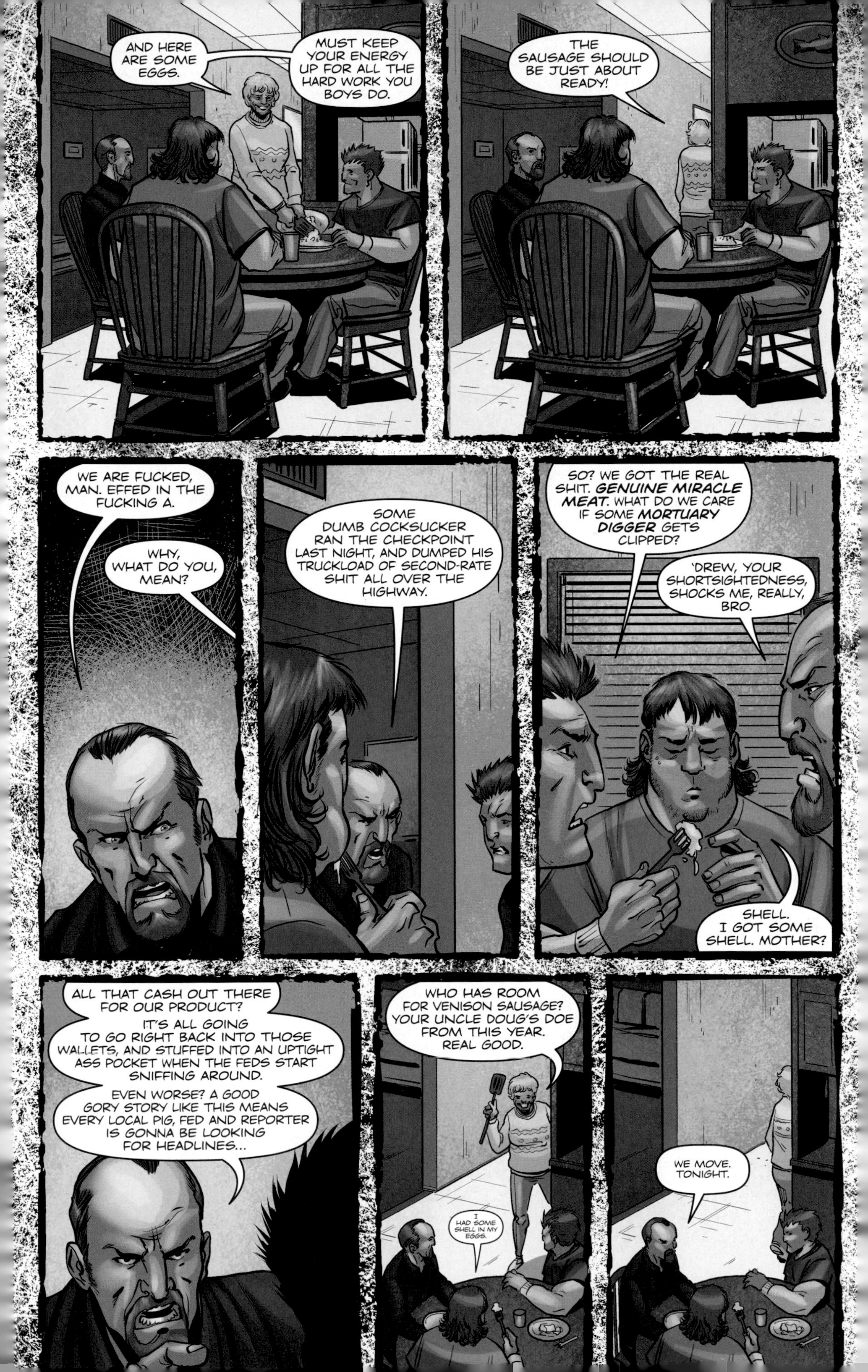
AND HERE ARE SOME EGGS.
MUST KEEP YOUR ENERGY UP FOR ALL THE HARD WORK YOU BOYS DO.
THE SAUSAGE SHOULD BE JUST ABOUT READY!
WE ARE FUCKED, MAN. EFFED IN THE FUCKING A.
WHY, WHAT DO YOU, MEAN?
SOME DUMB COCKSUCKER RAN THE CHECKPOINT LAST NIGHT, AND DUMPED HIS TRUCKLOAD OF SECOND-RATE SHIT ALL OVER THE HIGHWAY.
SO? WE GOT THE REAL SHIT. GENUINE MIRACLE MEAT. WHAT DO WE CARE IF SOME MORTUARY DIGGER GETS CLIPPED?
'DREW, YOUR SHORTSIGHTEDNESS, SHOCKS ME, REALLY, BRO.
SHELL. I GOT SOME SHELL. MOTHER?
ALL THAT CASH OUT THERE FOR OUR PRODUCT?
IT'S ALL GOING TO GO RIGHT BACK INTO THOSE WALLETS, AND STUFFED INTO AN UPTIGHT ASS POCKET WHEN THE FEDS START SNIFFING AROUND.
EVEN WORSE? A GOOD GORY STORY LIKE THIS MEANS EVERY LOCAL PIG, FED AND REPORTER IS GONNA BE LOOKING FOR HEADLINES...
WHO HAS ROOM FOR VENISON SAUSAGE? YOUR UNCLE DOUG'S DOE FROM THIS YEAR. REAL GOOD.
I HAD SOME SHELL IN MY EGGS.
WE MOVE. TONIGHT.

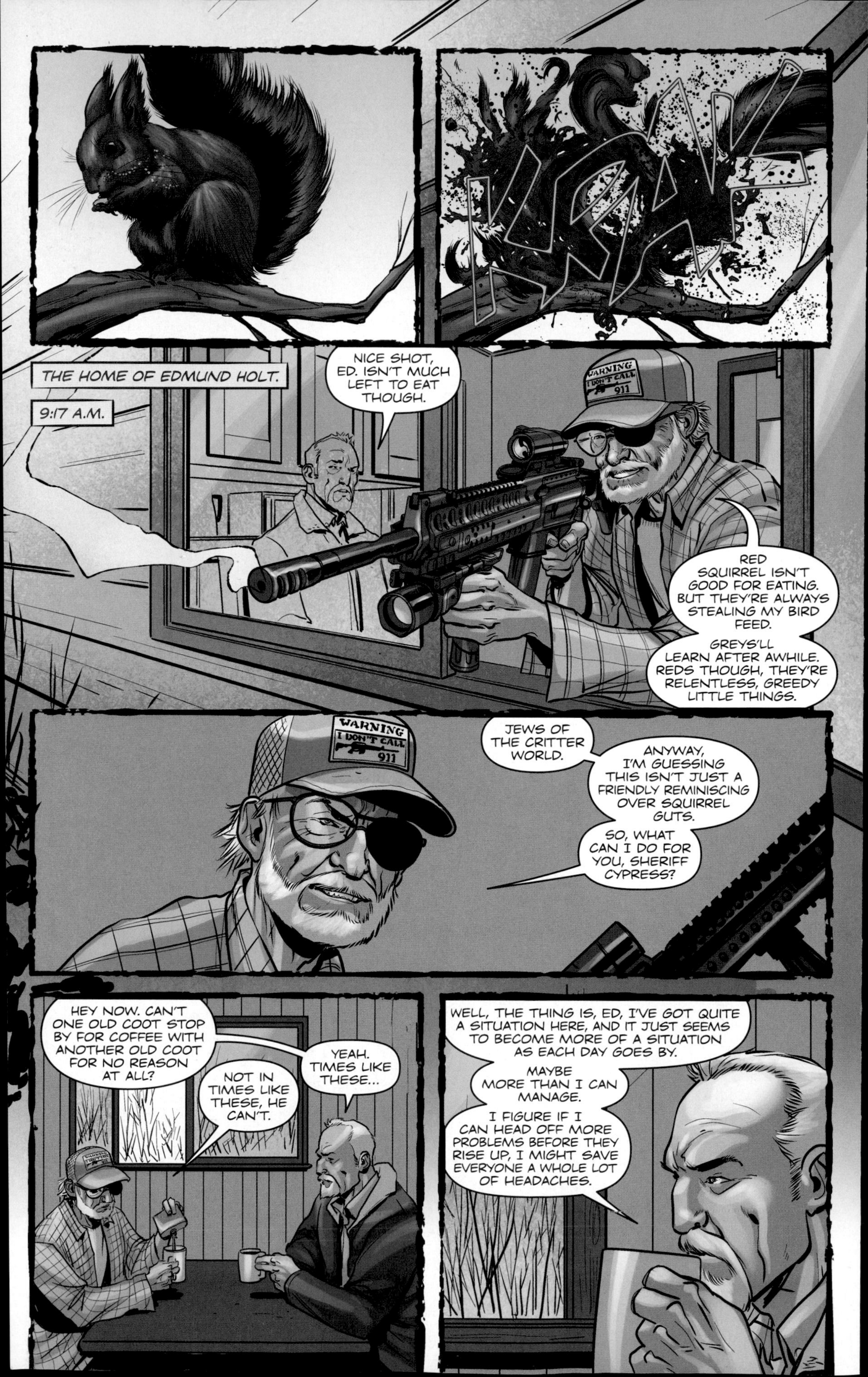
THE HOME OF EDMUND HOLT.
9:17 A.M.
NICE SHOT, ED. ISN'T MUCH LEFT TO EAT THOUGH.
WARNING I DON'T CALL 911
RED SQUIRREL ISN'T GOOD FOR EATING. BUT THEY'RE ALWAYS STEALING MY BIRD FEED.
GREYS'LL LEARN AFTER AWHILE. REDS THOUGH, THEY'RE RELENTLESS, GREEDY LITTLE THINGS.
JEWS OF THE CRITTER WORLD.
ANYWAY, I'M GUESSING THIS ISN'T JUST A FRIENDLY REMINISCING OVER SQUIRREL GUTS.
SO, WHAT CAN I DO FOR YOU, SHERIFF CYPRESS?
HEY NOW. CAN'T ONE OLD COOT STOP BY FOR COFFEE WITH ANOTHER OLD COOT FOR NO REASON AT ALL?
NOT IN TIMES LIKE THESE, HE CAN'T.
YEAH. TIMES LIKE THESE...
WELL, THE THING IS, ED, I'VE GOT QUITE A SITUATION HERE, AND IT JUST SEEMS TO BECOME MORE OF A SITUATION AS EACH DAY GOES BY.
MAYBE MORE THAN I CAN MANAGE.
I FIGURE IF I CAN HEAD OFF MORE PROBLEMS BEFORE THEY RISE UP, I MIGHT SAVE EVERYONE A WHOLE LOT OF HEADACHES.

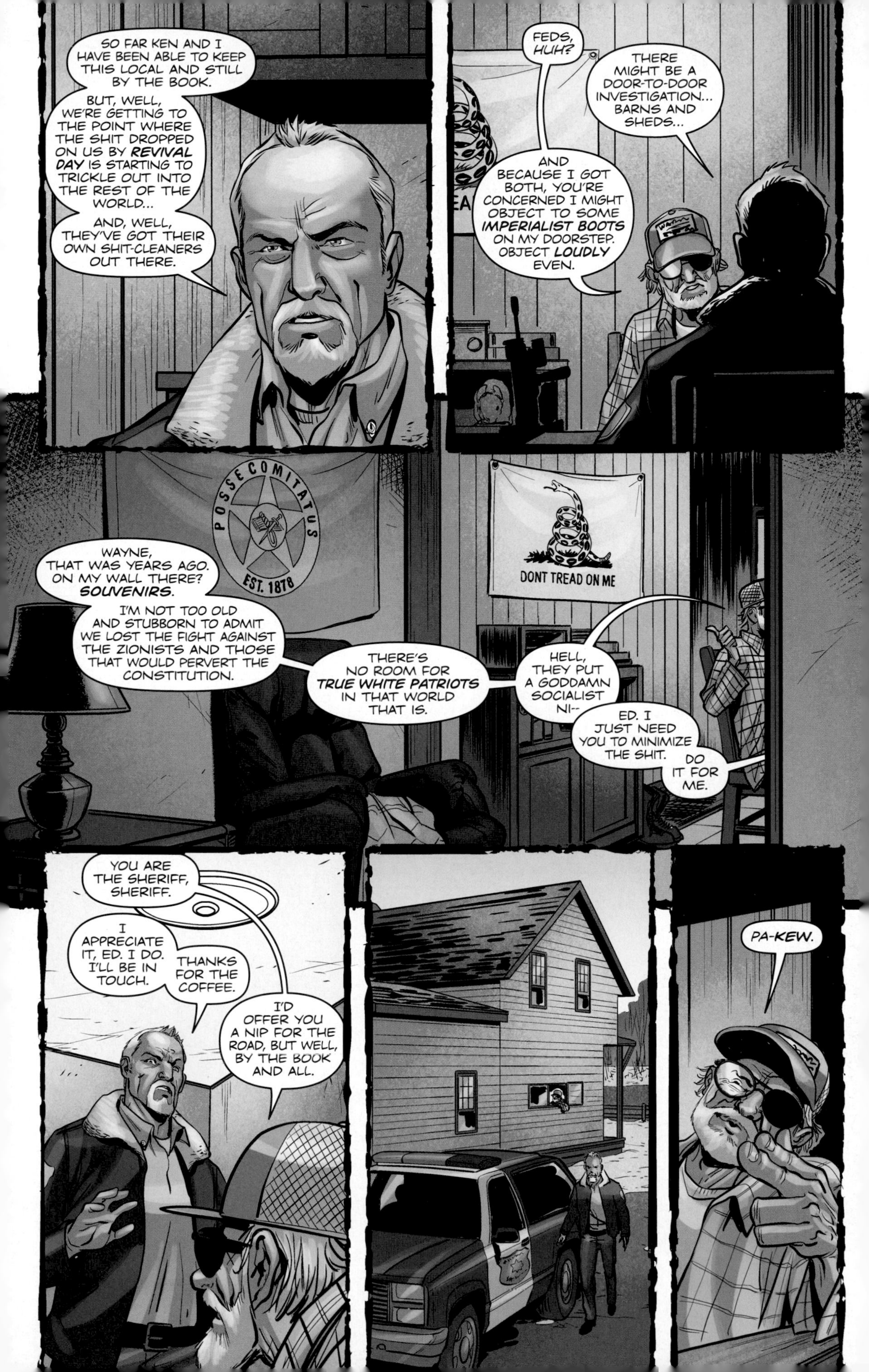

SO FAR KEN AND I HAVE BEEN ABLE TO KEEP THIS LOCAL AND STILL BY THE BOOK.
BUT, WELL, WE'RE GETTING TO THE POINT WHERE THE SHIT DROPPED ON US BY **REVIVAL DAY** IS STARTING TO TRICKLE OUT INTO THE REST OF THE WORLD...
AND, WELL, THEY'VE GOT THEIR OWN SHIT-CLEANERS OUT THERE.
FEDS, *HUH?*
THERE MIGHT BE A DOOR-TO-DOOR INVESTIGATION... BARNS AND SHEDS...
AND BECAUSE I GOT BOTH, YOU'RE CONCERNED I MIGHT OBJECT TO SOME **IMPERIALIST BOOTS** ON MY DOORSTEP. OBJECT **LOUDLY** EVEN.
POSSE COMITATUS
EST. 1878
DONT TREAD ON ME
WAYNE, THAT WAS YEARS AGO. ON MY WALL THERE? **SOUVENIRS**.
I'M NOT TOO OLD AND STUBBORN TO ADMIT WE LOST THE FIGHT AGAINST THE ZIONISTS AND THOSE THAT WOULD PERVERT THE CONSTITUTION.
THERE'S NO ROOM FOR **TRUE WHITE PATRIOTS** IN THAT WORLD THAT IS.
HELL, THEY PUT A GODDAMN SOCIALIST NI--
ED. I JUST NEED YOU TO MINIMIZE THE SHIT.
DO IT FOR ME.
YOU ARE THE SHERIFF, SHERIFF.
I APPRECIATE IT, ED. I DO. I'LL BE IN TOUCH.
THANKS FOR THE COFFEE.
I'D OFFER YOU A NIP FOR THE ROAD, BUT WELL, BY THE BOOK AND ALL.
PA-KEW.

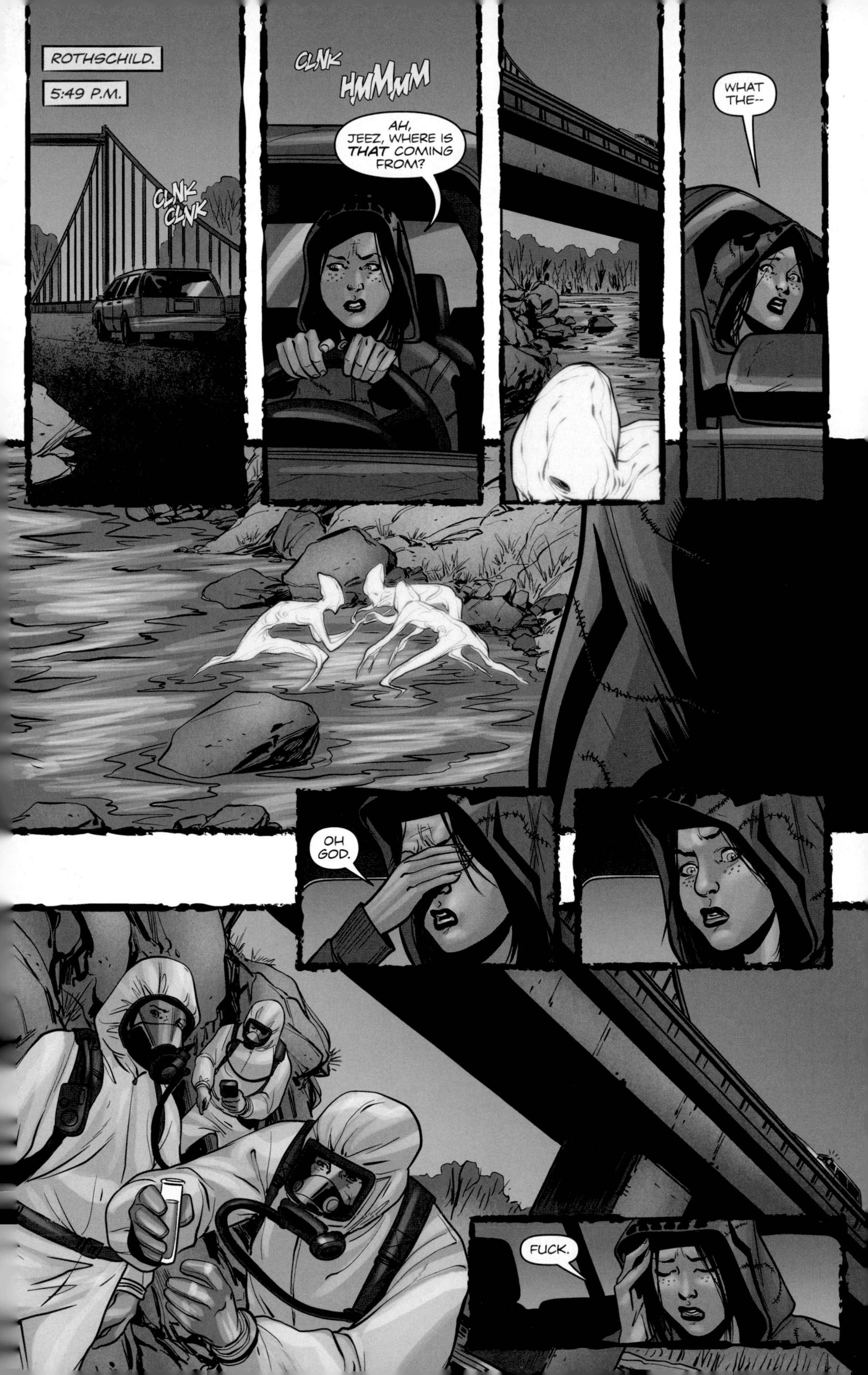
ROTHSCHILD.
5:49 P.M.
CLNK CLNK
CLNK
HMMMM
AH, JEEZ, WHERE IS THAT COMING FROM?
WHAT THE--
OH GOD.
FUCK.

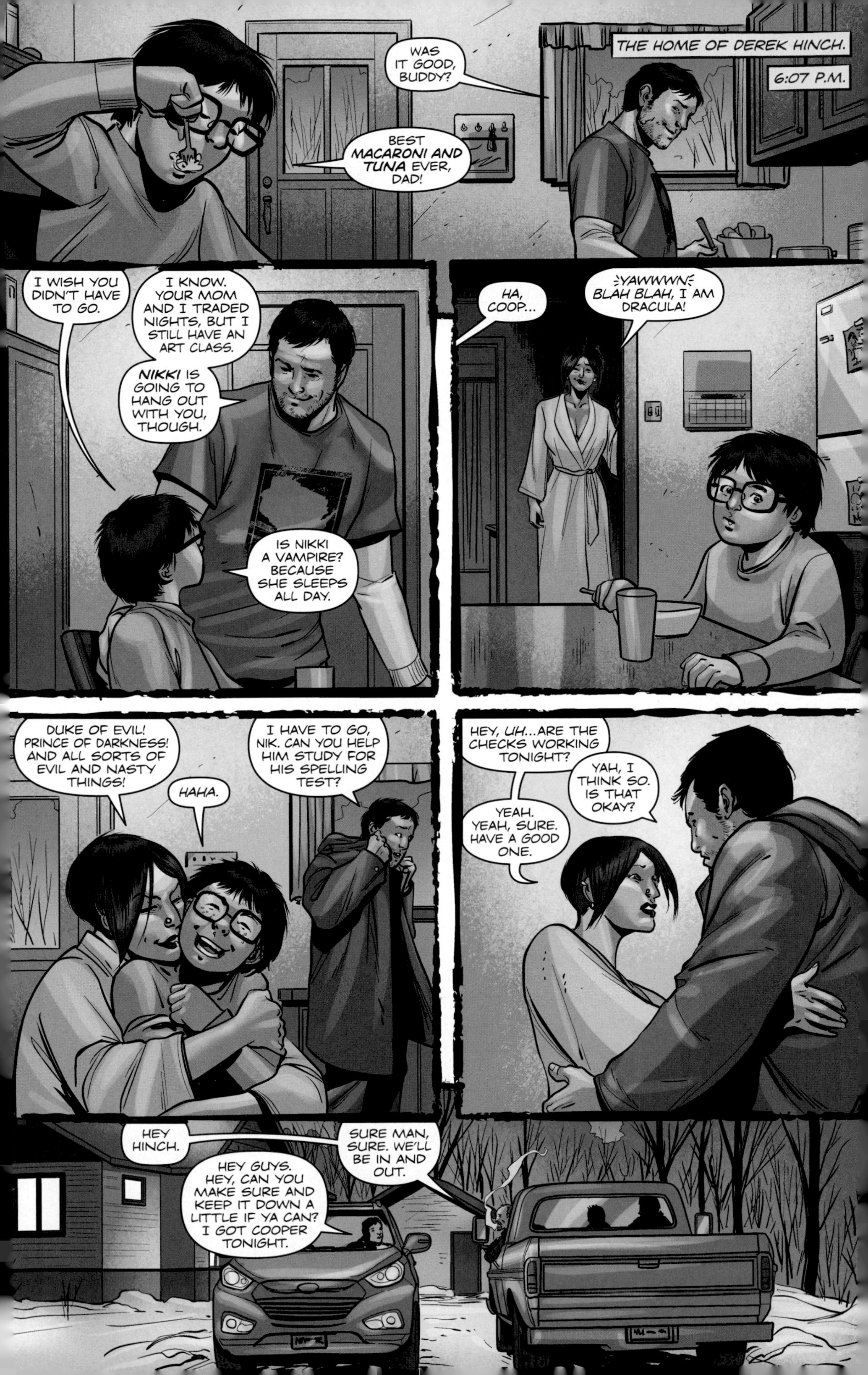
THE HOME OF DEREK HINCH.
6:07 P.M.
WAS IT GOOD, BUDDY?
BEST MACARONI AND TUNA EVER, DAD!
I WISH YOU DIDN'T HAVE TO GO.
I KNOW. YOUR MOM AND I TRADED NIGHTS, BUT I STILL HAVE AN ART CLASS.
NIKKI IS GOING TO HANG OUT WITH YOU, THOUGH.
IS NIKKI A VAMPIRE? BECAUSE SHE SLEEPS ALL DAY.
HA, COOP...
YAWWWN BLAH BLAH, I AM DRACULA!
DUKE OF EVIL! PRINCE OF DARKNESS! AND ALL SORTS OF EVIL AND NASTY THINGS!
HAHA.
I HAVE TO GO, NIK. CAN YOU HELP HIM STUDY FOR HIS SPELLING TEST?
HEY, UH...ARE THE CHECKS WORKING TONIGHT?
YAH, I THINK SO. IS THAT OKAY?
YEAH. YEAH, SURE. HAVE A GOOD ONE.
HEY HINCH.
SURE MAN, SURE. WE'LL BE IN AND OUT.
HEY GUYS. HEY, CAN YOU MAKE SURE AND KEEP IT DOWN A LITTLE IF YA CAN? I GOT COOPER TONIGHT.

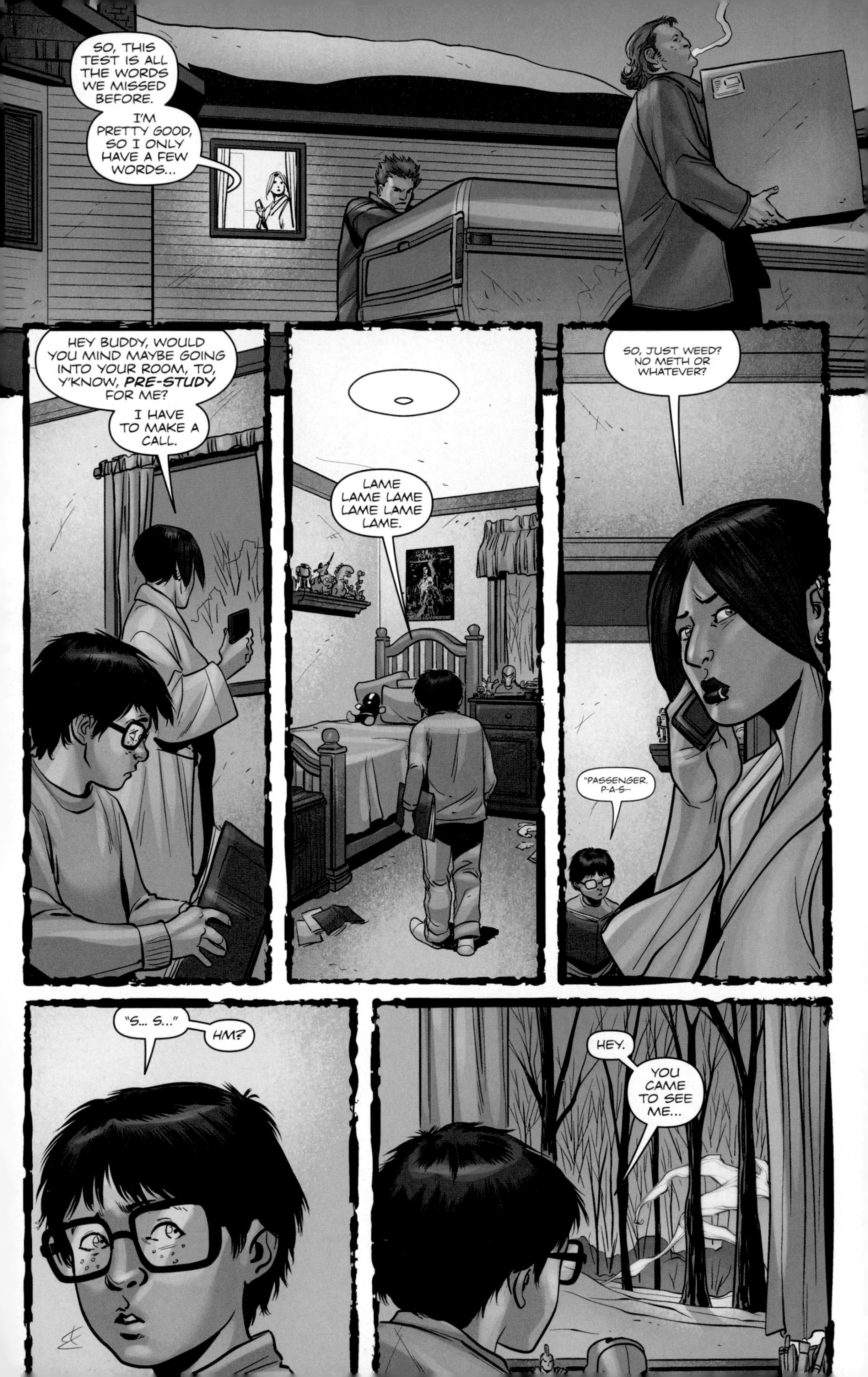

SO, THIS TEST IS ALL THE WORDS WE MISSED BEFORE.
I'M PRETTY GOOD, SO I ONLY HAVE A FEW WORDS...
HEY BUDDY, WOULD YOU MIND MAYBE GOING INTO YOUR ROOM, TO, Y'KNOW, PRE-STUDY FOR ME?
I HAVE TO MAKE A CALL.
LAME LAME LAME LAME LAME LAME.
SO, JUST WEED? NO METH OR WHATEVER?
"PASSENGER. P-A-S--
"S... S..."
HM?
HEY.
YOU CAME TO SEE ME...

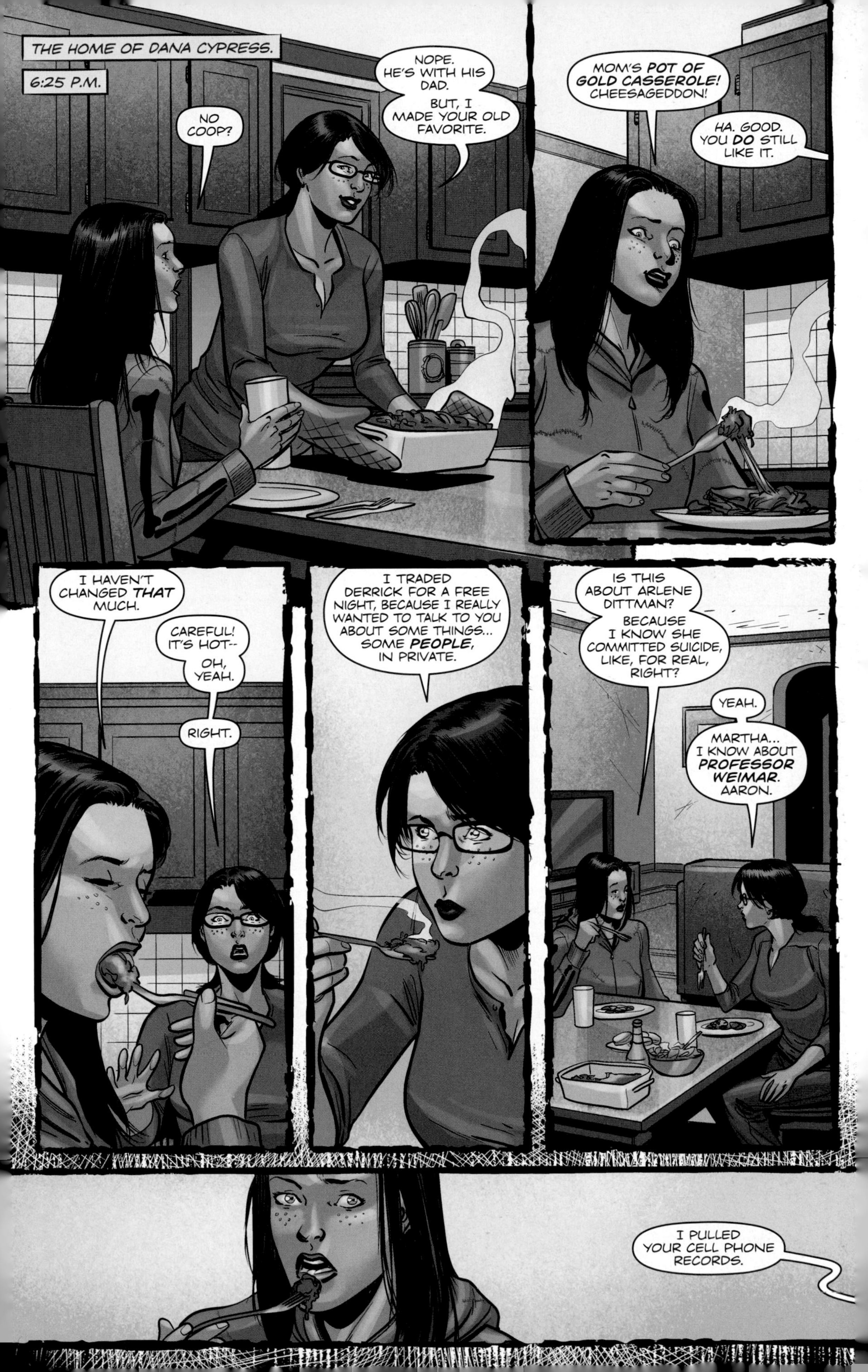
THE HOME OF DANA CYPRESS.
6:25 P.M.
NO COOP?
NOPE. HE'S WITH HIS DAD.
BUT, I MADE YOUR OLD FAVORITE.
MOM'S **POT OF GOLD CASSEROLE!** CHEESAGEDDON!
HA. GOOD. YOU **DO** STILL LIKE IT.
I HAVEN'T CHANGED **THAT** MUCH.
CAREFUL! IT'S HOT--
OH, YEAH.
RIGHT.
I TRADED DERRICK FOR A FREE NIGHT, BECAUSE I REALLY WANTED TO TALK TO YOU ABOUT SOME THINGS... SOME **PEOPLE**, IN PRIVATE.
IS THIS ABOUT ARLENE DITTMAN?
BECAUSE I KNOW SHE COMMITTED SUICIDE, LIKE, FOR REAL, RIGHT?
YEAH.
MARTHA... I KNOW ABOUT **PROFESSOR WEIMAR.** AARON.
I PULLED YOUR CELL PHONE RECORDS.

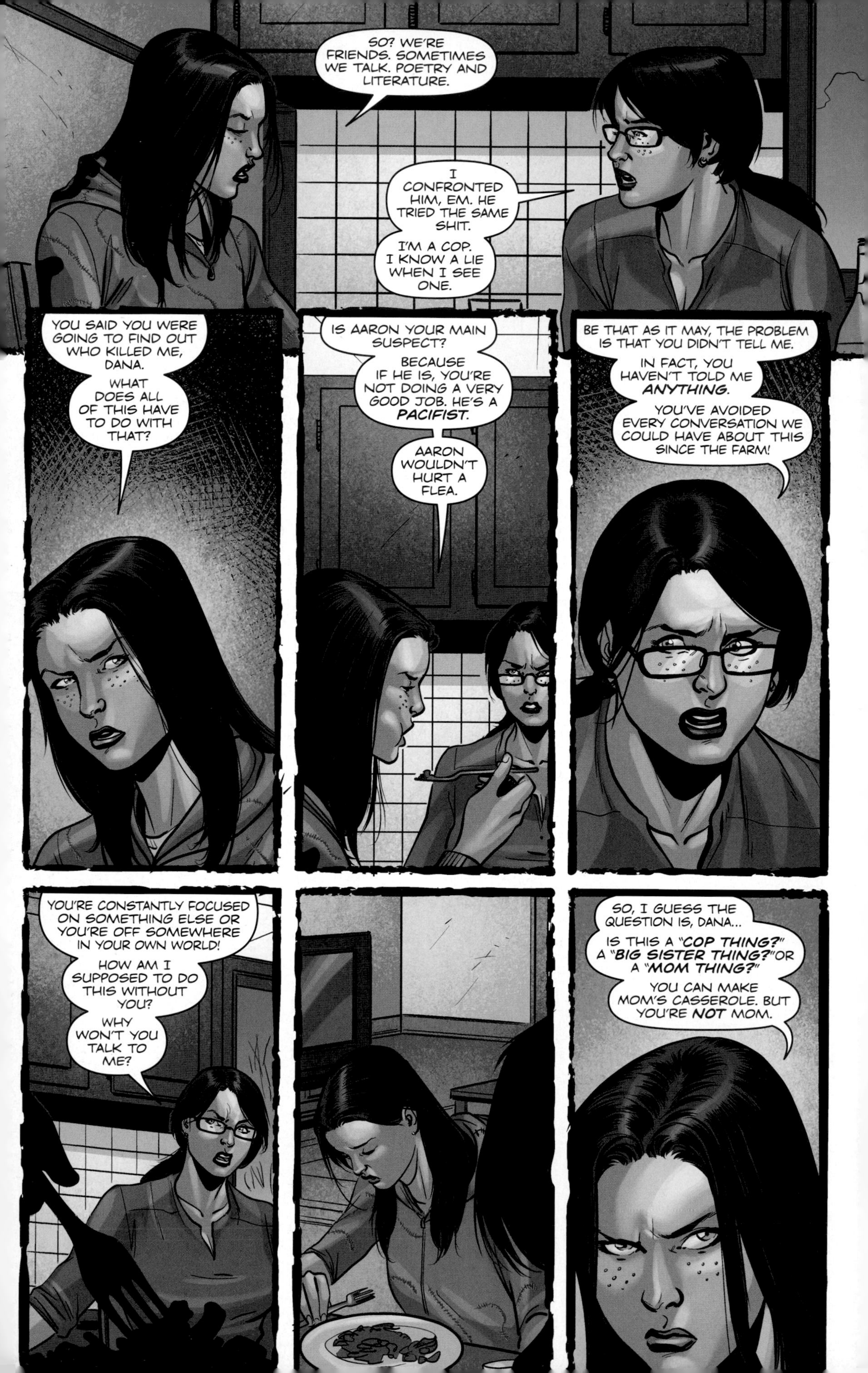
SO? WE'RE FRIENDS. SOMETIMES WE TALK. POETRY AND LITERATURE.
I CONFRONTED HIM, EM. HE TRIED THE SAME SHIT.
I'M A COP. I KNOW A LIE WHEN I SEE ONE.
YOU SAID YOU WERE GOING TO FIND OUT WHO KILLED ME, DANA.
WHAT DOES ALL OF THIS HAVE TO DO WITH THAT?
IS AARON YOUR MAIN SUSPECT?
BECAUSE IF HE IS, YOU'RE NOT DOING A VERY GOOD JOB. HE'S A ***PACIFIST***.
AARON WOULDN'T HURT A FLEA.
BE THAT AS IT MAY, THE PROBLEM IS THAT YOU DIDN'T TELL ME.
IN FACT, YOU HAVEN'T TOLD ME ***ANYTHING***.
YOU'VE AVOIDED EVERY CONVERSATION WE COULD HAVE ABOUT THIS SINCE THE FARM!
YOU'RE CONSTANTLY FOCUSED ON SOMETHING ELSE OR YOU'RE OFF SOMEWHERE IN YOUR OWN WORLD!
HOW AM I SUPPOSED TO DO THIS WITHOUT YOU?
WHY WON'T YOU TALK TO ME?
SO, I GUESS THE QUESTION IS, DANA...
IS THIS A "***COP THING?***" A "***BIG SISTER THING?***" OR A "***MOM THING?***"
YOU CAN MAKE MOM'S CASSEROLE. BUT YOU'RE ***NOT*** MOM.

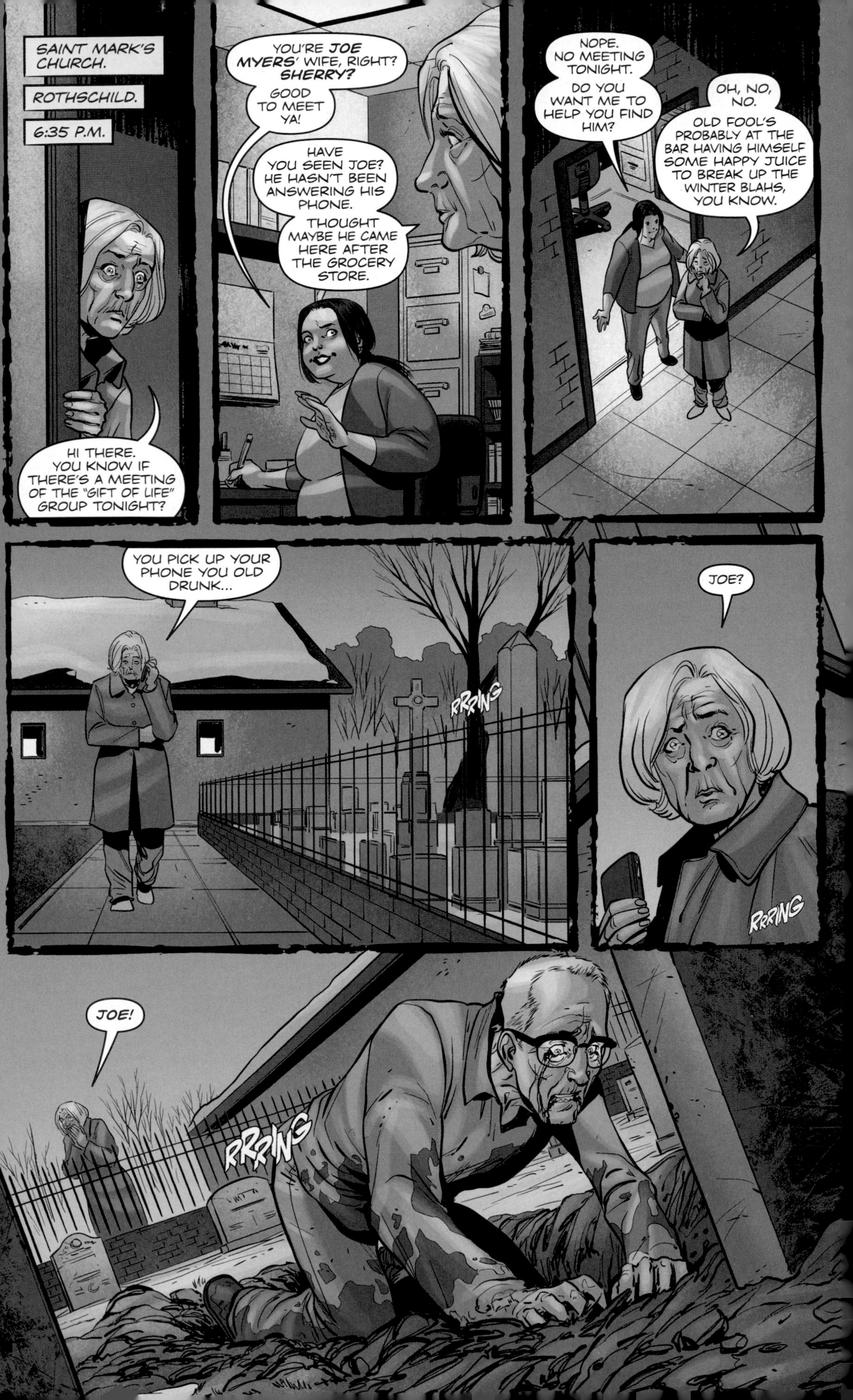
SAINT MARK'S CHURCH.
ROTHSCHILD.
6:35 P.M.
HI THERE. YOU KNOW IF THERE'S A MEETING OF THE "GIFT OF LIFE" GROUP TONIGHT?
YOU'RE JOE MYERS' WIFE, RIGHT? SHERRY?
GOOD TO MEET YA!
HAVE YOU SEEN JOE? HE HASN'T BEEN ANSWERING HIS PHONE.
THOUGHT MAYBE HE CAME HERE AFTER THE GROCERY STORE.
NOPE. NO MEETING TONIGHT.
DO YOU WANT ME TO HELP YOU FIND HIM?
OH, NO, NO.
OLD FOOL'S PROBABLY AT THE BAR HAVING HIMSELF SOME HAPPY JUICE TO BREAK UP THE WINTER BLAHS, YOU KNOW.
YOU PICK UP YOUR PHONE YOU OLD DRUNK...
RRRING
JOE?
RRRING
JOE!
RRRING

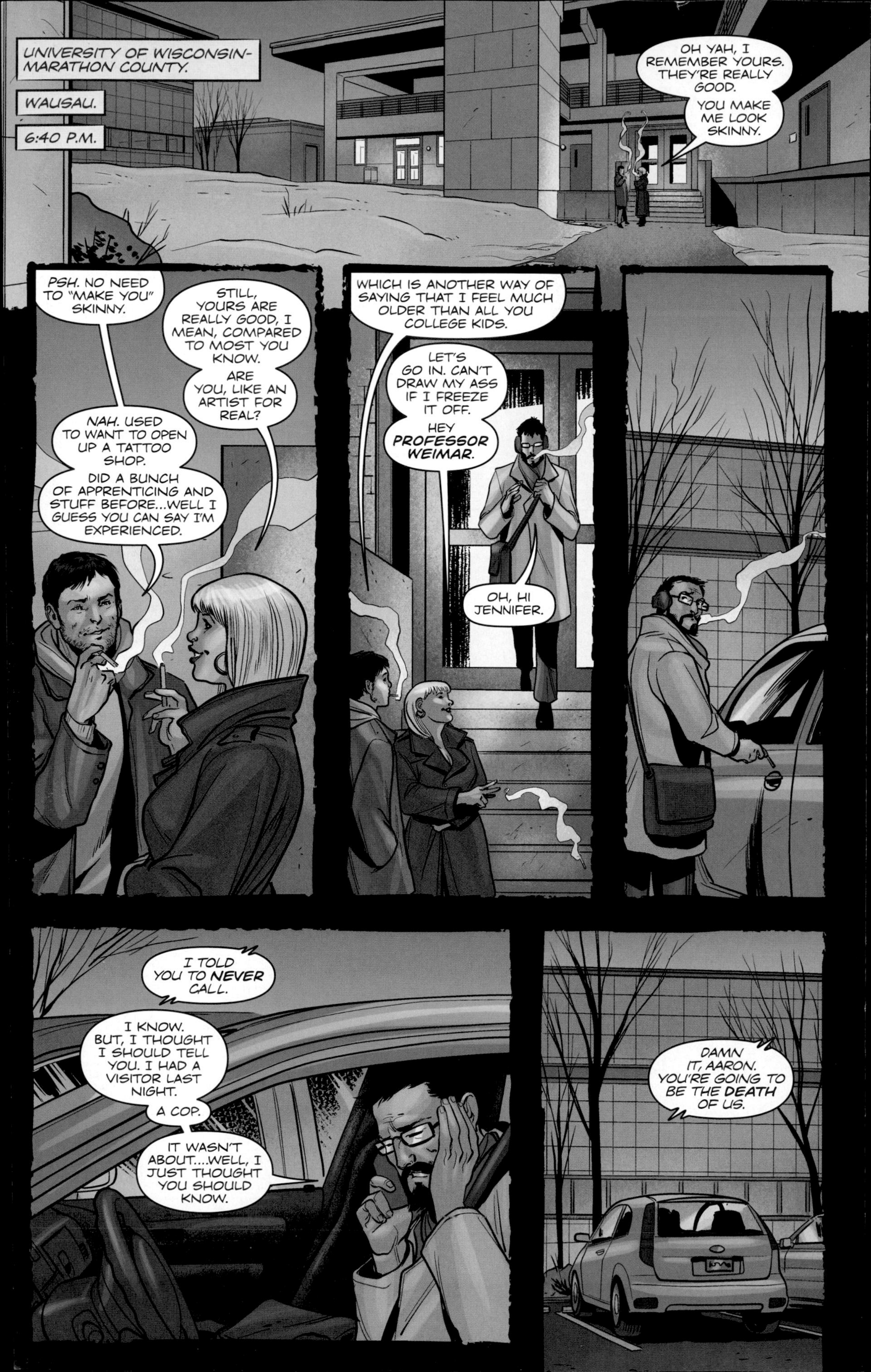
UNIVERSITY OF WISCONSIN-MARATHON COUNTY.
WAUSAU.
6:40 P.M.
OH YAH, I REMEMBER YOURS. THEY'RE REALLY GOOD.
YOU MAKE ME LOOK SKINNY.
PSH. NO NEED TO "MAKE YOU" SKINNY.
STILL, YOURS ARE REALLY GOOD, I MEAN, COMPARED TO MOST YOU KNOW.
ARE YOU, LIKE AN ARTIST FOR REAL?
NAH. USED TO WANT TO OPEN UP A TATTOO SHOP.
DID A BUNCH OF APPRENTICING AND STUFF BEFORE...WELL I GUESS YOU CAN SAY I'M EXPERIENCED.
WHICH IS ANOTHER WAY OF SAYING THAT I FEEL MUCH OLDER THAN ALL YOU COLLEGE KIDS.
LET'S GO IN. CAN'T DRAW MY ASS IF I FREEZE IT OFF.
HEY PROFESSOR WEIMAR.
OH, HI JENNIFER.
I TOLD YOU TO NEVER CALL.
I KNOW. BUT, I THOUGHT I SHOULD TELL YOU. I HAD A VISITOR LAST NIGHT.
A COP.
IT WASN'T ABOUT....WELL, I JUST THOUGHT YOU SHOULD KNOW.
DAMN IT, AARON. YOU'RE GOING TO BE THE DEATH OF US.

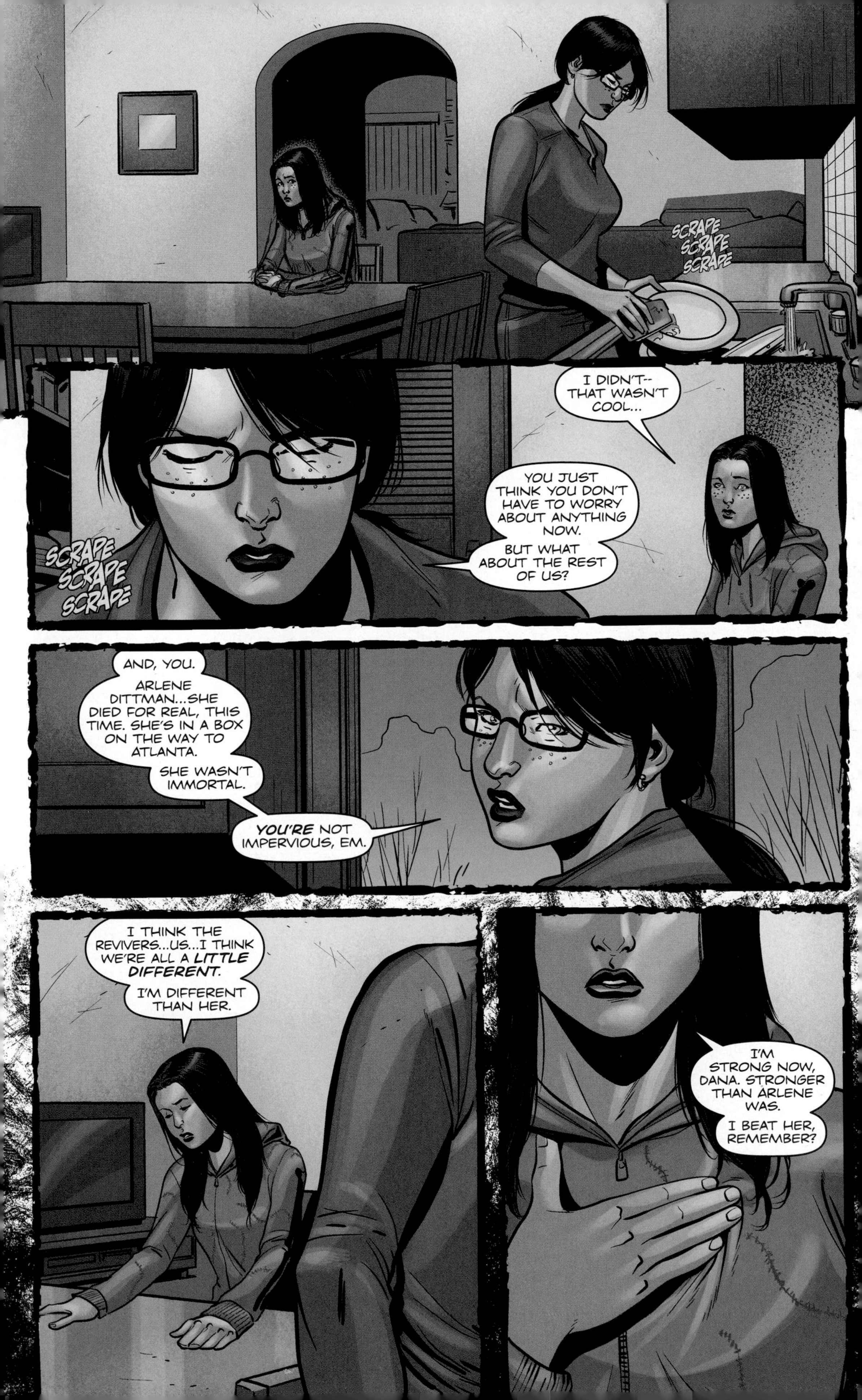
SCRAPE SCRAPE SCRAPE
SCRAPE SCRAPE SCRAPE
I DIDN'T-- THAT WASN'T COOL...
YOU JUST THINK YOU DON'T HAVE TO WORRY ABOUT ANYTHING NOW.
BUT WHAT ABOUT THE REST OF US?
AND, YOU.
ARLENE DITTMAN...SHE DIED FOR REAL, THIS TIME. SHE'S IN A BOX ON THE WAY TO ATLANTA.
SHE WASN'T IMMORTAL.
YOU'RE NOT IMPERVIOUS, EM.
I THINK THE REVIVERS...US...I THINK WE'RE ALL A LITTLE DIFFERENT.
I'M DIFFERENT THAN HER.
I'M STRONG NOW, DANA. STRONGER THAN ARLENE WAS.
I BEAT HER, REMEMBER?

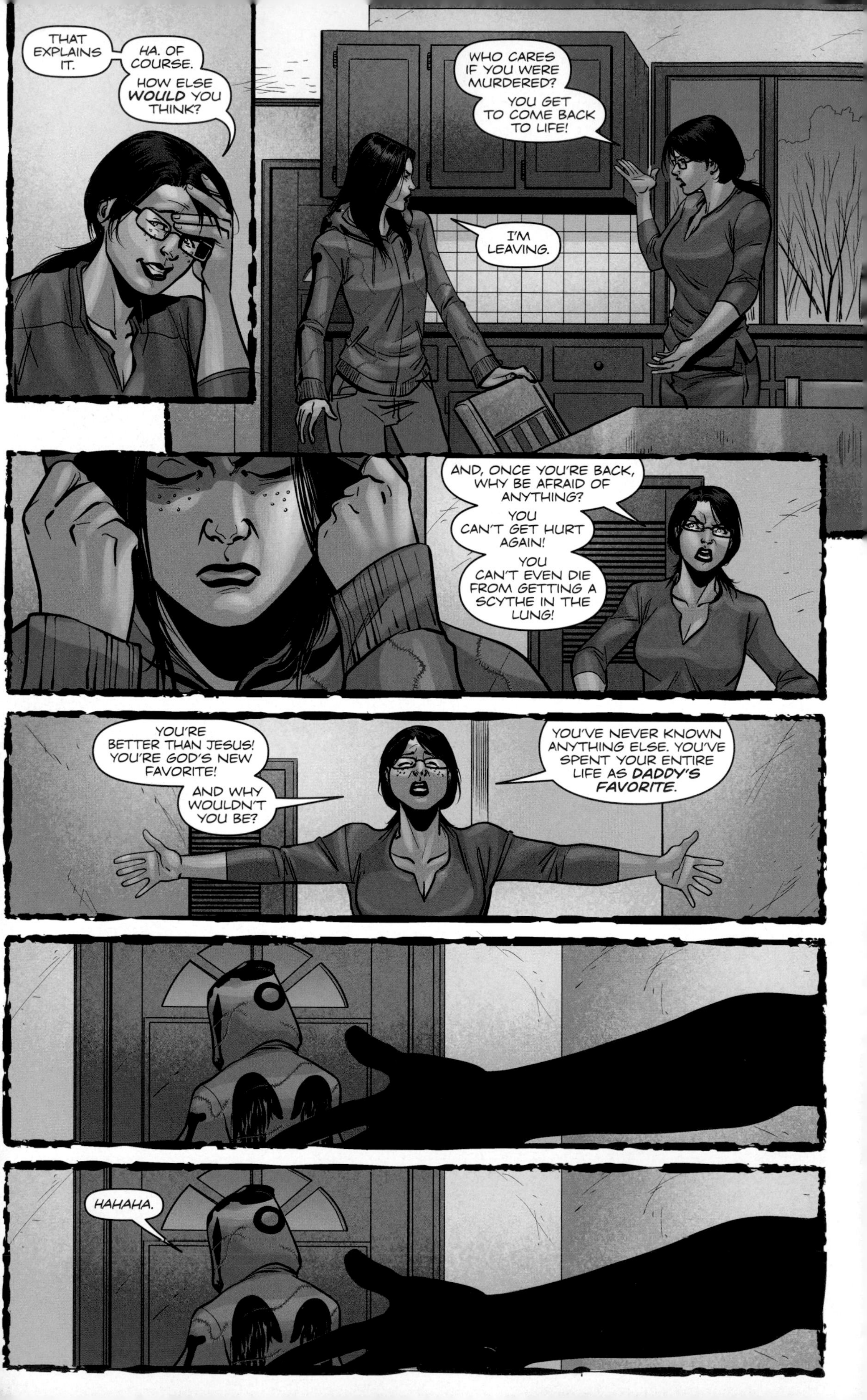
THAT EXPLAINS IT.
HA. OF COURSE.
HOW ELSE WOULD YOU THINK?
WHO CARES IF YOU WERE MURDERED?
YOU GET TO COME BACK TO LIFE!
I'M LEAVING.
AND, ONCE YOU'RE BACK, WHY BE AFRAID OF ANYTHING?
YOU CAN'T GET HURT AGAIN!
YOU CAN'T EVEN DIE FROM GETTING A SCYTHE IN THE LUNG!
YOU'RE BETTER THAN JESUS! YOU'RE GOD'S NEW FAVORITE!
AND WHY WOULDN'T YOU BE?
YOU'VE NEVER KNOWN ANYTHING ELSE. YOU'VE SPENT YOUR ENTIRE LIFE AS DADDY'S FAVORITE.
HAHAHA.

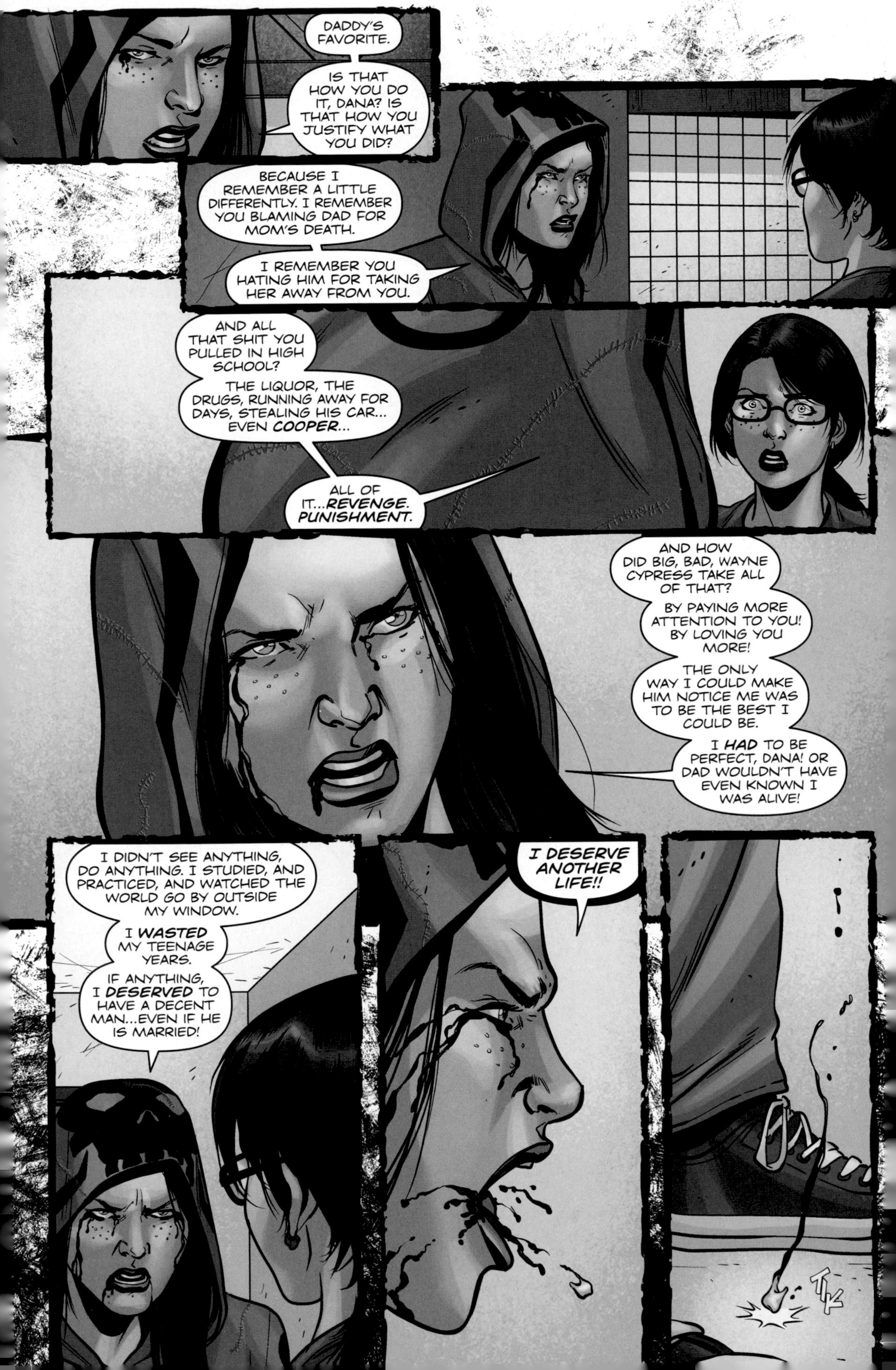
DADDY'S FAVORITE.
IS THAT HOW YOU DO IT, DANA? IS THAT HOW YOU JUSTIFY WHAT YOU DID?
BECAUSE I REMEMBER A LITTLE DIFFERENTLY. I REMEMBER YOU BLAMING DAD FOR MOM'S DEATH.
I REMEMBER YOU HATING HIM FOR TAKING HER AWAY FROM YOU.
AND ALL THAT SHIT YOU PULLED IN HIGH SCHOOL?
THE LIQUOR, THE DRUGS, RUNNING AWAY FOR DAYS, STEALING HIS CAR... EVEN COOPER...
ALL OF IT...REVENGE. PUNISHMENT.
AND HOW DID BIG, BAD, WAYNE CYPRESS TAKE ALL OF THAT?
BY PAYING MORE ATTENTION TO YOU! BY LOVING YOU MORE!
THE ONLY WAY I COULD MAKE HIM NOTICE ME WAS TO BE THE BEST I COULD BE.
I HAD TO BE PERFECT, DANA! OR DAD WOULDN'T HAVE EVEN KNOWN I WAS ALIVE!
I DIDN'T SEE ANYTHING, DO ANYTHING. I STUDIED, AND PRACTICED, AND WATCHED THE WORLD GO BY OUTSIDE MY WINDOW.
I WASTED MY TEENAGE YEARS.
IF ANYTHING, I DESERVED TO HAVE A DECENT MAN...EVEN IF HE IS MARRIED!
I DESERVE ANOTHER LIFE!!
TIK

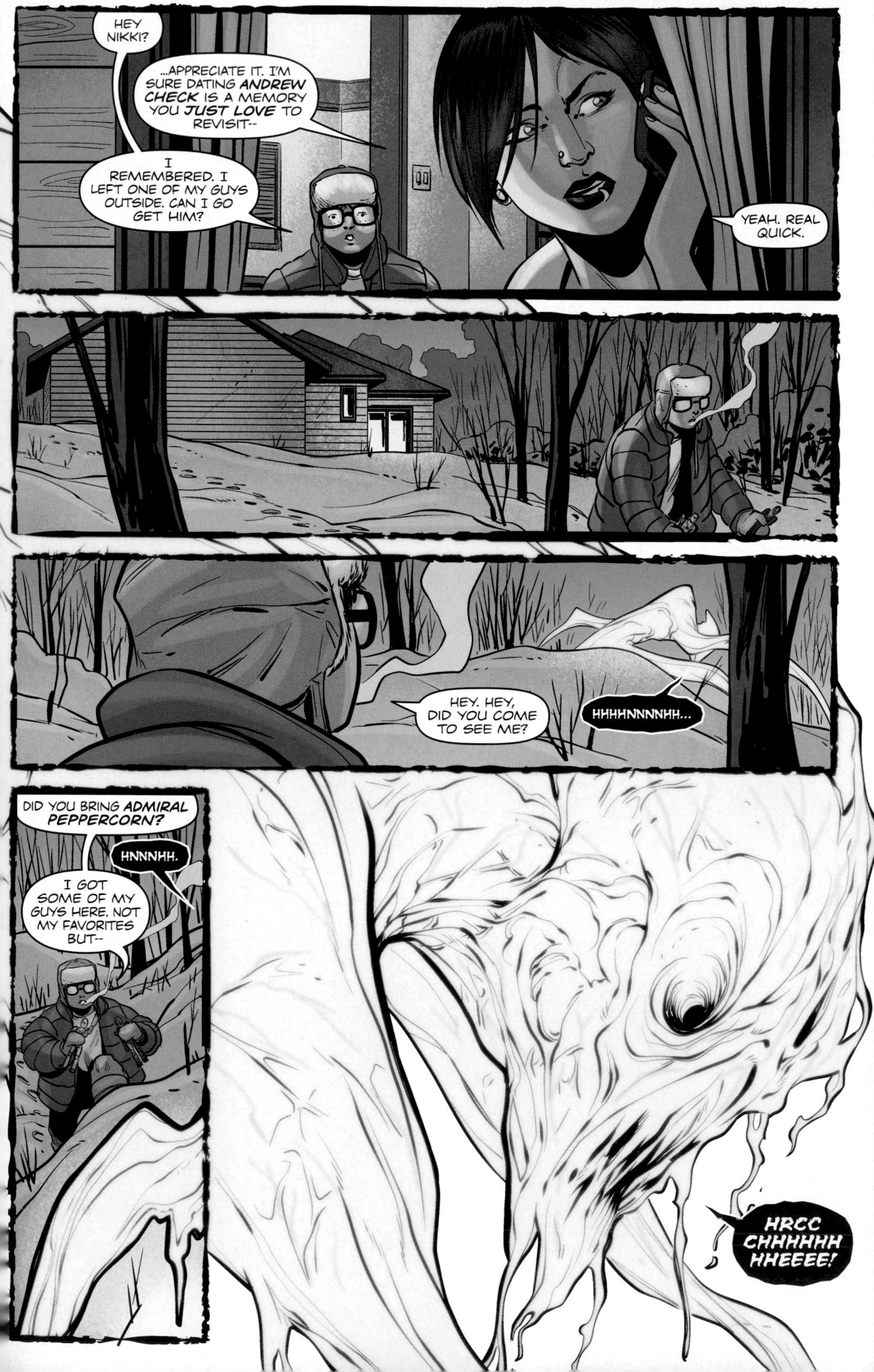
HEY NIKKI?
...APPRECIATE IT. I'M SURE DATING ANDREW CHECK IS A MEMORY YOU JUST LOVE TO REVISIT--
I REMEMBERED. I LEFT ONE OF MY GUYS OUTSIDE. CAN I GO GET HIM?
YEAH. REAL QUICK.
HEY. HEY, DID YOU COME TO SEE ME?
HHHHNNNNHH...
DID YOU BRING ADMIRAL PEPPERCORN?
HNNNHH.
I GOT SOME OF MY GUYS HERE. NOT MY FAVORITES BUT--
HRCC CHHHHHH HHEEEE!

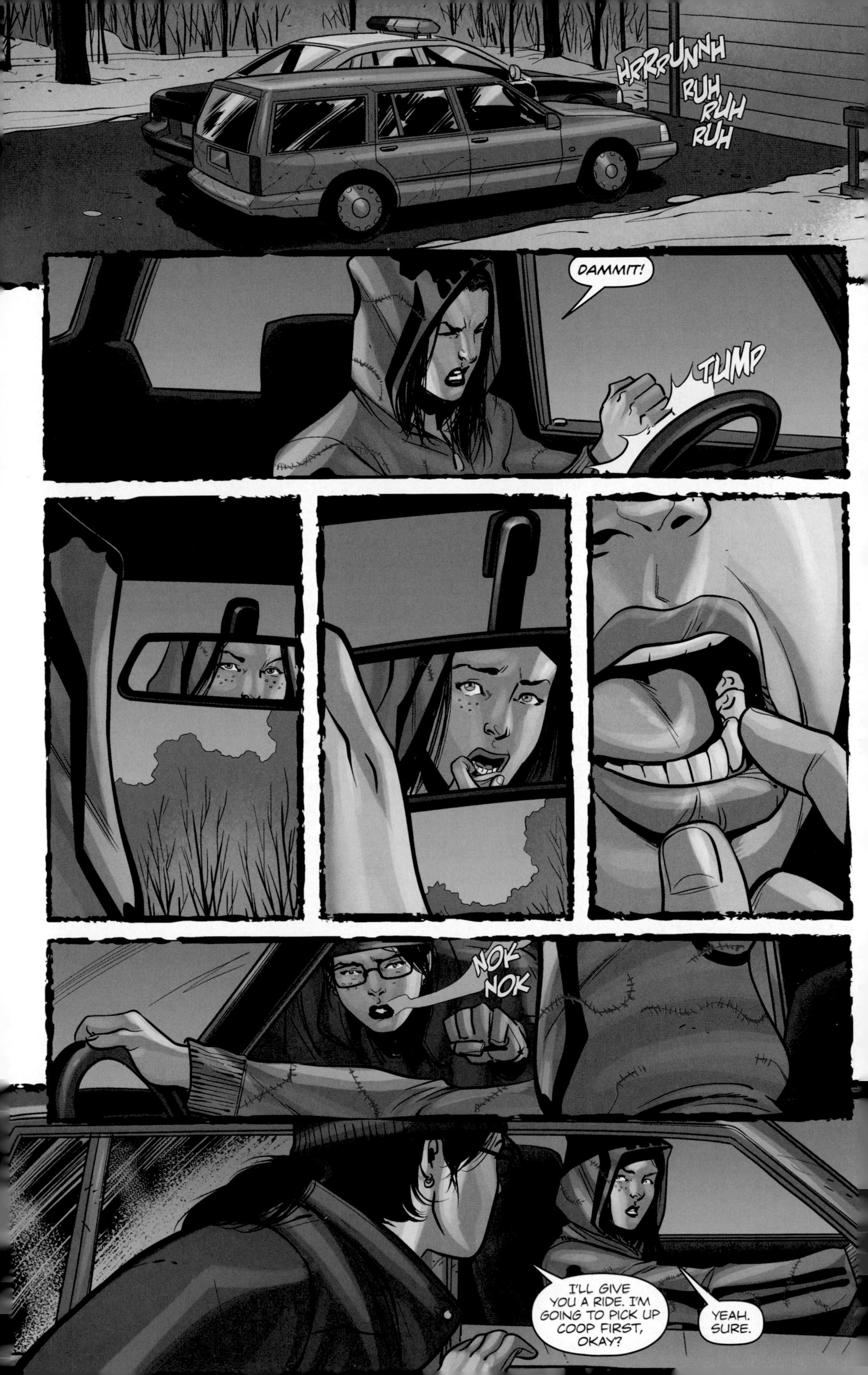
HRRRUNNH
RUH RUH RUH
DAMMIT!
TUMP
NOK NOK
I'LL GIVE YOU A RIDE. I'M GOING TO PICK UP COOP FIRST, OKAY?
YEAH. SURE.

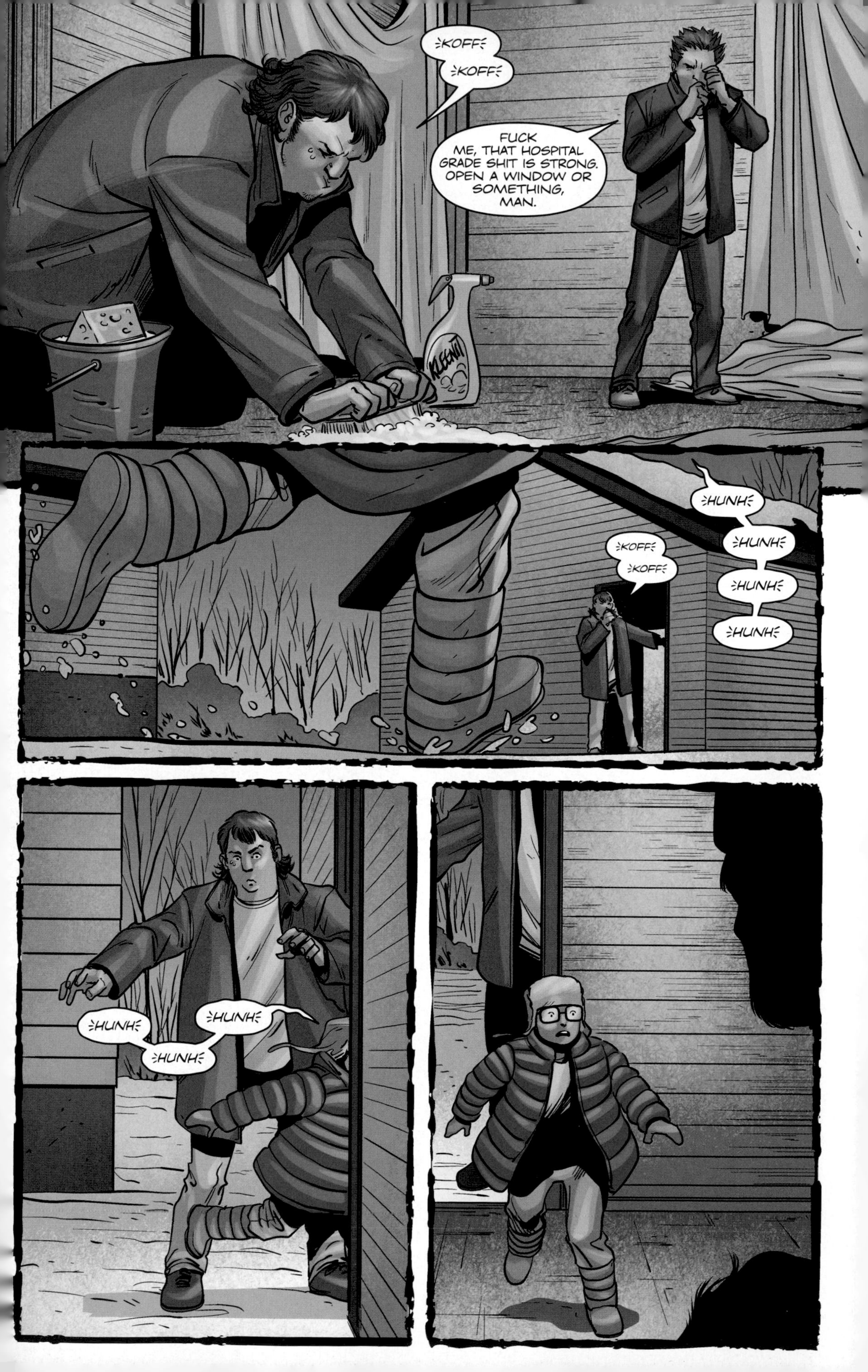
KOFF
KOFF
FUCK ME, THAT HOSPITAL GRADE SHIT IS STRONG. OPEN A WINDOW OR SOMETHING, MAN.
KLEENIT
HUNH
HUNH
KOFF
KOFF
HUNH
HUNH
HUNH
HUNH
HUNH
HUNH

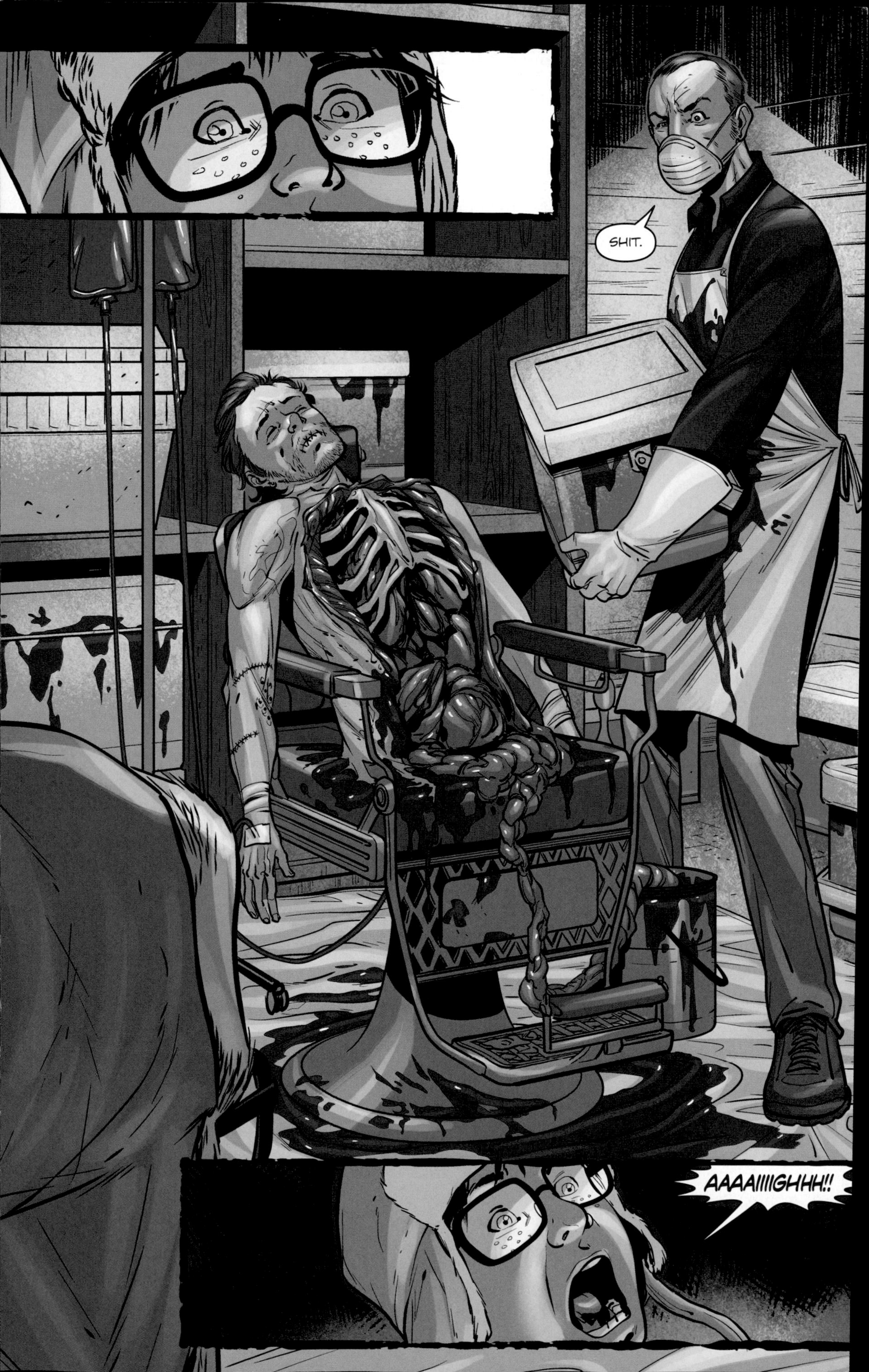
SHIT.
AAAAIIIIGHHH!!

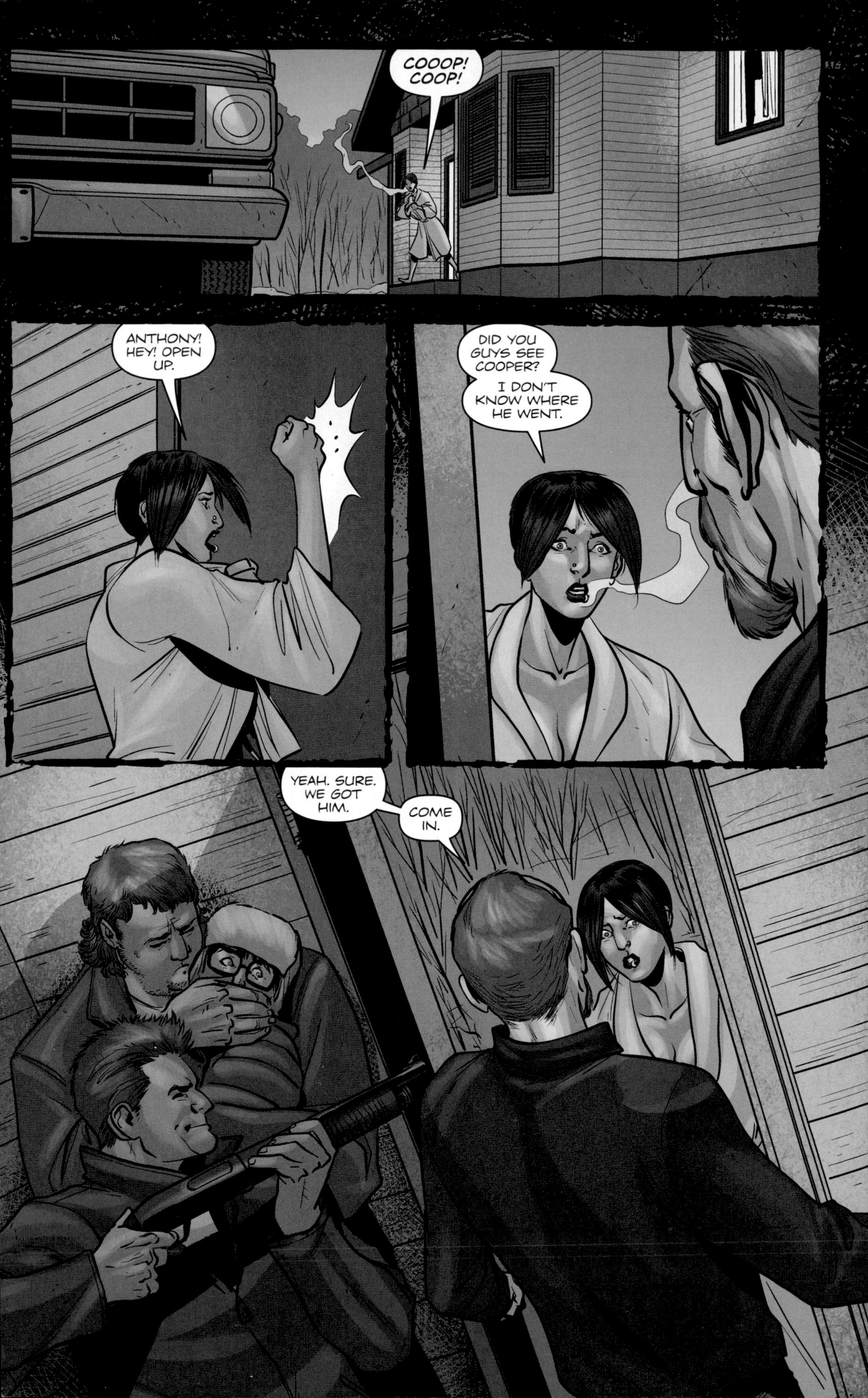
COOOP! COOP!
ANTHONY! HEY! OPEN UP.
DID YOU GUYS SEE COOPER?
I DON'T KNOW WHERE HE WENT.
YEAH. SURE. WE GOT HIM.
COME IN.

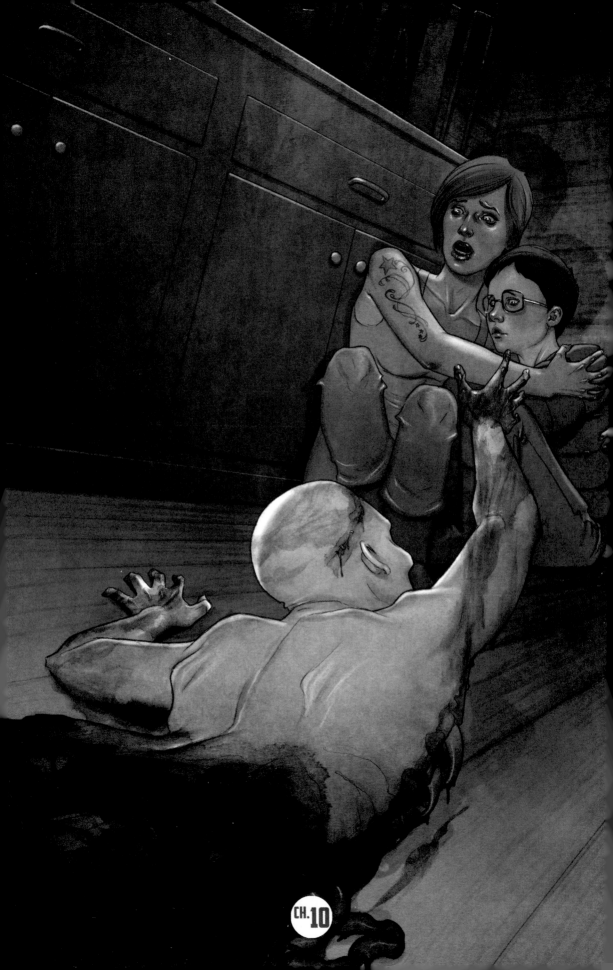

CH.10

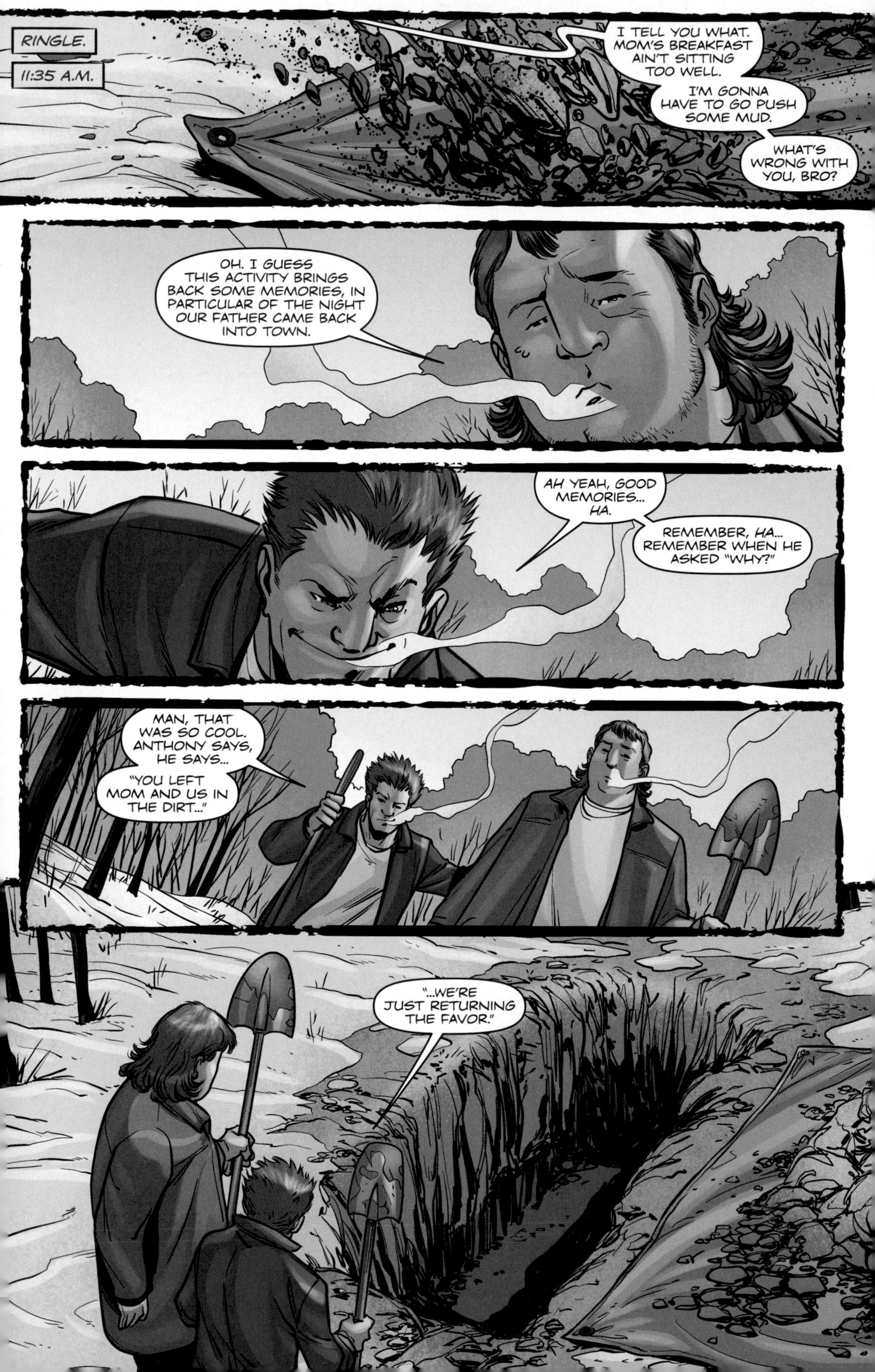
RINGLE.
11:35 A.M.
I TELL YOU WHAT. MOM'S BREAKFAST AIN'T SITTING TOO WELL.
I'M GONNA HAVE TO GO PUSH SOME MUD.
WHAT'S WRONG WITH YOU, BRO?
OH. I GUESS THIS ACTIVITY BRINGS BACK SOME MEMORIES, IN PARTICULAR OF THE NIGHT OUR FATHER CAME BACK INTO TOWN.
AH YEAH, GOOD MEMORIES... HA.
REMEMBER, HA... REMEMBER WHEN HE ASKED "WHY?"
MAN, THAT WAS SO COOL. ANTHONY SAYS, HE SAYS...
"YOU LEFT MOM AND US IN THE DIRT..."
"...WE'RE JUST RETURNING THE FAVOR."

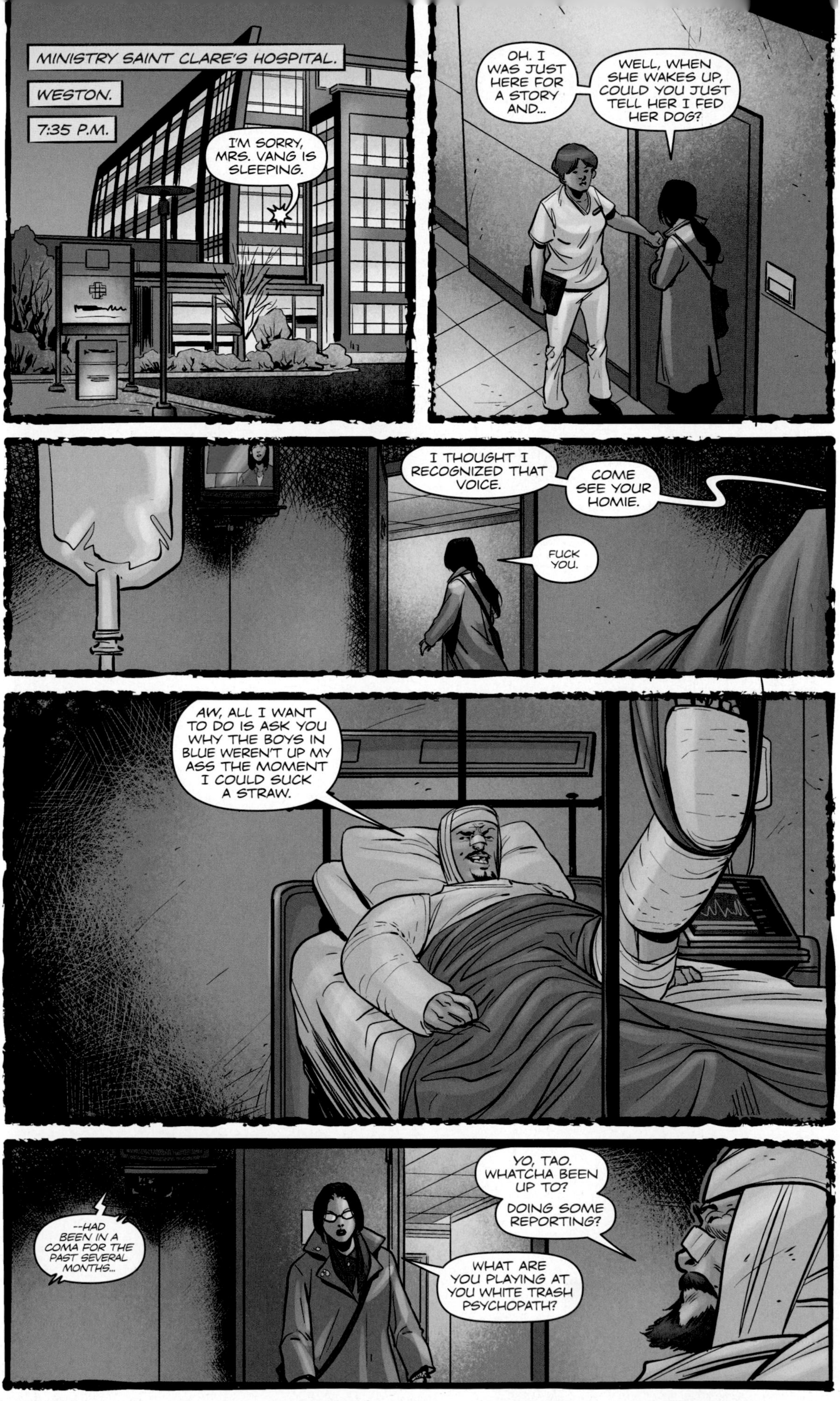
MINISTRY SAINT CLARE'S HOSPITAL.
WESTON.
7:35 P.M.
I'M SORRY, MRS. VANG IS SLEEPING.
OH. I WAS JUST HERE FOR A STORY AND...
WELL, WHEN SHE WAKES UP, COULD YOU JUST TELL HER I FED HER DOG?
I THOUGHT I RECOGNIZED THAT VOICE.
COME SEE YOUR HOMIE.
FUCK YOU.
AW, ALL I WANT TO DO IS ASK YOU WHY THE BOYS IN BLUE WEREN'T UP MY ASS THE MOMENT I COULD SUCK A STRAW.
--HAD BEEN IN A COMA FOR THE PAST SEVERAL MONTHS...
YO, TAO. WHATCHA BEEN UP TO?
DOING SOME REPORTING?
WHAT ARE YOU PLAYING AT YOU WHITE TRASH PSYCHOPATH?

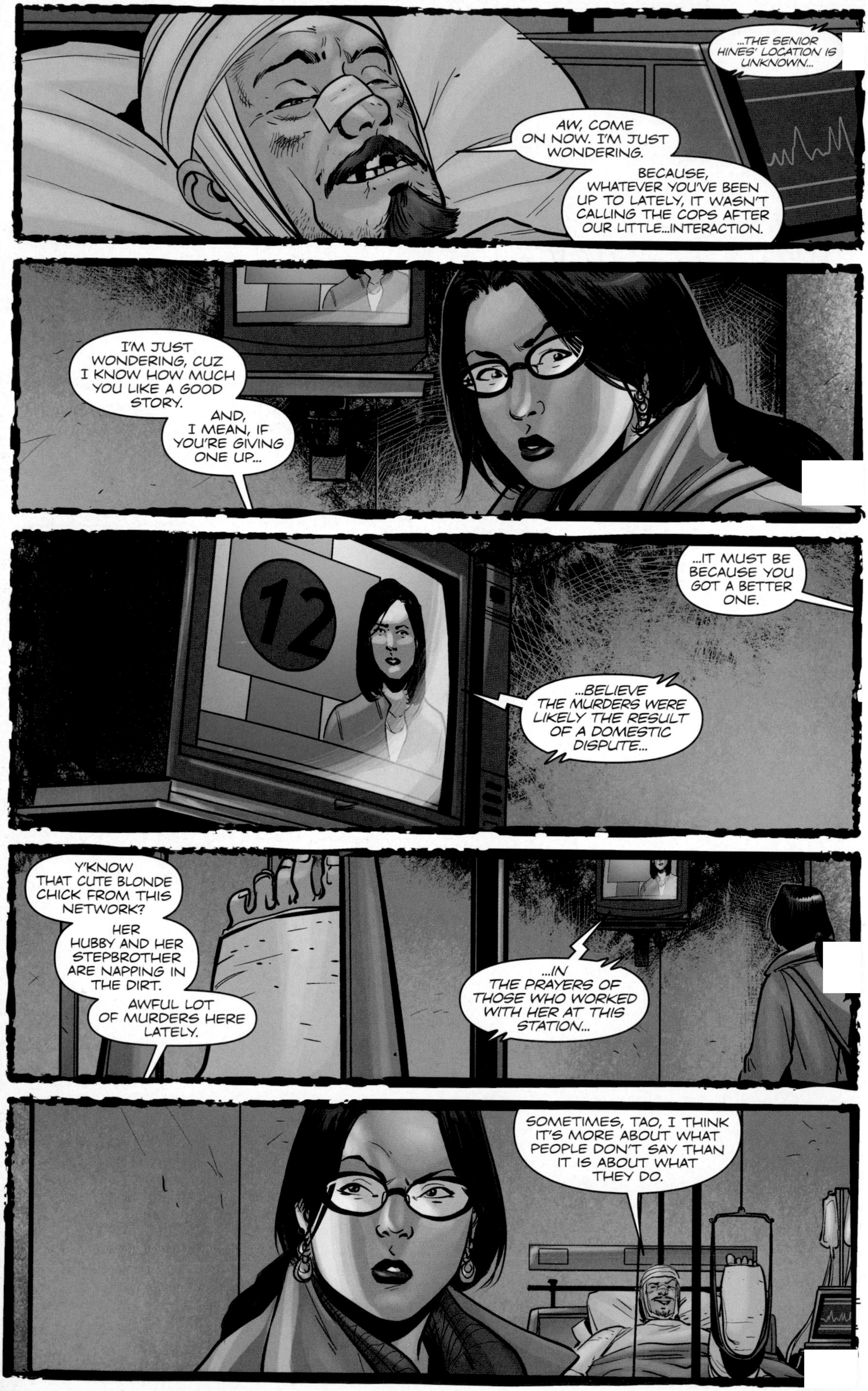
...THE SENIOR HINES' LOCATION IS UNKNOWN...
AW, COME ON NOW. I'M JUST WONDERING.
BECAUSE, WHATEVER YOU'VE BEEN UP TO LATELY, IT WASN'T CALLING THE COPS AFTER OUR LITTLE...INTERACTION.
I'M JUST WONDERING, CUZ I KNOW HOW MUCH YOU LIKE A GOOD STORY.
AND, I MEAN, IF YOU'RE GIVING ONE UP...
12
...IT MUST BE BECAUSE YOU GOT A BETTER ONE.
...BELIEVE THE MURDERS WERE LIKELY THE RESULT OF A DOMESTIC DISPUTE...
Y'KNOW THAT CUTE BLONDE CHICK FROM THIS NETWORK?
HER HUBBY AND HER STEPBROTHER ARE NAPPING IN THE DIRT.
AWFUL LOT OF MURDERS HERE LATELY.
...IN THE PRAYERS OF THOSE WHO WORKED WITH HER AT THIS STATION...
SOMETIMES, TAO, I THINK IT'S MORE ABOUT WHAT PEOPLE DON'T SAY THAN IT IS ABOUT WHAT THEY DO.

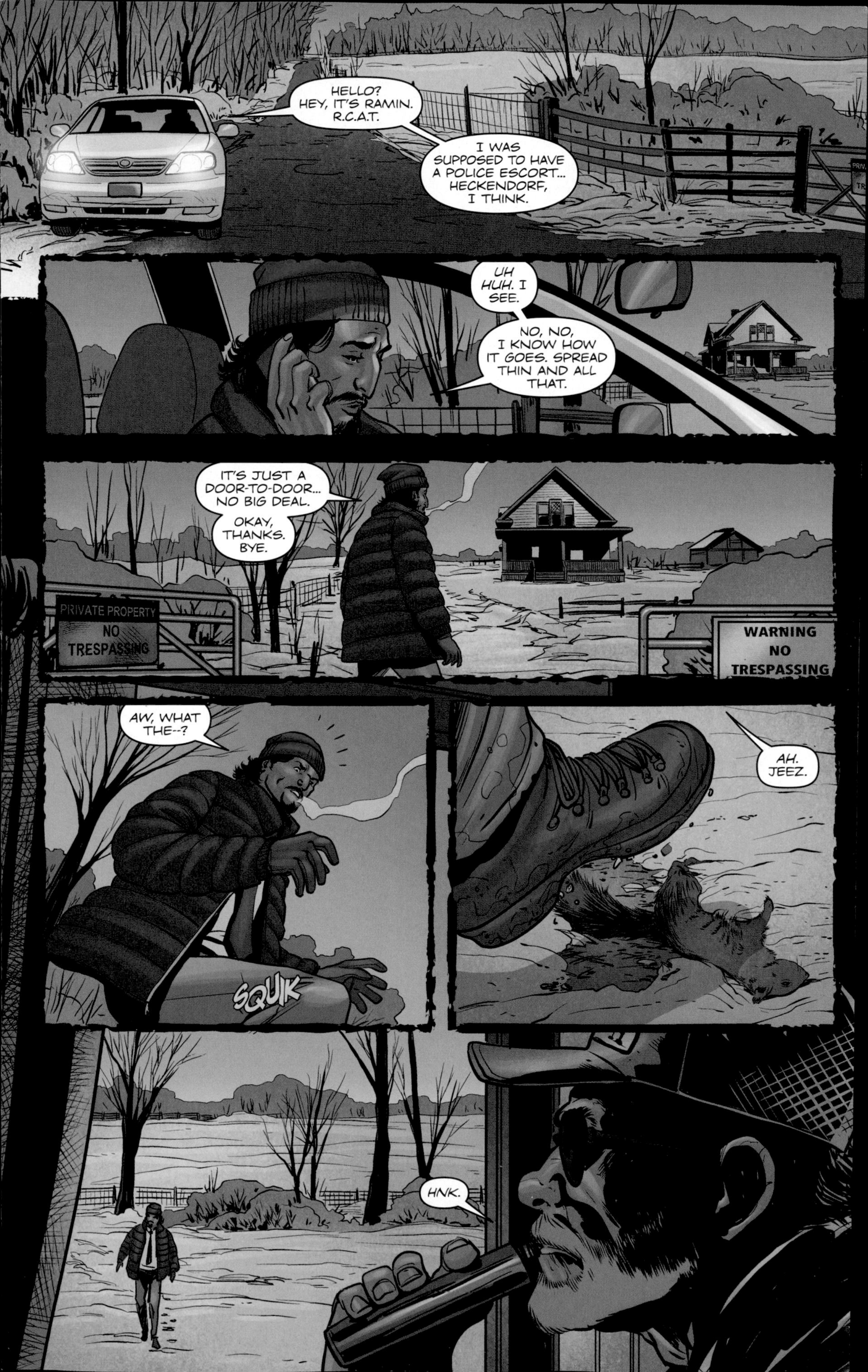
HELLO? HEY, IT'S RAMIN. R.C.A.T.
I WAS SUPPOSED TO HAVE A POLICE ESCORT... HECKENDORF, I THINK.
UH HUH. I SEE.
NO, NO, I KNOW HOW IT GOES. SPREAD THIN AND ALL THAT.
IT'S JUST A DOOR-TO-DOOR... NO BIG DEAL.
OKAY, THANKS. BYE.
PRIVATE PROPERTY
NO TRESPASSING
WARNING
NO TRESPASSING
AW, WHAT THE--?
SQUIK
AH. JEEZ.
HNK.

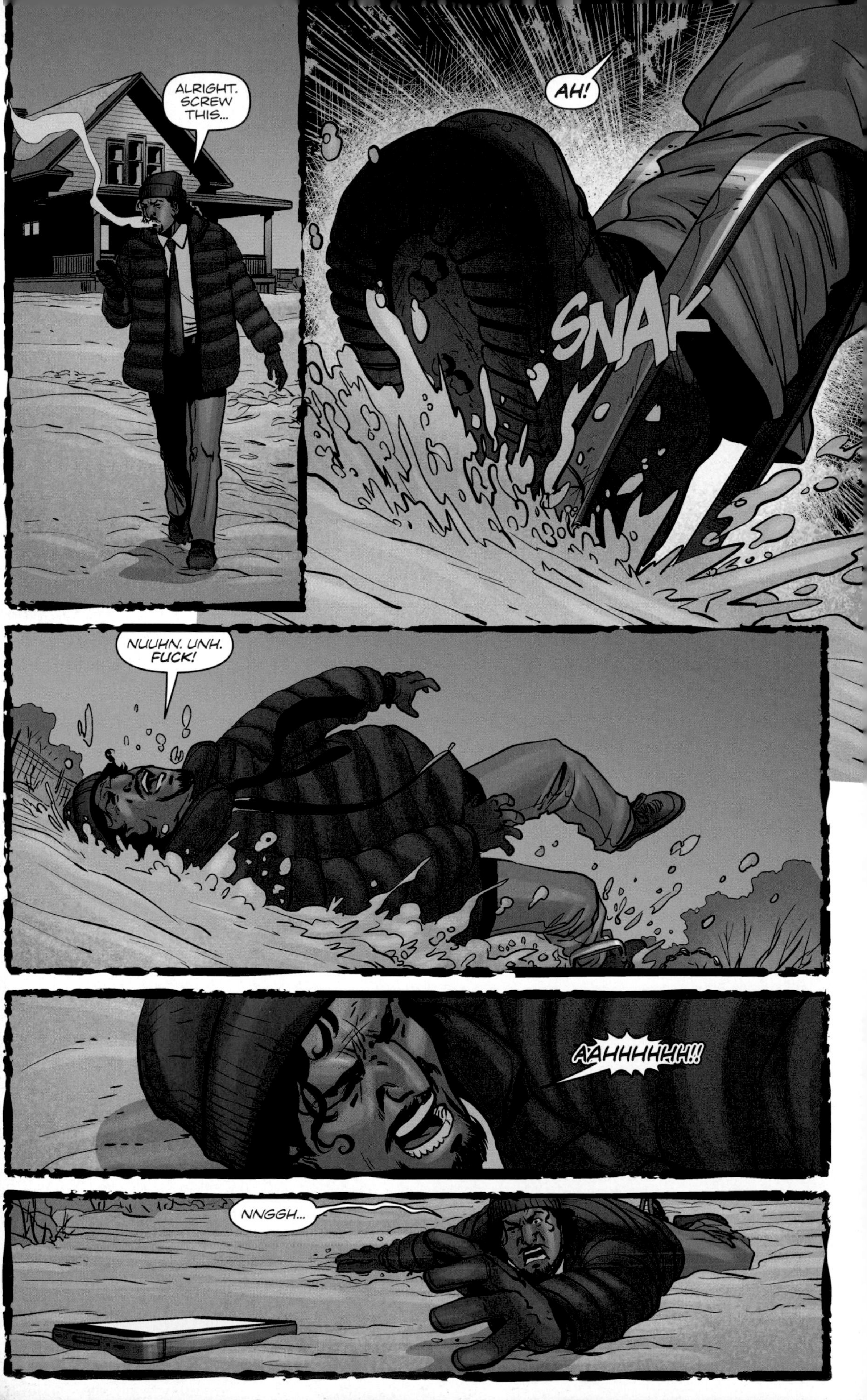
ALRIGHT. SCREW THIS...
AH!
SNAK
NUUHN. UNH. FUCK!
AAHHHHHH!!
NNGGH...

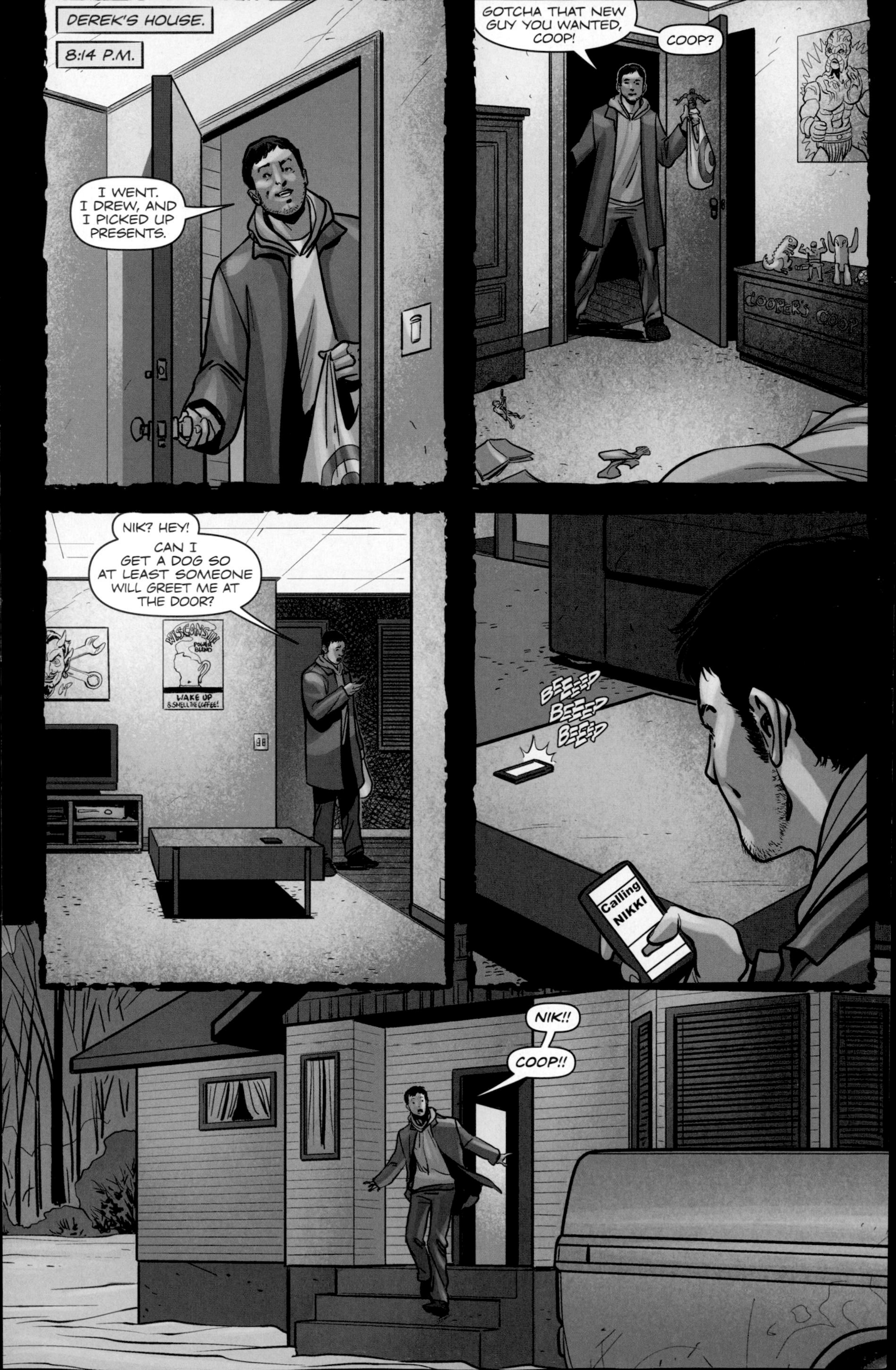
DEREK'S HOUSE.
8:14 P.M.
I WENT. I DREW, AND I PICKED UP PRESENTS.
GOTCHA THAT NEW GUY YOU WANTED, COOP!
COOP?
COOPER'S COOP
NIK? HEY!
CAN I GET A DOG SO AT LEAST SOMEONE WILL GREET ME AT THE DOOR?
WISCONSIN
WAKE UP & SMELL THE COFFEE!
BEEEEP
BEEEEP
BEEEEP
Calling NIKKI
NIK!!
COOP!!

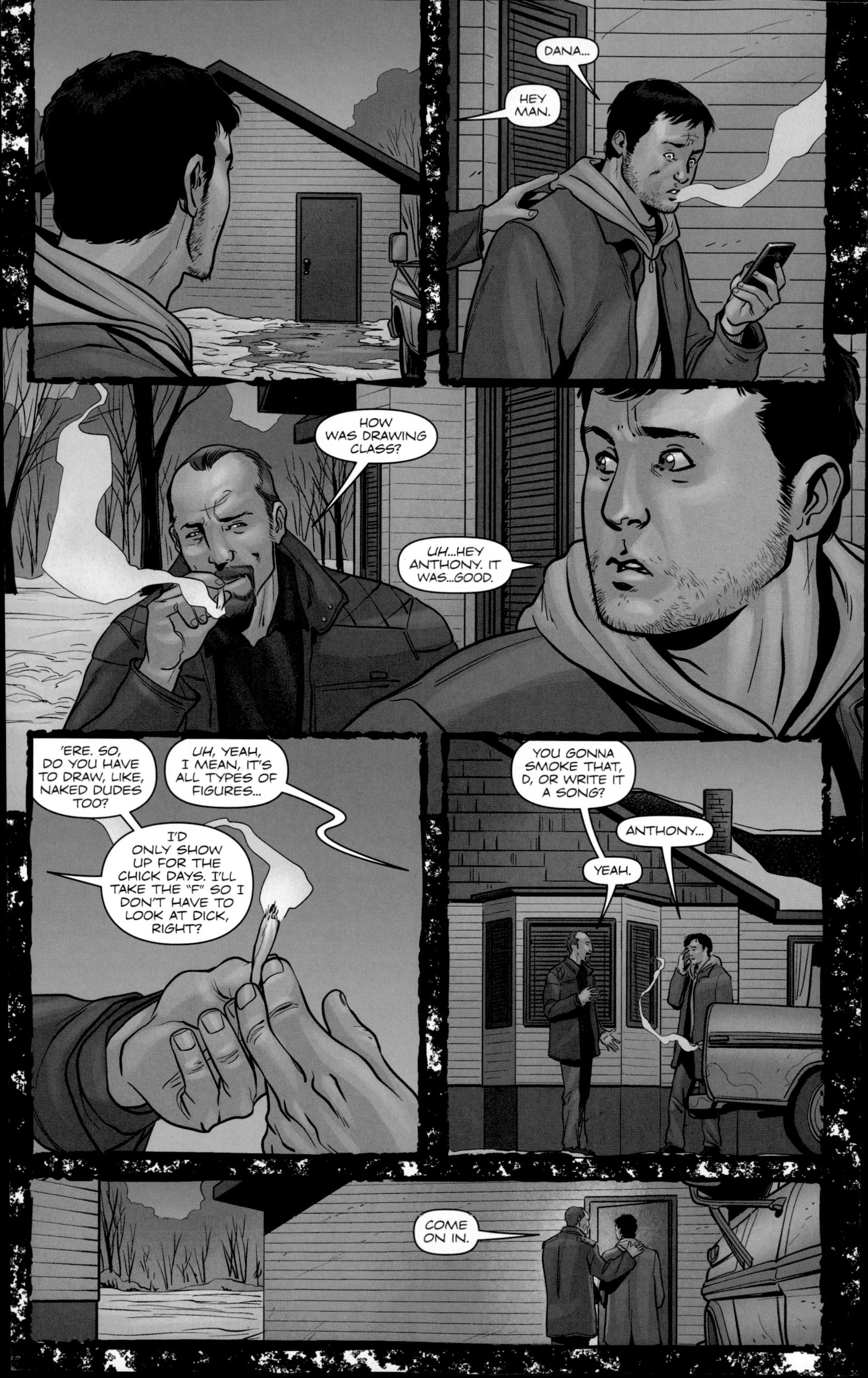
DANA...
HEY MAN.
HOW WAS DRAWING CLASS?
UH...HEY ANTHONY. IT WAS...GOOD.
'ERE. SO, DO YOU HAVE TO DRAW, LIKE, NAKED DUDES TOO?
UH, YEAH, I MEAN, IT'S ALL TYPES OF FIGURES...
I'D ONLY SHOW UP FOR THE CHICK DAYS. I'LL TAKE THE "F" SO I DON'T HAVE TO LOOK AT DICK, RIGHT?
YOU GONNA SMOKE THAT, D, OR WRITE IT A SONG?
ANTHONY...
YEAH.
COME ON IN.

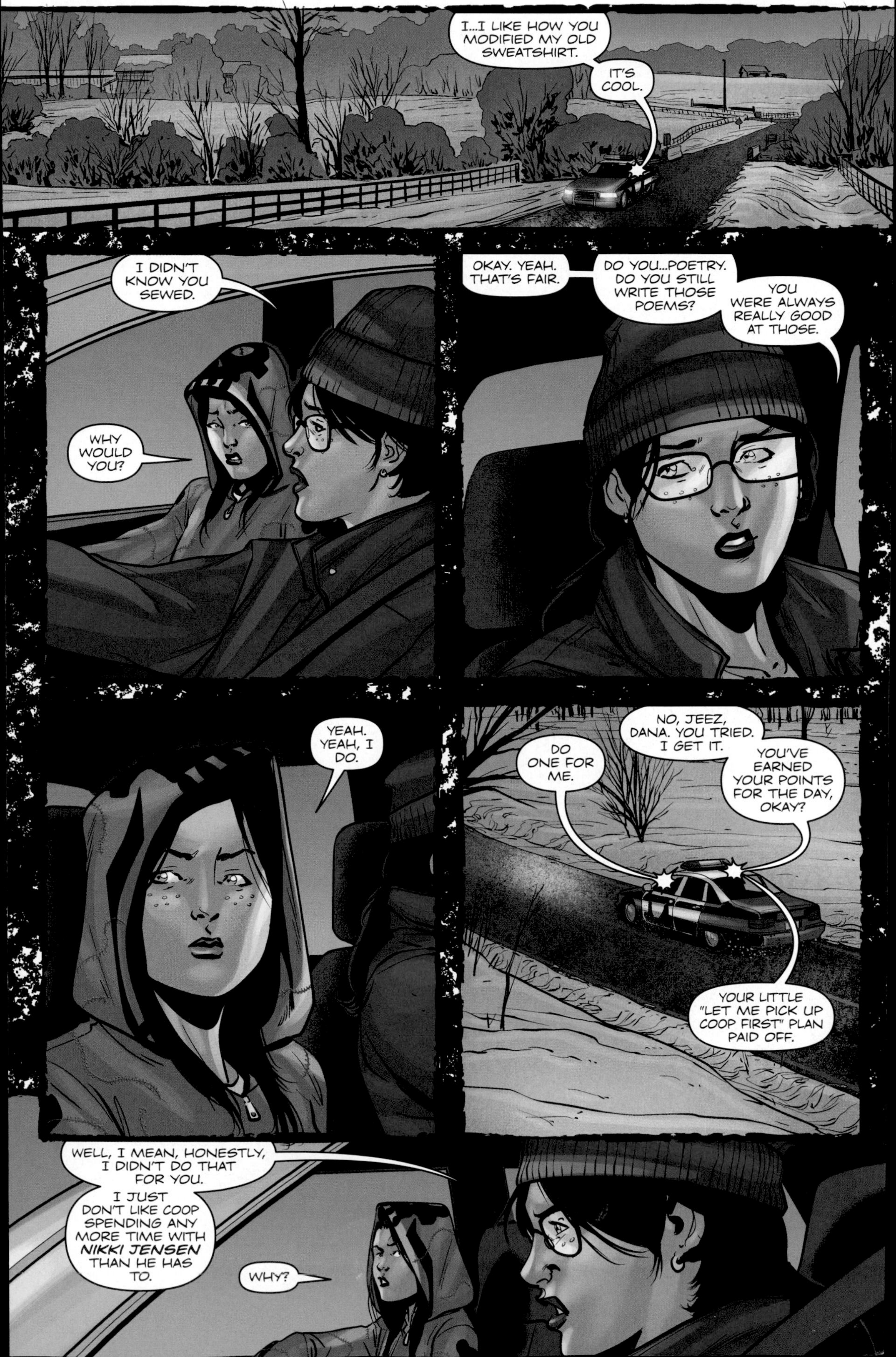
I...I LIKE HOW YOU MODIFIED MY OLD SWEATSHIRT.
IT'S COOL.
I DIDN'T KNOW YOU SEWED.
WHY WOULD YOU?
OKAY. YEAH. THAT'S FAIR.
DO YOU...POETRY. DO YOU STILL WRITE THOSE POEMS?
YOU WERE ALWAYS REALLY GOOD AT THOSE.
YEAH. YEAH, I DO.
DO ONE FOR ME.
NO, JEEZ, DANA. YOU TRIED. I GET IT.
YOU'VE EARNED YOUR POINTS FOR THE DAY, OKAY?
YOUR LITTLE "LET ME PICK UP COOP FIRST" PLAN PAID OFF.
WELL, I MEAN, HONESTLY, I DIDN'T DO THAT FOR YOU.
I JUST DON'T LIKE COOP SPENDING ANY MORE TIME WITH NIKKI JENSEN THAN HE HAS TO.
WHY?

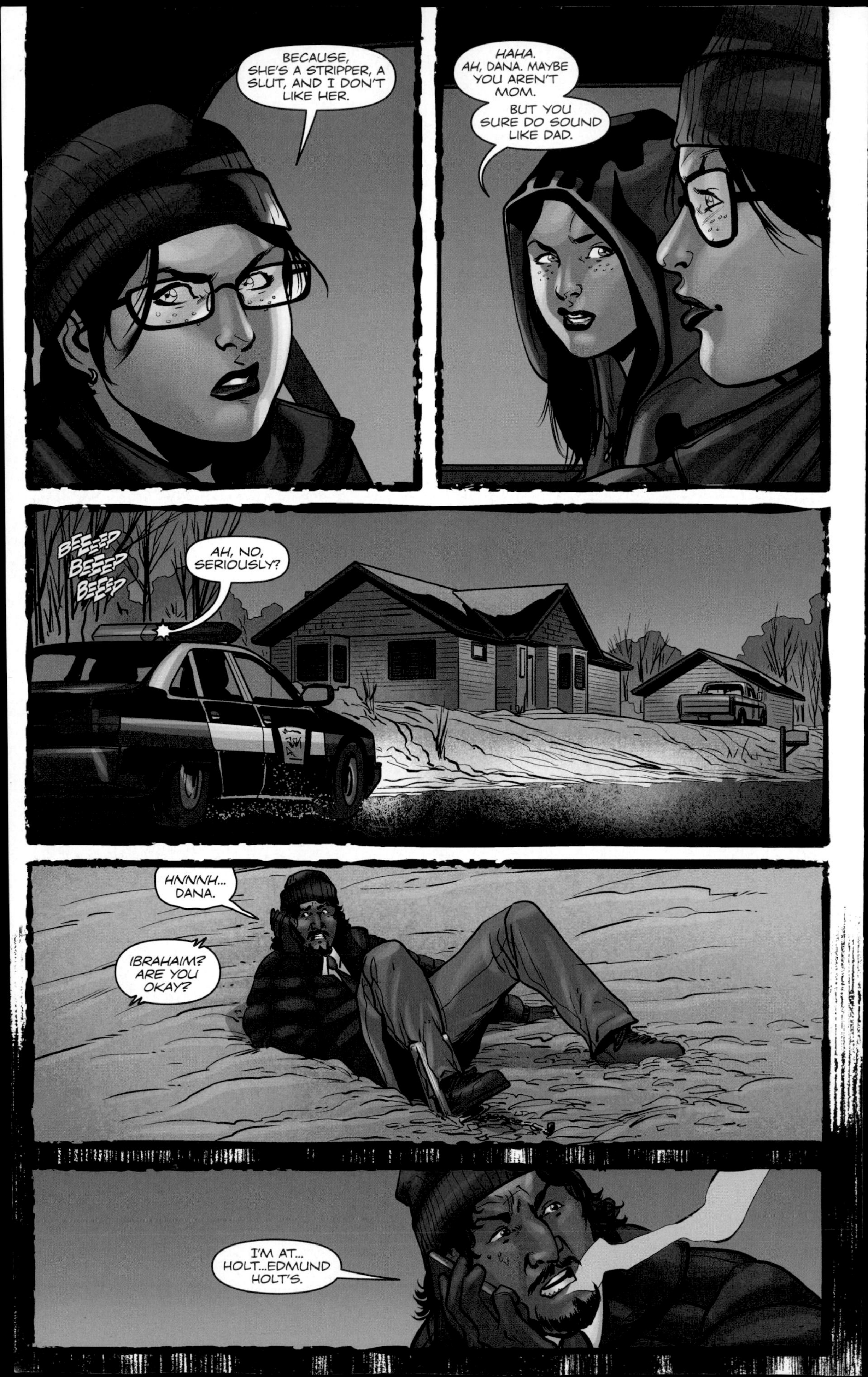
BECAUSE, SHE'S A STRIPPER, A SLUT, AND I DON'T LIKE HER.
HAHA. AH, DANA. MAYBE YOU AREN'T MOM.
BUT YOU SURE DO SOUND LIKE DAD.
BEEEEP BEEEEP BEEEEP
AH, NO, SERIOUSLY?
HNNNH... DANA.
IBRAHAIM? ARE YOU OKAY?
I'M AT... HOLT...EDMUND HOLT'S.

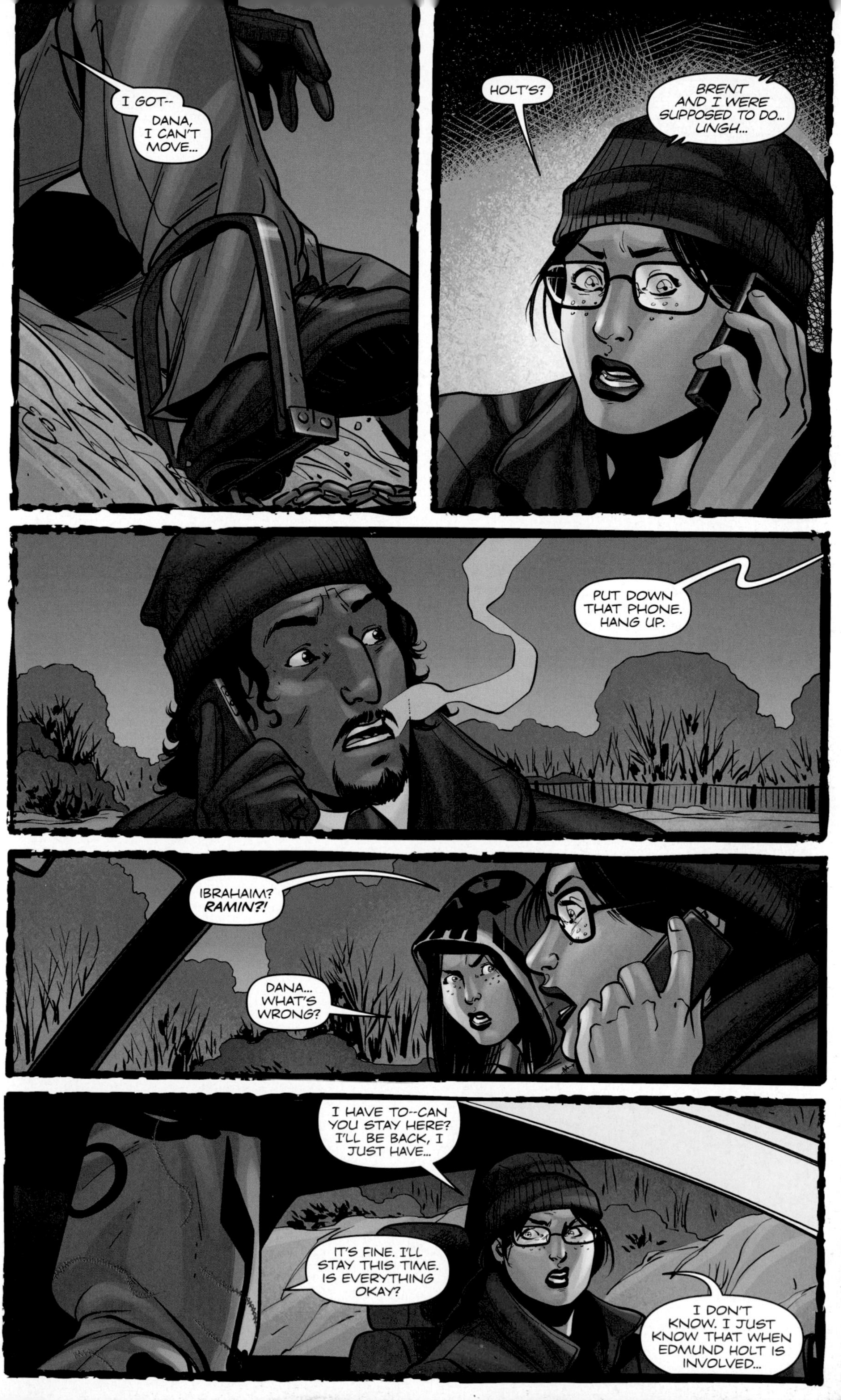
I GOT--
DANA, I CAN'T MOVE...
HOLT'S?
BRENT AND I WERE SUPPOSED TO DO... UNGH...
PUT DOWN THAT PHONE. HANG UP.
IBRAHAIM? *RAMIN?!*
DANA... WHAT'S WRONG?
I HAVE TO--CAN YOU STAY HERE? I'LL BE BACK, I JUST HAVE...
IT'S FINE. I'LL STAY THIS TIME. IS EVERYTHING OKAY?
I DON'T KNOW. I JUST KNOW THAT WHEN EDMUND HOLT IS INVOLVED...

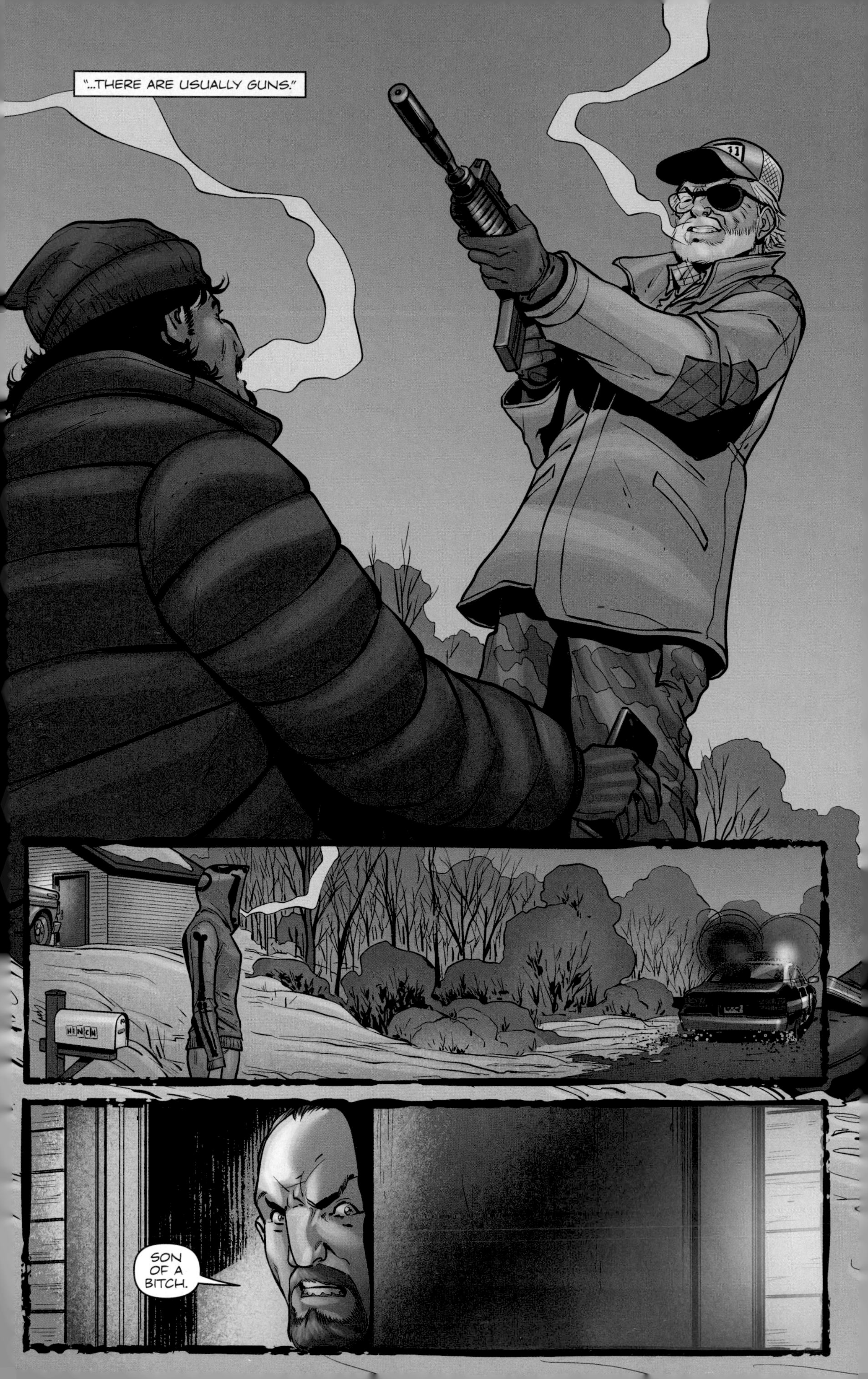
"...THERE ARE USUALLY GUNS."
HINCH
SON OF A BITCH.

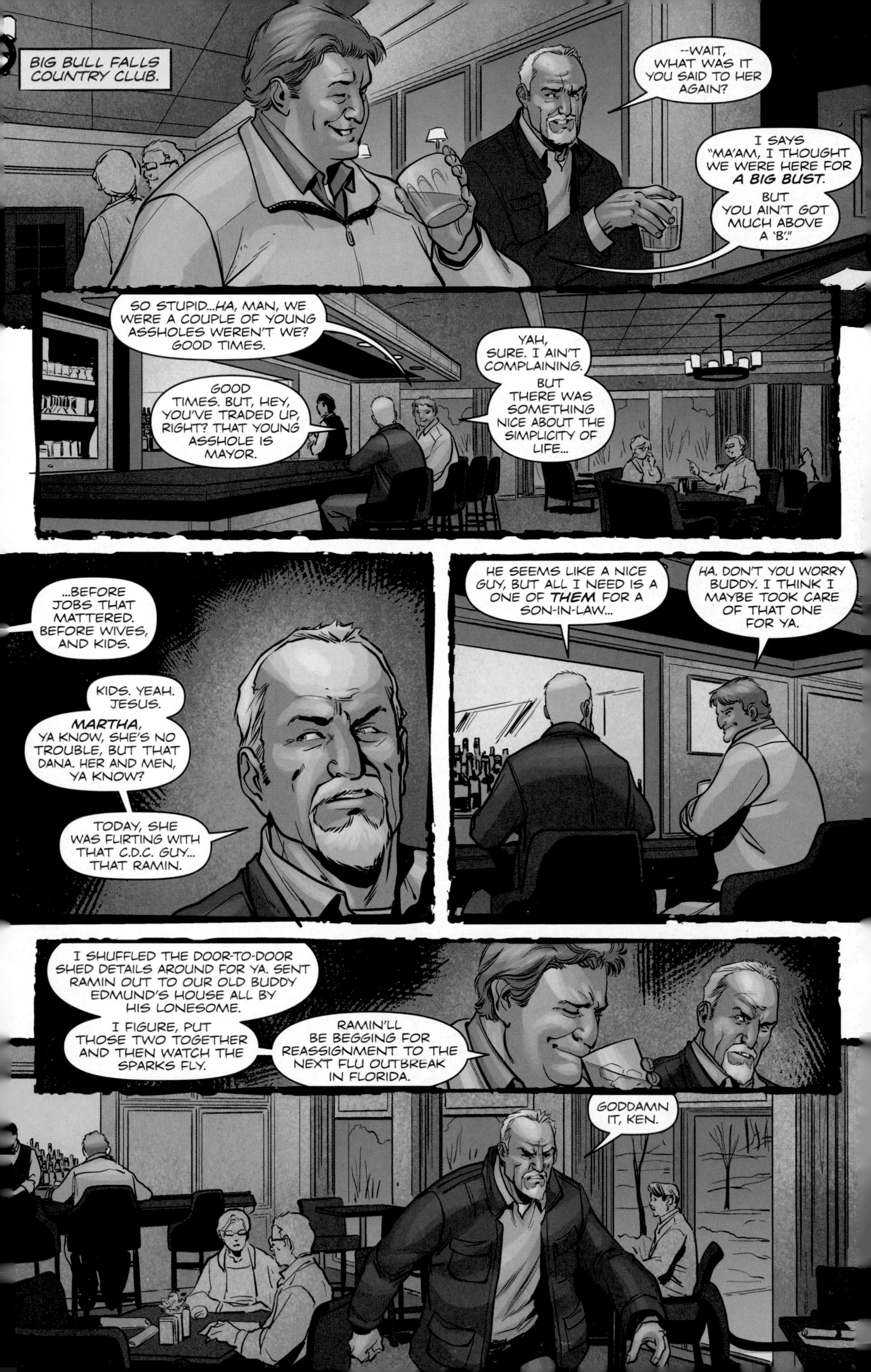
BIG BULL FALLS COUNTRY CLUB.
--WAIT, WHAT WAS IT YOU SAID TO HER AGAIN?
I SAYS "MA'AM, I THOUGHT WE WERE HERE FOR **A BIG BUST**.
BUT YOU AIN'T GOT MUCH ABOVE A 'B'."
SO STUPID...*HA*, MAN, WE WERE A COUPLE OF YOUNG ASSHOLES WEREN'T WE? GOOD TIMES.
GOOD TIMES. BUT, HEY, YOU'VE TRADED UP, RIGHT? THAT YOUNG ASSHOLE IS MAYOR.
YAH, SURE. I AIN'T COMPLAINING.
BUT THERE WAS SOMETHING NICE ABOUT THE SIMPLICITY OF LIFE...
...BEFORE JOBS THAT MATTERED. BEFORE WIVES, AND KIDS.
KIDS. YEAH. JESUS.
MARTHA, YA KNOW, SHE'S NO TROUBLE, BUT THAT DANA. HER AND MEN, YA KNOW?
TODAY, SHE WAS FLIRTING WITH THAT C.D.C. GUY... THAT RAMIN.
HE SEEMS LIKE A NICE GUY, BUT ALL I NEED IS A ONE OF ***THEM*** FOR A SON-IN-LAW...
HA. DON'T YOU WORRY BUDDY. I THINK I MAYBE TOOK CARE OF THAT ONE FOR YA.
I SHUFFLED THE DOOR-TO-DOOR SHED DETAILS AROUND FOR YA. SENT RAMIN OUT TO OUR OLD BUDDY EDMUND'S HOUSE ALL BY HIS LONESOME.
I FIGURE, PUT THOSE TWO TOGETHER AND THEN WATCH THE SPARKS FLY.
RAMIN'LL BE BEGGING FOR REASSIGNMENT TO THE NEXT FLU OUTBREAK IN FLORIDA.
GODDAMN IT, KEN.

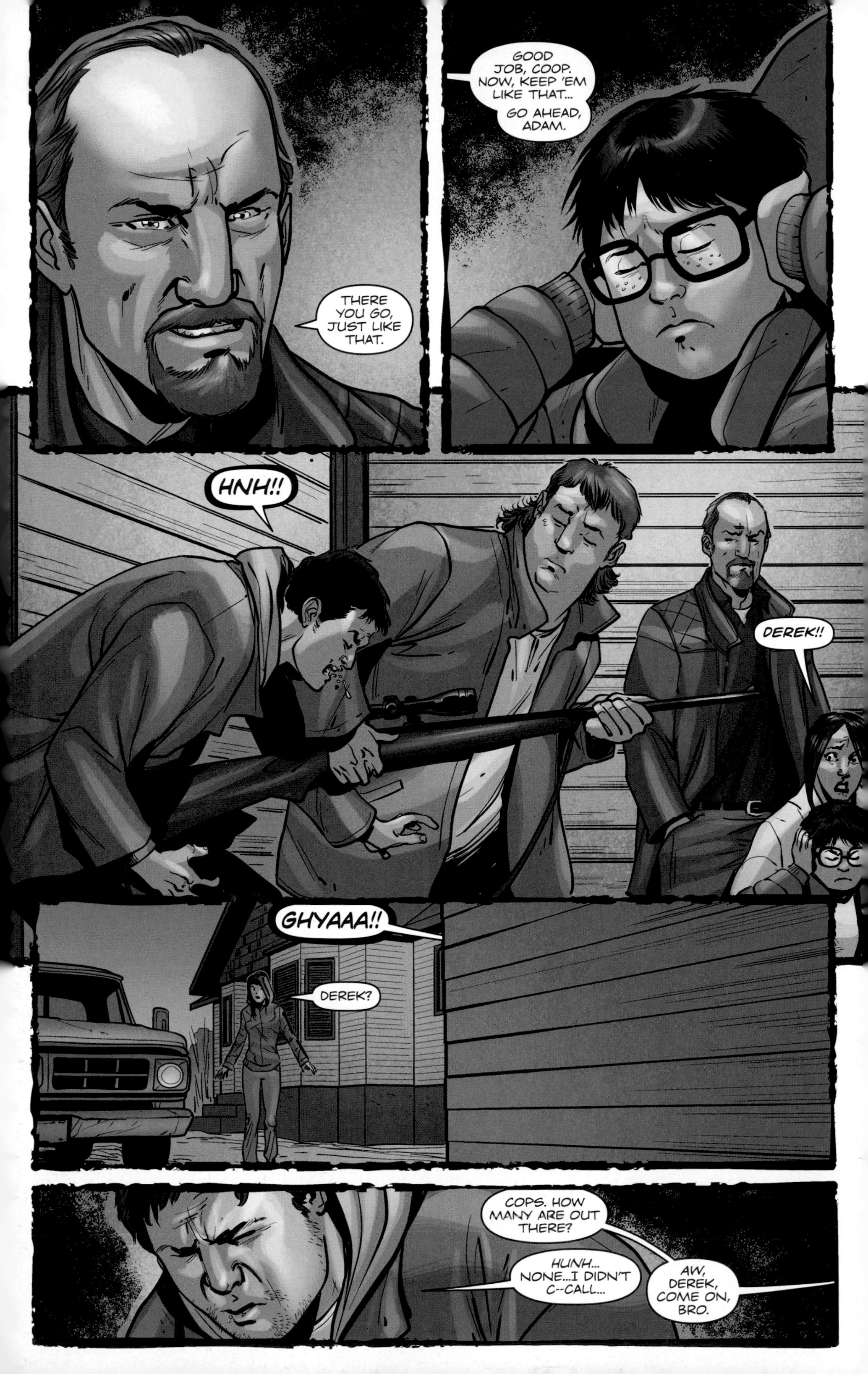
THERE YOU GO, JUST LIKE THAT.
GOOD JOB, COOP. NOW, KEEP 'EM LIKE THAT...
GO AHEAD, ADAM.
HNH!!
DEREK!!
GHYAAA!!
DEREK?
COPS. HOW MANY ARE OUT THERE?
HUNH... NONE...I DIDN'T C--CALL...
AW, DEREK, COME ON, BRO.

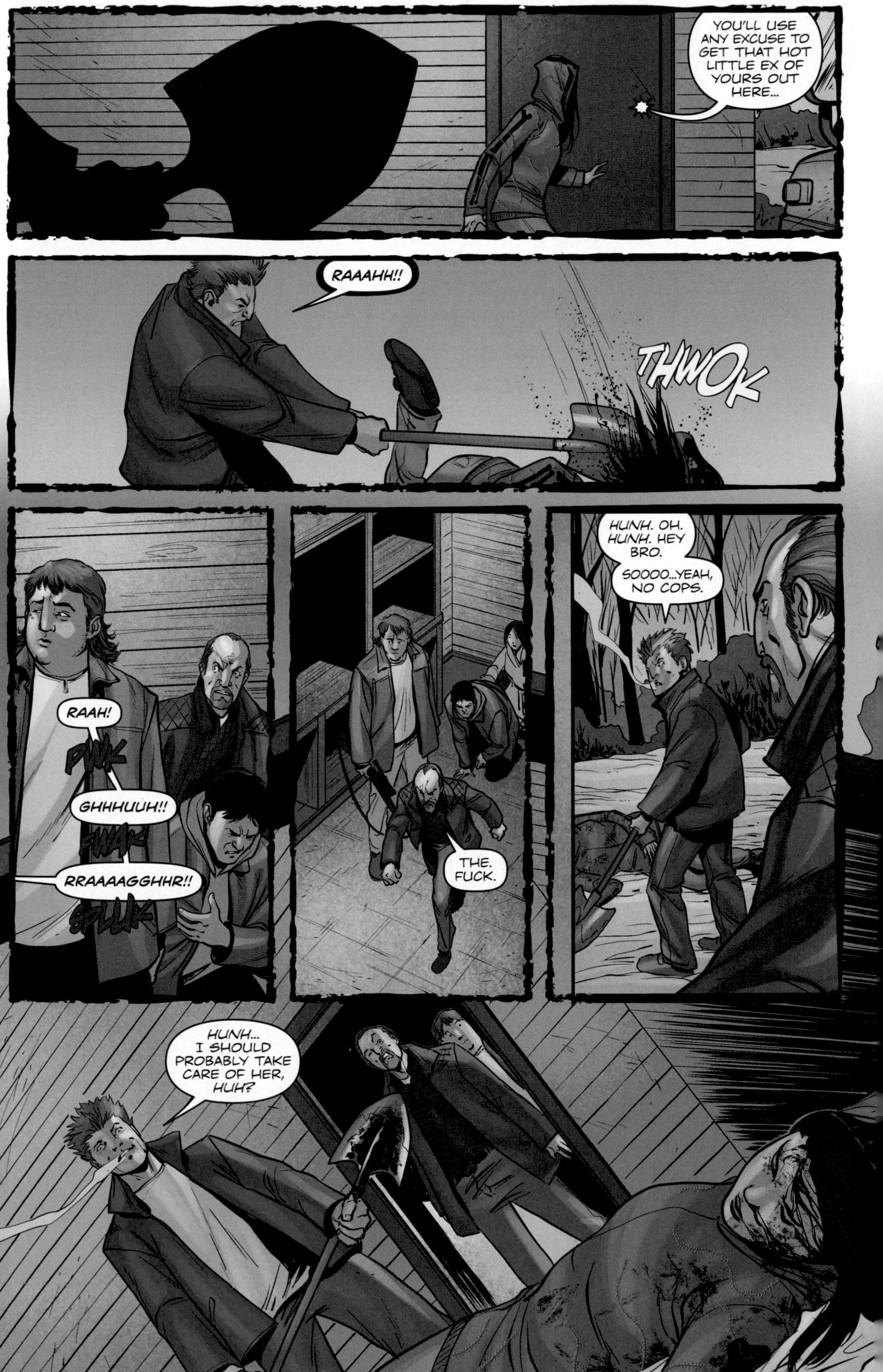
YOU'LL USE ANY EXCUSE TO GET THAT HOT LITTLE EX OF YOURS OUT HERE...
RAAAHH!!
THWOK
RAAH!
GHHHUUH!!
RRAAAAGGHHR!!
THE. FUCK.
HUNH. OH. HUNH. HEY BRO.
SOOOO...YEAH, NO COPS.
HUNH... I SHOULD PROBABLY TAKE CARE OF HER, HUH?

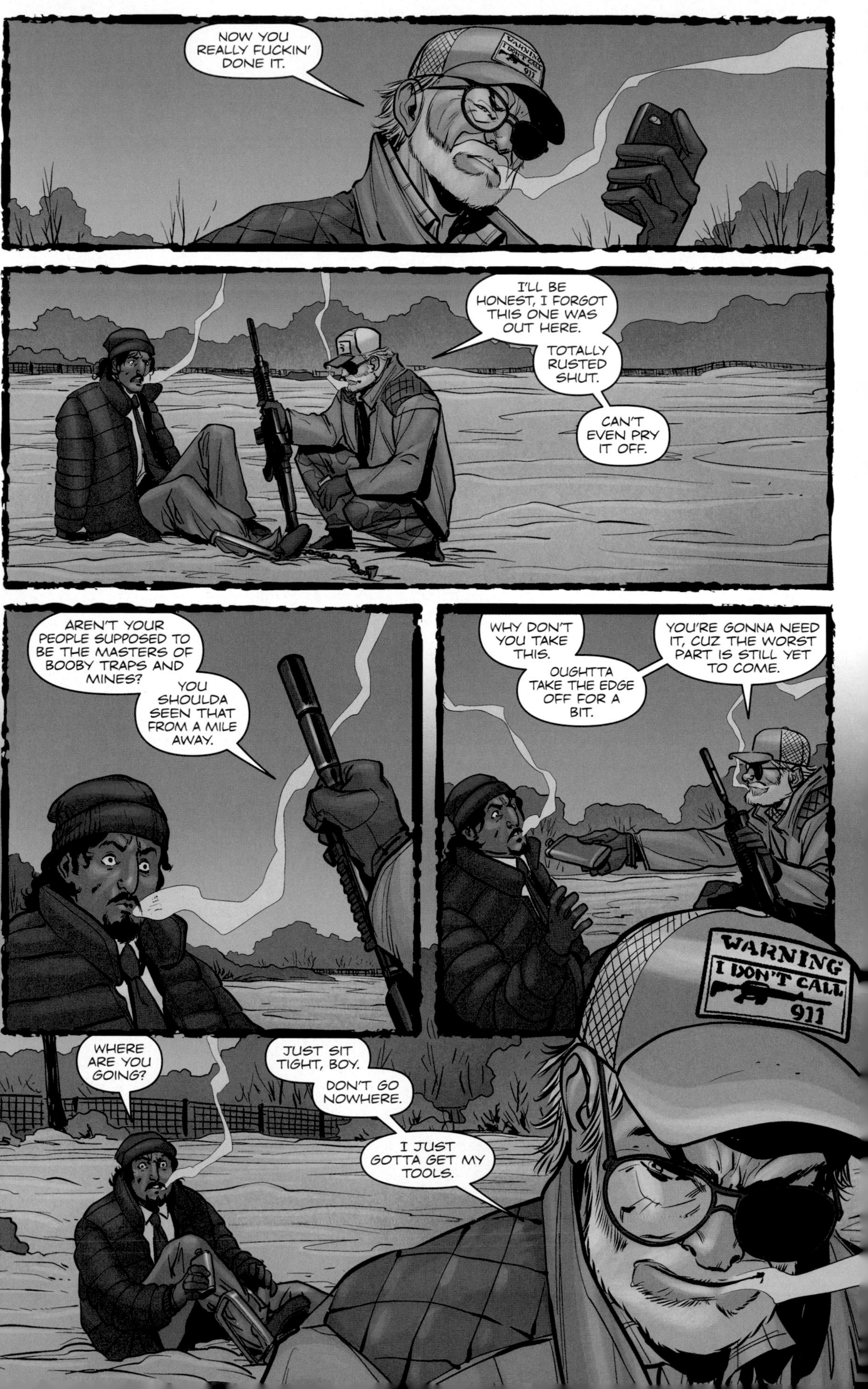
NOW YOU REALLY FUCKIN' DONE IT.
WARNING I DON'T CALL 911
I'LL BE HONEST, I FORGOT THIS ONE WAS OUT HERE.
TOTALLY RUSTED SHUT.
CAN'T EVEN PRY IT OFF.
AREN'T YOUR PEOPLE SUPPOSED TO BE THE MASTERS OF BOOBY TRAPS AND MINES?
YOU SHOULDA SEEN THAT FROM A MILE AWAY.
WHY DON'T YOU TAKE THIS.
OUGHTTA TAKE THE EDGE OFF FOR A BIT.
YOU'RE GONNA NEED IT, CUZ THE WORST PART IS STILL YET TO COME.
WARNING I DON'T CALL 911
WHERE ARE YOU GOING?
JUST SIT TIGHT, BOY.
DON'T GO NOWHERE.
I JUST GOTTA GET MY TOOLS.

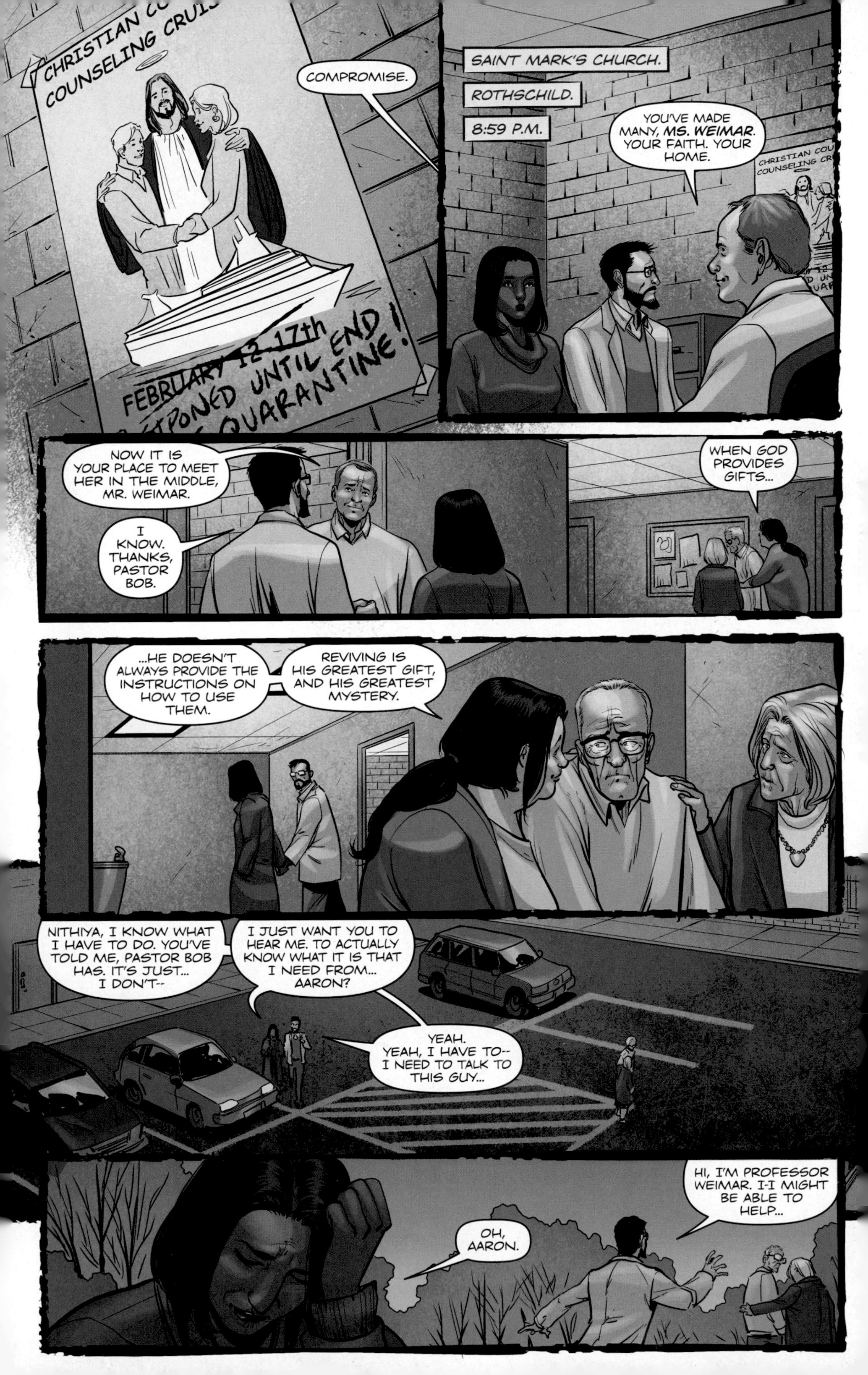
CHRISTIAN CO
COUNSELING CRUIS
FEBRUARY 12-17th
POSTPONED UNTIL END OF QUARANTINE!
COMPROMISE.
SAINT MARK'S CHURCH.
ROTHSCHILD.
8:59 P.M.
YOU'VE MADE MANY, **MS. WEIMAR**. YOUR FAITH. YOUR HOME.
NOW IT IS YOUR PLACE TO MEET HER IN THE MIDDLE, MR. WEIMAR.
I KNOW. THANKS, PASTOR BOB.
WHEN GOD PROVIDES GIFTS...
...HE DOESN'T ALWAYS PROVIDE THE INSTRUCTIONS ON HOW TO USE THEM.
REVIVING IS HIS GREATEST GIFT, AND HIS GREATEST MYSTERY.
NITHIYA, I KNOW WHAT I HAVE TO DO. YOU'VE TOLD ME, PASTOR BOB HAS. IT'S JUST... I DON'T--
I JUST WANT YOU TO HEAR ME. TO ACTUALLY KNOW WHAT IT IS THAT I NEED FROM... AARON?
YEAH. YEAH, I HAVE TO-- I NEED TO TALK TO THIS GUY...
HI, I'M PROFESSOR WEIMAR. I-I MIGHT BE ABLE TO HELP...
OH, AARON.

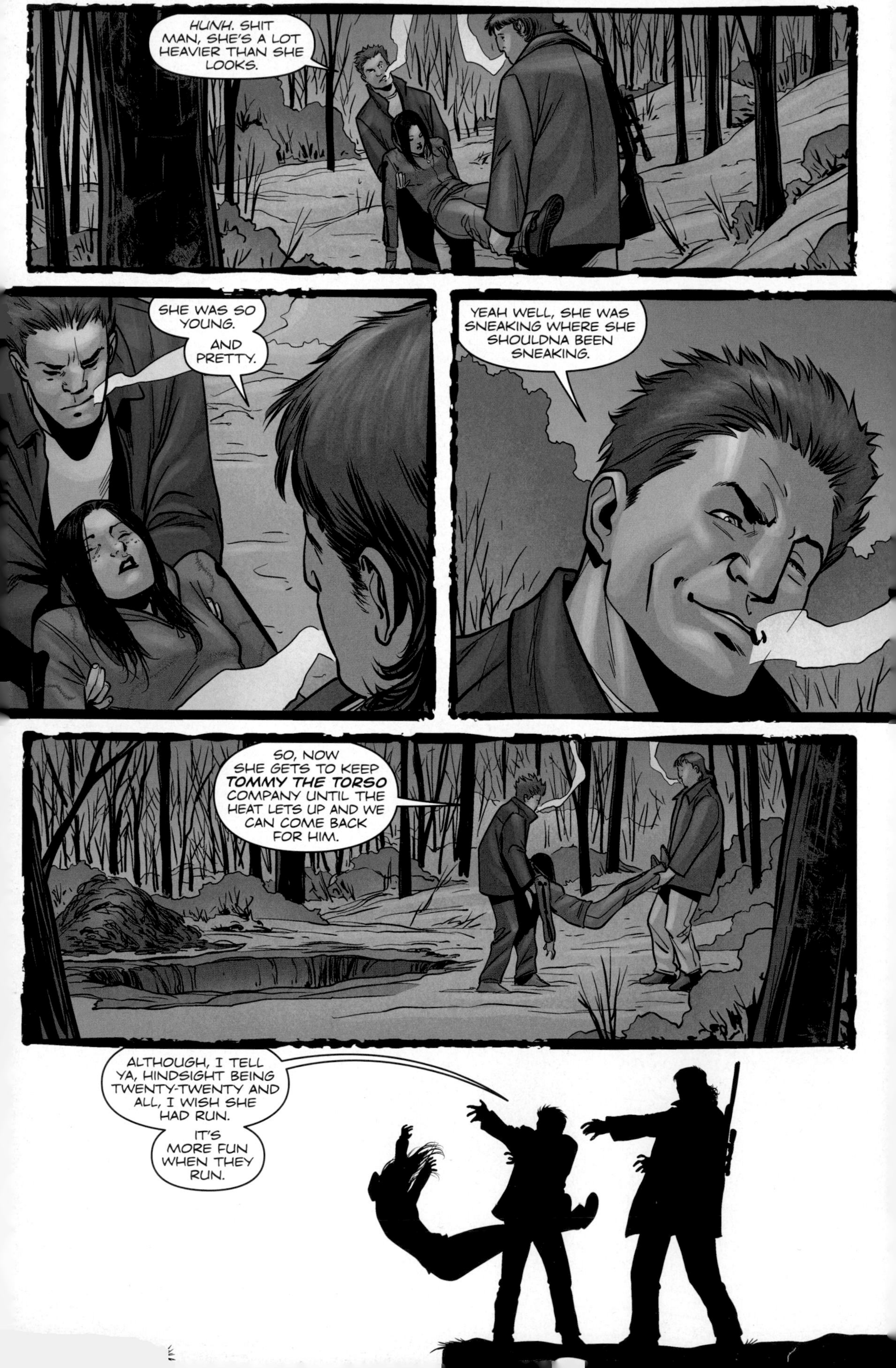

HUNH. SHIT MAN, SHE'S A LOT HEAVIER THAN SHE LOOKS.
SHE WAS SO YOUNG.
AND PRETTY.
YEAH WELL, SHE WAS SNEAKING WHERE SHE SHOULDNA BEEN SNEAKING.
SO, NOW SHE GETS TO KEEP **TOMMY THE TORSO** COMPANY UNTIL THE HEAT LETS UP AND WE CAN COME BACK FOR HIM.
ALTHOUGH, I TELL YA, HINDSIGHT BEING TWENTY-TWENTY AND ALL, I WISH SHE HAD RUN.
IT'S MORE FUN WHEN THEY RUN.

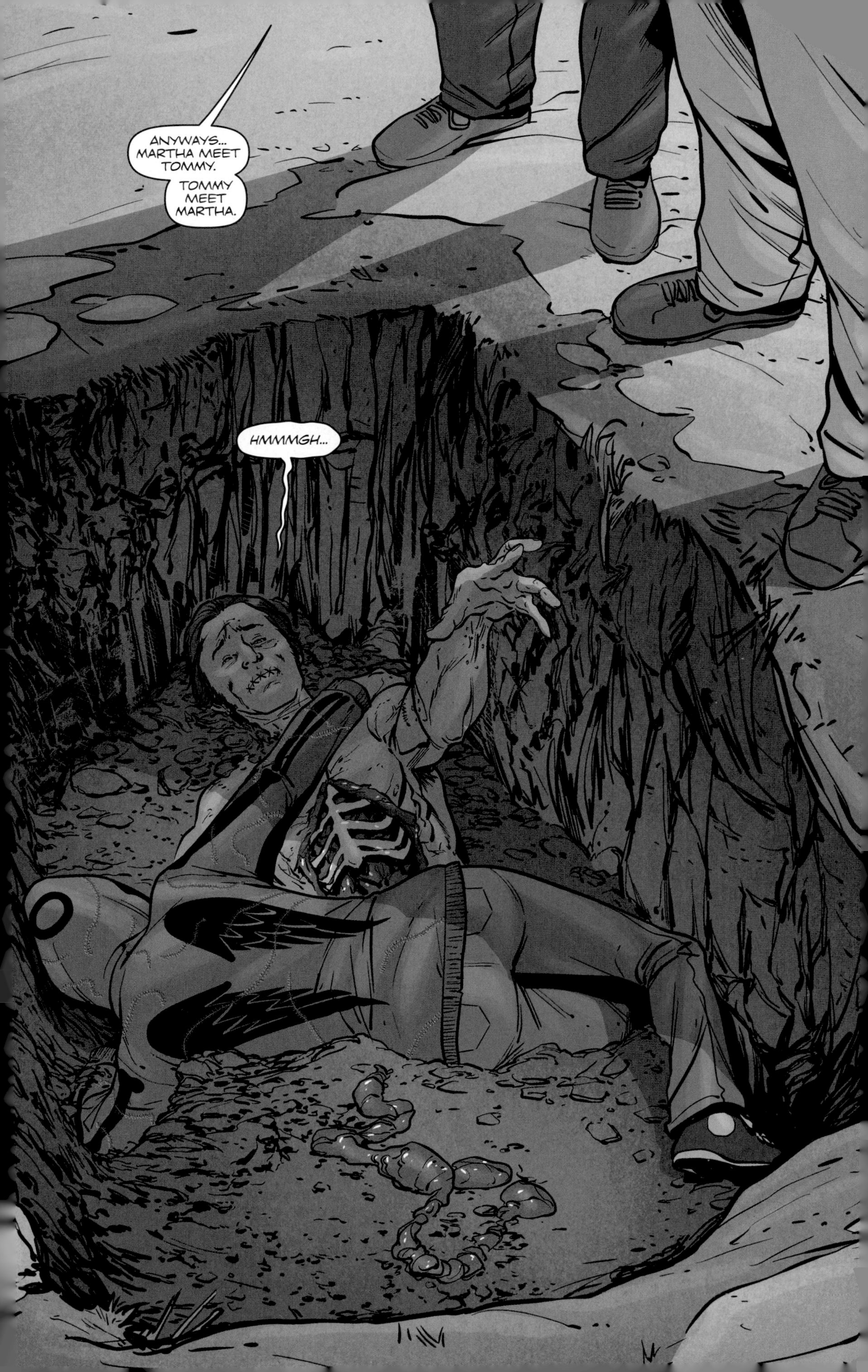
ANYWAYS... MARTHA MEET TOMMY.
TOMMY MEET MARTHA.
HMMMGH...

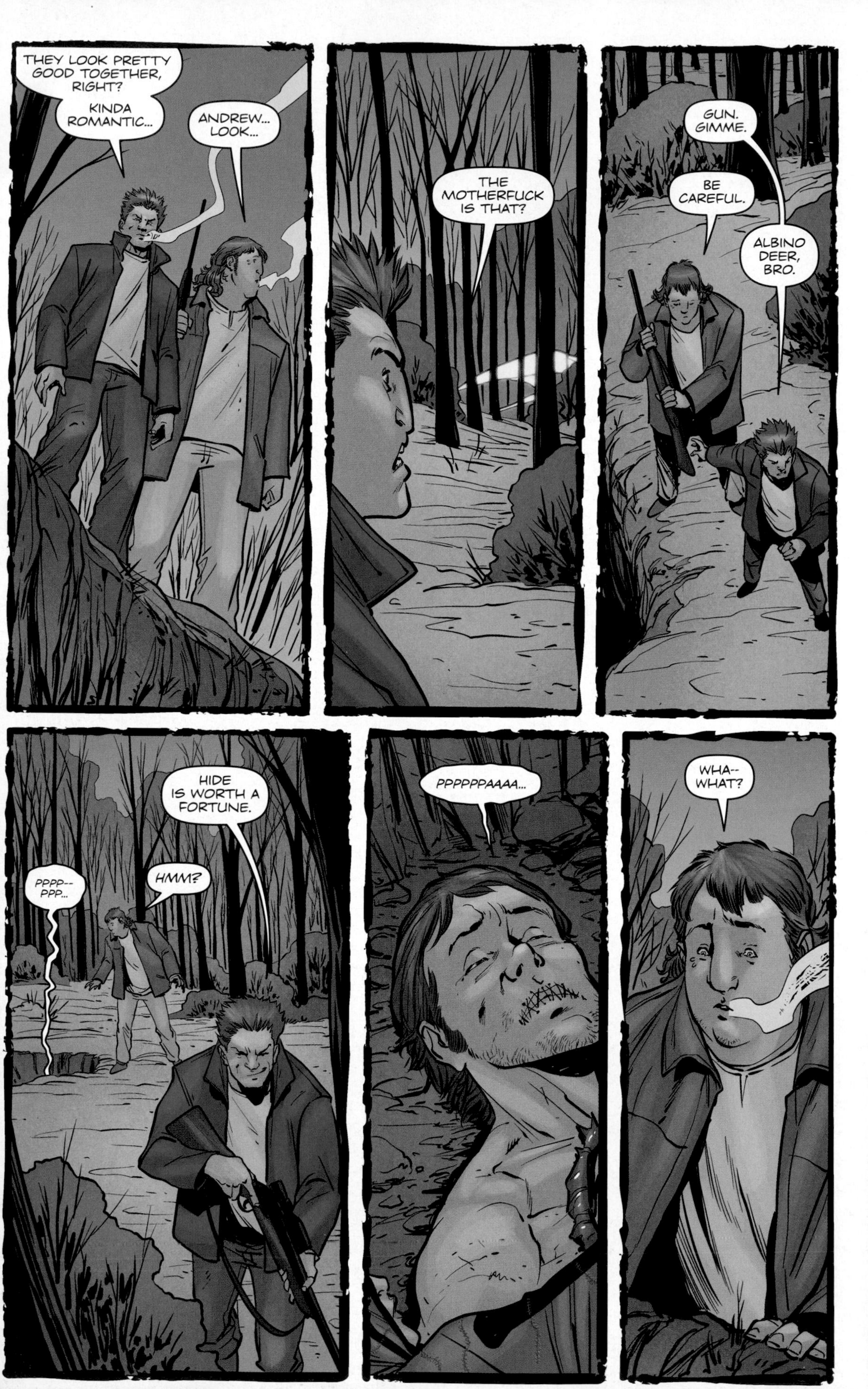
THEY LOOK PRETTY GOOD TOGETHER, RIGHT?
KINDA ROMANTIC...
ANDREW... LOOK...
THE MOTHERFUCK IS THAT?
GUN. GIMME.
BE CAREFUL.
ALBINO DEER, BRO.
HIDE IS WORTH A FORTUNE.
HMM?
PPPP-- PPP...
PPPPPPAAAA...
WHA-- WHAT?

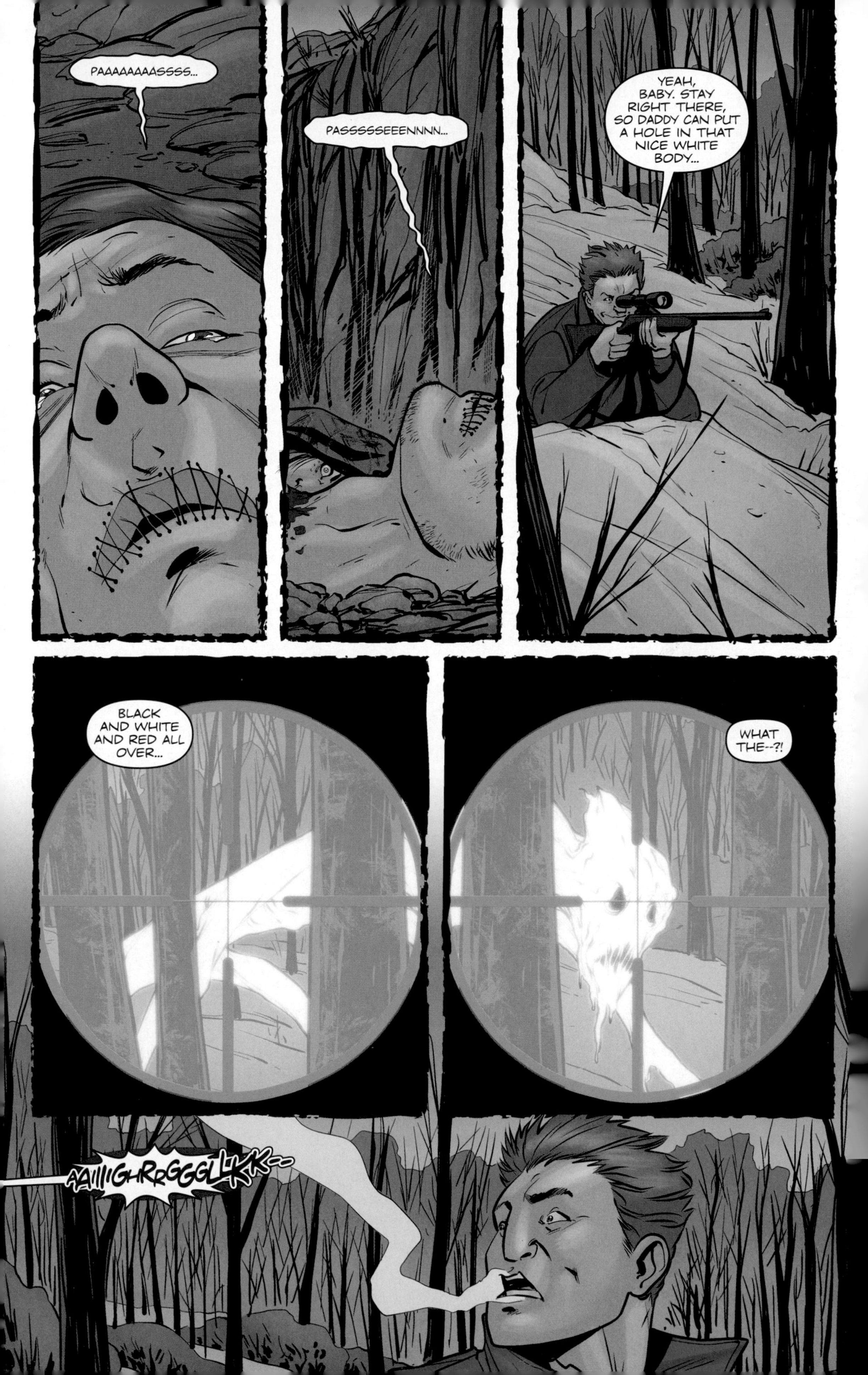
PAAAAAAAASSSS...
PASSSSSEEENNNN...
YEAH, BABY. STAY RIGHT THERE, SO DADDY CAN PUT A HOLE IN THAT NICE WHITE BODY...
BLACK AND WHITE AND RED ALL OVER...
WHAT THE--?!
AAIIIIGHRRGGGLLKKK--

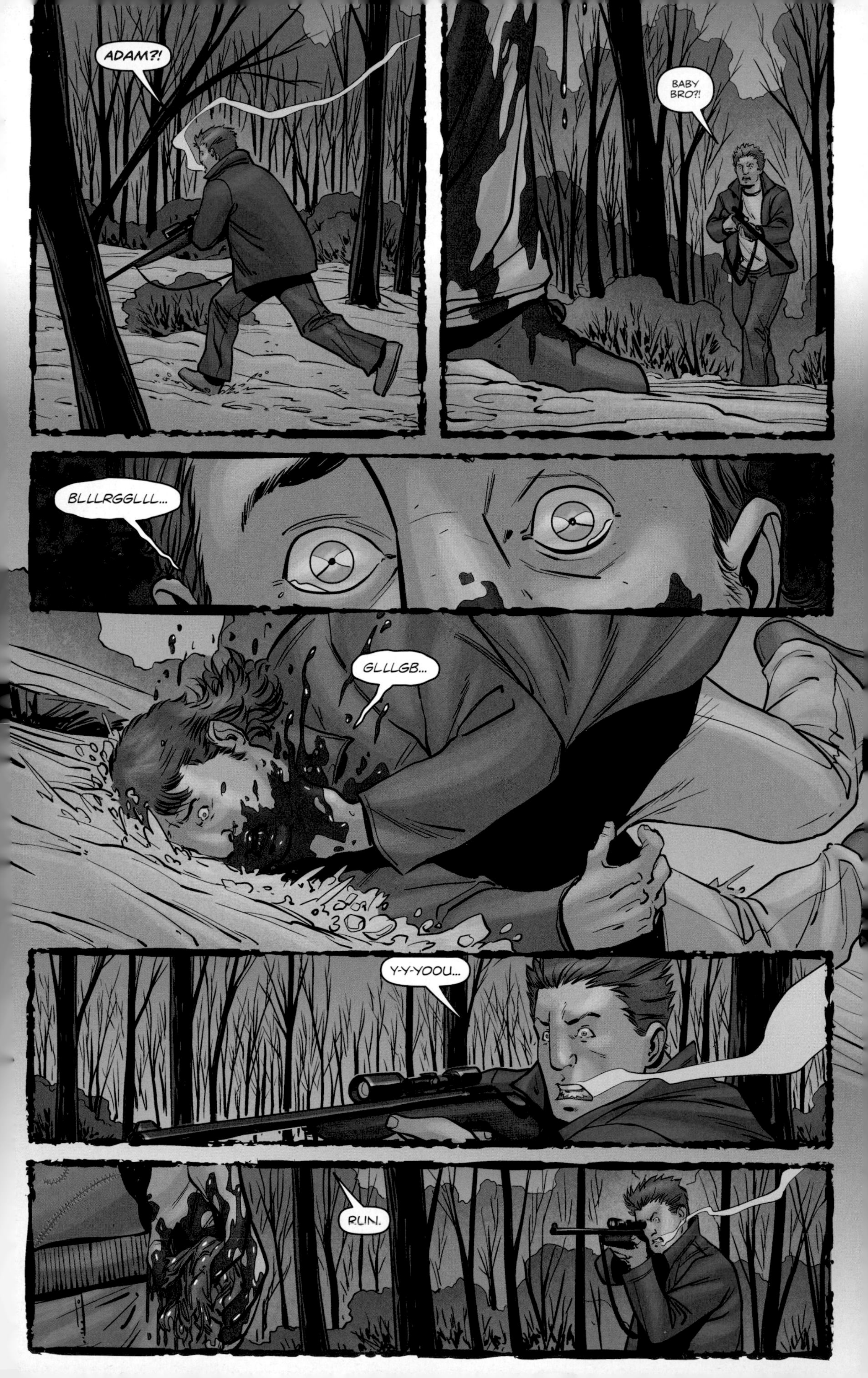
ADAM?!
BABY BRO?!
BLLLRGGLLL...
GLLLGB...
Y-Y-YOOU...
RUN.

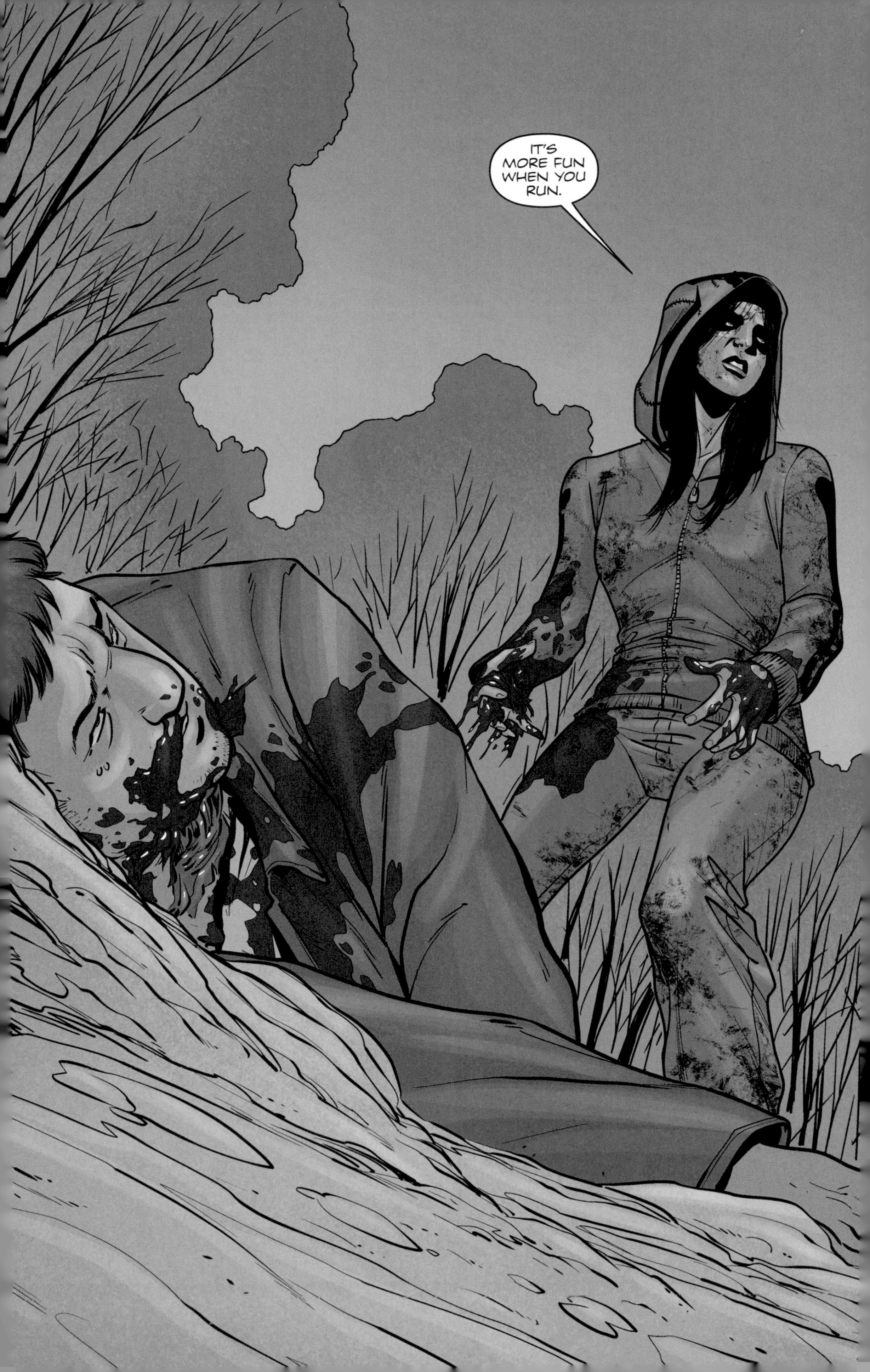
IT'S MORE FUN WHEN YOU RUN.

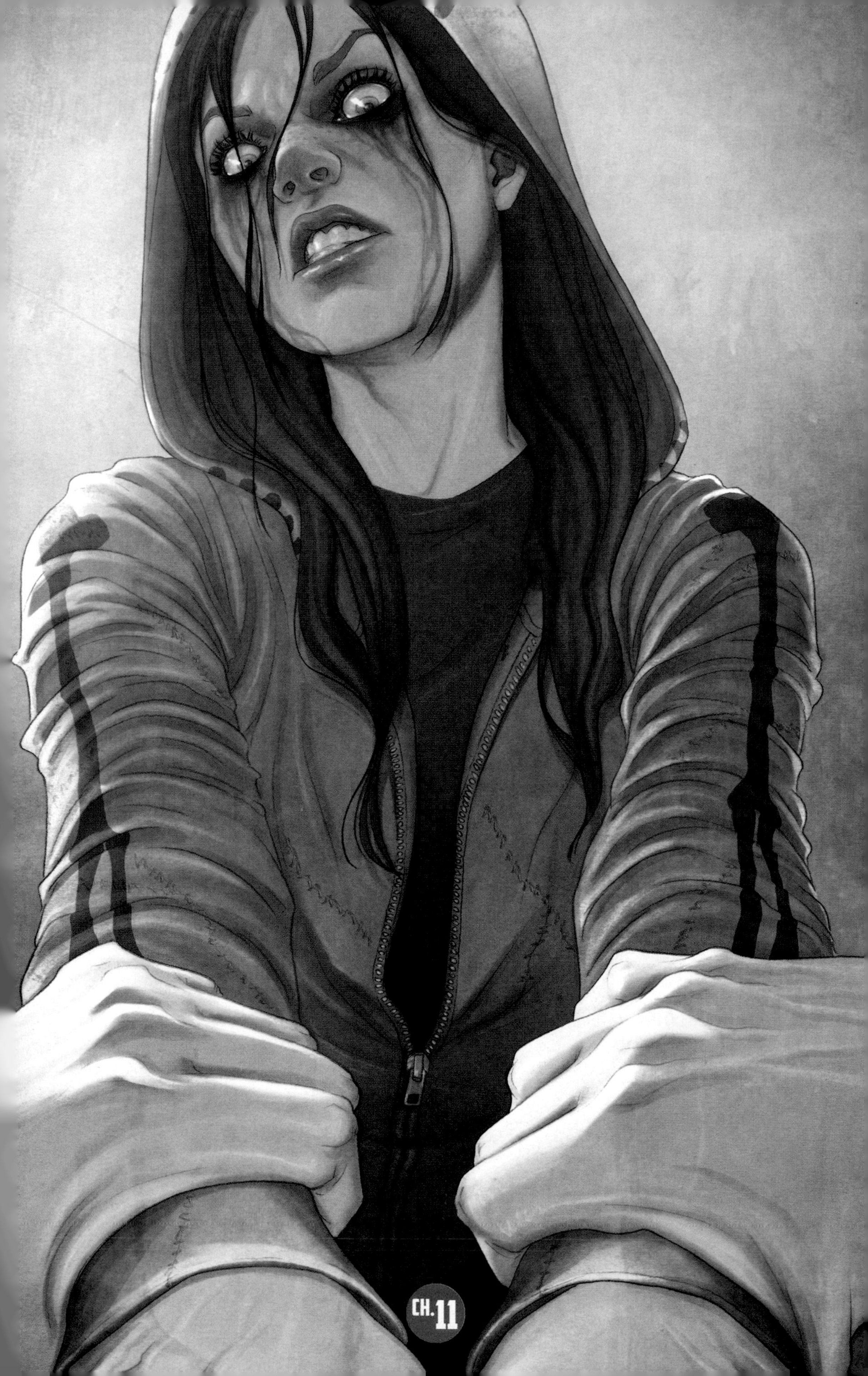
CH. 11

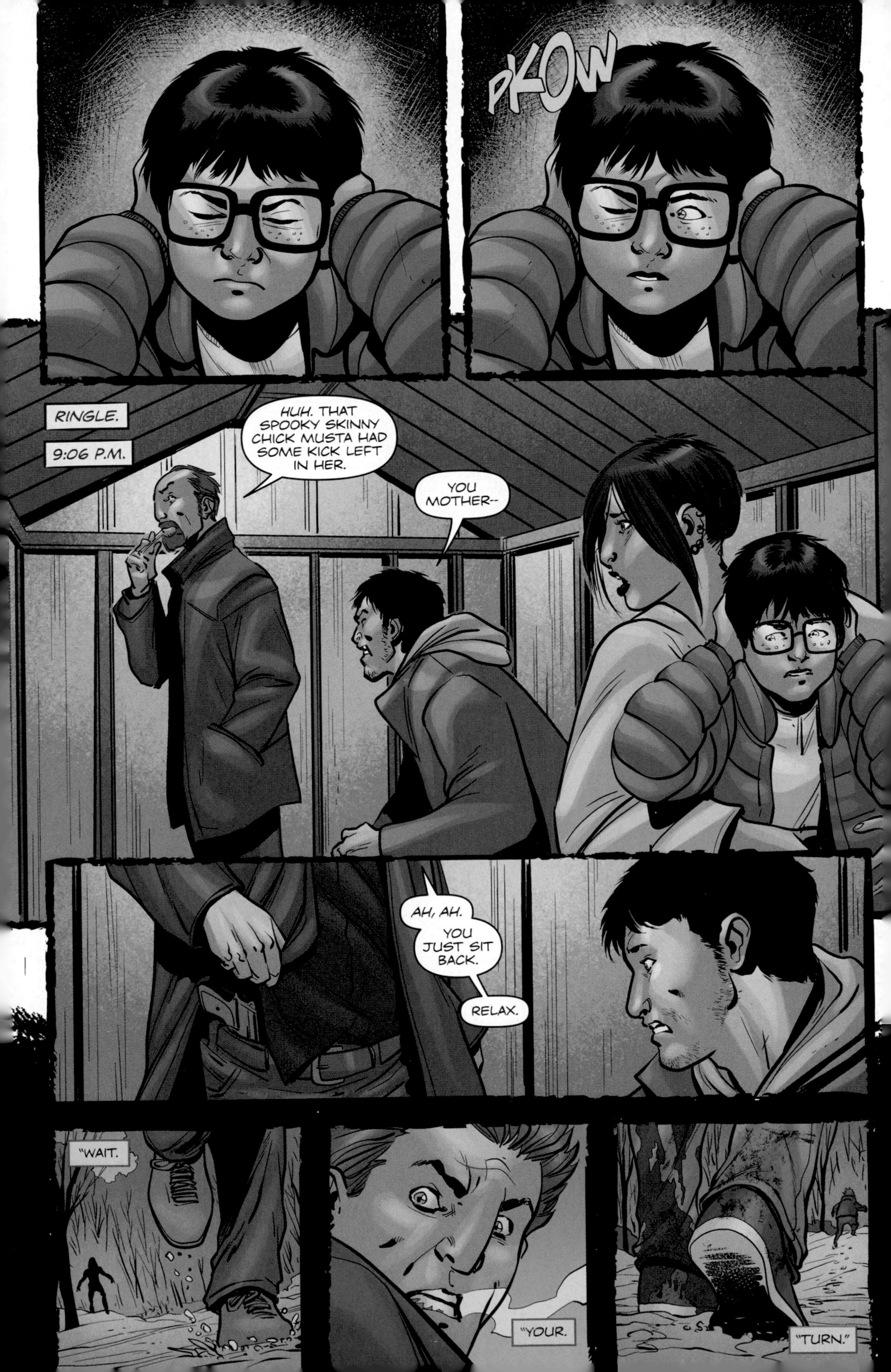
PKOW
RINGLE.
9:06 P.M.
HUH. THAT SPOOKY SKINNY CHICK MUSTA HAD SOME KICK LEFT IN HER.
YOU MOTHER--
AH, AH.
YOU JUST SIT BACK.
RELAX.
"WAIT.
"YOUR.
"TURN."

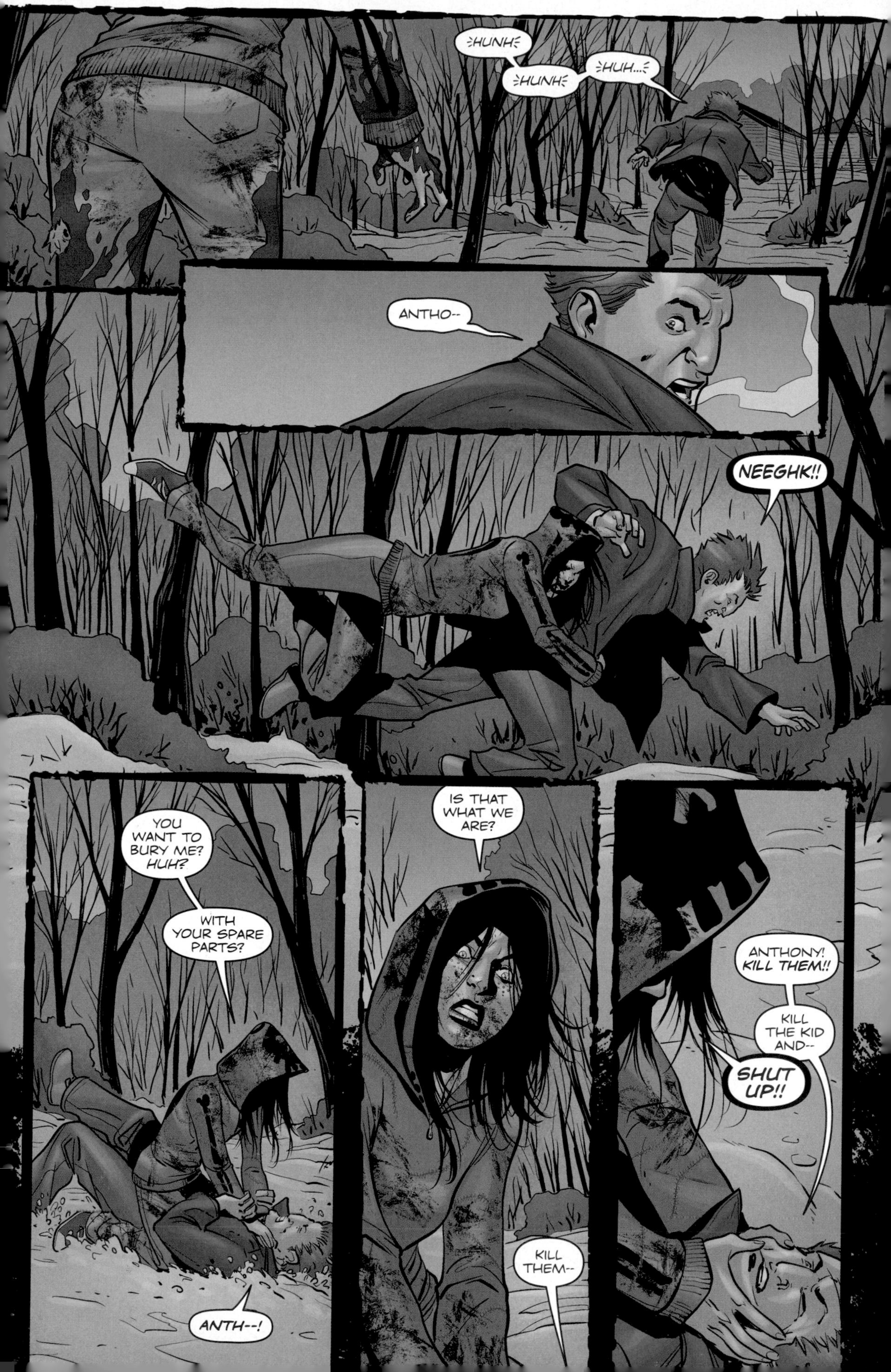

HUNH
HUNH
HUH...
ANTHO--
NEEGHK!!
YOU WANT TO BURY ME? HUH?
WITH YOUR SPARE PARTS?
ANTH--!
IS THAT WHAT WE ARE?
KILL THEM--
ANTHONY! KILL THEM!!
KILL THE KID AND--
SHUT UP!!

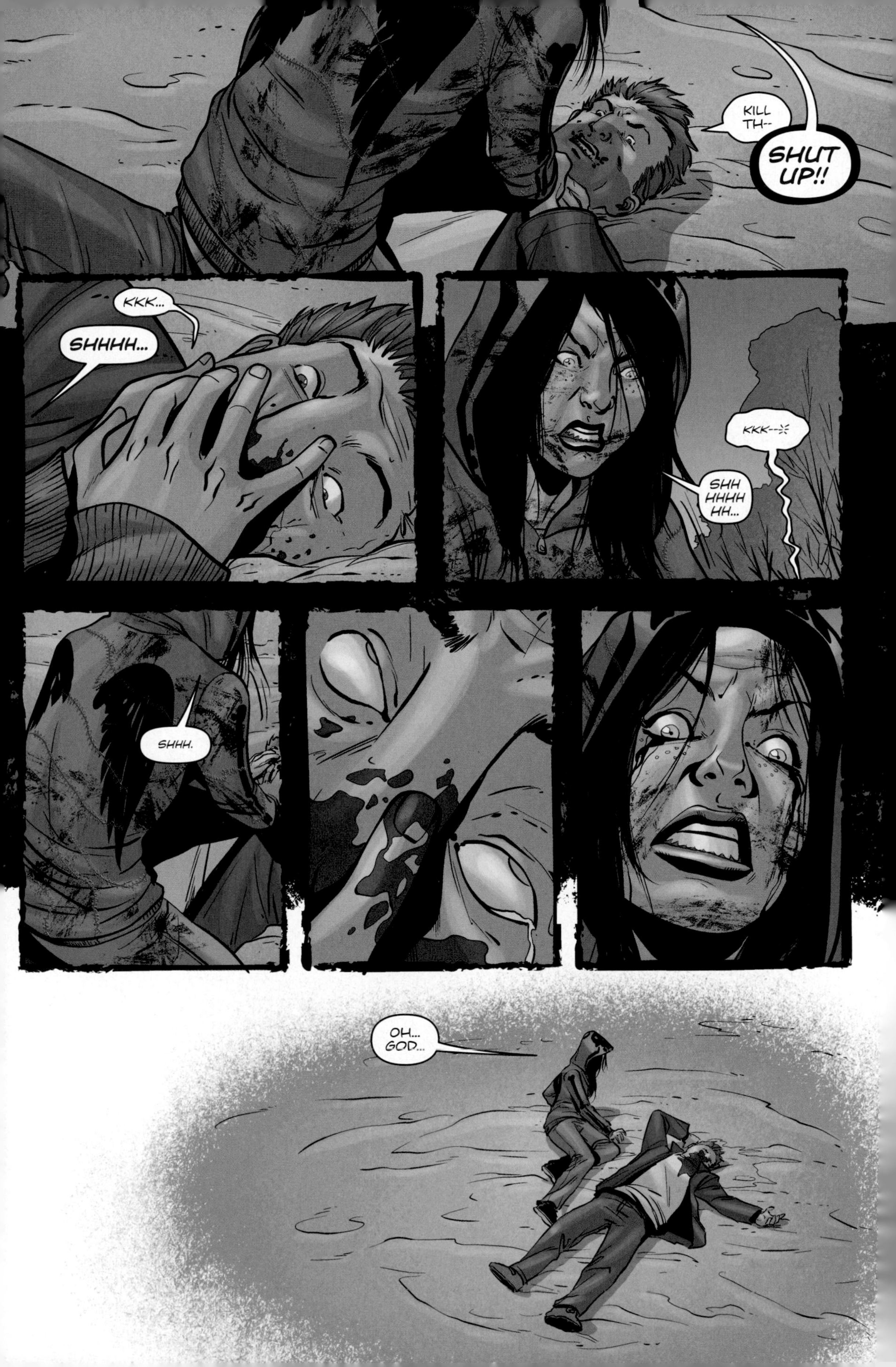
KILL TH--
SHUT UP!!
KKK...
SHHHH...
KKK--
SHH HHHH HH...
SHHH.
OH... GOD...

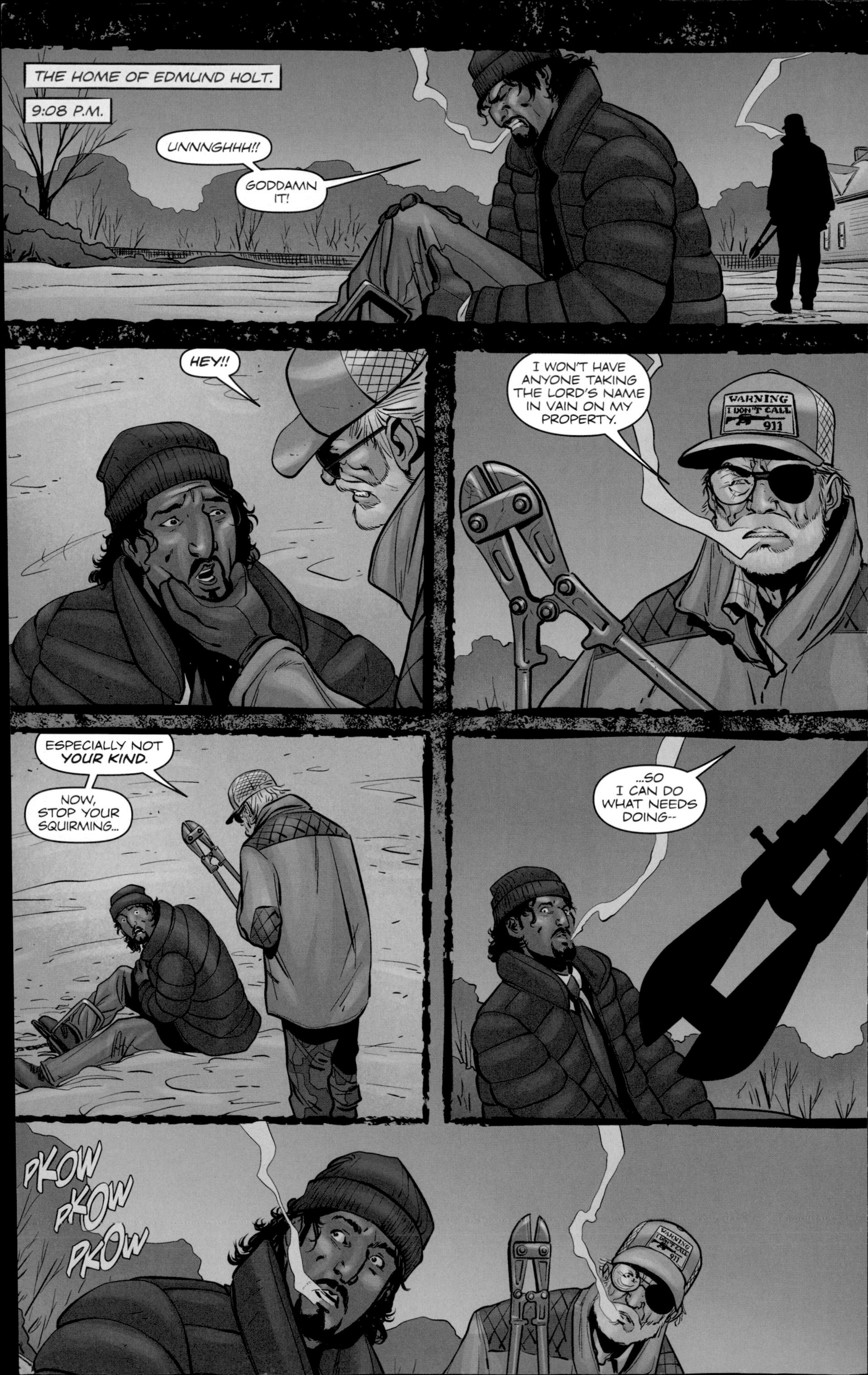
THE HOME OF EDMUND HOLT.
9:08 P.M.
UNNNGHHH!!
GODDAMN IT!
HEY!!
I WON'T HAVE ANYONE TAKING THE LORD'S NAME IN VAIN ON MY PROPERTY.
WARNING I DON'T CALL 911
ESPECIALLY NOT YOUR KIND.
NOW, STOP YOUR SQUIRMING...
...SO I CAN DO WHAT NEEDS DOING--
PKOW PKOW PKOW

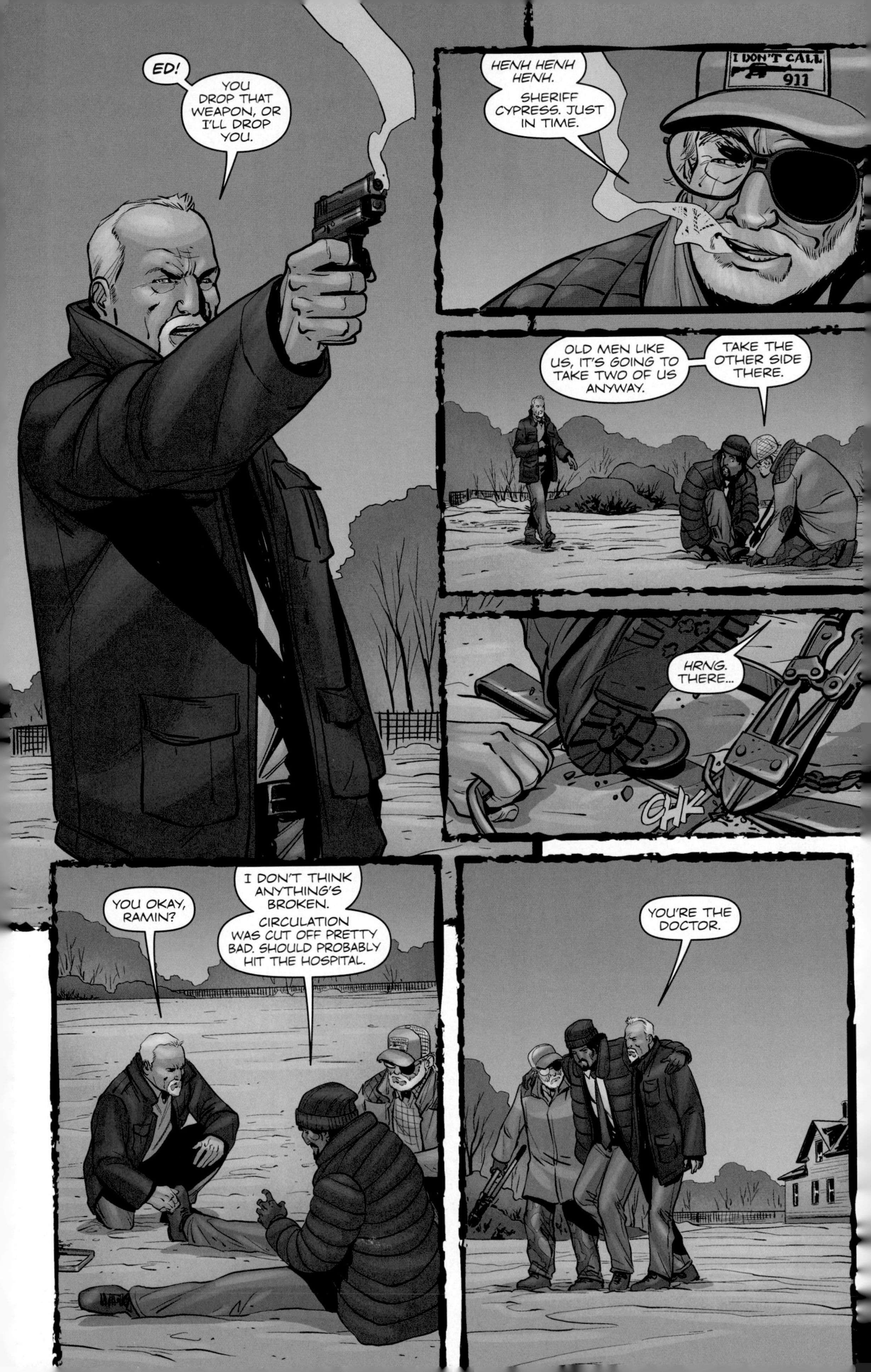
ED!
YOU DROP THAT WEAPON, OR I'LL DROP YOU.
I DON'T CALL 911
HENH HENH HENH.
SHERIFF CYPRESS. JUST IN TIME.
OLD MEN LIKE US, IT'S GOING TO TAKE TWO OF US ANYWAY.
TAKE THE OTHER SIDE THERE.
HRNG. THERE...
CHK
YOU OKAY, RAMIN?
I DON'T THINK ANYTHING'S BROKEN.
CIRCULATION WAS CUT OFF PRETTY BAD. SHOULD PROBABLY HIT THE HOSPITAL.
YOU'RE THE DOCTOR.

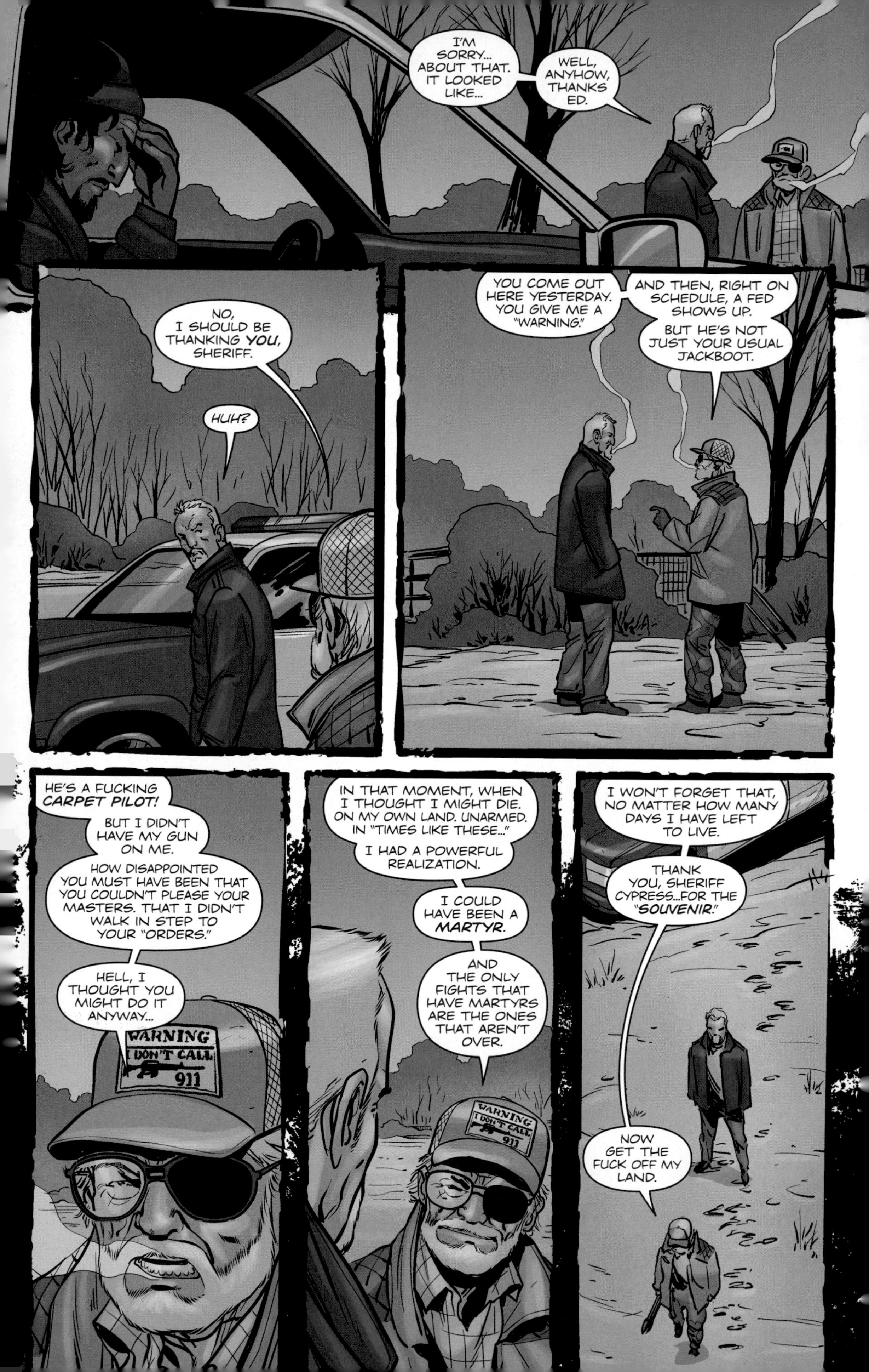
I'M SORRY... ABOUT THAT. IT LOOKED LIKE...
WELL, ANYHOW, THANKS ED.
NO, I SHOULD BE THANKING YOU, SHERIFF.
HUH?
YOU COME OUT HERE YESTERDAY. YOU GIVE ME A "WARNING."
AND THEN, RIGHT ON SCHEDULE, A FED SHOWS UP.
BUT HE'S NOT JUST YOUR USUAL JACKBOOT.
HE'S A FUCKING CARPET PILOT!
BUT I DIDN'T HAVE MY GUN ON ME.
HOW DISAPPOINTED YOU MUST HAVE BEEN THAT YOU COULDN'T PLEASE YOUR MASTERS. THAT I DIDN'T WALK IN STEP TO YOUR "ORDERS."
HELL, I THOUGHT YOU MIGHT DO IT ANYWAY...
WARNING
I DON'T CALL
911
IN THAT MOMENT, WHEN I THOUGHT I MIGHT DIE. ON MY OWN LAND. UNARMED. IN "TIMES LIKE THESE..."
I HAD A POWERFUL REALIZATION.
I COULD HAVE BEEN A MARTYR.
AND THE ONLY FIGHTS THAT HAVE MARTYRS ARE THE ONES THAT AREN'T OVER.
I WON'T FORGET THAT, NO MATTER HOW MANY DAYS I HAVE LEFT TO LIVE.
THANK YOU, SHERIFF CYPRESS...FOR THE "SOUVENIR."
NOW GET THE FUCK OFF MY LAND.

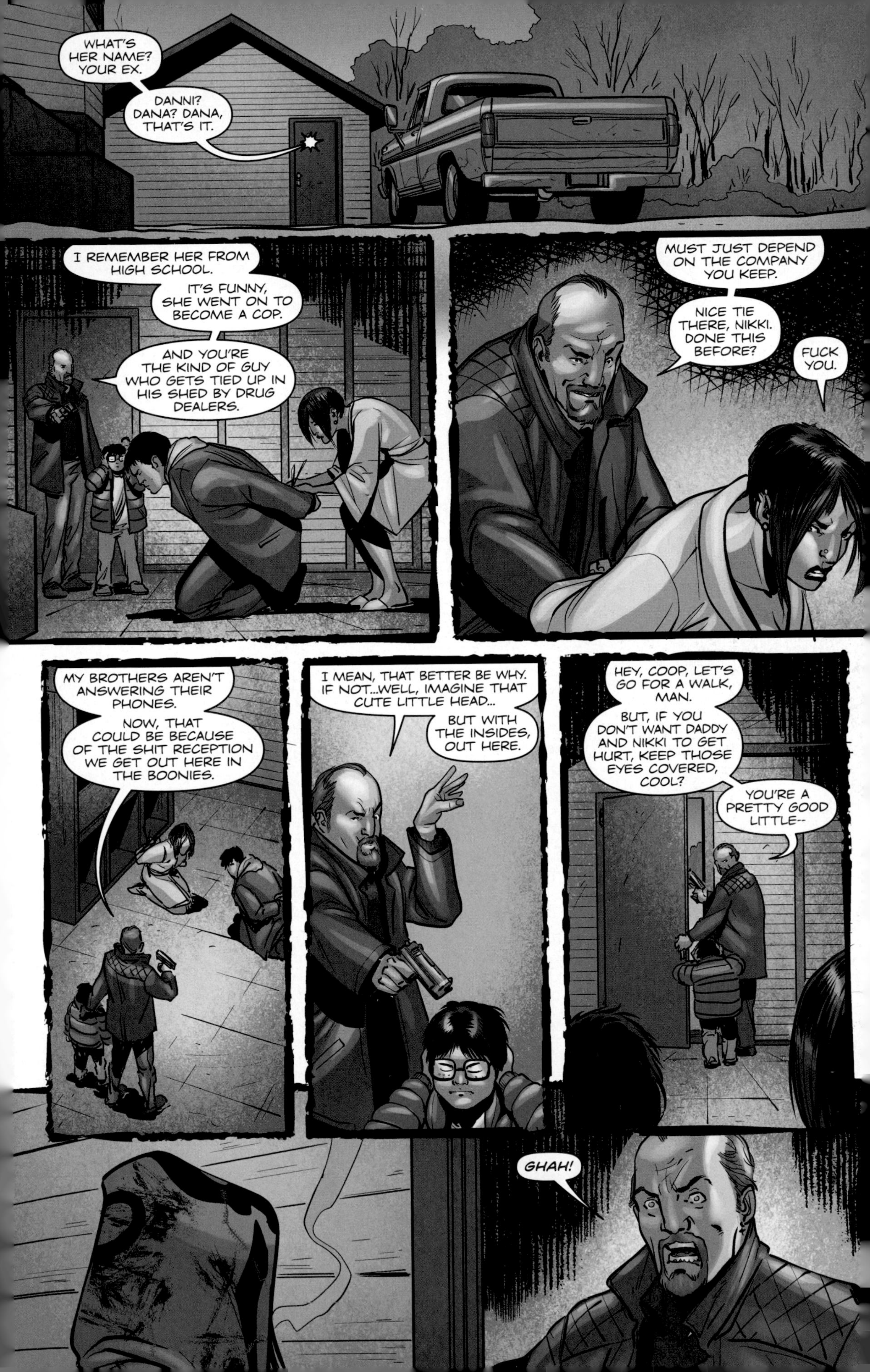
WHAT'S HER NAME? YOUR EX.
DANNI? DANA? DANA, THAT'S IT.
I REMEMBER HER FROM HIGH SCHOOL.
IT'S FUNNY, SHE WENT ON TO BECOME A COP.
AND YOU'RE THE KIND OF GUY WHO GETS TIED UP IN HIS SHED BY DRUG DEALERS.
MUST JUST DEPEND ON THE COMPANY YOU KEEP.
NICE TIE THERE, NIKKI. DONE THIS BEFORE?
FUCK YOU.
MY BROTHERS AREN'T ANSWERING THEIR PHONES.
NOW, THAT COULD BE BECAUSE OF THE SHIT RECEPTION WE GET OUT HERE IN THE BOONIES.
I MEAN, THAT BETTER BE WHY. IF NOT...WELL, IMAGINE THAT CUTE LITTLE HEAD...
BUT WITH THE INSIDES, OUT HERE.
HEY, COOP, LET'S GO FOR A WALK, MAN.
BUT, IF YOU DON'T WANT DADDY AND NIKKI TO GET HURT, KEEP THOSE EYES COVERED, COOL?
YOU'RE A PRETTY GOOD LITTLE--
GHAH!

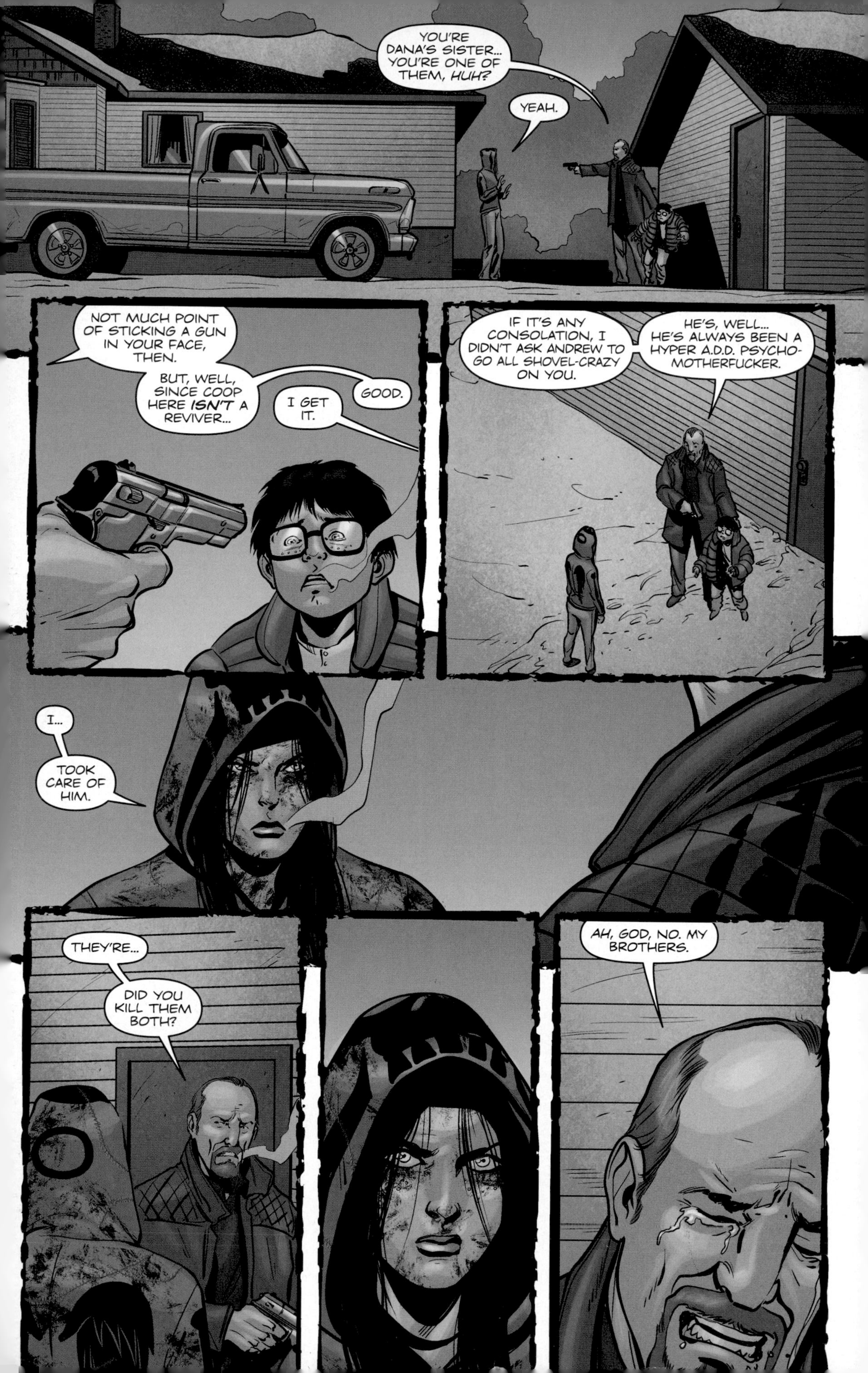
YOU'RE DANA'S SISTER... YOU'RE ONE OF THEM, HUH?
YEAH.
NOT MUCH POINT OF STICKING A GUN IN YOUR FACE, THEN.
BUT, WELL, SINCE COOP HERE ISN'T A REVIVER...
GOOD.
I GET IT.
IF IT'S ANY CONSOLATION, I DIDN'T ASK ANDREW TO GO ALL SHOVEL-CRAZY ON YOU.
HE'S, WELL... HE'S ALWAYS BEEN A HYPER A.D.D. PSYCHO-MOTHERFUCKER.
I...
TOOK CARE OF HIM.
THEY'RE...
DID YOU KILL THEM BOTH?
AH, GOD, NO. MY BROTHERS.

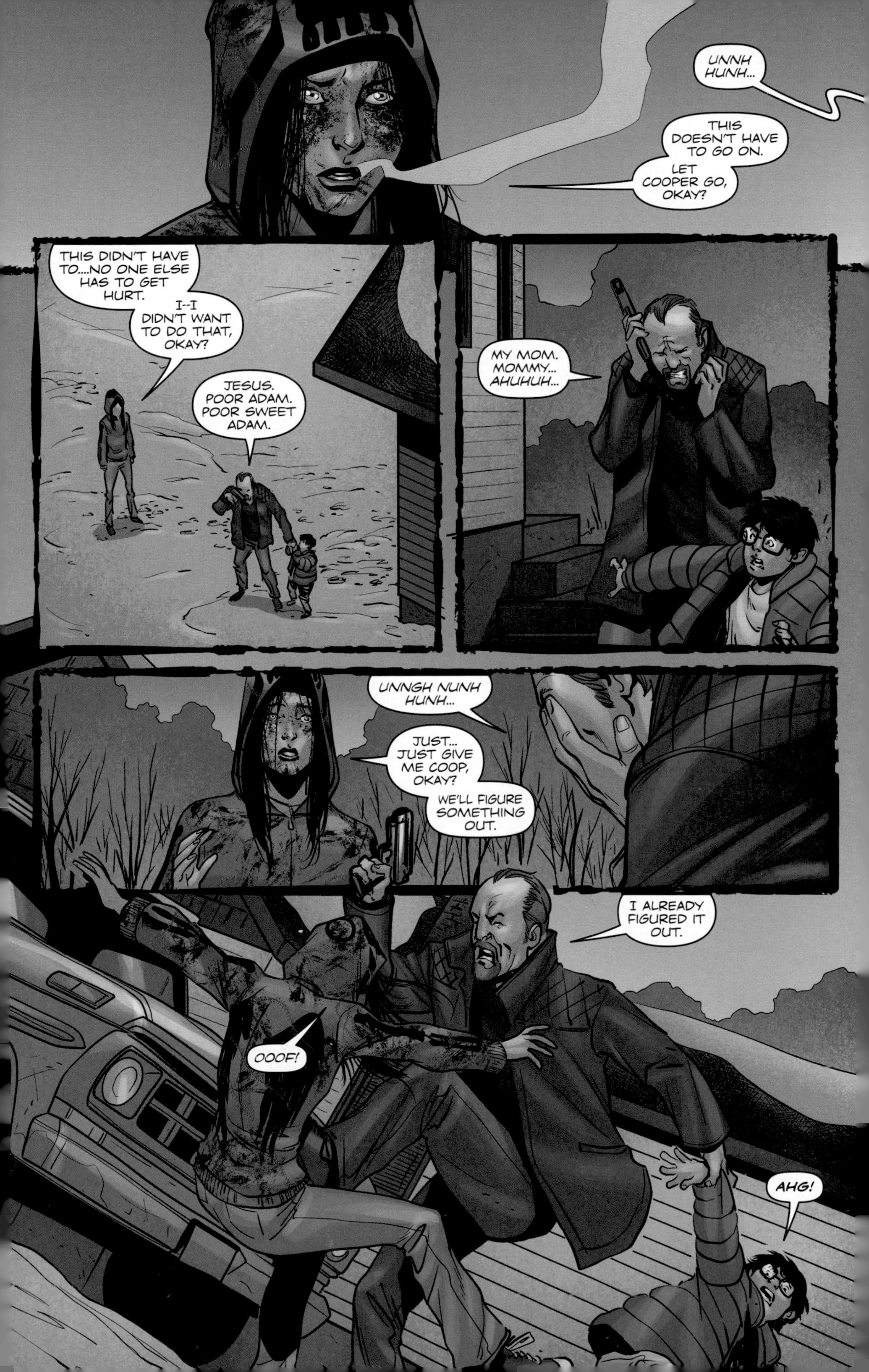
UNNH HUNH...
THIS DOESN'T HAVE TO GO ON.
LET COOPER GO, OKAY?
THIS DIDN'T HAVE TO....NO ONE ELSE HAS TO GET HURT.
I--I DIDN'T WANT TO DO THAT, OKAY?
JESUS. POOR ADAM. POOR SWEET ADAM.
MY MOM. MOMMY... AHUHUH...
UNNGH NUNH HUNH...
JUST... JUST GIVE ME COOP, OKAY?
WE'LL FIGURE SOMETHING OUT.
I ALREADY FIGURED IT OUT.
OOOF!
AHG!

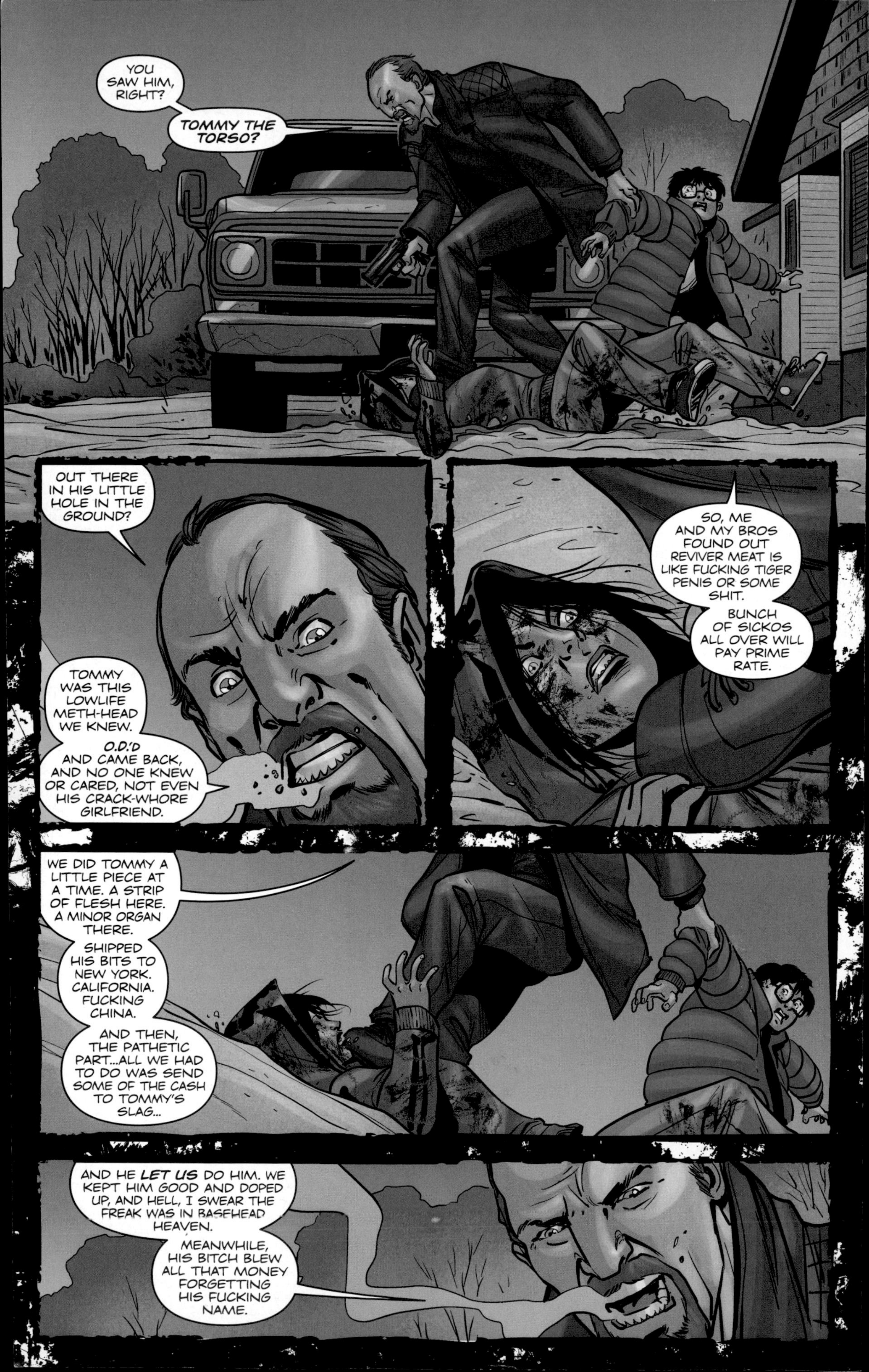
YOU SAW HIM, RIGHT?
TOMMY THE TORSO?
OUT THERE IN HIS LITTLE HOLE IN THE GROUND?
TOMMY WAS THIS LOWLIFE METH-HEAD WE KNEW.
O.D.'D AND CAME BACK, AND NO ONE KNEW OR CARED, NOT EVEN HIS CRACK-WHORE GIRLFRIEND.
SO, ME AND MY BROS FOUND OUT REVIVER MEAT IS LIKE FUCKING TIGER PENIS OR SOME SHIT.
BUNCH OF SICKOS ALL OVER WILL PAY PRIME RATE.
WE DID TOMMY A LITTLE PIECE AT A TIME. A STRIP OF FLESH HERE. A MINOR ORGAN THERE.
SHIPPED HIS BITS TO NEW YORK. CALIFORNIA. FUCKING CHINA.
AND THEN, THE PATHETIC PART...ALL WE HAD TO DO WAS SEND SOME OF THE CASH TO TOMMY'S SLAG...
AND HE LET US DO HIM. WE KEPT HIM GOOD AND DOPED UP, AND HELL, I SWEAR THE FREAK WAS IN BASEHEAD HEAVEN.
MEANWHILE, HIS BITCH BLEW ALL THAT MONEY FORGETTING HIS FUCKING NAME.

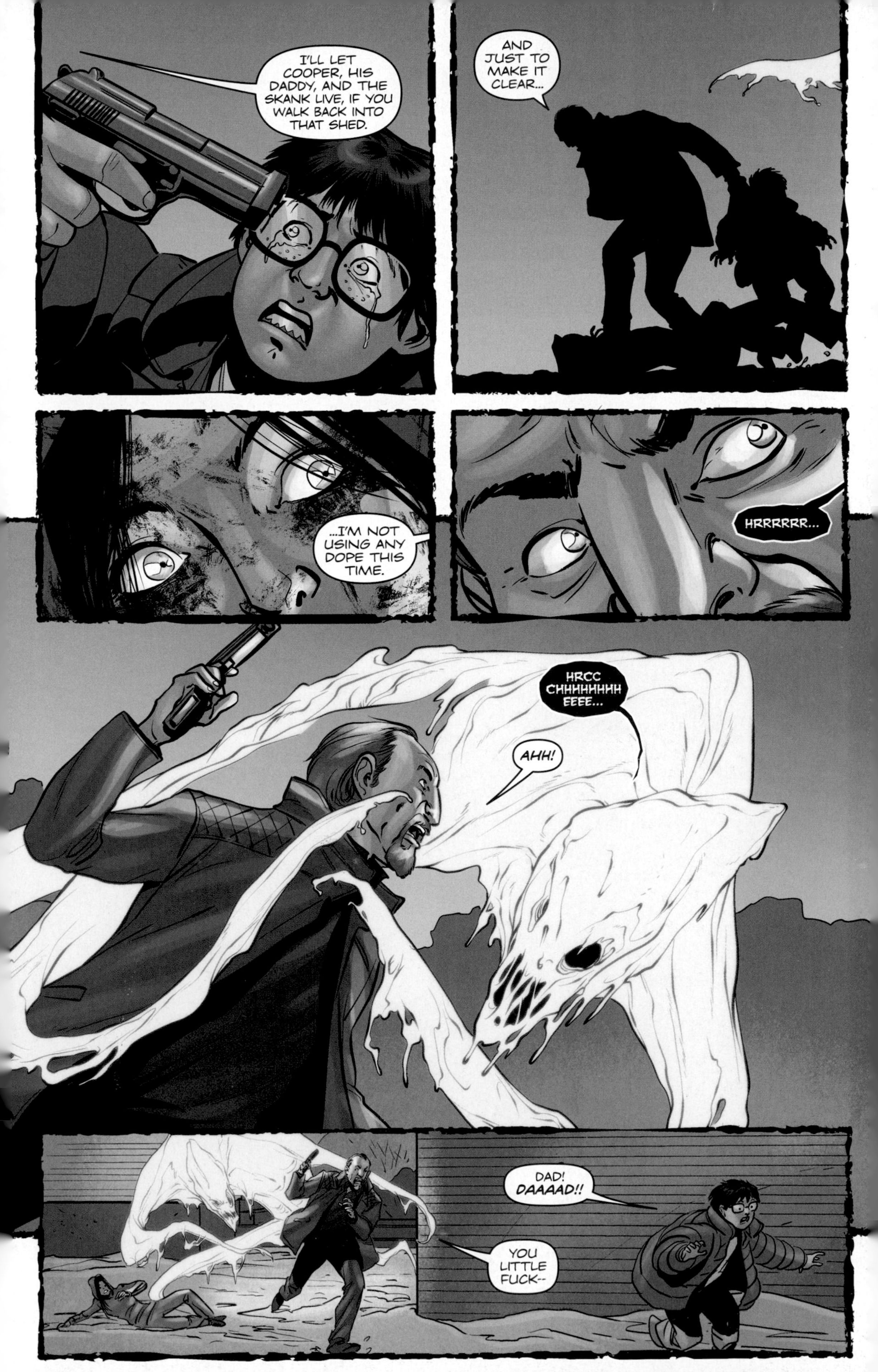
I'LL LET COOPER, HIS DADDY, AND THE SKANK LIVE, IF YOU WALK BACK INTO THAT SHED.
AND JUST TO MAKE IT CLEAR...
...I'M NOT USING ANY DOPE THIS TIME.
HRRRRRR...
HRCC CHHHHHHHH EEEE...
AHH!
DAD! DAAAAD!!
YOU LITTLE FUCK--

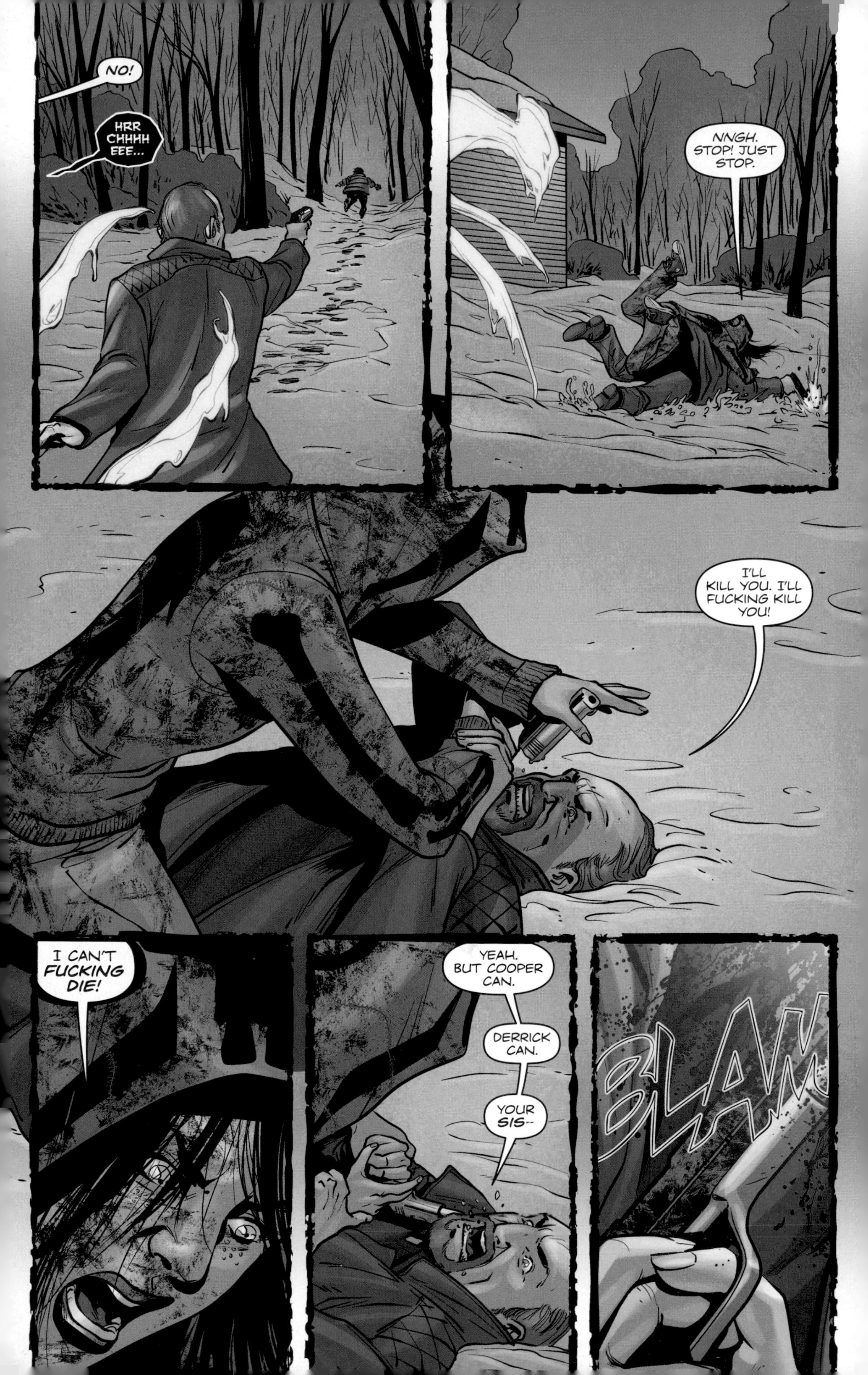
NO!
HRR CHHHH EEE...
NNGH. STOP! JUST STOP.
I'LL KILL YOU. I'LL FUCKING KILL YOU!
I CAN'T *FUCKING DIE!*
YEAH. BUT COOPER CAN.
DERRICK CAN.
YOUR *SIS--*
BLAM

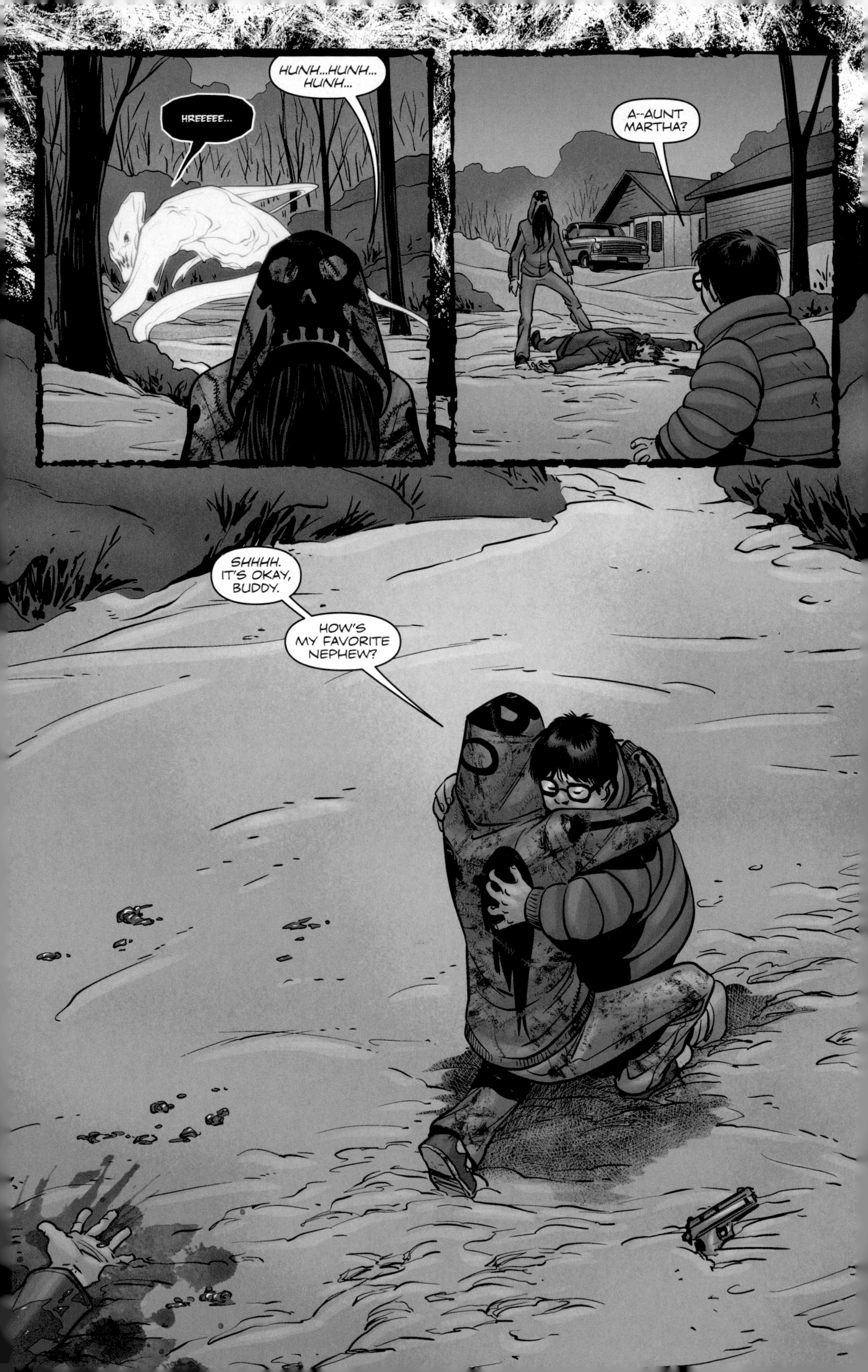
HREEEEE...
HUNH...HUNH... HUNH...
A--AUNT MARTHA?
SHHHH. IT'S OKAY, BUDDY.
HOW'S MY FAVORITE NEPHEW?

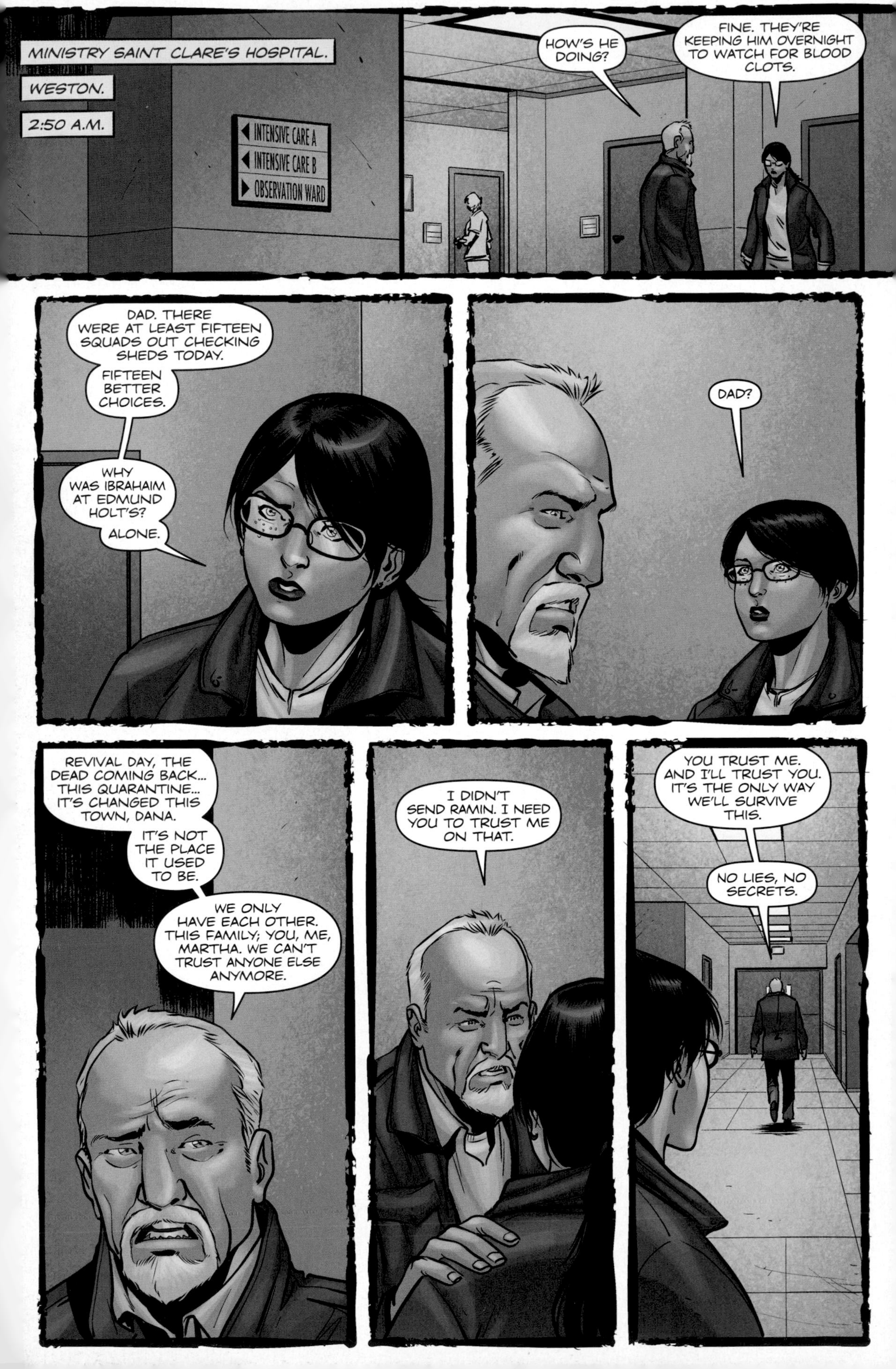

MINISTRY SAINT CLARE'S HOSPITAL.
WESTON.
2:50 A.M.
INTENSIVE CARE A
INTENSIVE CARE B
OBSERVATION WARD
HOW'S HE DOING?
FINE. THEY'RE KEEPING HIM OVERNIGHT TO WATCH FOR BLOOD CLOTS.
DAD. THERE WERE AT LEAST FIFTEEN SQUADS OUT CHECKING SHEDS TODAY.
FIFTEEN BETTER CHOICES.
WHY WAS IBRAHAIM AT EDMUND HOLT'S?
ALONE.
DAD?
REVIVAL DAY, THE DEAD COMING BACK... THIS QUARANTINE... IT'S CHANGED THIS TOWN, DANA.
IT'S NOT THE PLACE IT USED TO BE.
WE ONLY HAVE EACH OTHER. THIS FAMILY; YOU, ME, MARTHA. WE CAN'T TRUST ANYONE ELSE ANYMORE.
I DIDN'T SEND RAMIN. I NEED YOU TO TRUST ME ON THAT.
YOU TRUST ME. AND I'LL TRUST YOU. IT'S THE ONLY WAY WE'LL SURVIVE THIS.
NO LIES, NO SECRETS.

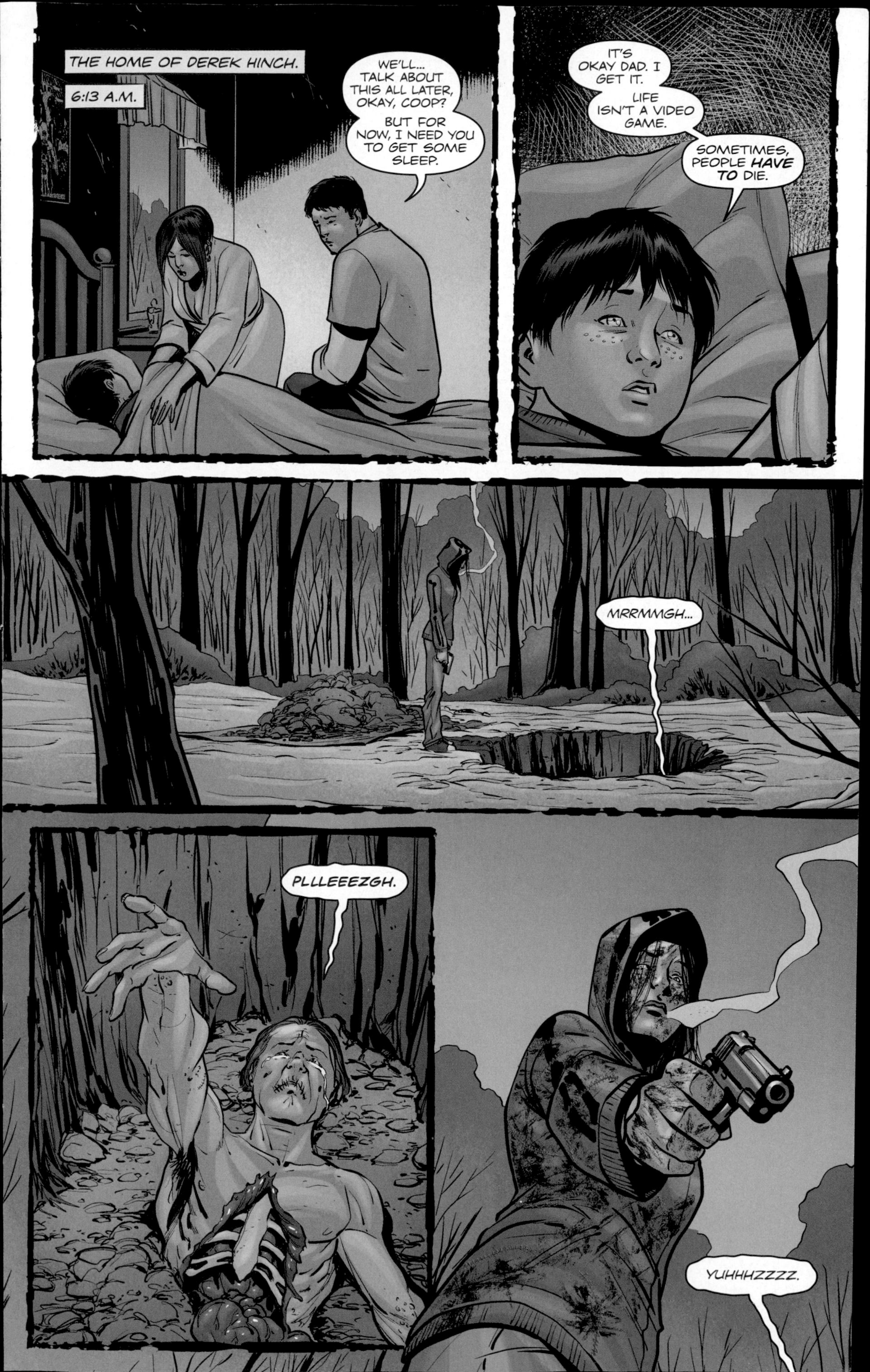
THE HOME OF DEREK HINCH.
6:13 A.M.
WE'LL... TALK ABOUT THIS ALL LATER, OKAY, COOP?
BUT FOR NOW, I NEED YOU TO GET SOME SLEEP.
IT'S OKAY DAD. I GET IT.
LIFE ISN'T A VIDEO GAME.
SOMETIMES, PEOPLE **HAVE TO** DIE.
MRRMMGH...
PLLLEEEZGH.
YUHHHZZZZ.

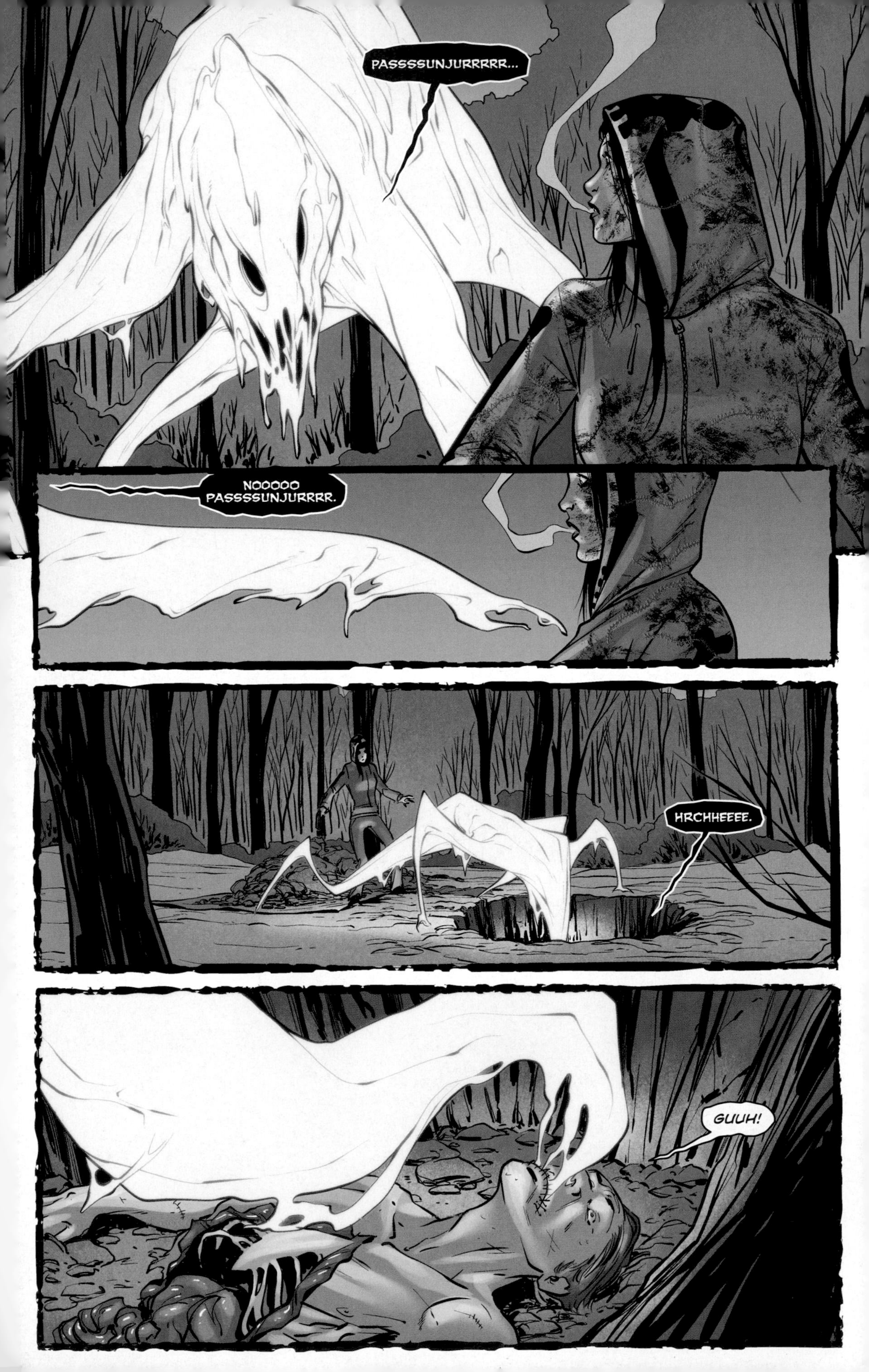
PASSSSUNJURRRRR...
NOOOOO PASSSSUNJURRRR.
HRCHHEEEE.
GUUH!

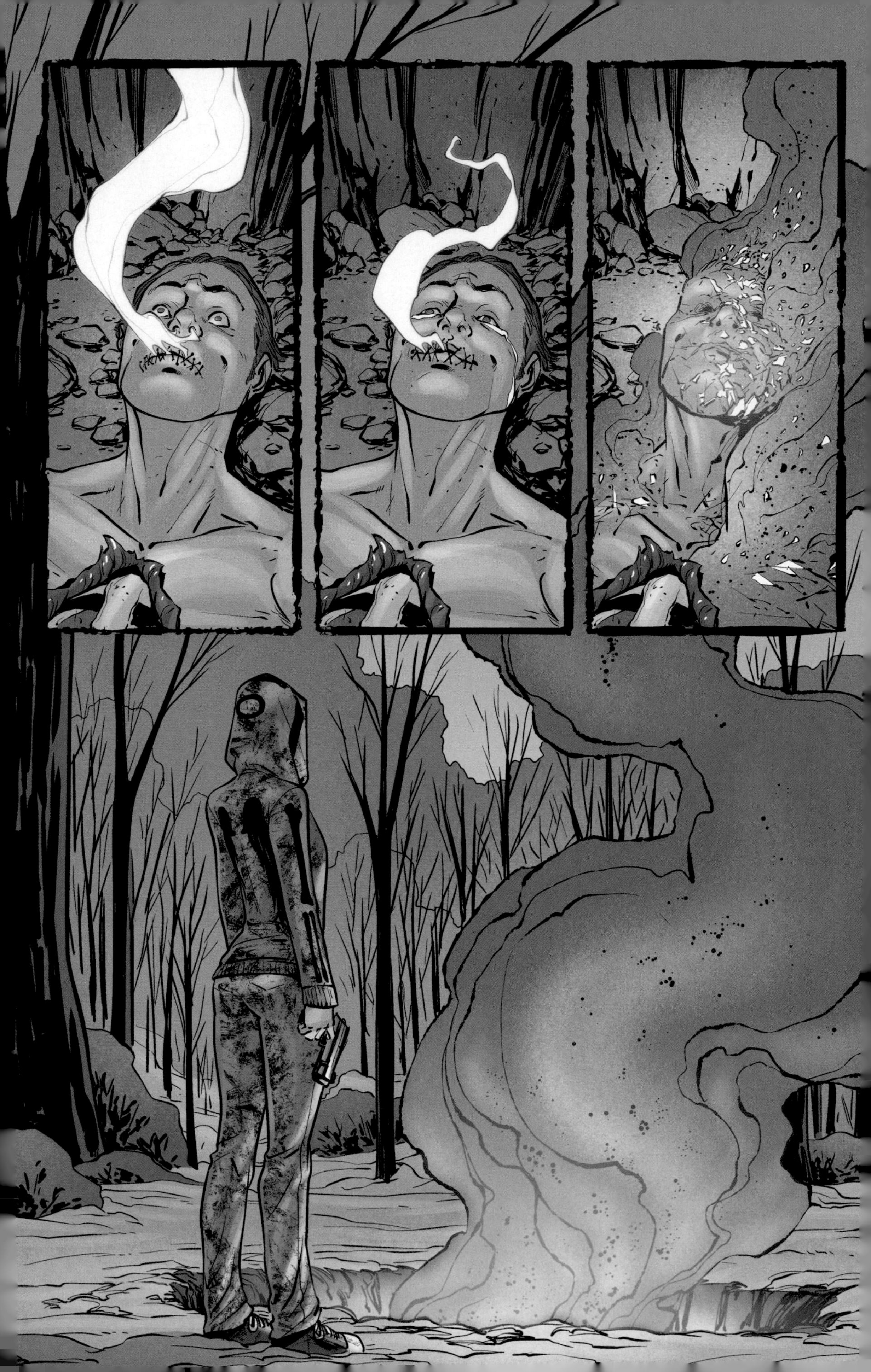

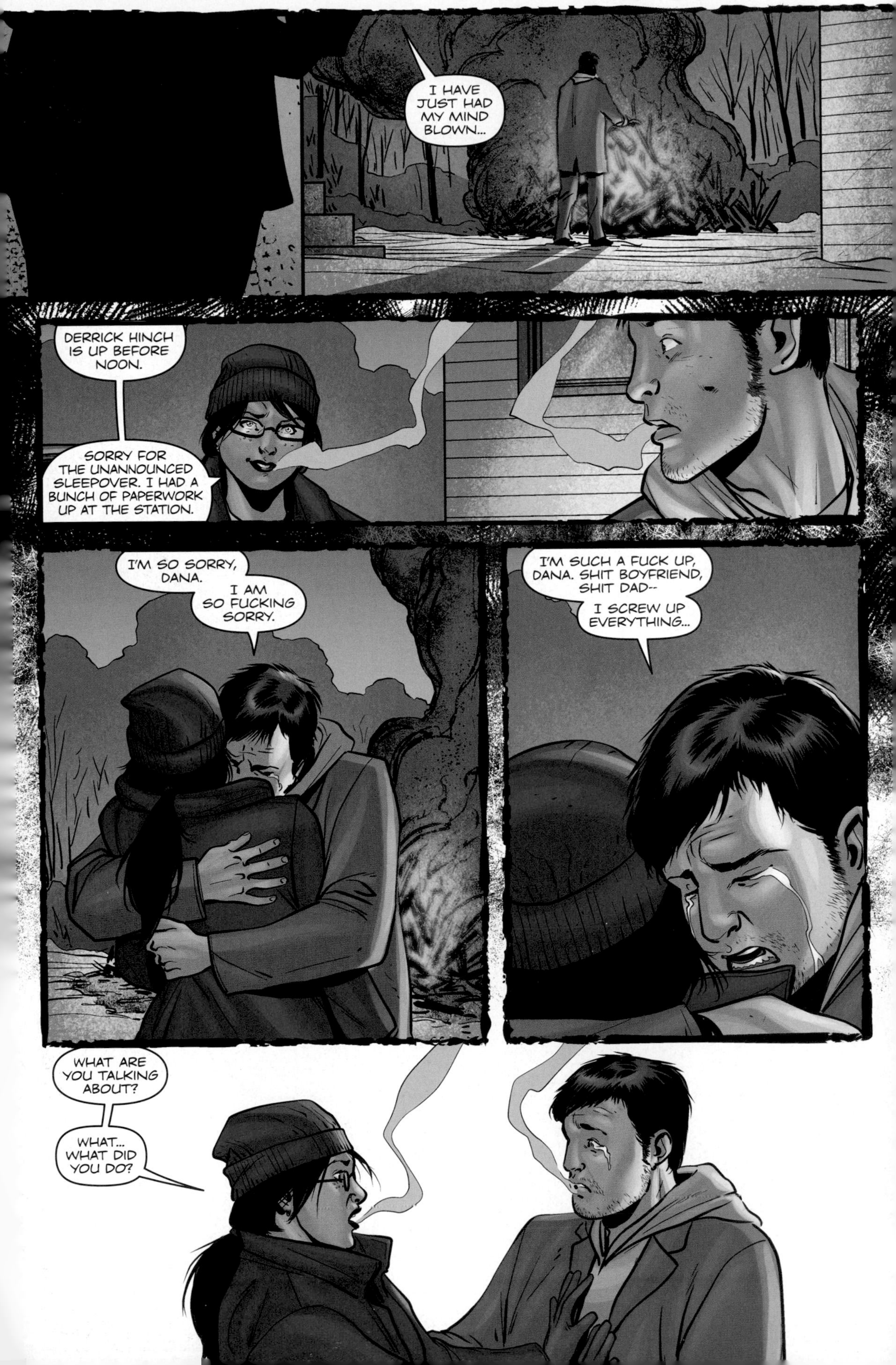
I HAVE JUST HAD MY MIND BLOWN...
DERRICK HINCH IS UP BEFORE NOON.
SORRY FOR THE UNANNOUNCED SLEEPOVER. I HAD A BUNCH OF PAPERWORK UP AT THE STATION.
I'M SO SORRY, DANA.
I AM SO FUCKING SORRY.
I'M SUCH A FUCK UP, DANA. SHIT BOYFRIEND, SHIT DAD--
I SCREW UP EVERYTHING...
WHAT ARE YOU TALKING ABOUT?
WHAT... WHAT DID YOU DO?

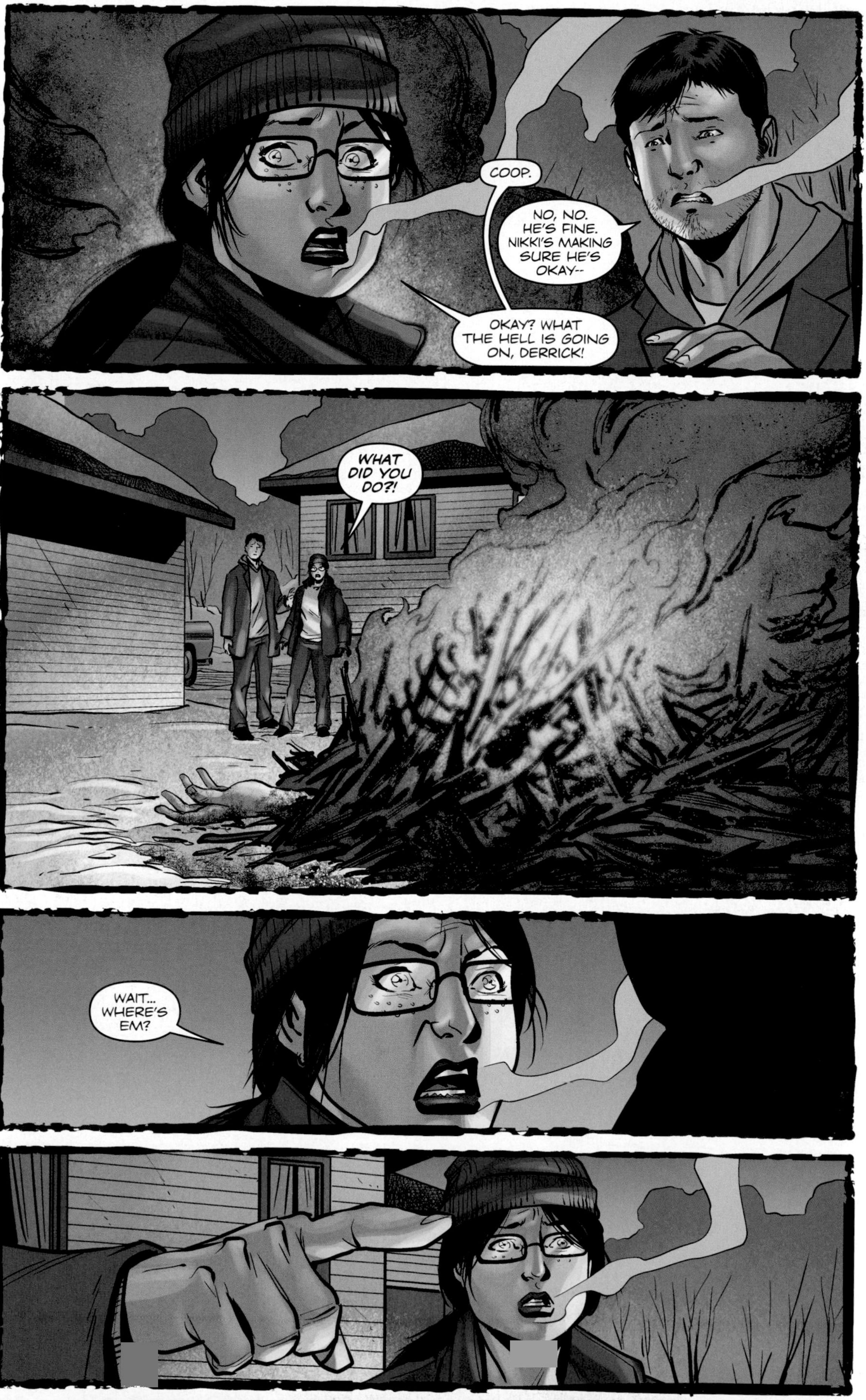
COOP.
NO, NO. HE'S FINE. NIKKI'S MAKING SURE HE'S OKAY--
OKAY? WHAT THE HELL IS GOING ON, DERRICK!
WHAT DID YOU DO?!
WAIT... WHERE'S EM?

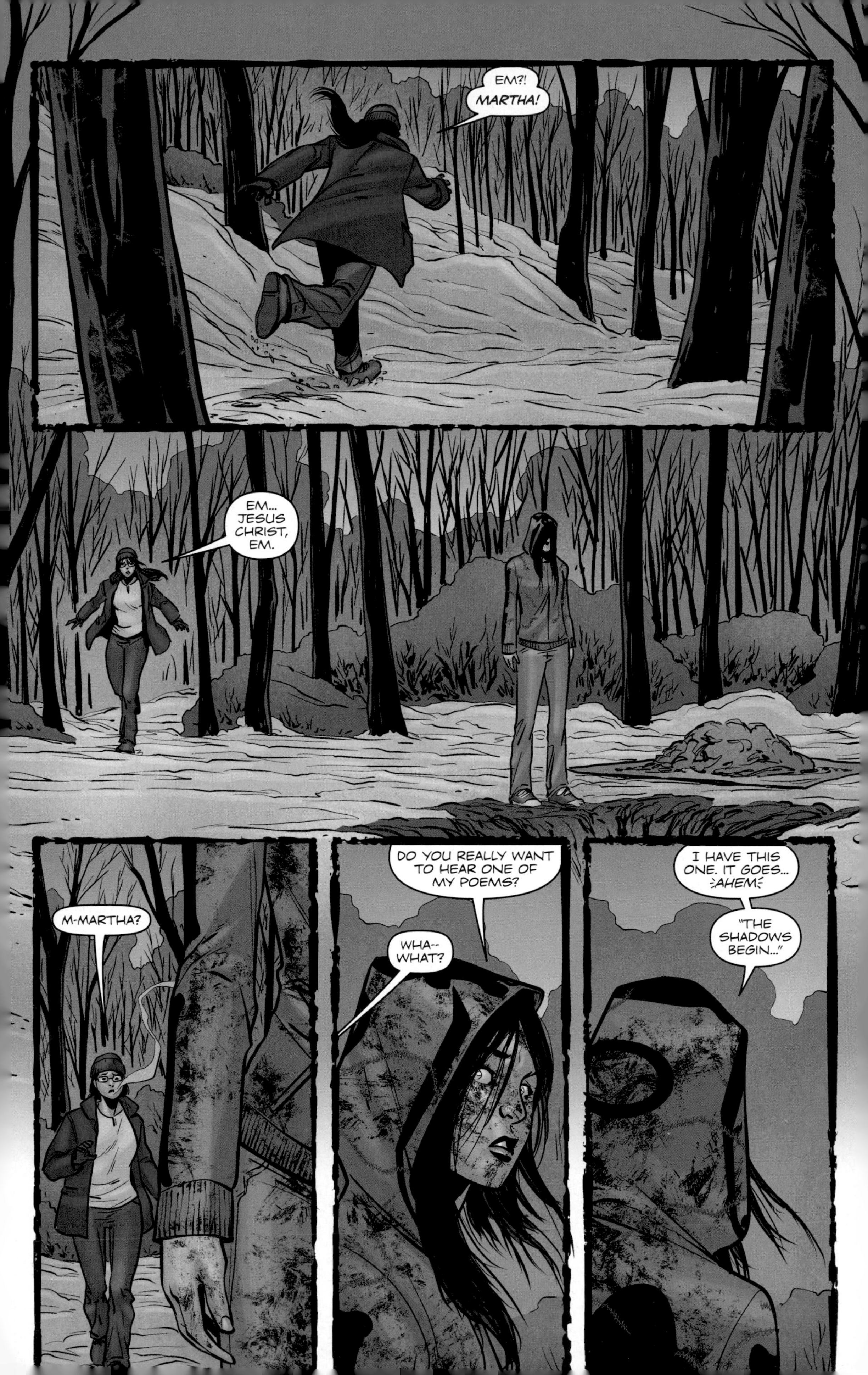
EM?! MARTHA!
EM... JESUS CHRIST, EM.
M-MARTHA?
DO YOU REALLY WANT TO HEAR ONE OF MY POEMS?
WHA-- WHAT?
I HAVE THIS ONE. IT GOES... AHEM
"THE SHADOWS BEGIN..."

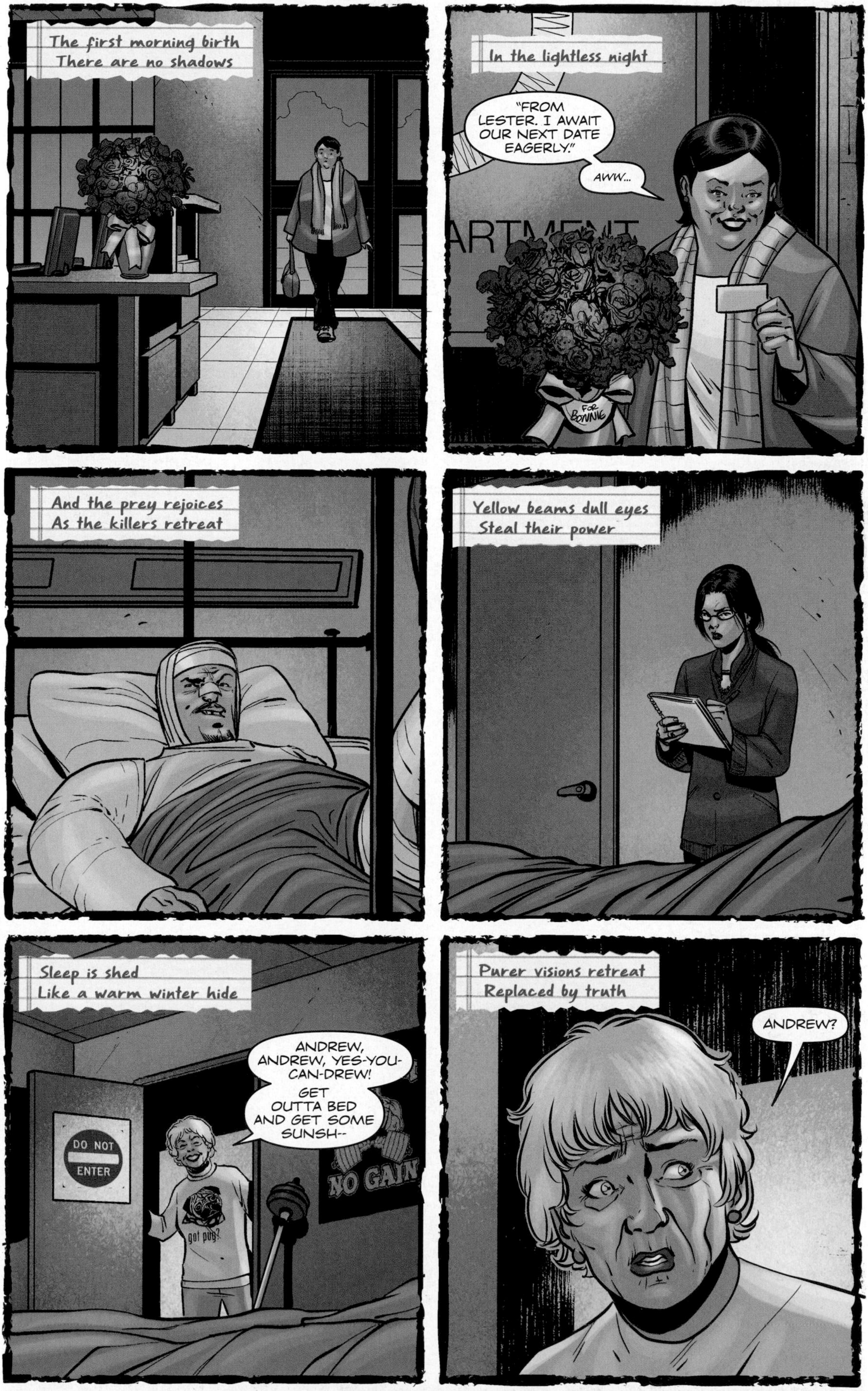
The first morning birth
There are no shadows
In the lightless night
"FROM LESTER. I AWAIT OUR NEXT DATE EAGERLY."
AWW...
ARTMENT
FOR BONNIE
And the prey rejoices
As the killers retreat
Yellow beams dull eyes
Steal their power
Sleep is shed
Like a warm winter hide
ANDREW, ANDREW, YES-YOU-CAN-DREW!
GET OUTTA BED AND GET SOME SUNSH--
DO NOT ENTER
got pug?
NO GAIN
Purer visions retreat
Replaced by truth
ANDREW?

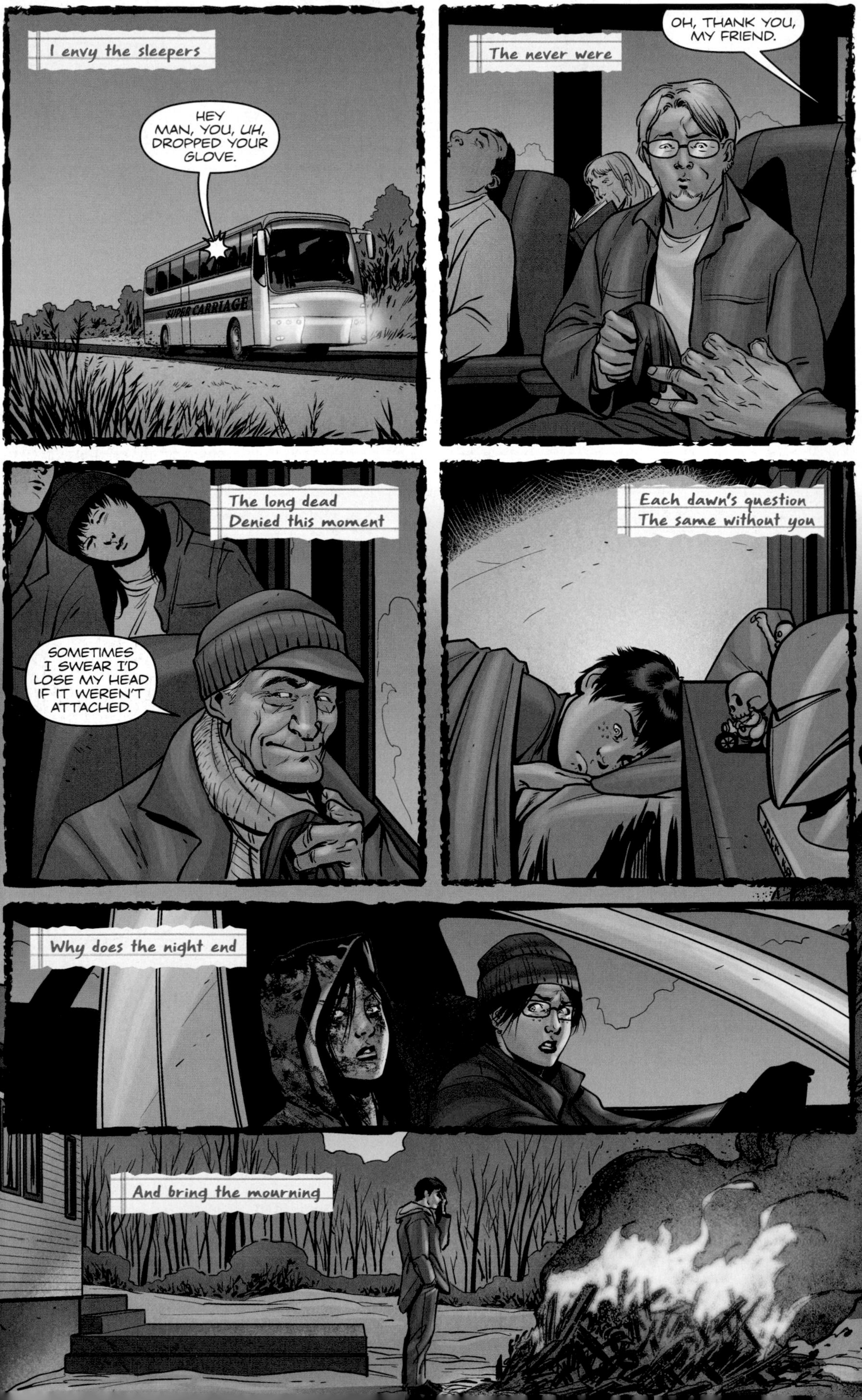
I envy the sleepers
HEY MAN, YOU, UH, DROPPED YOUR GLOVE.
SUPER CARRIAGE
The never were
OH, THANK YOU, MY FRIEND.
The long dead
Denied this moment
SOMETIMES I SWEAR I'D LOSE MY HEAD IF IT WEREN'T ATTACHED.
Each dawn's question
The same without you
Why does the night end
And bring the mourning

'EM'

TIM: 'EM' is another character I've been tinkering with for years, not unlike 'Jack Kraken.' But it took REVIVIAL for me to really figure out what to do with her.

MIKE: She's barely the same character anymore, huh? Pretty crazy how something changes in 20 years!

TIM: This design for her is circa 1996 when I was still reeling from THE CROW obsession. The idea was always the same: A young 'undead" girl dealing with her newfound immortality. The difference is the level of goth.

MIKE: I'm definitely not into the goth aesthetic as much as Tim, obviously. I really enjoy seeing how the character's look has evolved over the years. One of my favorite things about the book is that we actually made Dana the former goth and Em sorta wears her old clothes as a "costume". Well, at least that's as close to a costume we'll ever do in this book.

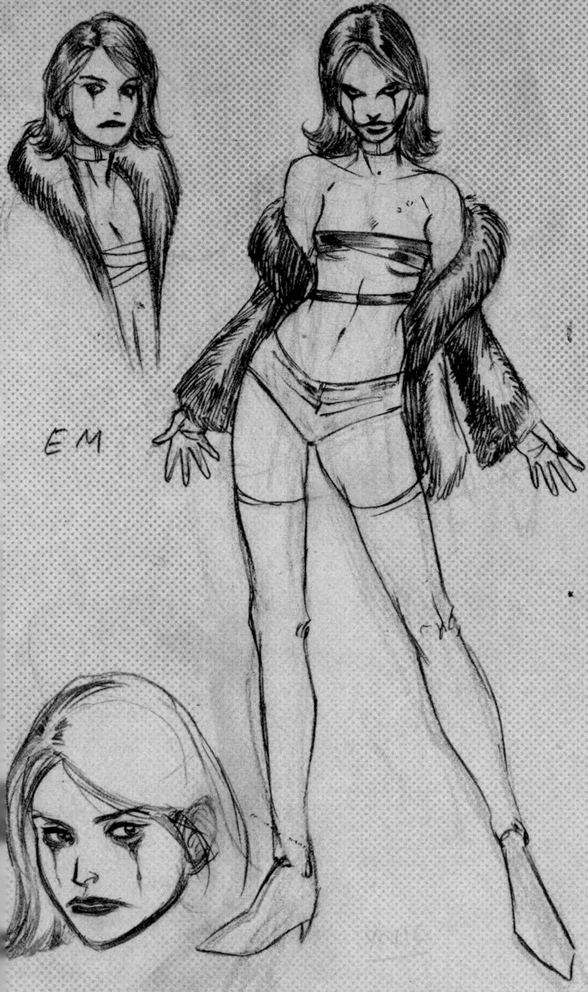
EM

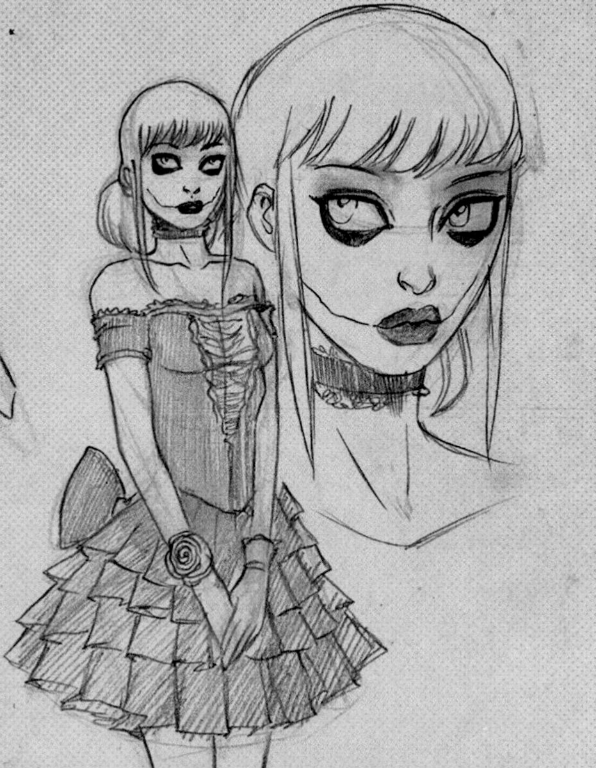

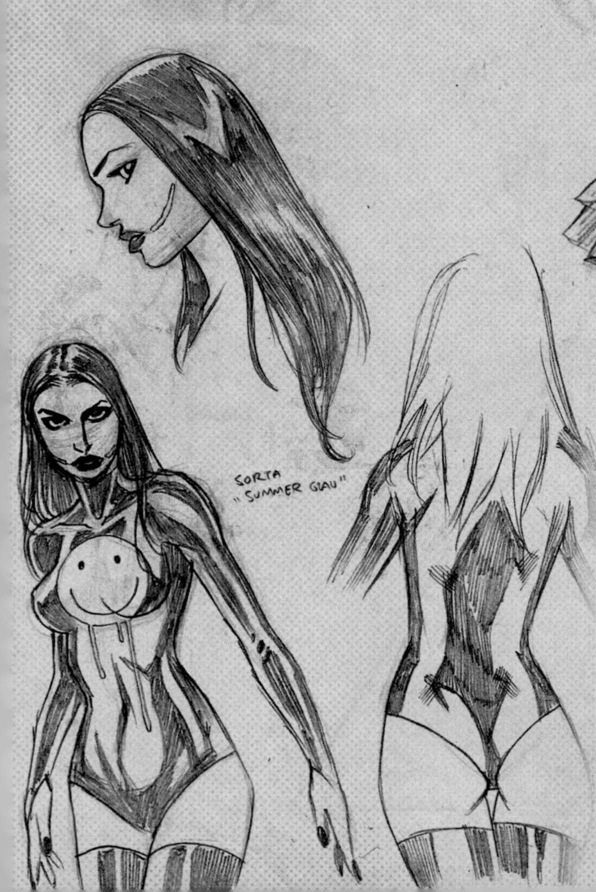
SORTA
"SUMMER GLAU"

TIM: In 2005 I was asked by Tokyopop to pitch a 'OEL' so I dug out Em, and gave her a "lolita" makeover. Some of the ideas from this pitch made it into REVIVAL.

TIM: In about 2006 or so, I considered using EM in HACK/SLASH. Eventually that idea sort of morphed into the slasher "Acid Angel."

CHEESE

THICK LASHES

EM CYPRUS
5'4
98 lbs

NO MAKE UP
LIGHT FRECKLES

BACK SKULL
WHITE HOOD

HALO

SCYTHE ON
EACH ARM

TIM: Once Mike and I had decided to do a comic together, I dug up ol' Em, and we started talking about a way to fit her into a "rural noir" type story we both knew we wanted to do. First things first! She had to be a "normal" girl, and not a Crow knock off.

MIKE: I think Tim probably draws some of the most attractive "normal" people I've ever seen. I think this is when it started to gell for me. I really took to the normal girl wearing the "angel of death" hoodie. It was important to me to make distinct body shapes for the characters as well. Em is pretty slim while Dana is older and more curvy. They still have the same eye color and freckles. I wanted them to actually look related.